W9-BTT-452

The

LATINIST

The

LATINIST

A NOVEL

MARK PRINS

W. W. NORTON & COMPANY

Independent Publishers Since 1923

Copyright © 2022 by Mark Prins

All rights reserved
Printed in the United States of America
First Edition

For information about permission to reproduce selections from this book, write to Permissions, W. W. Norton & Company, Inc., 500 Fifth Avenue, New York, NY 10110

For information about special discounts for bulk purchases, please contact W. W. Norton Special Sales at specialsales@wwnorton.com or 800-233-4830

Manufacturing by Lakeside Book Company
Book design by Beth Steidle
Production manager: Beth Steidle

Library of Congress Cataloging-in-Publication Data

Names: Prins, Mark, author.
Title: The Latinist / Mark Prins.
Description: First edition. | New York, NY : W. W. Norton & Company, [2022] | Includes bibliographical references.
Identifiers: LCCN 2021037031 | ISBN 9780393541274 (hardcover) | ISBN 9780393541281 (epub)
Subjects: LCGFT: Thrillers (Fiction). | Novels.
Classification: LCC PS3616.R554 L38 2022 | DDC 813/.6—dc23
LC record available at https://lccn.loc.gov/2021037031

W. W. Norton & Company, Inc., 500 Fifth Avenue, New York, N.Y. 10110
www.wwnorton.com

W. W. Norton & Company Ltd., 15 Carlisle Street, London W1D 3BS

1 2 3 4 5 6 7 8 9 0

PART I

Love is the cause of my pursuit.

MARIUS,
translated by Florence Henshawe

CHRISTOPHER ECCLES'S OFFICE AT WESTFALING College loomed over the cloisters where Tessa sometimes held tutorials, when the weather suited, and now as she listened to her student read from her paper on Ovid's *Metamorphoses* and the recurring theme of gods exploiting mortals, a cigarette butt dropped into the quadrangle a few feet from them, where it lay in the grass, used and smoking. Chris despised all constraints on his smoking habit, but this was the first Tessa had seen him use the quadrangle grass as an ashtray. Fines were imposed for dropping butts onto the footpath, let alone onto the quadrangle, let alone for smoking indoors, and it wasn't hard to imagine the red nub between Chris's fingers, the tip crackling as he stole one last illicit drag before ejecting it through his casement window.

"Entitlement in the Roman imagination was therefore conceptualized in these hierarchies of god, demigod, and mortal," Florence continued, her face buried in her pages, "and in so doing acts of entitlement of many sorts were justified as 'the natural order of things.'" Florence glanced at Tessa. "I'm sorry," she said. "Does this all sound like rubbish? Is it too abstract?" She hadn't seen the aerial cigarette.

"Did you read the criticism?" Tessa said, without taking her eye off the little plume that twirled into the warm March air. "The question for you may be, is Ovid reinforcing these ideologies or exposing them for what they—"

"Is that a butt on the quadrangle?" Florence interrupted.

Tessa paused. She resented having to manufacture some excuse for her mentor, distinguished head of classics at Westfaling, littering on the inviolable sanctuary of an Oxford quad.

"Oh, for fuck's sake," said Florence. "Talk about breach of etiquette." She set her pages down and stood.

"Where are you going?" Tessa asked.

"To throw it in the bin," said Florence.

"That's not your responsibility," Tessa said. It seemed essential that Florence not play maid to Chris's tobacco leavings, though Tessa was otherwise torn about how to proceed. "That's not your responsibility at all," she repeated, and remembered staring at the woolen sock fastened around the smoke alarm in Chris's office. "Pleading the Fifth," he'd said. He often sprinkled his speech with Americanisms in her presence. It was one of their running gags. "You're a knob," she'd responded.

Florence hovered in the shadow of the cloister, uncertain. "If Max sees that, he's going to go mental," she said. Max was the porter. Florence stepped out and squinted into the sun, inspecting the windows of Staircase 7, then crossed back into the cloister, smiling with the joy of seeing an adult, an authority figure, breaking a rule. "Chris's window is open," she whispered. "Should we tell Max?"

For a moment, Tessa envied Florence the worldview in which Max held authority over Chris. "What's the natural order of things?" Tessa asked.

"Pardon?"

"You mentioned god, demigod, mortal . . ."

"God, demigod, mortal, animals, plants, rocks."

"And do you think there might be an Oxford hierarchy?"

Florence stared at the smoldering butt.

"Max can't do anything," Tessa continued. "The best he can do is pick it up and hope the rector doesn't notice, because it'll be his fault if he does."

"Can I go and get it now?" Florence said.

"Just leave it," Tessa responded. "We haven't even gotten to Apollo and Daphne. Compressing two thousand years of critical response into a five-minute chat is only possible if you have five minutes to attempt it."

Papers crinkled in Florence's fingers as she looked for her place in the essay. Other students passed blithely along the footpath. The last strand of smoke floated out of view. Tessa hadn't mentioned it to Chris last night, but it was their argument yesterday that had precipitated her breakup with Ben. And then waking up in Chris's house this morning—*mistake*. She had slept on Chris's couch before—there was at least precedent—but now that Diana had left him, it was a bit different.

The staircase door squealed and Chris himself stepped out onto the footpath, moving briskly away from Tessa and Florence. "When Ovid's gods encounter mortals," Florence continued, not looking up from the last page of her paper, "they're likely to maim or kill them, or transform them into an inanimate or speechless entity, for arbitrary and self-serving reasons . . ." Another cigarette appeared in Chris's hands and then the small flame and more smoke swirling around him. As he turned the corner of the quadrangle toward the Porter's Lodge, he noticed Tessa and Florence on the bench in the cloisters and stopped, hovering for a moment, before turning to face them head-on. He approached slowly, looking at Tessa, inspecting her.

"It's you," he said.

Florence stopped reading.

"That it is," said Tessa. He would not usually interrupt a class. With anyone else she would have been duly annoyed and curt, but for Chris she made an exception.

"May I borrow your mobile?" Chris said. "I wouldn't ask if it wasn't a bit of an emergency. I've left mine at home."

"You can try," said Tessa. "I think it's nearly dead." She reached into her bag and handed him her phone. "By the way, Chris . . ." Tessa nodded at the butt in the quadrangle grass.

His head swiveled in the direction of the cigarette but returned instantly to her phone. "Oh yes, right, of course. One mustn't ash on the lawn. Finest lawn in Oxford and therefore the world. What's your code?" he said.

Typical Chris, what's your code? She didn't even tell Ben her code. Tessa reached for the phone and entered her password, wondering what Chris would need to make a call for so urgently. His mother was sick, she knew. "I don't know how far you'll get," she said. "It's at one percent."

"You can use mine, Professor Eccles," said Florence. "I've only just charged it."

Chris turned, as if he hadn't heard her.

"Anyway—" Tessa said, but Chris pivoted back again.

He had told her, the night before, that everything would sort itself out just fine, her applications, Ben, her life, and his words had comforted her. Now his face looked sallow and damp. He must have drunk even more than she. His shirt reeked of cigarettes, even from several feet away.

"Is everything all right?" Tessa asked.

"No," he said. "Mum's not well. Looks like it's dead." He returned Tessa's phone.

"You can still use mine," said Florence.

But he was already back on Staircase 7.

"He seems a bit out of sorts," said Florence. "And he didn't even pick up the cigarette."

He did seem out of sorts, but Tessa had other things on her mind.

At eleven, Tessa wrapped up Florence's tutorial with compliments on her paper and a recommendation that she look at Callisto,

Semele, and Io if she was interested in expanding it into one of the mandatory long essays in her next year. "And I'd be remiss if I didn't make you aware of a conference, here, just before break ends. If you find yourself bored of Dorset or just craving your tutor's thoughts on a minor author, you should come."

"Marius, right?" Florence asked. "I saw the conference proceedings. 'Minor Poets and . . . ?'"

Tessa thought for a moment: the conference had some convoluted title that she was embarrassed not to remember. "'Minor Poets and Pseudepigrapha: New Advances'?"

"'Approaches'?"

"'Approaches to Old Problems . . .'"

"'In Noncanonical Texts,'" Florence finished.

"I'm doing a great job of advertising," Tessa said.

Florence handed over the translation she'd been assigned. "I suppose I could tag along."

Pleased, Tessa wished Florence a good vacation—today was the last Thursday before the Easter holiday. As Florence ambled off into the sunny late morning, Tessa spent a moment looking at the butt and nub of the filter lying in the short grass. She had walked directly from Chris's house to the tutorial, had not even had time to change. The vodka and tonics from last night throbbed, though she blamed her headache on Ben. She honestly could have killed him for his timing. Her dissertation defense was next week. She'd had only one Skype interview and no callbacks for jobs next year. The butt seemed portentous, but she struggled to put her finger on why. It seemed to speak, maybe, to the grim truth lurking beneath her spring day—that after six years of crushing dedication to this life of the mind, on the cusp of officially receiving her doctorate, twelve of the universities she'd applied to had gone radio silent on her candidacy, with the exception only of Westfaling, which had coughed up a contingent faculty position, making it a baker's dozen of failure that she had not imagined possible in light of her work, her monograph under consideration at Oxford University Press, her first paper being accepted by *Classical Journal of America* (she'd finally been able to add *forthcoming* to her CV), and a recommendation letter from a titan in the field, Chris, that could be nothing other than glowing.

Tessa's future had only ever looked so uncertain in the year after her father died, nearly eight years prior. Tessa remembered him as a brilliant asshole with a short temper who would consume the *Lancet* from underneath a broad bucket cap on the few occasions he obliged the family with his presence at Neptune Beach, his pale legs stretched under a fat umbrella. He got away with absenteeism and open mockery of Tessa's philology habit ("we should use Latin instead of anesthesia") because Sheryl was also a doctor and Claire aspiring-to-be. Tessa had just been accepted to Cornell and the University of Florida, her safety, when they were blindsided by his diagnosis. For eighteen years she'd dreamed of escaping Florida, but suddenly Cornell was very far away and very expensive. She'd been made to see how selfish such a departure would be, with Dean terminal and Sheryl overwhelmed by work. Inscribed in these hushed conversations was the belief that Tessa's passion was less valid than, say, Claire's: she was signing a lease in Ann Arbor, and her future in medicine needed to be shielded.

After Dean died it struck Tessa that she might not have the personal or emotional resources left to launch her own life. She was twenty, she'd spent the last two years ferrying Dean to appointments, crushing his pain pills, providing companionship for his frazzled spirit, watching him die, watching him watch himself die. Her mother and sister's tears at the funeral had felt like personal insults, each orb a sort of acid on the fiber of her being, as she sat in dour, disciplined silence. Her grades were so-so, her personal life nil, her sister soon to be credited as first author on a published paper (she'd been able to tell Dean just before he passed), and the chalky scalp through his flossy hair, the translucent skin, the way he'd compelled everything in his life around achievement and then not quite achieved, the way he'd never fully appreciated her and yet she'd been his loving daughter, his docile helper, the witness of his most vulnerable seconds, his mother, essentially, it was all devastating.

That year, she translated vast swaths of the *Aeneid* in a twenty-four-hour Waffle House off the highway between Gainesville and Jacksonville—she had not yet moved onto campus, and the prospect of home terrified her. When he was alive, Dean had cultivated basically nothing inside or outside the house, and the very sameness of the before/after visited an inarticulable pain on Tessa, the solution of which lay in the smothered hash browns and bottomless coffee mug at the truck-stop Waffle House off 301, the kind anonymity of its eternal, synthetic daylight, and Virgil's twelve-book origin myth of the Roman Empire. She had lost any sense that her life after graduation might involve Virgil or Ovid in any formal way—Dean had murmured something about law school, at one point—and so these hours spent writing felt like a refusal of the very notion that she had a future. The thing reaped from those nights was a paper on piety and its relation to the master narrative, which Chris had seen and on the spot arranged a fellowship to whisk its author away from whatever American backwater it inhabited—until Tessa arrived, he had never heard of Jacksonville, or so he maintained.

A life had ensued. In Oxford, she had pursued her passion doggedly, without apology, through her relationship with Ben and even the death of Ben's father, whose funeral last month had coincided with a more or less crucial paper she was delivering in Edinburgh for the Association for Classical Studies. Ben's hand in hers when he asked her to stay had felt like the last thread tethering her to earth, but she had gone, and now Ben had gone, too.

She had thought he had forgiven her, but in fact he had been lying in wait. Last night, she had arrived late to make dinner. Ben had one more day before he left for the North Sea, and he had cooked the previous two nights. He had taken a proprietary stand about that night, which Tessa learned soon after arriving at her flat, breathless and sweating under her cardigan. She had been arguing with Chris about a request for a footnote in her forthcoming paper. One reader's report insisted that she acknowledge Apollo's "love" for Daphne wasn't always interpreted as being ironic. This was a minor point in her paper, but one on which she didn't feel she could budge.

"I'm so sorry," she'd called from the hallway, where she could smell marinara sauce and hear water boiling. "It was Chris—we got into an argument." In the kitchen, which doubled as living room and dining room, Ben had treated her to an ambiguous stare from his post at the counter. She kissed him on the cheek and continued talking as she changed in the bedroom.

"He took issue—he really latched on to this point about the 'amor' in the Daphne Apollo sequence being ironic or not. Because I wrote about 'love' used in an ironic sense, so Apollo is this great archer who saves the world from Python, and he challenges Cupid to an archery match and Cupid shoots him with an arrow, which inflames him with desire for Daphne, whom he then chases with such rapey persistence that she begs her father to transform her into something basically that Apollo can't fuck, and she turns into a laurel tree." Tessa ducked under the sloped garret ceiling, shouting over the sound of boiling water. "There's a great statue in Rome by Bernini of Apollo's hand latched around Daphne's torso as her skin transforms into bark and leaves sprout from her fingers. And remember what the laurel tree is? Literally a metonymy for trophy. There's even

a moment earlier in Book I where they're having an archery con-
test and don't know what to give as trophies because the laurel tree
doesn't exist yet. Anyway, Apollo's 'love' for Daphne is pretty clearly
meant in an ironic sense. Like, look where his love gets Daphne. And
meanwhile Apollo gets to keep being Apollo, no consequences."

She crossed back into the kitchen and approached Ben. The
block of Parmesan was nearly gone; he seemed primarily intent on
demolishing it. "Think we have enough there?" she said.

"This is all about a footnote?" he responded.

"Well, yes, in a way."

He kept grating.

"Are you just going to keep doing that? Are you upset with me
about something?"

"Christ. I'm making dinner again because you didn't turn up—"

"I apologized for that."

"And you're banging on about a single footnote."

Tessa focused on letting the anger go. Leave it at Westfaling.

"What do you expect?" Ben had continued. "Y'all right, love?
Shall I do you a plate? I leave tomorrow, we don't even have time for
a fight."

"Then why are you starting one?" she'd snapped.

Now Tessa pinched the white filter tip of the cigarette butt
between her fingers and disposed of it, still warm, in the nearby
bin. She continued on to Staircase 7, where she had spent most of
the past two years, with her first teaching responsibilities under
Chris's tutelage, and trekked past Chris's door, which was closed, up
to the office that she shared with Annie, the history and geography
postdoc. She turned the key and left the door open. Annie's leather
jacket was tossed over the ottoman like some felled animal. There
were two umbrellas shunted between the wall and the oak desk that
they shared. The room smelled vaguely of rain, even as light arced

through the casement windows. She unpacked her laptop, wondering if Ben had sent her a message since last night. Maybe he had forgotten something. Besides her. She went to her email. She scanned over a message from Apple informing her that her backup was complete, and after observing that there was no email from University College London, Brasenose College, St. Andrews, Case Western, UCLA, or any of the other institutions that held her once-promising future in their palms, she opened the missive from the Hotmail account that looked like a phishing scam.

You may want to reconsider asking Christopher Eccles for a recommendation letter in the future.

Underneath was a thumbnail of a picture. She immediately became aware of the open door at her back. She closed it, then clicked the thumbnail. It was an image of a letter from Chris on Westfaling stationery. She read the letter twice.

To Whom It May Concern,

I have known Tessa Templeton since 2006, when she began her Master's of Studies in Greek and Latin Languages under my supervision. Though our collaboration was minimal in her first year at Oxford, I have heard that she acquitted herself well in her Research Methods seminar class, and her score in the spring examinations, known here as Advancements Exams, was above average.

Tessa has made strides from a rocky beginning to her doctorate. Like many candidates new to the independent work habits required of professional scholarship, she has difficulty applying herself consistently to research and drafting, and we met more regularly in her first year than is normal with the students I supervise. Sometimes, she is hindered by a tendency to be argumentative, which is not always accompanied by the appropriate rigour. Over the three years that I advised her, however, and with encouragement, I've witnessed an improvement in her work ethic, and more confidence managing her own time, culminating in what I suspect will be a successful confirmation of her doctoral status this spring.

I'm confident in Tessa's willingness to apply herself, and I support her decision to pursue a career in the field. Please reach out to me by phone or by email per the below if you have any further questions about her qualifications.

Sincerely,
Professor Christopher Eccles
Westfaling College, Oxford University

. . . .

THE FIRST TIME Tessa finished the letter, she laughed at the ingenuity of whoever had forged it, even if she dinged them for shoddy research of her CV (publicly available)—no mention of her first in the Advancement Exams, her O'Neill Fellowship, nor the Daphne and Apollo paper she'd delivered in Edinburgh, among other elisions. She awarded points for the syntax and vocabulary, which, she had to admit, were decent imitations of Chris's own, for the Westfaling stationery, even for the use of Garamond, Chris's chosen font for paper correspondence. A lineup of suspects appeared unbidden in her mind—Lucrezia Pagani, Liam Sinclaire-Stoudemire, Claire, her sister. Another indistinct figure—wait, that was Dean Templeton, her father, who seemed briefly more viable than anyone, so dedicated an opponent he had been to classical philology as a serious pursuit. Ben stood at the edge, skulking—but that was not possible. For one, he was digitally illiterate. But also, the timing would be in too poor taste, and though he loved a good prank, he was too bighearted to lob one through the interweb like a parting grenade.

Dangling from one of many pens in a mug on her desk was a key chain Ben had given her last spring in the shape of a meat tenderizer, meant to evoke not only the back rubs he lavished on her sometimes nightly, but also a gag he liked to make of wanting to eat her, that if he did not love her so much he would absolutely make a repast out of her lovely arms, that each back rub constituted not a selfless act of love but a preparation of her delicious self for when he would finally be unable to resist, that even though she thought she had seen him first, talked to him first at the Covered Market, he had in fact noticed her beforehand and discovered an appetite for blond American academics. It had been a little much, actually, to use as a key chain. The size of a thimble, it was a bit ponderous, resembling a double-sided hammer from one angle, and something entirely different from another. She'd made an unobtrusive home for it in the office, where it could baffle anyone keen enough to notice it in the first place. Only Chris had ever guessed.

"Something to do with Ben?"

"How did you know?"

"I didn't. Seems a bit creepy, though, no? Intimations of phallic violence."

"True," she'd said. But that would be so alien to Ben as to seem absurd. "Yes, of course, the reading had occurred to me."

Had she not worried the balance of power in the relationship tilted, if anything, too far in her favor, perhaps she could have shared in Chris's speculation. As it was, her heart contracted around the idiotic little emblem, and she tore her attention away only with a pang of sadness.

The one person she could feel sure did not write the letter was its putative author, Chris. Chris's dedication to her career had been unflagging, at least since she'd switched her focus from Virgil to Ovid some years ago, after a challenging start to her time in Oxford. Since then, her work had blossomed, flowered, flourished, leafed, whatever you wanted to call it, in a way that had not only won her accolades (the forthcoming publication, the travel fellowship, presenting in Edinburgh on the same bill as Colm Feeney!), but also sharpened her understanding of herself, her beliefs about literature, her basic ordering of the cosmos and one's place in it, none of which could have been achieved toiling in the intellectual space where he'd found her, those barren Virgilian fields, that carcass of reactionary scholarship she'd long since harvested beyond any vital use. Chris had rescued her, for lack of a better word, from that . . . her eyes alighted again on the screen . . . "rocky beginning to her doctorate."

It wasn't funny, Tessa concluded, and the thinnest blade of anger sliced through her thoughts. She needed to call Lucrezia anyway. She would congratulate her on her execution and explain how unfriendly her timing was given the slew of rejections and deafening silence from numerous institutions she would have considered step-downs just a few weeks prior. Not to mention her boyfriend of two years walking off without so much as a proper goodbye, a fucking exit interview, or something.

Dredging her phone from her bag to dial Lucrezia, Tessa recalled it had died in Chris's palm just an hour earlier. Laughter spilled from the open window as she plugged it in. Tessa suddenly doubted Lucrezia could mimic Chris's written voice so effectively—Liam could have, probably, and thus she assumed

their collusion. Plus the stationery. As Chris's other doctorate student, Liam could easily have procured the materials and
written the letter and even known about Tessa's "rocky beginning." But Liam, big loping Liam, or, as Tessa had once called
him, hot-but-happily-hitched Liam, was as capable of shenan-
igans as a member of the Queen's guard, at least with women
he wasn't married to, good old good-natured and good-naturedl
y-nostalgic-for-empire Liam. Somehow he invited hyphenation,
perhaps because he had been the first hyphenated man Tessa had
ever met—meaning not that he had taken his wife's last name,
but that he descended from actual nobility, culottes and all: Liam
Sinclaire-Stoudemire. Tessa would feel the occasional pang of
guilt at the sound of his heavy tread on Staircase 7, through Chris's
half-open door, she and Chris locked in argument about the meta-
physics of a text or just shooting the shit, when she knew Liam
struggled even to get Chris to read his emails. He would somewhat pathetically scuffle about outside to announce his presence,
but Chris would press through fifteen, sometimes thirty minutes
past the start of their meeting, pretending not to notice. Tessa
would have felt worse had she not believed at her core that she
was a better classicist who had made exponentially more sacri-
fices, and that Liam's scholarship was crushingly unoriginal, even
if he was a good person and didn't deserve to be treated like an
invisible child.

Tessa's phone buzzed to life and she located Lucrezia's number quickly, eager to put the mystery to rest. This was not how
she wanted to be spending her day. She had a meeting with Chris
at one-thirty and a paper to begin on Marius and her viva next
week, for which she needed to allot ample time to fret over, if not
prepare for.

Lucrezia answered after two rings. "Tessa!" Tessa loved how Lucrezia said her name, elongating the double consonant, as if it were a song: *Tess-sa*. "*Dimmi*."

"You could have at least waited until April fool's," Tessa said.

A pickaxe fell rhythmically in the background. She could see Lucrezia at the Isola Sacra Necropolis baking in the sun along with the red bricks of the tombs. Tessa hadn't yet been able to visit, due to an inability, on both sides, to find funds for a trip.

"Waited for what?" Lucrezia said. "To ask you again when you're going to come?"

"You didn't send the email?" Tessa said.

"No," said Lucrezia. "What email? When are you going to fly down?"

"When is the funding going to appear?" Tessa asked, distracted.

"When you get that new travel fellowship."

"Or you scrape together some pennies from your boss."

"So many fragments, so many inscriptions, so much that's probably Marius."

"I'm hanging up."

"So much lost to posterity . . ."

Tessa ended the call and peered again at the image on her screen. She pushed her hair back, feeling between her fingers something fuzzy, a linty batch of gray and lavender yarn from the upholstery of Chris's couch. That she depended on him not only for midwifing her career, but also for mopping her up when her boyfriend disappeared, seemed perhaps extravagant, but in fact testified to the depths of their connection, both intellectual and personal. Take the meeting in which she had formally asked him for a recommendation letter, last October. A red-orange leaf had rustled through his cracked window just as she'd asked. "You'll hardly need me," he'd said, his eyes yielding hers in favor of the leaf—Chris was color-blind, though he could pick out reds. Usually Diana paired his olives with his grays, but he'd resembled, that day, a lump of clay in his forlorn monotone collared shirt and trousers. By then it had become clear that Diana had left him, and Tessa had asked if he was all right.

He hadn't taken her meaning at first, or if he had, he'd chosen to elude her with a more or less pedantic display of his learnedness, treating her to the latest on *Metamorphoses* I 544–547, the disputed lines in which Daphne appeals for help to some permutation of father, mother earth, or both. "This young man, or woman," he'd complained, brandishing a thin stack of pages for which, presumably, he was a blind referee. "I'm assuming they're young. This *youth* completely ignores the errors in agreement between the surviving codices, even the Marcianus and Neapolitanus."

Marcianus, a late eleventh century manuscript residing in Florence; Neapolitanus, a twelfth century in Naples. Tessa had arrived at Oxford with the notion that texts like the *Iliad* and *Aeneid* and *Metamorphoses* had passed immaculately from composition to present day as if by time warp—she knew intellectually that their authors pre-dated the printing press by well over a thousand years, but had not appreciated what fires and mice and mold could do to manuscripts in short supply already, because who had time to write out the *Iliad* by hand? The well water didn't fetch itself. Tessa didn't even have time to respond to her sister's emails, and her kitchen had faucets. The result was that the oldest surviving manuscript of the *Metamorphoses* postdated Ovid by roughly one thousand years, and some passages did not match up with other near-contemporaries. Had Ovid published two versions? Or had early scribes simply embroidered their own verses onto an original? Scholars hypothesized genealogies for different manuscripts, based often on the errors the manuscripts repeated—the same misspelling of a Greek name, for example, might be shared by two different manuscripts, suggesting a common parent. Thus "errors in agreement."

Though the thing that had really stunned Tessa was not the existence of different versions of the *Metamorphoses*, but the existence of poets, great ones, whose work hadn't survived at all, or only in the barest fractions. She considered Marius to be one of these poets.

"Slipshod," Tessa had agreed. Normally she would bite on any conversation related to Apollo and Daphne, but Chris hadn't actually agreed to write the reference yet, a reaction she could only attribute to external dislocation. Marital collapse. She worried about him. The fact that his father had killed himself always loomed somehow and worried her.

"What are the chances five scribes independently misspelled Melanchaetes as melanchates, in the great Actaeon dog catalogue?" he'd continued, with characteristic attention to scrupulous detail. Chris had named his black Lab melanchates, insisting on the lowercase misspelling even on her official papers, to celebrate the error in transmission. "Quite bloody low, I'd say."

"Chris," she'd interrupted. "Are you okay?" she asked with more meaning.

Chris's brow furrowed in surprise and he laid the offending pages to rest on the coffee table. A long silence enveloped them, which Tessa steadfastly refused to break. He seemed to contemplate denial. The red leaf brushed off the windowsill and fluttered to the floor. Finally he'd said, "Was just a matter of time."

When she revisited the recommendation letter in November, he'd shown all the enthusiasm she'd originally anticipated. "I'm such a fan of yours," he'd said. "I'll find it difficult to be objective."

"Don't feel you have to be," she'd responded, relieved, wondering what she'd been worrying about in the first place.

Now Tessa stared at the *W* in *Whom* with the unmistakable space between the two overlapping *V*'s—Chris disliked seeing Garamond in pixilation, as its serifs were subtly modeled, and easily blurred on a screen. He used Georgia in his emails. She wondered what Chris would make of the letter, what truths he might deduce—a forgery being, in a way, not so different from those lines of verse embroidered onto Ovid's poem, masquerading as Ovid's own. She enlarged the thumbnail and printed out a copy. One of Chris's maxims for studying literature was, "It is not the evidence itself, but the peculiarity of the evidence that matters," taken from a Poe story, and some part of her was curious what "peculiarities" he would draw from the text. Perhaps she would show it to him at their meeting, perhaps not. Literally flushing it might offer solace, as would incineration, both enticing options for the crisp page she removed from the tray and slipped into her bag against the hard green cover of her Oxford Classical *Metamorphoses*.

Tessa powered through her last tutorial of the term, in the Westfaling garden, hardly thinking about the letter at all. Arnold Cowen and Ed Duffey read aloud from their papers on Actaeon, the hunter who stumbles upon the goddess Diana bathing in Book III and, as punishment, is turned into a stag and eaten alive by his own dogs. Arnold bemoaned the fact that melanchates had not been spotted at Westfaling in months, and Tessa mirrored Arnold's melancholy puzzlement, affecting not to know that Diana had taken him when she'd left. At the end of the hour, Tessa asked for the Marius translation she'd assigned, and while Ed handed over several crumpled pages of what she was sure were agonized, literal renditions of each and every line, Arnold sat still as a gnome.

"Arnold?" Tessa asked.

"It's just—there's dashed little chance he'll turn up when we sit our finals," he said.

"Basically none," Ed echoed, merely because it was true.

Suddenly annoyed, Tessa found herself snapping, "And I suppose the only reason to do anything is because you might have to sit a fucking exam." Arnold and Ed's faces jolted to attention. "Why affect to be interested in the classics at all—"

"I'll have it in your pidge tomorrow," Arnold said quickly.

"Thank you," said Tessa, aware she had spoken sharply. But still, the gall—as if she didn't already know that Marius's scant surviving work polled poorly with the mainstream. It was clear Arnold had not even planned on bothering. Both young men murmured their goodbyes and traipsed across the lawn; Ed's face turned just enough to indicate he'd said something and Arnold responded by cuffing him across the head.

Tessa rested her left temple against her fingertips. Arnold had surrendered immediately. She knew stories of the Templeton temper preceded her. Some part of her wished he'd talked back. A sumptuous hot flash of anger would clear her mind and dispel her lurking hangover. A tongue-lashing, if properly administered, was better than electrolytes, or at least as good. Her father, the revered research physician, used to appall any and all company with the way he spoke to his daughters, and Tessa could not deny the crisp pleasure of anger's fluency, the way it sometimes ordered her words like perfect little soldiers.

Her last classes of the term were taught. Six weeks of vacation rolled out luxuriantly before her, if she could only feel satisfied with the offer she'd received: to teach next year at Westfaling, to continue here, and was that such a grim future? Had the college ginned up anything better than a stipendiary lectureship, the circumstances would be different. More dismal pay, no job security. Surely Chris wouldn't allow her to be terminated, so long as funds didn't run dry, but who knew what the future held for classics budgets? Tessa had worked herself to the bone to avoid just this—a tightrope walk over the maw of unemployment, the default mode of contingent faculty everywhere, even at Oxford. It was maddening not to know what was being discussed behind closed doors, why her application had been deemed unfit for an interview anywhere except Case Western Reserve University in freezing Ohio. And not to make too fine a point about it, but the Daphne and Apollo paper alone accomplished more than the dissertations of many of her peers. This was not a belief she held in a vacuum—it had been received at Edinburgh accordingly. The event had felt like a coronation.

Everything seemed to shimmer with an eerie uncertainty, and Tessa suddenly distrusted the idyllic calm of the garden, the lapping warmth of the sun. In *Metamorphoses*, the *locus amoenus*, or "pleasant place," was never to be trusted, and anytime Ovid began to describe the loveliness of a quiet grove, or the limpid surface of a tranquil pond, you knew some violence was about to occur. Apollo and Daphne's chase occurred in a Thessalian vale; mist from a waterfall flecks the leafy treetops. A river flows majestically through a wooded valley, et cetera.

She left the trio of chairs with time to spare before her one-thirty with Chris and wandered through the archway into the front quad somewhat listlessly, intent mainly on curbing the desire to check her email for news on applications, or a gesture of peace from Ben. In the front quad, a gaggle of undergraduates skirted the quadrangle grass on their way to Hall for a late lunch. An older couple in mealy parkas nosed shyly out of the Porter's Lodge—tourists. On the near façade, Agnes Westfaling presided in statue along with her husband, Hugh, and an effigy of Charles I, who had reigned when the college was consecrated. Because of Chris, Tessa knew that Agnes Westfaling wore something called a farthingale and, likely, a mourning veil, and that she'd been "a faithful executor of her husband," curious phrasing that in hindsight gestured as much to Chris's vague marital troubles as to Agnes's piety—she'd founded Westfaling in accordance with her husband's last testament, outmaneuvering corrupt administrators and vulturous heirs who'd hoped to bend her feminine will.

Chris had taught her many of these little facts, so that much of what she knew about Westfaling had come from him. She knew, to some degree, that she could speak sharply to undergraduates with impunity, despite being young, female, and podunk American, because she enjoyed Chris's unadulterated favoritism. Situated in an explicitly patriarchal England, Agnes had accomplished much, but in the founding of the College she'd acted always on the authority of her husband's legal document. She had been, despite her formidable character, a male proxy. It irked Tessa that she might continue under Chris with a contingent contract, which constituted, at the end of the day, a sort of serfdom.

From the shadow of the Porter's Lodge a tall, loping figure staggered into the sunlight and stood, frozen over a sheet of white paper. It was Liam, in full rugby kit, as still as Agnes. Tessa immediately remembered the letter of recommendation, that little page of slander in her shoulder bag, and she walked with renewed purpose around the corner of the quad.

"Liam," she said, caught up in extracting a confession. His face met hers; he wore an inscrutable expression, but in Tessa's urgency she rushed onward. "Did you send me that email?" she said, reaching into her bag.

Liam's face broke, suddenly, into an extraordinary grin, and Tessa was flooded with relief. Liam had done it. It was all a joke. Relief was just transmuting to righteous anger when Liam wrapped her in a bear hug—scent of sweat, grass, men—and just as precipitously let her go. "Email?" he said, the grin widening still. Finally she took stock of the page in his hand, which he slipped into hers, and the loose strands of its mangled envelope.

It is with great pleasure . . . position of Tutorial Fellow and Associate Professor of Latin Language and Literature . . . Brasenose College, Oxford . . .

Heat moved across Tessa's cheeks and down her neck. Out of some deep reserve of etiquette she mimed a perfect spasm of happiness and embraced him again, the ground seeming to shift, for a moment, under her feet. "Congratulations," she managed.

"Bloody hell," he said. "I'm speechless."

"You deserve it," Tessa heard herself say, a peculiar phrase because it was in fact the opposite of how she felt. Liam was lovely, but he'd published nothing and had nothing in the pipeline. Now she imagined a scrum of aged dons reading his dissertation aloud while tending a small flame under an offcut of her Daphne and Apollo paper. She preferred hot-but-happily-hitched Liam. She didn't know how she felt about this new, tenure-track Liam.

"To be honest, I was rather worried"—he dropped his voice slightly—"about Chris's recommendation, but it seems the old boy came through in the end."

"Speaking of," Tessa said, suspecting Liam had forgotten his prank in the red heat of victory, "were you the one who sent me that very unfunny email?" She watched his face, still dazzled with joy, for signs of guilt or recognition, as her hand crept under the flap of her bag and her fingers settled on the page.

"Right, an email. I haven't the faintest," he said. "What does it have to do with Chris?"

"It?" Tessa said. "What is it?"

"What do you mean, 'What is it?' You tell me." He laughed, then seemed to notice the cloud gathering on Tessa's face. "Is everything all right?"

It was not him, and suddenly she imagined the catastrophe of showing him the letter. Liam was a do-gooder; she risked provoking his earnest assistance. But worse, they weren't close enough for her to trust his discretion. A lump formed in her throat.

"It's nothing," she said. His eyes lingered on hers, searching for her meaning, but she sensed the traction of his need to celebrate, the enclosure of personal, nuclear imperatives between the vague wilderness of hers, and she cut off further inquiry. "Lara will be thrilled," she added.

His head turned in a sheepish grin. God, he was happy. He asked politely if there were any updates on her applications, and she managed to smile and say, "Just Brasenose," and send him on his way. As he marched back through the Porter's Lodge she stared at the flayed pulp of the envelope in his right hand, her own fingertips still pressed against the letter in her bag, kneading it into the slab-like cover of her OCT *Metamorphoses*.

Tessa checked her phone and saw it was 1:32—she was late. She turned toward Staircase 7 and walked quickly, her flats clapping the stone walkway. A shadow passed over the quad—two clouds were spreading across the sky, braiding together in weird, ominous shapes. Her lineup of suspects had not panned out, and if the letter was not a prank, if it was meant to terrorize her, the list of suspects broadened considerably. It might even have nothing to do with her: George Bale leapt to mind. An endowed chair at University College London, George wore nailhead suits and penned lightly condescending reviews of Chris's books. Chris hated George, and as far as she could tell the feeling was mutual. On the several occasions they had met—conferences, colloquia—George was always solicitous and overtly kind to Tessa in a way that made her feel like a pawn, and therefore vexed her. George was friends with Diana, and moreover, he was on the search committee at UCL.

A tremor of unfamiliarity passed through her as she climbed the steps. If only she could speak with Ben; she trusted him, and he existed outside the incestual pools of elite philology. An image of him on the train visited her, his head jostling against the window, eyes closed in slumber, and she felt newly dismantled.

She climbed the first flight—Chris's door was slightly ajar—and when she rapped her knuckles on the jamb, he did not lift his face from the book it was buried in. Tessa gave another knock to secure his attention. "Come in, come in," he said, without looking up.

His office was lovely and quiet. Sunlight spilled through the open windows. A breeze ruffled lazily the loose pages on the glass coffee table. The scent of his cigarette could only just be detected.

"Heard about Liam?" he asked, as Tessa slung her bag onto the leather expanse of his red tufted chesterfield.

"Yes," she said. "I'm happy for him."

Chris's eyes rose to meet hers. A mischievous smile curled across his face. "No, you aren't."

"He's overcome a lot," she persisted only somewhat playfully. "A negligent supervisor, for one."

"But not congenital blandness," he said.

Now she could not suppress a smile. "Chris, he's a good guy. A decent bloke."

"So is my mailperson, it doesn't qualify him to teach at Oxford."

"I once literally saw him walk an elderly woman across Turl Street," she said, tumbling onto the chesterfield next to her bag. She suddenly found that she was tired.

"A hazardous strait, it's true."

"He volunteer-leads a boxing class on weekends for Parkinson's patients. Gabriel used to go."

"Gabriel?"

"Ben's dad."

"Oh right," Chris said. His attention veered downward again.

"Liam was at the funeral," Tessa added.

"That's still eating you?"

"That's when everything started with Ben."

Chris stood. He'd sensed, perhaps, the tremor of emotion in her voice. "And when you dazzled the world," he said.

Not that that's yielded a job offer, she thought.

"You're young," he said, striding across the creaky floorboards. "There will be plenty more funerals."

"That's reassuring." She laughed morbidly. "Thanks for reminding me."

Chris's expression creased into a self-effacing laugh. He hadn't meant to be so ominous, this smile said. It was sometimes difficult to tell what his intended meanings were, but at least he could laugh at himself. As he took a seat in the armchair facing the coffee table, he placed his phone on the papers that were ruffling in the wind. "I've had to migrate several paperweights to the house," he said, by way of explanation. "Thanks to my pillaging wife. In other news," he added quickly, "Martin Wembley of Brasenose College is one of your examiners on Monday."

Tessa's mind clung to the phone for a moment, for reasons she couldn't construe, while Chris settled himself deeper into his chair. "The one who hired Liam?" she asked.

"Yes. Rather traditional, as you might imagine. Lacking originality. Exactly the type who'd hire a Sinclaire-Stoudemire."

Tessa groped in her bag for the pages she'd prepared for the viva.

"It's a pity they saw fit to reward him," Chris continued. "He was always the type to clock out at five. Hopefully Brasenose will witness an improvement in his work ethic."

This last phrase rang strangely in Tessa's ears as she drew forth several papers; the page now staring back at her was not the viva crib sheet she'd prepared earlier that week, but the printed image of the hoax recommendation letter. She snapped it straight, some of its insidious contents already returning by memory as she let her eyes rove over it again: *have heard that she acquitted herself well . . . above average . . . a rocky beginning . . . we met more regularly in her first year than is normal . . . a tendency to be argumentative . . .* Presently Chris's phone began to vibrate and he reached forward to silence it. *Over the three years that I advised her, however, and with encouragement, I've witnessed an improvement in her work ethic.* "Chris, I received a strange letter today," she said, even as her eyes were latching on to this last phrase. She paused and read it again: *witnessed an improvement in her work ethic.*

"A letter?" she heard him say.

Heat moved up her cheeks and around her neck. The imitation of Chris's voice in the letter had been a bit too good. Her body sank into the chair, as if collapsing. The words didn't match the person— the coaxing eyes and encouraging half smile and nervous laughter that had sometimes seemed odd, yes, and even marginally inappropriate, but never anything other than positive with respect to her career. Classics was where their minds met, classics was the overlap in the Venn diagram of their persons, where she was ceaselessly admiring of his abilities in the field, and he was ceaselessly kindling hers. Yet even as Tessa again presented the evidence to her imaginary jury: that Chris would have known about her O'Neill Fellowship and the Daphne and Apollo paper and the first she'd achieved in the Advancements, and therefore why would he have omitted them? Even as she presented this evidence for proper exegesis of the document at hand—that whoever forged this had done shoddy research of her CV—the peculiarity of their absences combined with the calculated attention to what would be the legal or ethical bare minimum of recognizing her credentials ("above average" on the Advancements) struck her suddenly as signature Chris scrupulousness. That was the peculiarity: that if Christopher Eccles were to write a rec sabotaging her career, this was the barbed subtext he would write it in—down to the condescending and insufferably male use of "argumentative," to the evaluation of her work ethic, to the statement about meeting more than usual in her first year (which he could prove with receipts or credit card statements from the Old Bank where he had made a standing reservation even if she hadn't finished a chapter or asked for feedback), down to the uppercase *W* in *Whom* with the unmistakable space between the two overlapping *V*'s—Garamond.

"Tessa?" Chris said. "Are you all right?"

She stared at him, his expression coiled into concern, and then looked down quickly. Her scalp prickled as her mind raced for a more plausible answer.

"Do you need water?" he said, rising solicitously. Tessa nodded and Chris rushed to the small refrigerator in the far shadowed corner of the office. He filled a small cup from a decanter; it would be flavored with cucumber slices, she knew. She knew so much about this man. He ventured back across the office and handed her the cool glass.

"I'm fine," she managed, after a sip of the cucumber water.

"You don't look fine," he said. "Are you seriously all right?"

The molecules seemed to have rearranged themselves in the room. She placed the glass on the sheaf of papers, next to his phone, and stood, her hand to her temple, the sheet dangling limply in her hand. She handed him the page. "Chris," she said. "Is this the letter you wrote for me?"

He began to read the letter. The narrative was gaining traction in her mind: "Is this why no one wants to hire me?" she added.

She could smell the tobacco off his blazer, see the dandruff cresting his shoulder, and as he read she remembered their first good meeting—they as a pair on the chesterfield. She recalled the moment he leaned over her pages and scratched the side of his scalp, springing loose a few flakes of Christopher Eccles's scurf that had flurried onto the thigh of her dark jeans. Underneath the repulsion had been a definite sense of awe and accomplishment, one that she had carried with her when she left his office with his enthusiastic praise. She hadn't brushed them off for at least twenty minutes, and she'd accounted for her excitement by telling herself that some of his success might rub off on her, at which she'd laughed. This was her way of hoping, she knew—couching it in wordplay, so that she could laugh about it. Otherwise hope was too dangerous, hope could lift you to unruly heights.

"I'm afraid someone's playing a prank on you, Tessa," he said. "Hardly good-natured."

"'Witness an improvement in her work ethic'?" she said, in disbelief. "It's on Westfaling stationery. That's your signature. It's Garamond, for god's sake. Chris, you didn't write this?"

"This isn't a recommendation I'd ever write for you," he said. He tried to hand the letter back to her, but she wouldn't take it. You're lying, she thought suddenly.

"I don't know if you want me involved in this, Tess, dear." He placed the page back on the coffee table and returned to his armchair. "If it went to the disciplinary committee it would have to be taken seriously. This could be perjury. It looks as if they've robo-signed my signature."

He took off his glasses and rubbed them with a handkerchief, looking at Tessa sternly.

"It came from George Bale," she blurted.

Now Chris visibly started. "You mean, he gave this to you?"

"He sent it to me, in an email."

"But how do you know it was George Bale?"

Tessa paused. "What do you mean, how do I know?"

"Hm?" He snatched the page up again and stared at it.

"What do you mean, how do I know?" Tessa heard her voice rising in pitch.

"I mean—he sent it to you in an email."

"Yes," she said.

"And you're saying it was from George Bale's email?"

"What else could I be saying, Chris?"

"I just want to make sure I have all the facts."

"But why would you ask if I knew it was from George Bale if I just said he sent it to me in an email?"

Chris paused and then seemed to become angry. "Well, because someone could have invented an account that says 'Georgebale at Hotmail' and sent you—"

"It came from his UCL address," Tessa lied.

"And moreover, how could George Bale have got it? He isn't even on the search committee."

"Got what? This?" she said, snapping it back from him.

Chris's eyes swiveled to the wall and then to her. "Tessa, you're twisting my words. I'm merely pointing out the holes in your logic, which can be porous. And you know, from the bottom of my heart, I'm sorry that you haven't had more luck in the job market, it's baffling to me, but I'm a bit shocked that you would lay the blame at my doorstep like this . . ."

Tessa looked away. The remark stung. He paused, clearly aware that he had hurt her.

"Especially when you have a perfectly acceptable offer to continue working here. I'm surprised that you would be taken in by this pernicious ruse."

She disliked the insinuation that she required a scapegoat for failure; yet it rang true.

"You're under so much pressure," Chris persisted. "I understand. Ben's left, you—"

"Did you write it or not, Chris?" she interrupted, trying to gather her thoughts.

"No!" Chris said, indignant again. "And I don't appreciate you coming in and accusing me of this."

"Okay—"

"Okay nothing. Clearly you need to phone George and ask him about it. If you really want to see the letter I wrote, I'll show it to you. This all makes me question how you perceive me in a way I don't like and in a way that's unbecoming of you." He paced around the table so that now he and Tessa were on the same side.

"I think you need to phone George immediately."

Tessa held up her hands. "Hold on."

"I think you need to phone him before we even discuss this further. Frankly, I don't even want to know about this. It just seems too outlandish. You understand, even if this was real, for him to divulge it to you is wholly unethical. In fact, phone George right now. We'll do it together. I'm sure I have his number."

Chris grabbed his phone from the sheaf of pages. Tessa's mind was racing—she had lost control. She did not know that Chris had written it. She felt an apology and self-disgust welling up inside her, and now George Bale was going to get roped in as well.

"I reckon you should be the one to talk to him?" Chris held out the phone.

Tessa looked at the matte black thing in his fingers that seemed suddenly so strange to her. He offered it again. "You didn't leave your phone," she said quietly, the queerness of this seeping in just as she said the words.

"What?"

"Just two hours ago, you asked to borrow my phone because you said you'd left yours at home, and now you have it right here."

Chris flinched again. In one motion he swiped the stack of papers off the coffee table, her cucumber glass clattering violently against the hardwood floor. Tessa retreated instinctively, her back arched, her heart caught in her throat.

"What is my having or not having my mobile to do with your printout?"

Tessa's skin prickled with the first intimation of fear. But overcoming the fear was anger at Chris's physical intimidation and the renewed conviction that he was lying. She backtracked toward the closed door. Chris wouldn't meet her eyes.

"So you don't want to call George Bale," he said.

"You're changing the subject," she persisted. "Why did you want to borrow my phone if you had yours? Why did you say you left yours at home?"

"I was mistaken. It was here all along. I just misplaced it."

"Chris, I'm sorry to—I'm sorry, why are you lying to me? What is going on?"

Chris looked at the ceiling now and breathed deeply. "We're supposed to be talking about the footnote. And your viva."

"Chris, I know you're lying to me about something. If I find out this is the letter that you wrote for me, which I will, and you continue to deny it—like, make a fucking calculation."

He stalked around the coffee table and came right toward her. She took just a slight step back. He brushed past her and swung open the door, pointing toward the empty staircase.

"If that is all," he said.

Tessa retrieved the letter from his desk and stuffed it into her bag, then marched past him, her heart thudding, into the utter stillness of Staircase 7. She left the college as quickly as she could, passing Lydia and Tully in their chef's whites smoking outside the dining hall, passing Max at the Porter's Lodge who nodded to her sternly, dodging tourists in visors drifting in through the wicket door. Chris's loss of self-control left her feeling utterly convinced that he had written the letter. He was the reason she had not been offered a single position outside Westfaling, hardly even an interview for next year.

Had she imagined the letter Chris would write? She had imagined it as a chastely positive missive—one in which he discharged his duty with typically repressed emotions, in which he made note of her abilities and withheld, piously, his own emotions toward her—or even allowed his own emotions to embellish a little. She had counted on some embellishment, maybe, and a thorough reckoning with her credentials, which were not inconsiderable. If this was Chris's, its recklessness and sheer audacity surprised her. But still, was this certainty? Beyond a reasonable doubt? Chris's authorship of the letter remained a hypothesis, not a conclusion, and to confuse those two would be a sort of moral failure. "Doubting Tessa," Chris sometimes called her, not without admiration, and it was true that in academia so far she'd been well served by her relentless skepticism, the legacy of being raised by not one, but two doctors, for whom testable hypotheses and the accumulation of data were a kind of religion.

To prove he had done it, she would need to get one of the departments to send her the letter Chris had sent them. Names of various classicists who might have direct or indirect access came to her—Ottamanelli? Sonja? Alistaire? But they were either too far from the search committees or too close to Chris for her even to contemplate. Higgins? Higgins—she and Phoebe Higgins had stayed out until three a.m. at the Edinburgh conference drinking claret and talking about their mothers. They had exchanged polite messages after Edinburgh. Higgins was on the search committee at UCLA and the rejection letter, when it arrived, felt especially barbed. Higgins had said nothing, and the rejection still stung, but she had offered to be of help to Tessa if she needed it. Even though she barely knew Higgins, she felt she could trust her. But could Tessa trust anyone? What other option did she have?

Deirdre Dewinter, her undergraduate thesis advisor. She wasn't on any of the search committees, but surely she knew someone who was, surely she could make back-channel inquiries on Tessa's behalf. It seemed the most reasonable avenue forward. Deirdre Dewinter—who, when Tessa first got to Oxford, told her there was never a bad time to call. Tessa could picture her now in her blue parka, jogging between lectures with her two terriers, Russkie and Dominic, talking on the phone with her husband, an anthropologist archaeologist who specialized in early Etruscan pottery and spent the majority of his year on one dig site or another in the eastern Mediterranean, Deirdre with earbuds in and the fog rising around her. Deirdre had seemed distant of late and she was very by-the-book, but still. Tessa had told her about job applications in the winter and Deirdre had given a brief but warm response—"You're a strong candidate. Good luck."

She walked along Broad Street toward the Trinity grounds and dialed, but it went straight to voice mail. *Hello, you've reached the voice-mail box of Deirdre Dewinter . . .* Tessa hung up. She went into her email, eyes skipping over a message from Lucrezia Pagani, subject line: *Visit?* She began a new message to Phoebe Higgins.

Dear Phoebe, . . . I don't have your number . . . I wanted to ask you a question . . . had such a wonderful time with you in Edinburgh . . . I assure you it has nothing to do with the position at UCLA . . . completely separate matter . . . I would be most grateful. She left her number.

•   •   •

TESSA LAY ON the couch, her face crumpled against a pillow and her feet, still socked, jutting over the other end. Was she not some sleeping goddess? Perhaps he should have put her in his bedroom, but that would have been too suggestive. He didn't want her to get the wrong idea. There's something chaste about a couch, and something that must be comforting to a young woman to wake up, clothed, blanketed, on a familiar couch after a good night's drinking. *Thank you for taking care of me,* she might say. Something gleamed off her skin. Sweat, maybe. Vodka from the vodka and tonics she had been drinking last night. But she always had a glow. One of her arms was propped under the pillow, but the other clutched the blanket, holding it up over her chest and neck, and for a moment he was transfixed by the downy hairs on her forearm. He had never seen them before, perhaps because he'd never had such an unchecked moment of gazing, and yet there they were. He could not help but imagine her as a grown-up Anne—Anne from the South Downs, the spring visits to his uncle's cottage, Anne whose cheeks would flush and reveal the same peach fuzz in the declining dusk light, the two of them chasing sand martins into the air around the gravel pits.

Chris walked away quietly, feeling spry. He glided through his bedroom and into the loo to brush his teeth. Every day for the past six months he had opened his bathroom cabinet to the sight of his toothbrush—red-orange, with Technicolor bristles that were meant to suggest a clean new white smile—and Diana's, a transparent clear plastic with plain white, soft bristles, of which she'd had literally dozens, but had left only one. It seemed the one place she'd missed in her ransacking of the house for her things was the bathroom cabinet—she'd even got the bar of soap from the shower. Now, as he routed all the grit from between his gums and spat into the running sink, he snatched Diana's toothbrush from the shelf and tossed it into the bin at his feet. He washed his own toothbrush and returned it behind the mirror, and took himself in. The cheeks could droop less, and his hair was out of sorts. When it became greasy it moved in all the wrong directions and more scalp showed than he would have liked. A shower was what he could use, but he wanted to wake Tessa with tea and some kind of light snack, a biscuit for her stomach to handle a paracetamol. He pushed his hair around. Not exactly Apollonian, but . . . Tessa lost her boyfriend, he lost Diana, the circumstances couldn't have been contrived better in their favor. What would be best, actually, was if he were too tall for the mirror. That was a problem he'd like to have.

When Chris made it back downstairs, paracetamol bottle rattling in his hand, Tessa was sitting forward over her knees, head held in both her hands.

"Painkillers?" he offered, as he approached.

"Yes, thank you."

He crossed into the kitchen and filled a glass with water.

"I'm sorry to have made such an ass of myself," she called after him. He brought her the water. She sighed, and threw back two of the pills.

"I think the circumstances called for a little excess." He took a seat on the ottoman, just next to her.

"I'm embarrassed. I could have made it back to my place."

"Maybe in a trolley." But she didn't laugh or smile.

"Where did I leave my handbag?" she asked. "Do you know?" She smoothed out the denim on her thighs, then pressed her fingers to her temples and looked around.

Chris said, deadpan, "You had a bag?"

"Yes."

He laughed. "You should have seen your face. I put it in the foyer."

Tessa stood and tossed the blanket over the back of the couch. "You've got a real knack for choice moments to deploy humor."

A spasm of anger gripped Chris's throat for a moment, and then passed. He took a sip of water from the glass. The tassels on the blanket's edge swished. The depression she had made in the couch cushion was lifting, things returning to the way they had been. She reappeared at the threshold of the living room.

"Can I offer you some tea?" he said.

"I feel I've depended on your hospitality enough, for the time being."

"It's not the first time you've been here."

"Slightly different circumstances."

"I wouldn't have had you here if I didn't think it had been in your best interest," he said.

"Admittedly not something I've been good about seeing to of late."

"Not so. Tessa, you're so near," he said.

"To what? A life alone because no one can understand how much this all means to me?"

"There are those who will," Chris said. "Who do."

"You're a saint for taking care of me," said Tessa, "but I need to prepare for Florence Henshawe at ten."

She moved toward the front door and opened it to a shaft of sunlight that illuminated the hall and, once again, the hairs along her forearm. She shut the door behind her; silence engulfed him. He went back upstairs to find his laptop to check Tessa's email, climbing the stairs slowly, as if trying to remember the route. He scanned his office but didn't see his laptop there, then his bedroom, then his office again, then he went to use the toilet, flushed, washed his hands, then saw Diana's toothbrush in the bin and felt dizzy. He put the toilet cover down and sat, gathering his thoughts.

Chris did know what it was like to not be understood. His mother had never exactly encouraged him to become an academic. She wore worsted wool, untreated, sheared and woven in Hampshire, and she had made Chris's clothes until he was just past eighteen and humiliated, not for the last time, by the posh public school boys at Trinity College, Cambridge. She respected people who did things with their hands. Chris's father had worked in the gravel pits until the gravel pits ceased to have any industrial use in the seventies, and then his mother, rather than try to enable her children to survive in the new economy that had left her husband jobless at forty-five and her entire family more or less dependent on the welfare state, had doubled down on callused hands and tried to send Chris to vocational school in Devon, despite his academic prizes, despite his scholarship to Cambridge, despite his contempt for his own father who had attempted to start a business with an investment in a certificate for heavy equipment operation and then a backhoe, which put them so far in debt that Chris had to wear his mother's wool caps and scarves and undershirts that made him feel like Thomas fucking Becket in his cilice and led the posh kids to call him woolly and then woolly mammoth on account of his daunting five-foot-seven stature. Chris had pointed out to his father that the same logic that had rendered the Eccles sheep farm and the gravel pits obsolete also applied to his loony equipment scheme, and Chris had been right. But he had never blamed his father the way he blamed his mother, his mother being intelligent but willfully submissive, his father only guilty of being stupid. When the backhoe scheme failed, Chris's father found work as a sub-department manager of meats and shellfish at the local Marks & Spencer, where he stayed for nearly ten years. At fifty-four he lined his windbreaker with ball bearings and rented a skiff in Portsmouth, charting a course east out of the Solent into the Channel. He hadn't counted on the tides, though, which in June are affected by the warmer waters generating currents heading north, resulting in an undertow, yes, but also a subsurface current that pushes back toward the shore. He was discovered the very next day, along with the boat, which was fine, along with alcohol, codeine, and xylazine, a sheep tranquilizer, in his bloodstream, upon which the life insurance company with which he'd taken out a policy made a strong case that the death by misadventure was self-inflicted.

It was true. Chris's father was stupid. Chris had nothing against sheep farmers, per se. He didn't think sheep farmers were stupid, per se. He just thought his father was. Had been.

But his mother knew the history of the area, and she had used it to bludgeon her son into accepting its traditions, none of which still existed. She was fastidious, like Chris. She praised the Eccles name and its pedigree while mythologizing none of her own ancestors, who didn't seem to exist, who seemed to have evaporated into the mists that collected off the escarpments.

Now his mother was dying, and his wife was gone. He didn't blame Diana for having an affair, but he was surprised by who she had chosen to do it with. He had tracked her phone to the canal not a kilometer from home. His first thought, when he looked at the map and saw her blinking location by the blue stripe, was that she had fallen in, and he nearly ran there. But she had been in a houseboat with the florist from the Covered Market. The hull squelched against the canal's wall when he stepped onto the deck, and there was a fetid algal odor all around. The florist came to the door when Chris knocked. The florist and the meat market man in the Covered Market were twins, so even though Chris recognized the face of the person who was cuckolding him, he didn't know if it belonged to the man who sold him sausages, or the one who had recommended the geraniums last spring. Diana didn't try to hide. When she heard his voice she asked, from the dark compartment, what he was doing there.

Cracking Diana's phone was easy—they shared passwords—but cracking Tessa's had required greater ingenuity. On a particularly frigid night last November when she'd canceled a dissertation meeting pleading illness, he'd used the free time to have a go at her email password. After two attempts on her personal account he knew that would be futile. He navigated to the Oxford University email portal and tried there, with the same results. The forgot-your-password link asked for the personal email to send a password reset to. Frustrated, he tried the cloud backup website. The user ID simply asked for your email, so he put hers in, then clicked the forgot-your-password link, which offered to send a password reset or to have him answer security questions. He clicked security questions. Galvanized by her betrayal—he knew she'd stood him up—he entered her date of birth, looked up her grandmother's maiden name on ancestry.com, then wrote down "name of childhood best friend" on a pad of paper. He was already thinking how he could contrive the conversation.

By the following week, he was in. Ben, her boyfriend, had convinced her to cancel the dissertation meeting for their second anniversary, the date of which they'd been arguing flirtatiously over. Should they celebrate their first date? Or the day they met? Chris was livid. Ben was a scruffy man-boy out of central casting who worked as a saturation diver in the North Sea. They lived in a sort of pressurized cabin, three men, a TV, and some jigsaw puzzles, for twenty-eight days at a time, so they wouldn't have to decompress between each dive. Twenty-eight days at a time in a "sat" chamber. Four days in that dank cistern at the end of each tour just to recalibrate! Glamorous in its own way, walking on the bottom of the sea, but Chris couldn't fathom the boredom. Stimulating conversationalist, Chris was sure.

Now Ben was out of the picture. Ben was gone. The previous night, Chris had been only too delighted to receive the news. Hardly three hours after meeting to discuss the footnote in her paper, he had run into Tessa again, smoking a rare cigarette outside the college. "What's the occasion?" he'd asked. She'd seemed harried, disheveled, vulnerable in the dim streetlight.

"Nerves. I haven't heard back from Case Western, Cambridge, Wake Forest, UCL, St. Andrews. I wish they would just tell me I've been rejected so I could stop thinking about it. And Ben just moved out, so there's that."

"Ben? Moved out?"

Chris had insisted she let off some steam. A glass of red wine at the KA led to vodka and tonics. They'd gone straight up St. Giles' toward her place on Leckford Road but she had inexplicably turned at Little Clarendon toward his. She'd had too much and he was carrying her bag and he'd offered his couch.

But if he had been carrying her bag, where were his things?

The laptop—that's where it was. He'd left everything at Westfaling. Chris stood, pleased that he'd solved the mystery without having to make a full search of the house. Since Diana had left, it had gone from breezy to drafty. The shelves were bare, the walls empty, the corridors bereft of melanchates's scuttling presence, her unconditional swaddling love. He had not moved her water bowl. He looked at his watch; if he left now he could be at College before ten.

Chris struck out on the street along the brick embankment on Jericho, in the unseasonably warm early March air. The unexpected loss of Ben made him buoyant; things were happening more swiftly than he could have hoped. He'd worried that keeping Tessa at Westfaling next year would favor the continuance of the Ben relationship; a post at an American university, while detrimental to Tessa and Ben, would also be detrimental to Tessa and Chris. It had to be Westfaling, and so far it seemed his recommendation letter had taken care of the other lectureships and assistant professorships and visiting assistant professorships she'd applied for.

He hit Broad Street just as a cloud was passing over. Bicyclists and shoppers were left in the shade for a moment. *Etiam si qua incidit cura, velut nubes / levis transit.* Seneca. *Even if some anxiety should fall upon him, it passed like a light cloud.* He stepped through the open doorway into the Westfaling quad, walked along the empty cloisters, and into the staircase leading to his office. There was his laptop where he'd left it, on the desk. He opened the casement window, which had been shut since the autumn. Crisp spring air washed through the office. He logged in. He'd had to find software that backed up data from the cloud onto a separate hard drive. All you needed was to log on to the account once, and as long as the account's password didn't change, there it all was. The cloud, the cloud. Nebulous data being pumped in and out at all times, there for the picking.

As the backup completed he glanced at his watch. Ten past ten. Tessa and Florence would have normally passed his door for their tutorial by now, but he'd heard neither. He clicked through the emails that started to populate from her inbox. Wedding invitation. Something from her sister Claire. Nothing from any schools.

But then, something from an email address that amounted to gibberish.

Qwerpoiuasdf1@hotmail.com. It was a single sentence.

You may want to reconsider asking Christopher Eccles for a recommendation letter in the future.

And attached to that a photograph of a letter on Westfaling stationery. Chris double-clicked the thumbnail of the photograph and, although he knew the text already, he read it again. *To Whom It May Concern.*

Could he delete it? No, he only had access to the backup. It was read only. He wanted to reach his hand into Apple's servers and yank it out. Out of the cloud.

Could he deny it? What was he going to say to her? He shut the office door and locked it. He fumbled in his pockets for a cigarette and lit it. How was she going to approach him? He would have to act normally, and if she said something . . . but she wouldn't be able to prove a thing. If she confronted him, he would simply show her the first letter he had written, the real one. None of the departments she applied to would furnish her with a copy of the recommendation letter. She'd have to resort to bribery or some underhanded exchange. But if he cast enough doubt, if he had his story ready, she might go for it. The alternative would be to admit that it was a true copy, and if he did that, well. She wouldn't have any option except to work at Westfaling next year, so she would have to remain in his good graces, and maybe they would be able to work through it. No, she wouldn't go for this. He'd had trouble enough wooing her without this. The deck was stacked against him enough. He flicked the butt out the window with a rash of sparks.

PART II

Were I deaf to you, my love, like divers to the
bird's call, Isimplycouldntbearit

MARIUS,
translated by Florence Henshawe

Can we please discuss?

The message from Chris traveled across Tessa's screen just as she finished marking the last essay. She flipped her phone over so she would not be interrupted again. The ambiguity of Chris's role in the letter was intolerable and so she shut him from her mind and focused on Marius in a spirit of defiance—Marius the minor, or "minor minor" poet, a "nonentity," per Chris. Tessa and perhaps twenty other living souls endured along the desks and tables of the Lower Reading Room. The quiet in the Bodleian seemed almost to take on its own texture, and she was grateful now for the way it enabled the work to engulf and insulate her.

Before her on the desk was *I Frammenti Completi di Publius Marius Scaeva*, a slim volume, hardcover, edited with commentary by Sergio Conti and published in Italian in 1940. It contained all five of Marius's surviving poems. She turned through its crackling pages to Marius III, and began to check Ed Duffey's translation against the Latin text. Ed was one of her best students, though very literal in his translations.

At what time you're absent, I listen and I hear your voice.
It drips down the fountain and mixes with the river waves,
and mutters with the doves, and indeed sometimes we join
   a silence.
(the voice) tells me hidden (things) you would be familiar
   with, intimate (things),

delicious (things), I would never commit to tablets.   5
(If) I were deaf to you (my) love, as a salvage diver
To a dove's songs, I would breathe my last (breath)

Everything was grammatically sound, not to her surprise. The Latin word for "salvage diver," *urinator,* was an unusual one, and Tessa knew the *Oxford Latin Dictionary* defined it merely as "diver." Ed had dived deep on the vocabulary. She gave him a check, then flipped back to the Conti to look at the last two lines in Latin.

> *ad te essem amorem surda, sicut ad cantus*
> *turturis urinator, ultimam efflarem*

Not much was known of Marius, and all his surviving poems were in a meter unusual for Latin poets—choliambic, or "limping iambs"— an awkward rhythm normally associated with works of invective, pioneered by a Greek poet several centuries earlier named Hipponax, and used only sparingly by Catullus, among others, in Latin.

The key to the limping iambs was the way each line gathered a short-long pattern, then reversed in the last foot: long-short, or long-long. Iambs were hard to achieve in Latin, and Tessa wondered if Marius had resorted to so much elision, here, in order to wrangle the iambic meter. Indeed, *te essem amorem* would be read all as one word, the *e*'s in *te* and *essem* joining, and the *m* in *essem* being dropped: "tessamoorem." *Ultimam efflarem* would do the same thing, and with the long vowels would read as "ooltimah-flahrem." Tessa felt herself making the argument that one performing the piece would have to take a very deep breath for the last two lines, just as the poetic persona herself would "breathe her last." Yes, and also there were the onomatopoeias, apt for a poem about hearing, which plays on the meaning of hearing itself and which seemed to be about love, not insult. *Turtur*, the Latin word for turtledove, was itself an onomatopoeia, a notion Tessa had stumbled upon early in life, when she imagined turtledoves as an exotic species of bird, or reptile, that had both wings and shell. Was she disappointed to learn they had nothing to do with turtles? No, she loved that they did not, that *turtur* was the Latin name for this type of dove because it made that sound *turtur*, and English in its amusing way had taken this root and turned them into feathered Franklins. She had confessed her early notion once to Chris, and he had sketched her, on the spot, a turtle with dove wings, a large bird-like eye on the side of its head, the creature in profile, looking at the viewer. It was one of those things over which she had wavered; was it charming? She had laughed at the time. But was it condescending? *Portrait of a Turtledove*, he'd written below. *For Tessa's Menagerie*. It still lay somewhere in her desk drawer.

Tessa flipped to Florence's translation.

When you're not there I listen for, I hear, your voice.
It trickles down the fountainsides, gets caught up in
the river tides, it mutters with the turtledoves
we even sometimes share a silence.
It tells me secrets you would know, intimacies   5
little sweet things, I would not trust to tablets.
Were I deaf to you, my love, like divers to the
bird's call, Isimplycouldntbearit

Tessa laughed as she read. Florence had cheekily rendered the elisions at the end. Sadly, she would get no points for poetic license when she sat her finals. But more subtly, Florence had taken a foot off the fourth line so the reader, expecting more syllables at line four, would hear a silence after the word "silence." There was lots of internal rhyme, but it was still iambic, which gave it a herky-jerky quality, like the limping iambs themselves. It was playful, it was fun. Tessa gave her a check, but wrote *Speak to me* on the pages.

Two years ago, when Tessa had first encountered Marius, she had puzzled over the last two lines of this poem. She had been checking references for *Hellenistic Derivatives in Classical and Late Classical Roman Verse*, edited by Chris, recently available from Oxford University Press, a menial though well-paid job that had required her to confirm the correct pages and line numbers in each reference in each author's unproofed essay. Why would a diver—*urinator*—be deaf to a bird's call? she'd speculated in a notes app on her phone. Did that simply refer to one not being able to hear a bird's call while underwater? The birds then would probably be gulls, but these were turtledoves, not the most riparian of birds. She had asked Ben what he thought—their vocations so rarely intersected—but he hadn't known, either. Maybe Marius *was* a bit of a loon, she'd figured.

In the Bodleian, she flipped to Conti's commentary, and the stray bit of information that had led her to Lucrezia in the first place.

Si pensava che fosse morto a Isola Sacra
He was thought to have died at Isola Sacra.

Even now it was funny—for as she scanned the rest of the page in Italian there was still nothing to support the statement about his place of death, just further hypotheses about the meaning of various lines in the poem and thoughts on the grammar and some of Conti's signature digressions. What a shit Conti was—what an obscure and delightful prick that he had written that down, for when Tessa had heard, some months later, that Lucrezia Pagani was to become site director for the excavation of the Isola Sacra Necropolis, her memory had somehow preserved the little gem.

Tessa had perhaps been overexcited in that first meeting with Lucrezia. But Marius's work had so nearly succumbed to time that even the smallest shred of new information could hijack her social graces. The five poems had escaped antiquity only by way of the Codex Salmasianus, an anthology of minor Latin poems, which dated him to the second century AD. The only other premodern source attesting to his existence was the *Suda*, a tenth century Byzantine encyclopedia whose terse entry Tessa had long ago memorized: *Publius Marius Scaeva. A poet writing in choliambs. He married Sulpicia.* The *Suda* referenced or directly quoted many scholia that had been completely lost—as such, it was in many cases the only link to recorded history in the ancient world.

At Tessa's request, she and Lucrezia had held a rushed meeting at dawn in the coffee shop adjacent to the Gloucester Green station, before Lucrezia caught a bus to Heathrow. Tessa had explained about Publius Marius Scaeva and the Conti reference. It might be nothing, but there was so little known about Marius that the smallest convergence of records, of any sort, would be of use. A cream-colored suitcase with leather trim had endured impatiently while Lucrezia listened in regal silence. She'd seemed unimpressed by Conti's lack of corroborating evidence. She was not unfriendly, had never been, but she gave off an air of expensive impenetrability. Finally, Lucrezia informed Tessa that she needed to leave to make her flight; they'd have to end shortly. Sensible queries occurred to Tessa simultaneously: What century were the graves at Isola Sacra? What was the class makeup of its inhabitants?

"Do you know any good reason," Tessa said instead, "why a diver wouldn't be able to hear a bird's call?"

Lucrezia smiled suddenly, as if Tessa had liberated her from the prison of a boring conversation. "But this is a perfect question," she said. "When you say diver, you mean the *urinatores*? The salvage divers?"

"Yes," Tessa said, sensing the change in Lucrezia's demeanor.

Lucrezia had then launched into what seemed at first to be a non sequitur: Did Tessa know that Nazaré, an old fishing village in Portugal, was a kind of surfer's mecca? Just offshore, a submarine canyon compressed walls of water into immense, heaving swells. From an old lighthouse on the coast you could watch men and women ride like specks on waves of up to twenty meters. Because of this irregularity in the ocean floor, surfers flew into Nazaré from all over the globe, and many surfers lived there too. Lucrezia had learned all this on a phone call with an ear, nose, and throat doctor local to the town.

The archaeology team at Isola Sacra hadn't made much of them at first, the millimeter-sized nubs in the ear canals of some of the skulls found in the necropolis. They were small enough to be attributed to ordinary irregularities in bone formation, they thought. But the growths had kept turning up, always in male skulls. Sixty-seven, now, and counting. "A genetic abnormality might be present in higher frequency if a society was isolated and everyone was, you know . . ." Lucrezia had seemed to search for an English euphemism.

"Interfucking?" Tessa had blurted, lacking a more concise verb for committing incest.

"Yes," Lucrezia said with a laugh, "you could say this. But Isola Sacra was part of a major port. This is not Papua New Guinea. Or British nobility."

Lucrezia had made inquiries and discovered that "external auditory exostoses" had been found in archaeological contexts and could be found even in lifeguards and surfers today. "Surfer's ear, it is called." She'd been put in touch with the ENT in Nazaré, an expert in removing "EAEs." He saw them all the time in professional surfers. Habitual exposure to cold water would cause soft tissue irritation in the ear meatus, then bone growths would begin to form. Over time, they could basically close the ear canal. "My boss seems to think they happened because of the *thermae*, the baths."

"Well, do you find EAE in non-coastal communities?" Tessa asked.

"That's what I say."

"The occupational profile of the salvage divers would match that of a surfer," Tessa said.

"Exactly! In terms of the habitual exposure to cold water—who is going to maintain the underwater foundations? Who is going to retrieve tons of expensive goods when a ship sinks in the harbor?"

Tessa had walked Lucrezia into the terminal while she continued to talk. "And what's more, each and every skull with these bone growths articulates with remains easily identifiable as male. The skeleton is sexually dimorphic to a degree, after puberty, but come on, the ears?"

Lucrezia had let the bus driver stow the fancy suitcase, insisted that they continue their conversation, gave Tessa two cheek kisses, invited her to Isola Sacra, and then swept onboard. Her blurry figure had navigated the aisle and found a seat, then knocked on the glass window. Tessa waved. Lucrezia started trying to say something to her, speaking. Tessa had stepped closer and pointed at her ear. Lucrezia's lips were saying, can you hear me?

Tessa shook her head. "No," she said out loud.

Lucrezia had laughed and signed two thumbs up.

Over the next year they'd become friendly, exchanging emails about Marius and Isola Sacra, meeting for coffee whenever Lucrezia came through Oxford. Lucrezia had promised to keep Tessa current on any developments with the population of *urinatores* at the necropolis, or of any evidence of Marius himself—though what that evidence might constitute remained vague.

The light had dimmed in the windows of the Bodleian. Tessa

packed the mess of graded papers into her bag, then opened her laptop to read the email from Lucrezia, subject line: *Visit?* Every so often she received a note like this. This one chided Tessa for hanging up on her earlier and informed her that the archaeological team had found "several interesting inscriptions." She'd reiterated that Tessa would need to pay for her own flights and closed with what felt like a warning.

Tell me your decision soon, alternatively I must ask
another Latinist about the inscriptions!
a presto
L

Was Lucrezia fishing for free labor? She consistently pled poor when it came to flying Tessa to the site, which was a problem. Chris wasn't about to open Westfaling's wallet, and Tessa herself had no money for flights—she was in perpetual overdraft with Lloyds. In any case, her dissertation defense was on Monday. She shut her laptop and stuffed it into her bag. Lucrezia had never threatened to bring someone else into the loop; maybe Tessa could ask Lucrezia to send her pictures of the inscriptions. She flipped over her phone, already composing the message in her mind. *Can you send me pics of . . .*

On the screen were two missed-call notifications from a number Tessa didn't recognize, twenty-nine and twenty-eight minutes ago. Slinging her bag over her shoulder, Tessa entered her password and filed out of the Lower Reading Room. 323 area code— California, her phone informed her. Phoebe? Tessa's pulse accelerated as she darted toward the exit under the Proscholium's hushed vaults, dialing as she went. In the paved square courtyard low voices echoed against the stone enclosure. *You've reached the voice mail box of Phoebe Higgins . . .*

Tessa left a brief voice mail for Phoebe and set off for her flat, mortified that she had missed her. That she had called back so quickly seemed to ratify Tessa's suspicions. Tessa walked quickly through jostling crowds and the weakening yellow light that still skimmed over the roofs and turrets and crenellated towers, anger and inarticulate sadness mingling with anticipation. By the time she reached the squeaky iron gate of the mid-terraced house on Leckford Road in which she lived, she felt wretched and alone. A gritty breeze had picked up, and the shadow of a cloud dimmed the still forecourt, devoid of flowers, with the small laurel climbing the house's front façade. Apparently the laurel's roots were growing into the stone, compromising the foundation. Her management company left notes from time to time indicating the tree was to be removed, but the appointment never seemed to materialize.

She swept up to her flat on the top floor, checking her phone for a call back, though she'd been clutching it the entire journey. All was quiet on Leckford Road, except the window in her bedroom that rattled in its sash every time the wind picked up. The same thing had happened last year when it began to warm—the wood in the frame expanded, the pane came ever so slightly loose. Ben had fixed it.

Tessa's phone vibrated in her palm. It was Phoebe's number.

• • •

CAN WE PLEASE DISCUSS? Chris typed.

He didn't press send. Instead he shut his office door and sat on the chesterfield. His mouth felt parched. He needed to hydrate. A tonic water in his fridge—he poured it over ice and added a slice of lemon. Then he decided he would prefer cucumber. He tossed the whole mix out the window and took a fresh cucumber from his fridge. He sliced, took four pieces and added them to the glass, then added ice and poured fizzy water over it. He shook the glass in his hand, dispersing the flavor.

It hadn't taken Diana long to understand that he had been tracking her. He knew she would figure that out. "Trust, but verify" had long been a joke between the two of them with respect to others—sure, Diana trusted her tennis trainer, but nevertheless Chris had offered to verify it was a fifty-quid session. "I believe Ashlynn," he'd said, when their broker was dawdling over the spring bank holiday with the escrow for their lovely house in Jericho, "I trust her." "She's never given you a reason not to trust her." "She seems trustworthy." "Good, we're agreed that we trust her." "Of course." "But how do you want to verify?" and Diana would smile. It got to the point where only one of them would interact with a caterer or a florist so that the other could pose as some anonymous stranger to check a price, or attempt to book the same venue on the same date for a higher price, any excuse to test loyalty, to divine integrity. They were obsessed with integrity—who had it, who didn't, the over/under on when someone would give in. Like Ashlynn. Diana had posed as an all-cash buyer with no co-broke. But Ashlynn didn't respond. Diana had gone higher, as Meredith Penkov, daughter of Vladimir Penkov, Bulgarian-born Russian gas magnate—a real person, by the way—and still Ashlynn didn't respond. They found out after the holiday that Ashlynn's mother had died quite suddenly in the Cotswolds from cardiac arrest. The kids were heartbroken. Chris saw them the next week in the Covered Market with their mother, who forced back tears as she told him, assuring him she had taken care of the paperwork that very morning. Twins, a boy and a girl, he never remembered their names, the girl had been wearing white stockings and a jumper that hung off one shoulder where her brother's face was buried the whole time Ashlynn spoke, harried, groceries spilling from her tote, resuming life. Trust, but verify. He didn't feel guilty—what about the time Diana's sister was dating that London banker who split his time between there and Hong Kong? Please, Ozzy, you're not fooling anyone. Just how to break it to Danielle that he was married and had a child with a learning disability.

They'd never discussed it, but of course it was only a matter of time until they started to verify each other. Chris had assumed Diana had from the start, had partially assumed from the start. When he began to suspect Diana was having an affair, he had a dream that he was following her up a winding staircase to the top of a tower where she was with, of all people, Charles Parnell. Diana was the married woman he was having his affair with, and there Chris was, discovering them, and something in him was flattered that Parnell had risked not only his own life and marriage, but that he'd risked all of Ireland to be with Diana. Chris yearned so much for that to be the case, had fantasized so often about the different men she had chosen that when he followed her to that boat on the river he could have slapped her out of sheer disappointment. Chris, who had never laid a finger on Diana, had never been closer to violence. He wanted to believe that this was simply because he had caught his wife cheating, that he would have had the same reaction if, contrary to the laws of science, he had found her with Charles Parnell, or with Paris son of Priam, but he remembered the excitement he felt in the dream as he climbed the tower, and he knew it was that he had found her under the hairy shelf of the meat man's paunch, that she couldn't, in fact, do better.

Yes, Diana knew he had taken liberties with her mobile device, and she'd mentioned it to him in their last conversation. But as far as he knew there was no precedent for prosecuting spouses under the computer misuse act. Certainly, with Tessa, that was a different matter. Shortly after experiencing the joy of first downloading her phone's contents to his hard drive, he spent a late evening reading case law and past judgments on the issue of "unauthorized access." Community labor was a common punishment. He saw himself on a roadway verge north of Banbury in a neon vest and orange gloves, skewering rubbish. But what frightened him more was being discovered by Tessa—the prospect of incurring her eternal disfavor was more immediate, more visceral. Yet he was also so curious to know how she would react. Would she forgive him? Could she love him enough to forgive him? It excited him, too, beyond all measure. It seemed the only pathway to wholeness, for him, for her to eventually know everything about him. It just couldn't happen yet, when things were so fragile.

And in any case, why should she be surprised that he would lie to her? He'd told her more than once that civilization is but a thin sheet of ice above an ocean of chaos and darkness, credit to Werner Herzog. Extrapolate, sweet student. Sometimes, as a thought experiment, he considered how he would feel about her if he she wasn't so radiant. He pictured her face and gave her a pug nose, a wart, a snaggle tooth, straggly gray hair, and cauliflower ears. But it didn't make a difference. She would have to be adjusted beyond all recognition for him to no longer be attracted to her. And even then, if her face were so warped, he knew that if he spent an hour in that creature's presence and recognized her gestures and the tone of her voice, he would love her again.

He had been surprised that Tessa would confront him so soon, without verifying the evidence. He swirled the cucumber around in his glass, crushed the ice between his teeth. He would come clean about the letter of recommendation. He saw this as but a ripple in the longer arc of their future together. Everything arced. They say the shortest distance between two points is a straight line. Wrong. It's a geodesic. Space is curved. So is the surface of the earth. There was no straight line between them, or between anyone or anything for that matter. Everything was curved, crooked, if you will. No other way to unity. And no other way to conceive of his love for her.

Was she going to be able to authenticate the letter? Maybe. Such is life. Everything grinds on. Chris had twelve tutorial papers he hadn't glanced at, two funding applications to decide between, a lecture on Persius he hadn't finished, and several unfinished papers each of which demanded its own labyrinth of references and addenda and mental unwinding, plus a buildings committee meeting he was presently skipping and a regent's meeting that evening on god knows what. The detritus of his official responsibilities accumulated in piles around his desk, though he knew where everything was—he was spatially gifted, had an excellent sense of direction, and near-photographic recall not of text itself but of where certain text was placed in a book, and on a page, a quality that he thought made him a good but not great scholar. A great scholar would remember the text itself; he would be so much more efficient if he could quote text and line number from memory. This was where Tessa often came in handy. He could say, That Persius quote from the prologue about Parnassus? And if she didn't know the Latin offhand, she'd get him the quote while he sat there and continued with the line of questioning, so that he wouldn't be distracted. It was so bloody useful. Unfailingly, she knew the line to which he was referring. No other student he'd ever advised could read his mind like Tessa. She was telepathic. Tessapathic, he had started saying to her. He had written three papers with her assistance.

Now Liam, his other advisee, was due to meet Chris at two-thirty. Chris had twelve minutes to make up an excuse or sneak away.

Liam, with greatest apologies but something has come up this afternoon. Could we reschedule? Please email. He scrawled on a note. Then he added as an afterthought, *CONGRATULATIONS.* He ripped off a piece of Scotch tape and attached the message to the outside of the door, gathered his things, and stepped into the hallway. As he was locking the door behind him he heard footsteps.

"Do I have the time wrong?" said Liam, his large head bobbing. "Or are we going out?" His pasty long hand restrained a suede bag with nickel buckles whose provenance Chris could trace all the way to Walters on Turl Street: How individuating, Liam. How interesting.

Chris pointed at the note on the door and then his throat, as if he were sick. He rasped, "Voice." And then put his hands beside his head to mime sleep.

"I'm so sorry, Chris," said Liam, now on the staircase landing, a full head taller.

Chris patted his shoulder and descended. He decided that he would find the original recommendation letter that he wrote for Tessa, the real one, and present it to her. He would apply pressure on Martesi, the editor in charge of the Oxford University Press Monographs Committee. If he could just get her to see how much better everything would be if she stayed at Westfaling, the letter of recommendation wouldn't matter. It wouldn't need to be interrogated. Life would grind on, as it always does, and they could put it behind them.

On the quad, a warm and peaceful afternoon had taken hold. He could feel the sun's heat rising off the stone footpath. Bethany and Tully chatted in their chef's whites outside the dining hall, and they waved to him as he passed, cheery masks of contentment. He turned and pulled out a cigarette and stopped by Bethany, one of the cooks, who was from Hampshire like him, and asked her if she'd been home yet this spring.

"Not yet," she said. A line on her forehead, which he'd never seen before, creased as she spoke. "I'm going for Easter. Big roast for the family. And who's cooking, d'you think?" She nodded at the dining hall and offered Chris a light. "Mum doesn't like me to get a vacation."

Chris tried to think of a proverb that he could warp for the situation at hand, but came up with nothing. Eternal servants? Mother proverbs? Children of? A modest proposal?

"Right. Quite the opposite for me when I visit home."

"Sure."

"Mum's sick."

"Oh, poor thing."

"The coast should be lovely this year," he added, as Liam came out of the staircase and looked at him, smiling, in conversation. Sod it. Bethany began to respond but Chris turned away and walked quickly toward the wicket door.

He struck out onto the road, then Broad Street, cut away from the Covered Market, where the meat man and the florist presided over their little kingdoms, and set off for home under the lengthening shadows of afternoon. Productive day! It was becoming precarious, the mound of responsibilities he'd been avoiding. Liam wasn't even the start of it. And yet he felt light, unburdened by the quotidian worries of teaching and administration. The walk up Botley Road to his house was cheery; was he on some drug? He bought a sandwich at the Buttery and ate it at home, the wax wrap, stained with mayonnaise grease, crinkling under his fingers. He opened a window, pleased by the lead counterweight in the sash as he always was—it's what Diana had been at first, for him, a counterweight that elevated his writing, his purpose, his energy, and then he'd become the counterweight, he knew, but instead of lifting Diana he had been sinking her, a pocketful of stones, a vest lined with ball bearings.

And was he now committing the same to Tessa, exerting the same downward force? No, Chris objected to this line of thinking. Marius hardly cropped up in the anthologies of minor poets; not only was his verse average, and inexplicably composed in limping iambs, it was also scant and lacunose. Virgil and Ovid survived in tens of thousands of lines; Marius perhaps one hundred fifty. Tessa believed that one of his fragments constituted the first literary reception of Ovid's Daphne and Apollo sequence—a monologue composed, perhaps, in Daphne's voice. Yet the only evidence he could see for this belief was her own bias. In fact, Tessa's phone held on it a living document in which she recorded thoughts about her own reception of Daphne and Apollo, deeply personal hypotheses about why she had been so struck, what the passage had meant to her, had done to her, when she'd first encountered it as a teenager. She'd added new readings over the years, not about the genre or any academic debate, but about how she'd personally perceived the passage at any given fulcrum in her life. Her own psychological growth could be observed like a flip-book in these snapshots, layered in time. Of course someone obsessed with her first reading of a passage would be drawn to the first literary reception of said passage, if it existed. Thus the root of her interest in Marius. And now she believed that all his poetry was wonderful (including the bollocks you couldn't read) and furthermore, she thought she'd connected him to Rome's ancient port city, Ostia.

He did not see it. The evidence was tenuous. And for someone like Tessa, with a fragile constitution—he would never forget finding her shivering in the AV closet at Edinburgh just moments before blowing the audience away—these webs of what-ifs and maybes could presage descents into hazardous psychological straits. With these low-quality, obscure fragments of poems, the more time one spent with them, the more one began to believe they held meaning. He had seen this occur in graduate school at Cambridge. George Bale, who had been his close friend and who also suffered from a fragile constitution, had become obsessed with the *Culex*, an obscure

poem from the *Appendix Virgiliana*, true author unknown. The titular *culex*, Latin for gnat, is an insect killed accidentally by a farmer,
whom it then haunts from the underworld. Of course, the short
poem was not the cause of George's mental breakdown, but an outward manifestation of it, a vehicle by which his mental disintegration
could occur—but Chris later regretted any and all encouragement
he had given. George had tried to kill himself. He was fine now, of
course. Distinguished man of letters. He'd never so much as looked
at the *Culex* again, so far as Chris knew. But Chris's memory of that
jagged bloodstain on the hardwood floor of George's Cambridge
flat—Chris had helped his parents move him out while George was
in the hospital—was something *he* could not unsee.

Now the breeze announced itself by scuffling a few pages around
in the living room, though mostly he'd secured the piles of his work
with saucers and mugs, since Diana had plundered all the paperweights. A few remained. Apollo and Daphne had been a gift to
him from Tessa, brought over from her summer in Rome, which he
had enabled with a travel fellowship, much to Liam's chagrin. The
statue secured a sheaf of correspondence for the Library Committee, whose input, Chris knew, the Bodleian warden was completely
uninterested in. Minutes and resolutions and debated suggestions
from junior faculty accumulated and were sent to Chris as head of
the committee, and there they accreted, requiring no attention from
him at all. He was good at finding sinecures—another quality of a
good scholar, though not a great one. The great ones didn't need to
find sinecures, they simply refused committee service and went on
with their lives, and no one bothered them about it. He noticed,
now, a cool glaze of sweat on his forehead as the air circulated, and
he remembered what he was looking for, the real recommendation
letter for Tessa.

He walked up the stairs to a cabinet in the study. His fingers, still greasy from the sandwich, slipped at first on the key that always sat in the keyhole, but on the second try he turned the lock and began to rifle through his Tessa folder. He found the original letter and looked at his phone. *Can we please discuss?* Chris sent the message.

•   •   •

"PROFESSOR HIGGINS?" Tessa said.

"Phoebe, please." Tessa recognized Phoebe's voice, which was at once high-pitched and grainy, a sort of rough velour.

"Phoebe," Tessa said. "Sorry for the phone tag." She needed to press on with her original inquiry—though in a way that wouldn't further compromise her future. "It's so good of you to call me back," she added. "I had such a wonderful time with you in Edinburgh and have been wanting to reach out—but then, of course, there was the UCLA application and I didn't want to seem meddlesome."

"Of course," Phoebe returned. "How are you?"

Her voice was warm. After the events of the day, the question was comforting. Rays of light filtered through the laurel leaves in the dormer window. "I could be better, to be honest."

"I see," said Phoebe. "I can understand how that might be true."

Encouraged by this cryptic statement, Tessa inclined toward transparency. "Well, how do I put this?" she began. "Something's come to my attention that would possibly be critical to my ability to find a position next academic year, after I receive my doctorate."

"Possibly in what way?"

"In a way that I don't have any ready means to confirm but about which I have suspicions," Tessa said.

"Yes," said Higgins, not like she was asking, but like she was confirming, waiting for Tessa to confirm. Tessa continued on, more confident. "My suspicions have to do with a letter of recommendation from my dissertation advisor."

"Yes," said Higgins again.

"Given you're on the search committee, and I've already been rejected, could you tell me, are they warranted?" Tessa asked.

"Yes, they are, I'm afraid," was Phoebe's reply.

Tessa's foot trembled. She found, to her own surprise, that she still needed more evidence. "Would you, I'm sorry, tell me if I'm being improper, but would you tell me just a word or phrase from the letter, if you can remember?"

"I recall 'argumentative.'" Phoebe's voice was clipped. "I recall 'rocky.' I recall 'lack of rigor.' None of which square with a first on the Advancements and an O'Neill and the paper you gave at Edinburgh, and you, from what I gather."

Tessa let her head pitch back on her shoulders. The weight and shock of reality struck her with peculiar force, and for a long moment she was sensible only of the exposed bulb in her sloped garret ceiling. She was absorbed into it; its glassy curve, its unlit filament.

"I'm sorry," Phoebe continued. "I could not do anything about it on our side. I would have taken you if I could, but I didn't have a consensus. I did call your dissertation advisor and talked to him. He seems very dedicated to whatever it is he's pursuing. I worried about you. If there's any way I can do something, if I can help . . . How did you find out?"

"Then you weren't the one who sent it to me?" Tessa asked. She was returning to herself and to Phoebe's voice slowly. Her heart writhed to understand what her mind now knew.

Phoebe laughed lightly. "I'm not the only one who took issue with it, then. No, I didn't send it to you."

"Do you think any institution will take me?" Tessa said.

"It would be difficult; anyone on the committee who preferred a different candidate could use that letter against you, even if they questioned its origins. And as you know, it's a competitive field. People like to pick favorites."

"I cannot tell you how grateful I am, Phoebe," Tessa managed.

Phoebe asked that Tessa consider their discussion as off the record, and Tessa reassured her that she would. "Well, I'm supposed to be teaching five minutes ago," Phoebe said, and the call ended as quickly as it had begun.

Tessa remained motionless on the bed for several minutes. She could hardly believe the reality presented before her. And yet the motive was clear: Chris had never intended to let her leave Westfaling in the first place. Thus his initial dodginess about the recommendation letter. Perhaps he disliked her, or loved her, or thought he loved her, or all of the above. It didn't matter much at all; she simply needed to be out from under him. It was really quite a straightforward situation, and for several moments she burned with simple hatred. The waxy leaves of the laurel tapped against the dormer window. It seemed they were both set for the chop. She saw in the tree's predicament something like her own, hovering between survival and annihilation. Even knowing that Chris had sabotaged her, she would be forced to accept the appointment at Westfaling. She felt paralyzed by this reality, even as she began to search for ways to elude it, to soften what Chris had done.

Tessa moved into the kitchen and took an apple from the counter, which she began to peel with a sharp little knife, if only for something to do with her hands. It was impossible to organize her emotions. Yes, Chris was controlling. When Tessa had first entertained ideas of studying Marius, Chris had pounced on her aspirations. Even recently, when he had seen that she planned to give a talk on Marius at the April conference in Oxford, he had vocalized his regret for finding her spot on the podium.

But the extremity of Chris's behavior here, she never would have presumed. It was beyond anything, and some part of her was pathologically curious about the preoccupation the letter seemed to be confiding to, about what it said about his feelings toward her—but his motives were irrelevant. She took it as no less than an attempt to metamorphose her, terminally, into something lesser than what she was—

Tessa yelped at a sharp pain at the base of her finger. She had snapped the small knife against her hand. Blood rose to the surface and made a little red rill in the contour of her palm. She let it trickle down the groove and onto her wrist, remembering, as it did, the way Claire had used to bandage her cuts and bruises as a child. She had not wanted to involve Claire, but now she felt that perhaps she should. She had to talk to someone, though she dreaded the enigmatic silence that would follow her account of the letter. Claire would be outraged by Chris's behavior, no doubt, but she never would have gotten herself into the situation to begin with. Last year, whenever Tessa had mentioned their collaboration, Claire would suddenly go mute. "He's married," Tessa had added once. "I didn't say anything," Claire had responded. Now Tessa sent Claire a text. *Call me.*

In the medicine cabinet, behind the mirror, she found a bandage, but was startled by a sudden rapping on her front door. Two sharp knocks. She left the bandage on the sink.

"Hello?" she called. She crossed into the living room. The flat had a buzzer that had been out of order since the winter. Still, one needed a key, or the lock code, to get in downstairs.

"Tessa?" Chris's muffled voice came meekly through the door. "Can we please discuss?"

Tessa froze. She could feel her pulse quicken. This was the type of thing—sometimes Chris would just appear out of thin air. For years, Tessa had found this endearing.

"Chris," she ventured, nearing the door. "How did you get in?"

"Your neighbor was leaving," he said. "Pardon the intrusion. You weren't answering your mobile."

Tessa waited for him to say something more. He cleared his throat. Clearly he had assumed she would open the door. "May I come in?" he finally asked.

"I have a question," Tessa countered. "If you're not going to respond, then please walk away."

Silence.

"Did you write the letter?"

"I have the real letter with me," he said.

"The real letter?"

"If you'd just let me in."

"You can push it under the door."

"Please, Tessa, this is a bit humiliating."

"I'm walking away," she said.

"Wait."

Two pages whispered under the door and then curled upward slightly at her feet. She took them in her left hand, the other still trickling blood. Garamond. No Westfaling insignia. Just text on paper.

Dear Members of the Search Committee

She read the pages at the door.

It is my pleasure to recommend Ms. Tessa Templeton for [ ] at [ ]. I have known Ms. Templeton since 2006, when she began

*her Master of Studies in Greek and Latin Languages under my
supervision. Ms. Templeton first caught my eye, however, months
previous, with a paper she wrote for her BA in Greek and Latin
Languages. This paper showed a passion for criticism and dazzling
intellect, all the more so because it was written before engaging in
any graduate work at Oxford.*

*It would not do justice to Ms. Templeton merely to mention her
high first in her Advancements Exams, the C. O'Neill scholarship
for study of Latin Verse that she won in 2008, the consideration
being shown by the Oxford Classical Monographs committee for
her dissertation-in-progress, the paper on Daphne and Apollo that
she will present this spring at the Association for Classical Studies
conference in Edinburgh, and the unusually high scores associated
with her pupils in their Modifications and final exams—Ms. Templeton is a model mentor and teacher, a first-rate classicist with an
unparalleled facility for language, and a brilliant mind with an
uncanny attention to detail and ability to juggle multiple ideas,
lines of thinking, and points of view.*

This was heartbreaking. To think that this letter could have been
in her applications, but wasn't. There were two paragraphs remaining; she opened the door for Chris and continued reading as she
walked through to the dining table.

"Your hand—" he said, but she waved him off.

*I have personally looked on as she's undertaken an ambitious project
in her dissertation. What began as her commentary on the nature of
power and subversion in Ovid's* Metamorphoses *has evolved into
a commentary on nearly his entire body of extant work. It is a penetrating study of the nature of power and tradition, a project with*

a bright future that has required great technical skill and research prowess on her part, which I believe will advance our understanding of the subversive in Ovid's works and contribute a compelling new interpretation of his exile.

Ms. Templeton is often the first to know about new developments in the field. Her wit and passion are leavened by a charming personality and uncommon grace. She would be a gift to any department. She is consistent, determined, and in my experience, a person of the highest integrity. She is one of my finest colleagues—a talented teacher and brilliant researcher.

In short, I give Ms. Templeton my highest recommendation.

Yours Sincerely,
Christopher Eccles
Westfaling College
Oxford University

Tessa slumped into the chair at her dining table, laying the pages on its surface. Chris hovered in the cramped room, his hands fidgeting. "Please don't smoke in here," she said preemptively.

"You're bleeding," he pressed. "Let me—do you have a plaster?"

As he took a few tentative steps farther into the room she recalled the way he'd nursed her hangover that very morning, the Tylenol rattling in its container. Did he think he was helping her? He looked diminished himself, unslept, dark pouches forming below his eyes.

"Chris," she said. "I know you didn't write this."

"But I did write it."

"What? This afternoon? You just went back to your office and dashed this off? This isn't what you sent to the universities I applied to!"

"That's what I wanted to tell you," he said.

"Why would you do that?"

"Because—" He stammered, looked away. "Listen, I had wanted to talk about the footnote, in the *CJA* paper, about 'love' being meant in an ironic sense."

"Will you just sit down?" she said, her voice rising. She saw him twitch. He wasn't used to being talked to this way. She lowered her voice as much as she possibly could. "If you would stop trying to change the subject," she said, almost gently. "It's a simple question." She watched him as he stepped forward and took the opposite chair.

"Because you're not ready, Tess, dear," he said eventually, making eye contact again. "You've only written ten out of the twelve chapters your dissertation really needs, and even those ten are still malleable. You're trying to move too quickly. You should have taken a fourth year for your degree, but you insisted on three. I knew if you'd gone to Princeton or UCL or UCLA, for heaven's sake, you wouldn't have developed it into the book it needs to be."

"And so you took it upon yourself—"

"To also push Martesi to accept it as his monograph at Oxford University Press," he cut in, "but he says that until he sees the book-length project he won't know how brilliantly you're going to tie it together. I would have explained to him but he didn't want to hear it—he wants to hear it from you. Read it from you. Come to OUP drinks with us on Wednesday. Or High Table. I'm having him to High Table."

"I think it's possible that you've lost your sense of boundaries," she said. Her hand throbbed; it was probably bleeding still. "And it seems to have caused you to do something quite unforgivable."

"Unforgivable? But how?"

Momentarily speechless, Tessa felt herself groping for the pages on the table as if for the remnants of sanity. "You," she said, standing, the letter now gripped in her fist. "The one person charged with being the custodian of my best interests in the profession and of my development as a scholar sabotaged my professional applications—when I put trust in you to write a true representation of my abilities in your letter, to the extent that I waive my right to see it, and you knifed me in my back and then look at me every day like everything's the same, and I have to track down your fuckery myself on a hunch?"

Chris stood, too. "I know what's best for you—" he said, placating.

"You don't know anything! You're psychotic!"

"That's certainly not the case. Please, Tessa, you must see how this will work out for you. Please don't say unforgivable."

"And why did you deny it this afternoon?"

"Because—I didn't think you would handle it well."

"As if there's someone who would?"

"I worried that if you knew, you wouldn't want to continue with the project."

"And so you were going to just let me wallow in a personal hell of rejection."

"But you would still have the acceptance at Westfaling, I don't see how, why you ever even needed that other validation."

Tessa was quiet. Chris moved as if to join her on the other side of the table, which only annoyed her further, and she turned away from him.

"Please don't say unforgivable," Chris said again, advancing. "Can you forgive me?"

Tessa unclenched her fist and smoothed out the now-crumpled pages. "What choice do I have?" she said, moving past him into the kitchen. She placed them under the electric kettle.

"Stop," he said.

Tessa was still startled that Chris had done this, had moved the boundaries of acceptable behavior so far from where she had believed they were. She wanted to hurt Chris, in a way that she couldn't quite articulate, that she was just grasping at but hadn't taken a verifiable shape.

"I wouldn't have thought that you would sink this low," Tessa said, returning to the dining room table.

"Please understand. Perhaps it would be best for you to get some rest. It's been a very long day. What have you done with the letter?"

She stood between him and the kitchen.

"I want to keep it."

"I'll let you have another copy—I'll send you one." Chris said these things all the time. He would never send it.

"I can't bear—I can't bear to have the other letter in my mind," said Tessa.

"Then let me send you a copy."

"No," Tessa insisted. "I need to have this one. It's important to me. As a token of your real opinion."

* * *

A LIGHT RAIN pattered against the windshield of the taxi as Chris rode home. A pyrrhic victory, the day had been. Strenuous, for sure. Position lost, yes. He licked his dry lips and tasted the residue of sweat, salty. But a victory nonetheless. The problem was solved, at least temporarily. As he stepped out, rain sprinkled the bald stretches around his brow and he could taste a mixture of rainwater and dried sweat, too, as it trickled down the delta of his upper lip. Inside, he was tempted to log in to Tessa's email and see if anything had come through since the afternoon, but then decided to be good and respect her privacy. Perhaps he could turn over a new leaf. There was a new understanding between them, and he felt vaguely euphoric. They had exchanged truths. This trust. When she had asked to keep the letter, he nearly said, *One might wonder if you would use the letter as evidence against me if you felt that you were being unfavorably treated, and if you wanted to make it a formal matter,* but he didn't say this, because in some way it was important to him that she did have the real letter, even if it made him vulnerable. And wasn't vulnerability the essence of trust? And wasn't trust the essence of love?

So he did not log in to Tessa's phone that night, but instead poured himself a finger of scotch and had a cigarette in the back-yard, among the early primroses and narcissi, where the rain mizzled away on the leaves and he could feel the mist clouding in the offing and making sport of the lights that were still on in neighboring win-dows. Cool gauzy curtains of mist billowing in the vague wind, to which he contributed his own smoky jets. It was there, in the strange serenity of the wet night, that he received a phone call.

"Christopher Eccles," a woman's voice said.

"Yes," he answered.

"This is Elizabeth from Hampshire Hospice. Your Mum's taken a fall . . ."

PART III

It is a love indeed if to have me
You account it cheap to have me treed.

MARIUS,
translated by Florence Henshawe

THE NEXT DAY, TESSA WOKE JUST AFTER DAWN to thoughts of Claire. Daylight cut through the muslin curtain. Her hand shivered at the cool brass foliate of the headboard as she dug out of her pillows. Under the hot shower she thought about her sister, perhaps still working after midnight in her lab at Merck, and then about what she would wear that morning, which led back to Claire: Claire had given her a wool knit sweater for Christmas, a beige thing with no silhouette, much like the sweaters that she, Claire, was partial to. Tessa had tried it on and planned to leave it in the States. Then she'd changed her mind and worn it on the plane. Claire's Christmas news for Tessa was that she had been promoted; she now made perhaps five times more than Tessa, but it was true Claire spent less on clothes, a fact their mother still joked about. Even after being her younger sister for twenty-seven years, Tessa couldn't have said whether there was a subtext to Claire's gift, and if so what it was. *You should attract less attention*, she might have been saying. But equally, *I think it would be sweet for us to look the same*. But perhaps most likely, *I ran out of time*.

Tessa stepped out of the shower and followed a wisp of steam back into her bedroom, where the air prickled her skin. She selected a pair of black jeans from the mess of clothes carpeting her floor and a pair of socks tangled between the sheets and footboard. As she dressed, her eyes returned to the footboard of the brass spindle bed and the discoloration along the base of the urchin-like finial that Ben had soldered on. When Ben had officially moved in he had shortened the balusters below the lip of the mattress so he could lie at length, then recapped them himself with brass shapes he'd salvaged from god knows where.

Normally he would do similar odd repair jobs at one hundred meters' depth: Ben had been a musician and what's called a "sat" diver, though when his dad fell ill he dove far less frequently, opting instead to be a part-time purveyor of fruits and vegetables at the Covered Market to make up for the diminished income. Tessa had already fallen for him from afar, during a date that Liam had set her on, at the O2 Academy where Ben was the opener. For three days following the concert she'd worn the green bracelet that got her in, was wearing it conspicuously when she perused his wares at the Covered Market and found herself laughing privately at the stack of bright red pomegranates—the underworld meal that dooms Proserpina to winter in Hades for all eternity. Chris had assigned a 1919 tome on the episode, in German, and Tessa had been immersed. Submerged.

At the register, he'd rung up the two cucumbers for Chris and several apples for herself and said, "You were smiling at my pomegranates."

He had large puffy lips, a long sloping figure. "Is that not allowed?"

"You smiled at them and then didn't even take one." He finished ringing her up and let his eyes rest on hers.

"I didn't know you were running a fruit orphanage," she'd said.

He'd laughed. Then, "You don't want Bramleys," displaying one of the apples she'd chosen. "Take the Braeburns, they're fresher. And better behaved."

She began to make a habit of dropping by the fruit and vegetable stand on her way home from the library. Usually Ben would be humming some low tune and he'd narrate what he was doing in a singsong way, recrating persimmons la da da di da. He always wore the same apron and a different sweater. Tessa would be wearing bloodshot eyes and a thousand-mile stare after ten hours in the Bodleian. It felt good to talk to Ben and run her fingers over the bristling fur of a peach.

Sometimes they would meander toward Tessa's flat, laden with rotten fruit, and throw fastballs at the abandoned boat in Port Meadow. He seemed to take pleasure in softening her, eliciting laughs, improvising songs that cast her as the hero in an epic journey to become a professor of classics. Sometimes she would ask how his dad was doing, and he would say fine, could be better, not great, he had a good day. He was her escape from work, and she was his escape from home.

The first time she invited him upstairs, he didn't leave for a week. Am I a groupie? she wondered. This must happen to him all the time. Yet, he couldn't have been comfortable in the bed—a full mattress, too short for his long body, with crescent-shaped foot and headboard. She would leave in the morning for the library and he would be curled up like a child, or his toes would poke through the brass rods and she would know they'd be freezing. (He had poor circulation.) Sometimes he wrapped some of the sheet around his foot and punched the whole apparatus through the rails. Even though this tactic left her sometimes sheetless, she felt it was good to keep him from getting too comfortable. She did not have the time or inclination or mental bandwidth for a serious relationship. But after six months, conversations were had.

"I don't like your bed," he'd admitted.

"The footboard?"

Nod.

"You're getting cold feet, is what you're saying."

"Yes. Literal cold feet."

"Not figurative."

"Not even the slightest."

Eventually, the bed became very much theirs, a DIY success, but at the time, a rusted bolt in the rail had led to a hacksaw and an afternoon of clattering brass dismemberment that had somehow echoed her anxieties about the domestic arrangement, its vague promise of deformation. The odors of resin and copper shavings had lingered for a week, and sometimes, especially in states of exhaustion, she thought they lingered still.

Claire called Tessa back at eleven a.m. Oxford time. Six in New Jersey.

"Tessa."

"Claire."

Tessa flagged her place in the translation she was marking and set it aside on the dining room table. Over the line came the sound of cooking—whisking. "Cooking breakfast?" Tessa asked. Claire didn't respond immediately—she knew Tessa knew she was. Tessa could see her at the stovetop with the phone hugged between her ear and her shoulder. There would be coffee gurgling nearby, and fresh fruit. Usually melon. Tessa knew others who made breakfast like this, but she didn't know anyone who could multitask quite like Claire. Tessa didn't worry that she wouldn't get her full attention. Sometimes, Claire seemed to think even better while she was doing seven other things.

"What's going on?" Claire asked.

"How are you?" Tessa demurred.

"Oh, we were with Stan's parents all last night."

"How are—Claude and Lorraine?" Tessa remembered them from the wedding.

"They're good," Claire said. "They seem very interested in grandchildren. Like, very interested. Stan confessed to me that Lorraine sent him all this literature on cryopreservation. I can see zygotes in her eyes. They were only here for a night and then dinner. How are you?"

"I'm fine," Tessa lied. She wanted to ease Claire into this. "How's the new position?"

"Just calling to chat?" Claire laughed. "We're seeing abnormalities that we know mean something but we don't know what. I have three researchers working for me, which is a godsend. Anything we accomplish is going to be a line item in my selfless employer's income statement, but such is life. That's what's happening here. When's your defense? How's Ben? Dare I ask about job applications?"

There was so much disappointment, it was like Tessa had built a dam around it, just to hoard it. "Ben's back in the North Sea," she said, lying by omission. She'd have to mete out her troubles. "And the viva? It's Monday." At least she was on track for that. "I still have an offer for a stipendiary lectureship at Westfaling." She heard Claire cutting something, chop chop, and something sizzling. "I'm presenting at a conference here next month on Marius; actually, the research on that front has been going well."

"I'm sorry, I don't remember who Marius is."

"I've mentioned him, he's this second century iambic poet . . ." Tessa trailed off. Trying to whip up enthusiasm for the classics in Claire always drained her. "Here's the thing," Tessa said. "I'm having a problem with Chris."

Claire said nothing and the chopping paused for a moment, losing its rhythm just perceptibly, then resumed. "Oh? What kind of problem?" Her voice modulated, became more relaxed but also more intense.

"So, I didn't tell you this before, but in the fall he was being cagey about his recommendation for other schools." A silence seemed to ramp up on the other end. Tessa's grip on the phone tightened. "Eventually he wrote it, and it felt like everything was normal. Then I get an anonymous email the other day with the recommendation he wrote for me, and it was an unmitigated disaster. Like, there was no way to read it other than that he was intentionally trying to keep me from getting a job."

"*No*," Claire gasped. "You're kidding me."

It wouldn't have mattered what Claire's supervisor wrote about her; she'd cracked the cell-replication process that made patients with a drug resistance no longer have that resistance. No one could have stopped Claire from getting a job. *Tessa has made great strides from a rocky beginning to her doctorate.*

"I wish I was."

Claire was silent. Both were capable of great tempers, but Claire's were always more clinical than Tessa's, and therefore more frightening. "Oh my god, Tessa. Well." Tessa heard something begin to sizzle, and then Claire interrogated her on the specifics, what she meant by an anonymous email, whether she had confronted Chris, what other schools she had heard back from. "And he wants you to work at Westfaling?"

"Yes." She couldn't say it without sarcasm. That she had received an offer from the person who wrote the torpedo rec letter seemed particularly twisted.

"Did he ever try anything on you?" Claire asked.

"No," Tessa said.

"Do you think there is a . . . a romantic dimension?"

"I don't think that's impossible," Tessa said.

"I think you need to get the hell away from him, first, and second have him censured. And the best way to do that is to make a complaint."

"I've thought about this, but it wouldn't be straightforward. In the letter, he says things like, 'we met more in her first year than is normal with the students I supervise.' One hundred percent true, but he twists it to imply incompetence on my part. Like, no, we met because he was so enthusiastic about my work. He says things like, 'I'm confident in Tessa's willingness to apply herself.' In a rec letter it sounds like someone has a gun to his head, but it's not objectively untrue."

Claire asked if Tessa would send her the letter, and Tessa agreed. The thought of Claire reading it compelled her to add that she had seen his "real" one, which was falling-on-top-of-itself complimentary.

"Use *that* in the complaint," Claire said.

"It's just text on paper, there's no signature or anything. He could—he would say, *I've never seen that before in my life.*"

Claire was quiet.

"And even if I did prevail through whatever disciplinary process Oxford has, where am I then going to work next year?"

"This is so beyond that. Are you serious? This is totally out of control. I don't think you're understanding the gravity of the situation."

Now Tessa was annoyed. "Believe me, I understand the gravity of the situation. It's my life. That's my point. I would think you of all people would understand how difficult my career would be, starting off without even a lectureship."

"My advice, Tessa, is to bring a complaint."

"Meanwhile, I'm presenting on Marius at this conference in April and I genuinely am on to something compelling."

"Tessa, do you really think this is the right time to be going on a lark with some pet project?"

Now Tessa gripped the phone tighter and the anger rose. On Marius, Claire sounded just like Chris.

"Did you just call me so you could do the opposite of what I say?" Claire asked.

"No, of course not."

"I'm not going to talk you out of whatever you want to do."

She was disappointed that Claire hadn't told her that her work would vindicate her in the end. But of course she hadn't given Claire enough evidence to make that argument. Knowing this didn't make it hurt less.

"I mean, tell me if I'm being presumptuous," Claire said.

"You're not. I'm going to talk to someone."

"Go outside the department if you can, because people talk."

"I know."

"And let me know what happens."

Tessa ended the call. The Oxford dPhil handbook lay somewhere in her bedroom, and she knew it contained a section on initiating an academic complaint. Claire was right, of course. Still, Claire had never quite understood the Latin, nor had their parents, for that matter, though at least Claire had tried.

It suddenly occurred to Tessa that she had never replied to Lucrezia yesterday—she had intended to ask for pictures of the inscriptions, but she'd been severed from the task by Phoebe's missed calls. Tessa sent the email and then worked for several hours, correcting the rest of her students' Marius translations. She would need to return them to their pidges sometime today. Before she left she saw a new email from Chris, a reply to the Daphne and Apollo acceptance with its attached readers reports, including the one requesting a footnote about the tone of "love."

It does not go addressed.

He was referring to the tone of "love," of course, but the statement could apply equally to his failure even to address the events of yesterday, to his own batshit attempt at normalcy. She thought of the passage, which had never really struck her as sad. Tragic, maybe, but in a manner of high drama, where Ovid's gymnastic handling of desire could be termed beautiful without irony, a passage of such spherical density that the first specks of her self had materialized around it. That could not be regained, she saw now: the texture of that moment. Her mother's flowers were blurred, the ripples along the pond's surface nothing other than ripples along a pond's surface. She would gradually forget what it meant to her. She reached for her phone instinctively; went to the notes app, opened the document she'd used over the years to chronicle her own reception of Apollo and Daphne, then stalled. The cursor blinked. She'd always thought the episode ended ambiguously, with Daphne, now a tree, "seeming" to accept her laureled form. *She nods and seems to move her canopy-like head* ("*in full consent*," one translator had added, inexplicably). "Seems" was the operative word, Tessa felt. She typed now to herself: *adnuit utque caput visa est agitasse cacumen.*

On her reply to Chris, she spent only a moment, feeling something strain in her chest, some delicate latticework of feeling whose knots still crisscrossed inside her.

* * *

THE DRIVE DOWN to Southampton General was uneventful. Chris lapsed into daydreams as he drove, his red Fiat performing admirably, the sun that was there at dawn slowly being curtained by clouds, but with a glimmer still, always on his left, reminding him that he was driving south. Back down to from whence he'd come.

Chris's task was to pick his mother up from the hospital, where she had gone after she had taken a fall at the hospice. Who made these decisions, he wondered, to send someone to the doctor when they're in hospice? It was like refurbishing a chest before using it for kindling. But, he presumed, dying was done with especial care at the hospice. They wouldn't let you bleed out in the games room, for example. You couldn't do it too slow, or too fast. It was like landing a plane, more or less.

The Southampton General entrance was empty as Chris walked toward it; empty in a way that concerned him. Was this not a hospital? Shouldn't there be flashing lights and gurneys entering, or patients being discharged at all times? He wanted the hospital to say something to him, this entrance, this mouth, but it was entirely mute, and he could just make out a single receptionist through the tinted glass of the automatic doors. A row of wheelchairs, folded up, on his right. Another automatic door. The young man at the desk, in scrubs, his hair dyed blond and gelled, took Chris's information. "Dorothy Eccles," Chris said.

His mother had been diagnosed with colon cancer almost half a year before. The first week of Michaelmas. The diagnosis had been uncertain; they did not know if they would be able to get all of the affected tissue, they did not know if the cancer was contained within the muscle wall or if it had spread, they did not know anything, it seemed, and the only way to illuminate her condition was to operate. A three-hour surgery, they presumed, and Dorothy was already physically quite frail. She'd never quite recovered from a hip replacement a few years back—she complained that her mind was fuzzy, that the anesthesia had done something to her brain. "I feel I'm being inhabited by a ghost," she'd told Chris when she last saw him, after they discovered the cancer. She had survived breast cancer in her sixties. She had not wanted to undergo another operation or chemotherapy. She was seventy-six. Chris had thought this a sensible decision. But in the weeks following he had felt himself nagged by a physical discomfort, like a pebble in his shoe, or a phantom itch on his back, and he could not decide whether it was because his mother was dying, or because his mother was willing to die. That she had told him to his face of her decision bothered him peculiarly. Because it meant that she would be leaving him. That she could utter these words to him as she looked in his eyes irked him considerably.

"It's your decision, Mum," he'd said. "You don't need to be a hero for us."

What the doctors thought would be a rapid deterioration had not occurred. Dorothy had continued in her daily routines: tending the three sheep, Feddy, Neddy, and Betty, guiding her vines along the trellis back of the kitchen, planting flowers in her garden, living alone in the house that had belonged to generations of Eccles shepherds. Chris suspected that the doctors had simply wanted to open someone up. One of them had perhaps had a boring shift. The doctor had given him a speech that Chris remembered resembling the U.S. defense chief's rationale for going into Iraq. "There are known knowns and known unknowns," he remembered the doctor saying. "Then there are unknown unknowns."

Yet then, quite suddenly, the deterioration had happened. It did not seem to have had a beginning, or if it did, Chris had missed it. She lost weight and was constantly in pain. She could no longer tend the sheep, and their neighbor, Old Nutley, had taken over. She had wanted to have hospice at her home, but Hampshire Hospice was a charity, after all, and not prepared to provide her with a full-time caretaker, and Chris was not about to move back in with her. Chris had felt she had realistic expectations for her illness; she had wanted to live through another spring. She always had daffodils and hyacinths and tulips; witch hazel, cowslip, camellias. In the years since his father's death, she had made the home beautiful, Chris had to concede, a garden as replete with fragrance as it was with audible reminders of life, gentle baying and chirping. In the end, she had had to leave for hospice before the daffodils and hyacinths.

The elevator dinged at the first floor and at the third he stepped out, following room numbers through a series of hallways. He thought of Theseus in the labyrinth trailing Ariadne's thread behind him so that he could find his way back out when he killed the Minotaur—he was Theseus, confronting nothing less frightening: a parent. How would he get out of this? Inside a room he saw a doctor weaving stitches into . . . it looked like someone's forehead. There was a woman, a lovely doctor, dictating something to a young man with a clipboard. Medical equipment rattled on a wheeled cart as it bumped the threshold of the doorway. Another door, another hallway, new voices. Let this journey continue, he thought. I'd love to never get there.

Around one more bend was 372. The door was open, a window visible and a stool next to it, empty. The rest of the room was obscured from the hallway. He approached slowly and knocked on the jamb. When he heard nothing, he crossed the threshold and saw a woman sleeping in a hospital bed.

It could have been any woman, was his first thought. He could not see the face, because it was tilted toward the ceiling. Her body was covered in a white blanket—some kind of synthetic hospital blanket. His mother despised synthetic fibers. He could see her hand—a clip on her finger, and her wrist was in a cast. She looked like the demographic of Dorothy Eccles, like a stand-in. He could have been volunteering at the local hospice, and been sent to this room. She had not responded to his knock; he took a seat in a corner of the room and checked his email, his heart lunging at a response from Tessa.

I do not understand. Who out there still thinks that love isn't meant in an ironic sense here?

Had he been given the chance on Thursday, Chris would have been able to hint that Wembley from Brasenose was not only on her dissertation defense, but also very likely the referee on her paper. His fingers began immediately to mash out a reply.

> 1955, Yelland, "Apollo's Love for Daphne." 1972, Chambers, "Cupid's Arrow." 1980, Hoy, "Vectors of Romance in Latin Verse," should I keep going? I can tell you right now if they publish this without a footnote you'll look sloppy. If you don't even engage with such an issue how am I supposed to promote your work?

He sent the email and turned his attention back to his mother. He noticed that her eyes were now open, and he stood. They tracked him. "Mum," he said.

She nodded faintly. She took several hoarse breaths. Her breathing was different—he couldn't quite place how. She seemed to breathe delicately, but also with great exertion. All her focus seemed to be on breathing. At her bedside, he saw that her irises were just slightly gray—it was a gray he'd seen before, in his old Cambridge mentor's jaundice. Yellow to others. Chris had been born without short-wave cones in his retina, which meant his vision skewed toward red hues with their longer wavelengths. His hue-skew, he called it.

He was confident that she recognized him, but not entirely. She was much thinner. He was looking at his mother's skull, he felt. Her hand stirred and reached up toward him, cast, oximeter, and all. He held it and knelt down, and pushed a hair back from her face, and he saw her lips, which were very dry. Her breathing accelerated and then slowed. Two of her fingers wrapped around his. Finally, her breathing began to relax. "I'm here, Mum," he said. "It's Chris."

There was a rap on the door and Chris turned to find a doctor. He seemed to be in his early forties, wore a white coat and a stethoscope around his neck. He carried a clipboard and wore orthotic trainers. "Hullo," he said. "I'm Dr. Nichols."

Dr. Nichols gestured for Chris to follow him. Chris followed his squeaking shoes outside of the ward and into the hallway. A nurse was pushing an empty gurney past them. Everywhere he heard the noise of wheels on the clean floors. He could taste death on his tongue.

"Your mother has a scaphoid fracture from the fall," the doctor said. "She'll wear a brace on her hand for several weeks."

Chris nodded. He doubted she would live long enough for it to heal. "Do you know how this happened?" he asked.

Dr. Nichols shrugged. He had kind eyebrows, Chris noted. A definite asset in his business. And in life. Chris's eyebrows were bushy and horizontal, with no feeling in them, no arches. This man's eyebrows rolled gently, like down land. "These things happen," he said. "It's a good hospice, but they can't look after everyone every minute. Sometimes you take a fall. Just be glad it wasn't worse."

"Her eyes . . ." Chris said.

Dr. Nichols shrugged again. "I'm an orthopedist," he said.

"They seem to be yellow," said Chris. "The oncologists are always giving me the slip. The doctors at the hospice don't—I mean, there are none, really." Chris looked at him with what he hoped was a pleading expression. He wanted to know how much time his mother had.

"Look," Dr. Nichols said. "The diagnosis is colon cancer, right?"

Chris nodded.

"Very normal for colon cancer to spread to the liver. It's probably jaundice."

"So it's spread?"

Dr. Nichols put his hands up. "I'm an orthopedist."

"Okay," Chris said. "Thank you."

As Chris returned to Room 372, he felt a pang of longing for Tessa to be there with him.

*   *   *

"IT COMES IN like a cramp and then it settles there. Grabs a hold of me insides. And it just twists. Like it's got fingers of knives. And it just holds on. It just holds there. And it seems to be that if I can get me breathing under control to where I can get a breath, where I can slow me heart, it just lets up a bit, and slowly, slowly, it releases."

They were cutting across Lee Down toward the hospice. There was a great field of wheat on either side of the road. As far as he could see in every direction were pylons for high-tension electric wire, running along the gentle slopes. Dorothy was in the passenger seat, her forehead resting against the window.

"Mum, this is what morphine is for."

The Fiat hit a seam in the road and Dorothy's forehead bumped against the window. She winced.

"I don't see why they shipped you off to the hospital for a fall. Why did you fall? What were you doing?"

"Take me past the house, lovey, will you?"

Chris was worried enough about getting her back to the hospice. He wasn't about to detour fifteen kilometers into the wilderness. "Not today, Mum."

She put her head back against the window, but another seam jostled her.

"Don't rest against the window like that, Mum."

"What are you even talking about?" she mumbled.

Chris reached across the transmission and pulled her shoulder so that her head was against the headrest. He wondered what state of disrepair the garden was in, whether it would be worse for Dorothy to see it. When he was young, he used to guess the colors of the flowers, and Dorothy would tell him if he was right. The daffodils would be out now, most likely. Maybe even the bleeding hearts, with the warm early spring. It would likely be overgrown with sedge and hawth, as his mother liked to call it, and it would depress her even more, or, worse, she would try to lift a pitchfork or a rake. No, it would not do to bring her back today. He continued driving along the quiet road in the calm sunshine. Another seam pounded the struts of the car and Dorothy's head bounced safely against the upholstered headrest.

Chris pulled into the hospice's familiar forecourt, where he helped his mother out of the Fiat with its hazard lights on. Inside he saw Elizabeth at the reception desk, wearing her blue and white Hampshire Hospice polo and spectacles. He smiled at her and guided Dorothy toward the bay where her ward was.

"Just the wing, then?" Elizabeth said. She glanced at Dorothy's arm brace.

"Scaphoid fracture," Chris confirmed. "In layman's terms."

"Perhaps Chris will help with the knitting, then," Elizabeth said to Dorothy.

"The house," she said. "I want to go to the house."

"You're too ill, Mother. Another day," Chris said.

"I'm just a bit green."

Chris noticed Connor, another palliative care nurse, pushing a cart of fresh linens toward them from the other end of the bay. "All taken care of?" he said to Dorothy with a smile. She smiled back at him. Connor—an avatar of competence—had a roly-poly figure and a goatee and a soft voice that came from such a funny-looking and gentle face that it sometimes seemed to acquire a mystical property. "Look at you," Connor said. "Skiving off to see the doctor. We missed you."

"It's just me wrist," Dorothy said. "The rest of me's tip-top."

Connor took her good hand and left his cart of linens. He peered into her eyes for a moment. "Are you in pain, beautiful?" he said.

"Not now," she said.

"Good," said Connor. "Let's get you lying down. Come along." To Chris he said, "She'll be all right."

Connor walked her to her ward, talking softly to her, his hand on the small of her back so that her shirt was pulled taut and Chris could see, along with the ridges of her spine, how little space she occupied. The pang of desire for Tessa intensified, as if the space being forfeited by Dorothy's body were creating a corresponding hunger for Tessa's. It had gone beyond sexual, he knew, had become a yearning for something other, different, more? He didn't know how to articulate it. He simply needed her there with him.

"Mr. Eccles?" he heard. A hand rested on his shoulder. It was Elizabeth. "We'll need you to move your car—it's blocking the entrance."

"Yes," he said absently. He followed her toward the exit.

"There's something I need to discuss with you after."

Chris parked the Fiat and returned. Elizabeth led him into a small office. He wondered if she was going to give him some kind of supportive talk. She was perhaps thirty, with a fringe and piercing eyes and burgundy lipstick that complemented her dark coloring. She seemed impossibly cool. Perhaps this was what the cool kids did these days, work in a hospice.

"Chris, whenever we have new patients we do an itinerary of documents that we often need, and when your mother came to us she said that she had an advance decisions document. However, we haven't seen it."

Chris nodded.

"It's very common for colon cancer to spread to the liver. You may have noticed the yellow in her eyes. We suspect that the tumor is blocking the bile duct. This can cause infection. We have her on a low dose of antibiotics right now, but some advanced decision documents prohibit the use of antibiotics, or other medicines meant to prolong life. We'll need to see it in order to determine our course of care henceforth." Elizabeth reached across the table and put her hand on his. "Chris, it's time to find it."

•   •   •

CHRIS DID NOT have his spare key to his mother's house on him, but she kept one under an urn in the garden, and Old Nutley would be able to help him in in the event that it wasn't there. He had a much-needed cigarette in the car park, ashing into the wild bushes on its outskirts. He remembered encountering Tessa having her rare cigarette, just a few nights ago, the encounter that seemed to have set off this entire hectic week. There was so much hope unleashed in those words, "He's moved out."

The Fiat made a satisfying crunch over the gravel at the hospice center exit, and out into the service road. The service road snaked for a kilometer or so over a rise, and as he broke out of the tree line he could see the escarpment on the north downs. He drove along slowly. How scenic, the Hampshire Hospice. Down in the scarp foot. Sun caught and congealed around the grassy edge of it. As a child he had thought it taller than Everest. Now it seemed to loom even larger than that. The ragged edge of it, the erosion that was so gradual, just erodes and erodes, until you're left with a mortal drop. He accelerated back into the tree line. The road led him into the downs. He drove faster after reaching the crest of the hill, causing his stomach to lurch.

Elizabeth's hand on his had felt electric. It was as if she had lit up a new circuit of desire for Tessa. And indeed, it had felt good not to check her mail after they had met last night, he had felt like he had been given a clean slate, of sorts. And fortunately, it seemed, Tessa would need to remain in Oxford next year, as she had not yet received any other offer. And yet, that was as of yesterday, and in addition, she had not accepted the offer to teach at Westfaling, which was troubling. Surely she would not be so self-destructive as to leave Oxford altogether, and attempt to pick up some sort of adjunct position. The application season for temporary hires came later than for full-time, and in fact it was just beginning. That was a possible option for her, if she had such a death wish. She wouldn't be able to adjunct in the UK for long—her student visa would quickly expire, and it would be impossible for her to get a new one without sponsorship. Yet she could likely do so in the States, a thought that hadn't occurred to Chris until just now. Could she stomach that? No system peddled false hope quite like the American adjunct industry, more predatory than payday loan programs, in its own way, not to mention humiliating, if you were willing to look at it for what it was. If Tessa were applying, it would probably crop up somewhere in her email—notifications that her online application had been received, for example. Chris felt himself yielding to the impulse to check Tessa's email when he returned home.

Another precipitous drop. Crowning the next rise was one shepherd's hut. It did not appear noble to Chris, but tragic in its solitude. A high-voltage cable raked across the down land on a chain of steel pylons. Where sheep once grazed, cereals as far as the eye could see were cultivated by machines. He continued along the road, which was no longer a road, really, just a lane, and over a few more downs the lane became no longer a lane, but an unpaved way. Billows of dust rose behind him. He pulled off to the byway for a small tractor that growled past. After another mile there was the unmarked road with the palsied elm, and after a few hundred meters down that, the brick and granite of the old house flickered through the bare branches of three mulberry trees.

Chris found the key under the urn and entered, worrying idly that Old Nutley would see him, not recognize him, and fill him with bird shot. Inside, the smell of sheep confronted his nostrils. Clearly Dorothy had taken them in with her during the winter. Through the front room, he passed the photograph of Samuel Eccles with the prize Southdown ram of 1926. Dorothy had always kept her most important documents in the icebox, with the assumption that if the house burned, that would be left. He doubted the likelihood of this, but was gratified by the ease of his search. In the icebox he found a sheaf of papers bound with twine, cold to the touch. As he rifled through he heard one of the sheep baying and knocking against the walled garden. "*Baaa*," it went. Neddy? Feddy?

I have the capacity to make the decisions set out in this document.

There it was. Her name, signed. Her handwriting was stable. He wondered if she could write like that now, she was so weak. Her signature a relic from another time. After was a page for reaffirmations of her decision, with four more signatures, dated. Once a month until January. So perhaps she had begun to have second thoughts?

I wish to refuse all medical treatment intended to prolong my life.

It suddenly occurred to him that this was why his mother had wanted to come home. Perhaps it wasn't some sort of metaphor. Perhaps she hadn't wanted to see the flowers. She just wanted to die, and her signed and notarized directions for doing so were its most direct route.

Baaaaa.

Or perhaps she had wanted to amend it, and live?

He walked out the door, with the document still in his hands, to take a look at the garden. The fragrance was pleasant and layered. That scent of lignin that comes from green plants, not flowers. The soil was almost tangy—it had rained recently. And then as he entered the garden the flowers themselves. Perfume. If you thought about it you could separate the scents. The heady aroma of the hyacinths. A hint of pear in the primroses. The narcissi, you couldn't smell: they were wilted and hardly visible under a canopy of ragwort. Weeds had mainly reclaimed the space. You would need a good chemical weed killer to rid it all, or an able body.

One of them cantered around the stone wall.

"Hello, Feddy," he said.

Baaa, Feddy replied.

Neddy and Betty came around the wall, too, more coyly.

They were hungry.

Chris felt an urge to feed them the pieces of paper he held in his hand. Feddy, the most intrepid, licked the fingers of his other hand. He held the pages down to see if he would bite. Feddy licked his chops and reached for them with his mouth. Chris yanked them away. Perhaps Feddy was acting on some primal impulse to protect his master's life. Prolong?

If he brought the pages back, they would take his mother off antibiotics.

It hadn't always been a garden, Chris recalled. It had simply been a grass strip between the house and the barn, where his father had parked the backhoe when he bought it, and in fact Chris was surprised that much could grow there, the way that thing's wheels used to grind up everything it traveled over. Then again, the chalk grassland in the downs was so fertile, you could throw a battery into a divot and leaves would sprout, Chris presumed.

"What to do, what to do?" he muttered. Might Old Nutley find the NHS logo in their cud? He folded the pages and jammed them into the inside pocket of his coat, then smoked a cigarette while the three sheep nosed around the foliage.

•   •   •

CHRIS COULD HARDLY keep his mind calm as he drove home on the A34. The decline in his mother's health had startled him. Her skin was detaching itself from the skeleton, gradually. Gravity was taking its toll. The effects were visible in the crags and fissures that appeared in her cheeks and forehead, on her arms when she lifted them up. Aging. It happened. What could he do for her? His father used to rub her bunions before he died.

In the passenger seat lay the advance decisions document. He hadn't decided yet what to do with it.

It was dark, and his headlights illuminated just enough space ahead for him to make it to the next stretch of pavement, but what of the stretch after that, and that? The darkness was interminably longer. He accelerated a bit, kicked the car into fifth gear, then accelerated more. The engine whirred. Lane markers flitted past. The dial on the binnacle read seventy-five, then eighty. Chris closed his eyes for a second, then two, three.

The Eccleses were not known for their mastery of self-preservation, or their interest in it, for that matter. And yet Chris had thrived all his life, no thanks to his mother, life-giver.

He parked the red Fiat around the corner from his house in an open space on the street and walked briskly home. It had cooled significantly. He produced his key and opened the door into the vestibule, where he hung up his tweed. A breeze scuffled several papers along the floor. It seemed he had left a window open. He crossed into the kitchen and ensured it was not the French windows onto the garden—any idiot could walk into the house if that were the case—but they were secure. It must have been one of the sashes upstairs. He snatched up the pages that were strewn on the parquet floor and turned on a kitchen light: Apollo and Daphne, an early draft of Tessa's *CJA* paper. The second section he had guided her on, the whole thing redrafted twice at his behest, and then to *CJA*, where he knew they were peer-reviewing through Forecaster and Sidney, both gaga, somehow, for love sequences that involved trees, and both equally uninterested in reception studies. No, if a lover turned into a tree it was enough for them. Forecaster had written an entire book on Philemon and Baucis. Chris knew they would love Tessa's paper, Daphne being of course such a seminal transformation herself into the laurel tree, and Tessa's charming reading of the sequence, not to mention lucid and learned prose. And yet, she had no idea the extent to which he'd orchestrated the acceptance for her, how he'd gone out on a limb for her . . . What he needed was to make her more aware that he had helped her career, to combat her perception, now, that he had been working against it.

Chris went up the dark stairs to the second floor and into the bedroom, where he found the sash window just slightly ajar. He remembered opening it on Thursday evening before he went to sleep, when it had been so warm out. He shut it with a reassuring

thud and locked it. The room was cool from the outside air, and
dark. Chris took a sweatshirt from the chest of drawers and traded
his turtleneck for it. He still had not made use of the other half of
the hulking chest, which Diana had cleared of her sundries—socks,
underwear, trousers, blouses, jumpers. There was a time when some
feeling would attend these absences, but now there was nothing.

In the study, as he waited for his laptop to boot up and he took
stock of the work he needed to do before his lecture on Monday,
he considered how he might make Tessa more aware of his importance. There were the OUP drinks on Wednesday, which Edmond
Martesi would be attending. Chris checked his email and felt a
pang of irritation as the inbox populated with perhaps fifty unread
messages—many of them students asking for his input or for clarification or for life advice, as if he were one to dispense it. He only
responded to emails on a basis of pure necessity and ninety-nine
percent of what he received did not qualify. One from Liam asking if
nine Monday worked for their rescheduled meeting—Christ, Chris
had forgotten about that. Monday mornings were generally free for
him, and Liam knew that. Chris responded simply, *Yes*, and clicked
through the rest of the missives. How boring these were! *Professor
Eccles, I'm a 2nd year from . . . I'm looking forward to . . . Do you have
any extracurricular book recommendations for your paper next term:
Selected Imperial Latin Verse?* Delete. He couldn't imagine responding to all this nonsense. Often Tessa would, and he ascribed it to the
American tradition of coddling students. A hackneyed argument,
yes, but no less true. There, professors were like items you chose from
a shop shelf, and the student was always right.

Chris felt an urge to log in to Tessa's email and see if she had
heard from any schools, but he reminded himself that he needed
to cease and desist. Instead, he went downstairs and opened a bottle of scotch and poured himself two fingers. Swapping vices. He

opened the French windows and went outside into the dark garden with the scotch and a torch from the top drawer in the kitchen. He was worried about the garden. The daffodils and hyacinths he had planted in autumn were not getting enough water, he suspected. He had been distracted. The flower beds looked parched to him, though of course how could he really tell in the torch light? He went back inside and finished the scotch, then filled the watering can in the sink. They looked sad, dry and sad and disconsolate out there. Perhaps he should add a nip of Laphroaig to the watering can.

Maybe it would be best to text Tessa, and yet he wanted to have something to bring to her. In the garden, the wind was frigid, and he poured the contents of the watering can quickly, then returned inside. It wouldn't do to wait until the OUP drinks on Wednesday to talk to Martesi, he felt. He would need to have a discussion with him sooner.

* * *

HELLO OLD FRIEND, Chris typed into his phone early the next morning. *Do you have a moment to spare today?* He didn't want to sound too imperious and vague, yet he also wanted to sound imperious and vague. *Do you have a moment to spare today at your convenience?* seemed to soften the request and the urgency of it, while still getting across the necessity of "today." It was still rather early, before six-thirty, but Chris wanted to put in his request as soon as possible. He sent it.

Chirr—up! Chirr—up! he heard from outside. Hooded warbler? It wasn't quite daylight, the sun clearly somewhere on the horizon but not above it yet. Chris flicked on the desk lamp on the end table and began his day with a renewed sense of urgency. He couldn't do anything about his mother, he considered, as he started the shower in the en suite. But about Tessa there was still opportunity. The window was closing quickly, however. He could see how, at face value, the recommendation letter he had written for her would be upsetting. He took solace in the notion that hers was a temporary irritation with him, rather than a deeper resentment.

Downstairs, Chris pulled provisions for his breakfast: eggs, some bacon rashers, butter, some chopped onion he had left in plastic, the frying pan, a bowl. He cracked the eggs over the edge of the bowl, done perfectly, all the sappy white and yolk captured for his repast, and tossed the crinkly shells in the bin. He took a fork and just as he was about to skewer the mess and mix it all up, three hard knocks rapped on the front door, startling him. Chris went to the door and opened it. There, in tennis shorts and a blue anorak, high white socks and white trainers, was Edmond Martesi, jogging in place.

"I saw your text," he began, and paused for breath, "and my day is chockablock. Then I thought, I'm cutting through Jericho anyway. Fancy a jog?"

Damn, Chris thought. It was the last thing he fancied. But he knew he needed as much of Martesi's goodwill as possible. Cool air was sweeping in from outside. Martesi hadn't seemed to notice that Chris's hair was still slightly wet from the shower. "Give me five minutes," Chris said.

"Splendid."

Chris put the bacon rashers and butter and bowl of eggs in the fridge. He rushed upstairs and threw on a pair of sweats and found his trainers, deep in the back of the closet.

"Port Meadow?" said Martesi.

"Marvelous," said Chris.

They took off on Walton Street toward the canal. The streets were quiet still. A bicycle sagged, chained to a drainpipe. A single door slammed shut somewhere far off behind them. They broke apart at the thin sidewalk on Wyckam Lane and Chris jogged in the street, then they spliced back together when they hit the footpath over the canal.

"Been trying to get back in shape for the old doubles game this spring," Martesi huffed.

"Getting back into it? Have you chosen a partner?" Chris asked.

"Howards and I have bandied the idea about."

"Christ Church Howards?"

"Right," Martesi said. He clapped a hand on Chris's shoulder. "Haven't seen you in a while!"

Martesi was running short of breath already. After the kissing gate, Chris slackened his pace. They started off into the meadow without conversation; Chris let Martesi catch his breath.

Chris himself had once been Martesi's doubles partner in the humanities division tennis tournament. Chris, though of average athleticism and less than average stature, was nevertheless an excellent tennis player, able to cover the court on short but speedy legs, with precise, even devious strokes, an excellent game at the net, and a peppy serve that caught his opponents off guard, in a league where half the points were achieved by double-faults from old dons barely able to grip a racket. Unlike many of his peers, Chris was coordinated. Martesi, though taller and with an all right game at the net, was not particularly fast or coordinated, and he never would have had a chance at the doubles cup with anyone other than Chris as his partner. Chris knew Martesi coveted the award—his father-in-law had rowed Blues at Cambridge, his brother-in-law had spent a year in professional rugby, and Aryanna had married him, a wimp. Thanks to Chris, Martesi had some accreditation for something other than his brain. Something for little Benjy and Braun to admire, even if they would soon understand how irrelevant a Faculty Doubles Commemoration Trophy was to a Cambridge Eights Medal, for example.

"Howards has a good stroke," Chris said. "Solid serve." This wasn't true at all, but Chris didn't want to get roped into playing with Martesi again.

"We wouldn't be playing for the trophy, that's certain," Martesi managed. "Good fun, never'less."

They rounded the north end of Port Meadow. Cows lowed somewhere in the fog. Every so often, picnickers got attacked by cows around here. Mauled, Chris imagined. Trampled, more likely. He could smell manure and grass and dew, the scents mingling into one perfume that would have to be called Fertility, if it were bottled and sold. Chris slackened his pace, as it was clear Martesi was going to tire quickly. Moreover, Chris wanted energy to collect his thoughts.

How was he going to ask Martesi for what he wanted? He needed to strategize.

Chris had been the classics delegate to OUP for four years and so he knew the procedure: two outside readers were given the submitted manuscripts from graduating dPhil candidates, and each manuscript was ranked on a scale from one to five. The classics delegate to OUP, formerly Chris, now Martesi, voted as well. The submissions were blind, but the delegate could usually guess whose work was whose; even the outside readers could figure it out easily enough, if they were so inclined. Chris had fought hard for one of Martesi's doctoral advisees in 2008, Timothy Hickey, when Martesi had first made overtures. Hickey's dissertation, as Chris recalled, was about Suetonius, the Roman biographer. It was a solid paper, but not virtuosic. It was distinguished only by some recondite implication toward historiography theory that Chris couldn't have cared less about, but which he knew could only cause Martesi's work to be more heavily cited, given how indebted Hickey's scholarship was to certain theoretical frameworks advanced by his mentor. Hickey, though his interests didn't align with Chris's at all, was clearly very bright and diligent, well liked and well married, and would prove a valuable ally for Martesi in years to come. Chris had held his nose and given Hickey a sterling endorsement at the delegates meeting, tipping the review in his favor, though a bolder project by Anne-Marie Papadopolous on Hellenistic and Latin meters was of conspicuous merit, and had scored slightly better with the outside readers. Nevertheless, Hickey had won the award.

The net result of this was that Martesi owed Chris a favor.

Martesi had simply asked Chris over tennis that year. Chris had presumed Martesi to be a more effective tennis player than he had turned out to be; he talked about his tennis game regularly. As it turned out, the tennis relationship had been more advantageous to Martesi than it had been to Chris. "I'm asking you a favor. Take a good hard look at Mr. Hickey. I won't forget it if you do." What had he said? A nudge?

The following spring, Chris had opted out of his doubles partnership with Martesi, mainly for the sake of optics—to the practiced eye, Chris's endorsement of Hickey's work was vulgar and opportunistic—but also because tennis bored him.

Now there were beads of sweat on Chris's brow and he, as well, was breathing hard. Their trainers scuffled along the gravel roadway.

"Four kilometers today," Martesi said. "Let's slow down at the edge of the meadow, have a stretch, shall we?"

Chris agreed and they chugged a bit farther. The sun was a silver glow in the east. A flock of geese took off from the west suddenly, their wings beating the air.

They skidded to a halt at the south end of the meadow, not far from the gate, along a stretch of cattle fence that Martesi promptly mounted with one of his heels.

"Hamstrings," he said. "Always the bloody hamstrings."

Chris wrapped his hands around the top rung of the fence and dug himself forward, stretching his calf muscle. The rung was wet and flaking. "You know what you should do?" Chris said.

"Yes?"

"Smoke more cigarettes."

"Ah yes, the old tobacco diet. I've given them up for Lent, though. Aryanna's idea."

"You don't say."

"She seems to think they cause cancer." Martesi switched his leg and groaned as he leaned forward. "You'd of course known, but I see so little of you these days!" he added.

Chris chuckled. "Nonsense, complete nonsense!"

In fact, it had been a little while, but Chris also knew that Martesi was trying to cultivate the illusion that Chris was asking him for something out of the blue, that he hadn't sufficiently been tending to their "friendship." It would be better manners, Martesi was saying, if he and Chris were at least able to pretend their relationship was something more than transactional. This annoyed Chris, given that Martesi clearly owed him. It wasn't a bank teller's job to make it as difficult as possible to withdraw funds. The bank would quickly lose all its business!

"So, Edmond," Chris began, changing to a quad stretch, as if the conversation's transition were to be just as casual. "I have a favor that I need to ask you."

"Oh, you do?" Martesi said. Was there a trace of amusement in his voice?

"I need a, well, how did you phrase it to me? I need to ask you to take a good hard look at someone for this year's monograph publication."

Martesi brought his limb down from the fence. "I was wondering when this moment would come," he said. "And I had a feeling it would be this spring, and not the next one," he added with a smile, as if to say, *You're a no-good dog, and don't I know it*. Chris smiled, too, and even emitted a strained chuckle, because he needed to curry Martesi's good favor, though he found Martesi's insinuation repellent. "But I say, Christopher. It's a damned inconvenient year for you to ask."

"Mildred LeClaire?" Chris said.

"She's the 'real deal,' as they say in America."

Was he using this phrase to suggest that it was an additional encumbrance to give the award to an American?

"I can't speak to Ms. LeClaire's work," Chris said. "But I assure you, so is Tessa."

Martesi shrugged.

Chris switched quads.

It would be beneath him to point out Martesi's specialization bias toward LeClaire's work, which was supposedly an exceptionally broad and erudite study of Tacitus and Livy with a concentration on medieval historiography. The type of thing to make Martesi salivate. But it was also reportedly exceptional work. Chris didn't know for himself. He hadn't read it. He didn't care.

"The Ovid manuscript is groundbreaking. It will lead to a fundamental shift in Ovidian studies. The style is exquisite, and it unites several lines of thinking that have never been resolved before. It has every right to win publication."

"I confess that I don't understand the request," Martesi said. "Based on the manuscript I've seen, it won't really help your scholarship. It's more like it would replace some of your key arguments in *Subversion and Play*. It's almost as if you're letting someone else publish your next book."

"Have you any idea"—Chris despised how he became more posh around posh people like Martesi, a relic of his Cambridge years, trying to fit in—"how many times I wanted to cite Papadopolous when I was editing *Hellenistic Derivatives*?"

"Papadopolous?"

"Anne-Marie, who was, you know, favored by Katz and Lincoln to win. And instead we gave it to Timothy Hickey, and did I grouse about it?"

"Let's not bring the past into this—"

"Says the historiographer." Chris could have laughed if he weren't so annoyed. Martesi gave him a look, shook his head, and leaned over, attempting to touch his toes. Several geese came grackling back from the west. The gate clanged nearby; someone was beginning their jog. Chris pulled his carton of cigarettes from his sweatpants pocket and lit one.

"I know it's a bind," Chris said. "But what I'm asking is for a nudge. I know that if it's close, you're going to give it to LeClaire. What I'm asking you is, if it's close, give it to Tessa."

A ring of smoke snarled in the breeze and blew toward Martesi. He lifted his head.

"Fancy one?" Chris said.

Martesi waved him off and curled his arms upward, reaching for the sky. "Diana make you give anything up?" he asked.

Chris searched Martesi's expression, but of course Martesi was facing the sky. So he had not heard? It seemed impossible. "No," Chris answered truthfully. *She's left me, if you must know*, he nearly added.

Martesi finished his stretch and moved closer to Chris. Chris offered him a drag. Martesi hesitated.

"It's not a cigarette if you share it. It's a fraction of a cigarette, and if it's less than half, it rounds down."

"Is that how it works?"

"Standard accounting procedure."

Martesi took the cigarette and took a long, satisfied drag. "One more," he said. He took another drag and handed it back to Chris. He leaned against the cattle fence and sighed.

"Okay," he said. "I'm not going to make you grovel."

Chris wanted to slap him. Instead he said, "So we're agreed?"

"Agreed."

"I can count on you?"

"If a nudge is called for, a nudge she shall receive."

"Good," Chris said. He was exasperated. He took his pack out and lit another cigarette. Martesi had smoked too much of the first one. He started off toward the kissing gate. Martesi followed behind.

At the kissing gate, Martesi said: "One more thing though, Chris."

"Yes?" Chris said. The damn thing took so long to get through.

"I'd like us to be doubles partners again, this spring."

"What about Howards?" Chris said, wanting to run off.

"Howards is rubbish, and you know it."

Chris stood at the fence. As Martesi moved the gate from the little cylinder, he grabbed the cigarette out of Chris's mouth and took a drag. He put the gate back in place and they started to jog off.

Jesus Christ, Chris thought. "Fine," he said. "You drive a damned hard bargain, Martesi."

"Good, then it's settled," he said.

"You're going to have to get in shape this year," said Chris, as they returned to Walton Road.

"What do you think I'm doing?" Martesi said.

"Then stop smoking cigarettes, for chrissakes," Chris said. He whipped it out of Martesi's mouth and threw it into the canal.

They passed over, back into Jericho. The streets were far busier now—bicycles whizzing, cars honking, doors slamming. Instead of going straight up Walton toward Summertown, Martesi followed Chris along Bicester Lane all the way back to his home.

"Say, Chris—have you any mints?"

Chris rustled in his change case for one of the wrapped mints he always kept there and found one while Martesi waited outside, the door ajar. He tossed it to Martesi. "Say hello to Aryanna," he added.

"Cheers," said Martesi. Chris watched him jog away from the threshold of his front door. Had he got slower? His right leg seemed to hitch with each stride, a tick he hadn't noticed before. It could have been due to an undisclosed injury. Still, Chris had accomplished his objective. He could say to Tessa outright: *If you accept the Westfaling position, you will win the OUP award.*

Inside, he took his breakfast from the refrigerator. He cooked the eggs and ate quickly. He then went upstairs and took his second shower of the morning, this one cold, vasoconstricting. It felt excellent. He dressed in a fresh pair of pressed trousers and a button-down underneath a black cardigan, which he thought quite modern and cool. He checked his email and saw a reply from Tessa regarding the footnote.

I don't care.

The terse response churned dangerously along one of the deeper reaches of his mind. Here he was at all hours trying to salvage her career. She was acting like a child. He replied with quick severity.

• • •

THE DAY OF Tessa's viva, the sun ceded the bright Oxford sky to scuds of metallic clouds. The wind picked up, and Tessa woke to the sound of her window bucking in its sash. Her sleep had not been comfortable. Over the weekend, she'd exchanged several emails with Lucrezia, who refused to send her photos of the inscriptions or release any more information unless Tessa committed to lending her assistance. She hadn't responded to Claire's missives wondering if she'd taken steps to register a complaint—she hadn't, and she did not care to examine the possibility further. Finally, Chris's response on the footnote issue had infuriated her.

Glad to see you're feeling free to fail.

The defense was at Westfaling, not far from Tessa's office, in one of the few proper classrooms in the college. She did not know if Chris was planning to attend; she hadn't invited him, but before the events of last week, she wouldn't have needed to. It would be assumed that he would be present, even though the supervisor was not allowed to speak during the examination. In her flat, she laid out the black skirt and tights, the long black gown with frills, the mortarboard, a white button-down blouse, and the black ribbon. As she looked at the assembly of garments on the bedspread something turned in her; a stark sense of isolation, and a physical hunger for Ben, if only to make her world cohere for an instant.

⋅ ⋅ ⋅

EDINBURGH.

In the months leading up to the conference, Tessa sometimes allowed herself to marvel at her change in circumstance, from truck stop waffle house to plenary session speaker in six short years.

Chris drove them in his Fiat, speeding the length of the isle of England to compensate for the flights they'd missed, casting cigarette butts into the annihilating rush of the open window. "I—we— already missed flights so I could be with Ben when Gabriel passed," Tessa justified. "This is not something I can afford to skip. He understands—I mean, I think he understands." Chris nodded and smoked, and occasionally Tessa smoked, too. He had brought a package of tobacco and papers—Tessa's preference. Chris listened with solemn intensity, and gradually the conversation became more personal. Maybe she was nervous about the 322-person seating capacity. Maybe she needed weighty conversation to distract herself from the guilt that gnawed at her sleepless brain. Maybe she found in Chris an essential audience for the decision she had made. But in that journey she felt herself hovering on the brink—of what, she did not know exactly; she knew only the trajectory of her life thus far and the imperative of persuading the car's inhabitants of that narrative.

She told Chris about the first time she'd heard Ben play music: how the guitar ruffled the air and then his voice flooded the concert hall with a low vibrato, how she'd felt a chill along her arms and in her heart; the music moved her. Who was he, and how had he just happened like that—because that was how it seemed to her, that he had happened, or that the music had happened, in the same way that her most sublime encounters with poetry felt like happenings, lodged in the time and space of her past as deeply and irrevocably as major life events: Apollo and Daphne, her high school graduation, those passages from Blake's *Jerusalem*, her father's funeral.

Soon they were skirting Birmingham, then Manchester, and her thoughts began to spill out muddled but constant as she rolled new cigarettes, white cadaver-like tubes.

The important thing was not Ben, right now, but her relationship to these moments. She told Chris how she still possessed the yellowing notebook page on which she'd written her high school translation of those hundred lines beginning "*Primus amor Daphne Phoebi*," how that first encounter with Daphne and Apollo had struck her at her core, made a claim on her, raised her hairs on end, and dragged her soul, just for a moment, out of her body. (She'd

talked to Chris about these things before, but always through a curtain of irony or self-effacement—she'd never shared this part of herself, this deeply, with anyone.) As brittle trees on the median strip
flitted by, she told Chris how she'd translated *in frondem crines, in
ramos bracchia crescunt*, as, *into foliage her hair, into branches her arms
developed*, and how "develop," at the time, was still being bandied
about as a sanitized descriptor for the mutations she and her classmates were undergoing. Her arms had still felt like ever-lengthening
noodles. There was apparently certain hair she was allowed to have
and certain she was not. She was still growing used to her own
odors. Her body had transformed—was transforming—and since
it was her first trip through adolescence she had no reason to think
she wouldn't transform into another species next. The euphemisms
of sex ed had formed a kind of rip current against the profanity that
spilled from music, TV, the lips of her classmates, and she recalled
noticing the last four letters of the Latin verb even as she translated
it to its most staid English equivalent. She recalled something rebel-
lious and alluring about this observation, how language could be
layered and insurgent. And maybe it was this that had caused the
world to stop and be perfectly articulated in the text.

But there was also her sudden fluidity reading that passage, in
that moment. Because, needless to say, Latin was difficult. Unscram-
bling syntax indifferent to word order had sometimes felt like scal-
ing a sheer cliff, other times like corralling headless chickens. She
couldn't recall whether it was *arce* on 467, which normally would
have troubled her, *arce* resembling *arcus*, bow, but in fact constitut-
ing a variant of *arx*, hilltop, or if it was when she knew *leves* to be a
variant of *levis*, light, not *lēvis*, smooth, because the first *e* scanned
short—but suddenly the language had yielded to her, its delicate
springs and wheels operated on their own, her eyes flowed over the
characters almost without effort.

It was January in Florida. Her mother's row of Taiwan cherries was erupting into hot pink inflorescences. She had the house to herself—Claire at college, her father likely at the lab, her mother possibly at the clinic, or on some errand, maybe shopping, or getting a manicure with girlfriends, though perhaps Tessa was only associating the bursting flowers in the backyard with the angry fuchsia polish Sheryl sometimes like to wear. In any case, Tessa was alone, she was sure, because she lay out in the living room, neutral territory she wouldn't have basked in so freely with either parent around, for she preferred to assemble dictionaries and grammars on the floor when she translated, and so was sprawled out before the curtain windows that admitted a view onto the backyard (short rolling lawn, angry fuchsia bloom, placid surface of the pond, creasing from time to time in the breeze).

The soft pastel of the flowers, the ripple of light across the pond, her fingers digging into the braids of the woven carpet, as if for a better grip—a so-called out-of-body experience, though Tessa considered the sensation more akin to merging than to leaving, in the same way a bird merges with the air when it first flies, or the way a narrow inlet joined the pond to St. Johns River and then the sea, so that the pond might almost be said to constitute the same body of water as the ocean. The chills she'd felt rippling along her arms, the helium-like insurrection that announced, *You are encountering beauty*, had something to do with empathy, she felt, the dissolution of the borders of oneself, the merging of her consciousness with the incomprehensibly vast reservoir of others. Yes, consciousness, that was the element, like water or air, that she dissolved into, not only Ovid's but infinite throngs of others. Tessa had felt so transformed by this mystical experience that when Daphne suddenly sprouted roots and foliage it had seemed logical. "And that's when I knew I would not become a doctor," she told Chris.

She loved Ben, she said, "but you have to understand what this means to me." She had felt that Ben could understand her love of poetry—the animal thing that lurked beneath all the academic posturing, the expository language, the learnedness. But the story she had risked on him, the story he could understand, was different from the one she could show to Chris.

"When I talk to him about it, it's more, 'There isn't some dramatic origin story for how I came to the classics, like, *Latin saved my life*.' I'll tell him something like, 'I think I was just attracted to the discipline of it as a child, and I wasn't the most social of kids. Latin was the one language you didn't have to speak to others. I thought, Great. Sign me up. I was kind of a loner.' You know, that's the narrative, which isn't untrue. But there's more than that. It's, 'the Project of Literature.' It's, 'speaking the ineffable,' and 'merging with what is unchanging and unchangeable in life.'"

"Well, there's bugger all in this profession without that," Chris said. Of course, she was preaching to the choir. But she needed a choir. Chris had worshipped in this cathedral his entire adult life; he was flock and laity. He told her, in turn, about his disciplinarian mother, the intellectual tundra of his hamlet in Hampshire, the stamina reviewing for his sixth form exams inspired by the idea of Cambridge—the yearning to be among others like him—only to be tossed into the Trinity fountain his first week there. It was unfailingly worth it, he said, if only because of those first nights reading *Eclogues*, and that thing telling him, not intellectually, but physically, carnally, *This is who you are*. "You can't ever walk away from that," he said. "You have to enshrine it. I really believe that."

They stopped at a Tesco Superstore in Lockerbie for gas and sandwiches, and when they rolled back onto the highway, she told him that she knew he would have to drive the Fiat back down on Sunday, and that, "I'm not taking my return flight, obviously." He protested that it would behoove her to get back to Ben as soon as possible, but she insisted. They rode up together, they would ride back together. In the drive's last hour her confidence seemed to tremble and expand, to reverberate in the tobacco-stained interior and drape itself over the tracts of countryside rushing past them. Chris had already coached her through the paper and her written presentation, but in the final stretch he had her rehearse to him from the passenger seat, smiling as she hit notes of humor, grimacing in pleasure when she nailed the major points home. They crossed the ring road and coasted in silence through Mayfair, then swept into the parking lot of the hotel, a refurbished royal building, an aggressively vertical stone structure with conical towers and thin airy finials, which reminded Tessa perversely of the Cinderella castle in Orlando, the iconography of children's dreams.

They changed quickly in their respective rooms and marched the short distance to the conference center, her blazer flapping in a gust of wind, the cold air nipping at the edges of her shell top. A young woman whose name Tessa recognized from logistical emails and her image on the university's faculty page—a doctoral student like herself—manned a table alone near the entrance with a clipboard and conference packets while voices leaked from the plaza upstairs. They checked in and ascended the flight of steps into a wide, high-ceilinged room filled with people who mingled and chatted in the margins of twenty-odd tables set with plates and cutlery. Tessa stole a glance at the schedule and saw her paper slotted directly after dinner for the plenary session as people began to notice Chris and to swirl toward them. Everyone else had playful titles like *Styx and Stones: New Readings of the Underworld from Julian Funerary Inscriptions*, where Tessa's now read innocent and stale: *An Interrogation of Genre in Ovid's Apollo and Daphne*. Chris introduced Tessa to a panoply of faces that unfailingly intimidated when she matched the

name tag to this or that illustrious paper; she was glad to have Chris
at her arm to navigate the shoal of people. Armond Poitou, dark
salty hairs standing on end. Colm Feeney, with an actual human
hand, a wiry figure and sharp, penetrating eyes. Phoebe Higgins,
with a swish of gray hair and crooked teeth bared. Half the fucking
endowed chairs in the Western world were there, it seemed, and the
moment everyone sat for dinner (Chris and Tessa placed at opposing
ends of the room), a savage sense of loneliness descended, unexpect-
edly, upon her.

The man seated next to Tessa, a ruddy-faced Scottish chap with
enormous hands and a dewlap, attempted to engage her in conversation, but she was suddenly fixated on the one wilting flower in
the center arrangement, and the obscenity of her presence there, in
Edinburgh. What in god's name was she doing here? Who would
leave their grieving boyfriend to present at a conference for dead
languages? Who were these people and who was she? Someone
filled her glass with white wine and a fillet of Scottish salmon was
plated before her. As her fingers nervously clasped the white cloth
that spilled over the table, memories of Ben and Gabriel began their
assault. The wine shimmered with dappled light and ambient conversation, the sound of voices gathering to an almost unintelligible
frequency, as Tessa was suddenly transported to the night she met
Ben's parents.

Gabriel, his face flushed in the candlelight, kneading the white
tablecloth between his fingers. "Hand-woven in the hills of Thes-
saly," he said. "You can feel the cotton fibers against the ridges in
your hands, not like most tablecloths nowadays, mind you, made
from synthetics."

Tessa could sense Ben rolling his eyes next to her—they had
begun dinner in the Duncans' little conservatory at a chaste distance but gradually their chairs had migrated nearer, so that their

shoulders now touched, and she sensed him stiffen. He had warned Tessa that his father had a bit of the raconteur in him, and he fancied himself a well-read man, often treating his guests to tales from folklore and mythology relevant to his favorite topic of conversation: textiles. Gabriel had been a carpet dealer for forty years.

"Do you know how long Penelope spent on Odysseus's shroud?" Gabriel asked.

"Maybe thirty years?" Tessa said.

"Twenty years! Bollocks to your Oxford schooling," he said with a laugh. "But Penelope's shroud—think of the craftsmanship. The level of detail. Weaving's no longer what it was, I'll tell you."

It struck Tessa as an odd point, and the notion that he had repeated this vignette over the course of a forty-year career, each time depriving Homer's premise of some of its essential beauty, did pain her slightly.

"In the poem, though," she said, "it also serves as a ruse to her suitors—Penelope having told them she would marry only when she finished the shroud, while every night undoing her work to buy time for Odysseus to return from Troy." A sheepish smile began to work its way onto Gabriel's candlelit face as Tessa spoke as delicately as possible. "I'm sure it was a beautiful shroud. But perhaps the twenty years were not a testament necessarily to the intricacy and detail of the work, but instead to her shrewdness and, one could argue, her devotion to her husband."

Ben and Matilda laughed at Gabriel, who flushed red, and Matilda said in a high, whiny voice, "Bollocks to your schooling," causing Gabriel to laugh outright.

"Fair play," he said to Tessa. She was struck by the softness in his face and his willingness to concede a point, so different from how her own father had been, whose facial expression would retain an impassive stare while that fucking bald head of his generated rebuttals, objections, quibbles, even when he knew he was wrong. She saw her own family life as she had when she was a girl—there was an innocence at the Duncans' that did not exist at the Templetons', had perhaps never existed, though some part of her believed it had at one point, and had merely been eradicated by a routine that elevated personal achievement over something like family bonds.

Afterward, on the bus home, Ben had asked, Am I Odysseus, or am I a suitor?

When she left for the library he'd say, Working on the shroud?

Last night he had said, I understand if you go to Edinburgh. But I felt it would be wrong not to ask, just to ask, for you to reconsider.

Later, Chris discovered Tessa in the AV closet, minutes before she was meant to go onstage. She had torn herself away from the table, dialed Ben unsuccessfully in the freezing night, then found herself physically unable to socialize. In the AV closet, she'd achieved a sort of Zen oneness with the dark and its warmth, its humming machinery.

"Christ," Chris said. A sash of light from the doorway blinded her. The hallway outside was quiet, which meant everyone had assembled in the plenary room, waiting for her.

"I don't know if I can do this," Tessa said.

Chris didn't speak for a moment, inhaling, exhaling. He was out of breath. He had been searching for her.

"Listen," his shape said in the dark. "Something in you decided to come here. Not just to Edinburgh, but to Oxford."

"Right."

"Allow me to suggest that you accept that part of you. Wrestle with it, fine. Kick it, scratch it, do judo to it. But don't lock it up." His hands now grasped her shoulders gently. "You are human, you may have faults. You construe them as demons. Don't. They're a part of you, no matter how hard you try to deny it."

"But what are we even doing?" she said. "Why are we even here?"

"Because, Tessa. This is who we are, is it not?"

•   •   •

TESSA'S EXAMINERS WERE Martin Wembley from Brasenose College, Leonora Strauss from Balliol, and Daniel Flemish from York University. They were aligned facing Tessa, each in subfusc as well. Tessa didn't know which one was Wembley and which was Flemish until they introduced themselves. Flemish had a patch of curly hair and thin lips, a hard time making eye contact. He was past middle age, tall, and thin, but then she met Wembley, whose hair, what remained of it, was silver, and he was even taller and even thinner. He gave her an overly friendly handshake and wished her good luck—the handshake was a little too enthusiastic, the grin a little too wide. Flemish and Wembley both wore white bow ties, whereas Strauss and Tessa wore black ribbons. Strauss was a bit shorter than Tessa, with frizzy dark hair, thick glasses, and some remnants of red polish on her fingernails. Strauss's research was mostly in reception studies, Tessa knew, which wasn't her strong point, nor was it Chris's. She hoped she would not have to come up with some argument on the fly.

"It is March fifteen, 2010," Flemish began, when they had taken their seats on the small proscenium, at chairs and tables arranged for the purpose. There was one administrator and one graduate student, apparently interested in Ovid, sitting in the room as well, in the five rows of seats below the stage. "We are convened here to examine Tessa Templeton of Westfaling College, Oxford University, for successful completion—"

The brisk unsealing of the door interrupted Flemish, who looked to his left, to see who had entered. Tessa didn't need to look; she knew already that it was Chris. Somehow, that she didn't want him there made it impossible for him to be absent. In the periphery of her vision she could tell he was wearing that light gray blazer with the neon threads that you couldn't see unless you were close. Flemish turned back to his script and continued, "for completion of her doctor of philosophy in Greek and Latin languages." Chris was hovering. "Take a seat, Professor Eccles, and as supervisor you're reminded that you're not allowed to speak in the proceedings."

Tessa looked now. Chris sat and mimed a zipper sealing his lips and leaned back in the chair. He didn't return her gaze. He seemed to be rolling a cigarette.

They started out slowly and predictably. Tessa introduced the topic, the *Fasti* as a codification of Roman morality and tradition, the irony of Ovid's exile, the second half of the *Fasti*, never written, the tragic fallout of censorship. Flemish lobbed her some questions about German commentators on the *Fasti*, Wembley asked about her research methodologies, and Strauss about how the *Fasti* had led her to the *Metamorphoses*—Tessa had wanted to explore the same ideas of power and censorship in Ovid's cosmology, the ways in which he was also codifying or subverting norms in the Roman imagination.

"As an example," Strauss said, "the Daphne and Apollo sequence in Book I?"

"Correct—" Tessa said, beginning to speak.

"Ah yes," Wembley interrupted her, not seeming to understand that he had done so. "Ms. Templeton, one of the reasons I asked about your methodologies is that you seem so precise and exhaustive in some areas, while in other areas your references to the extant body of scholarship seem, well, rather sparse. The Daphne and Apollo sequence struck me as one of these areas."

"Professor Wembley," Strauss interrupted now. "Maybe you

could allow her to finish answering my question before she returns to methodologies."

Wembley made a calming gesture with his hands. "Of course, of course," he said. "I'll wait my turn. My apologies." He sat back and grinned like he had when he shook Tessa's hand. It was more of a leer, Tessa decided.

"Well," Tessa resumed. "It seems clear to me that the sequence is an occasion for power and censorship to operate across a few lines. God and demigod, male and female. Cupid strikes Apollo with an arrow, which inflames him with love, and he chases Daphne through the woods. Ovid describes Apollo's passion, and he gives Apollo much time to speak, and then Daphne gets a yelp at the end when she begs her father to change her into something that Apollo can't copulate with. I had not meant the discussion to be a cornerstone of my thesis, but I think it illustrates a moment where a potential poetic figure is silenced, and that we lose her voice is tragic."

Wembley chimed in now. "This was one of those spots, regarding methodologies. Could you comment on the absence of core texts on this section from your bibliography? In particular, you refer to Apollo's love for Daphne as being ironic, without further discussion or conversation with other opinions on the matter."

Tessa was beginning to suspect Wembley was the peer reviewer for her Apollo and Daphne paper, the one who had written the dissenting review.

"Methodologies, let's see," she said, the heat beginning to run to her face, her heart rate increasing. "I'd say I took it as a given that in a passage where the word '*amor*' is used alongside lines such as '*auctaque forma fuga est,*' I'll translate: 'her beauty was enhanced by flight,' and '*Videt igne micantes / sideribus similes oculos, videt oscula, quae non / est vidisse satis,*' again: 'he gazes on her eyes gleaming like twinkling stars, he gazes on her lips, which are not enough only to be gazed at'—one wouldn't be required to make such a clarification."

"But have you consulted Yelland—"

"'Apollo's Love for Daphne,' 1955?"

"Yes, or—"

"Hoy? 'Vectors of Romance in Latin Verse'?"

"Or Chambers—"

"'Cupid's Arrow,' 1972? Yes. Yelland writes with frankly bizarre esteem for the 'spark of romance,' Hoy refers several times to the 'tragedy of their uncoupling,' and Chambers calls Apollo's 'courtship' 'eager, unalloyed love,'" Tessa said, annoyed that Chris had prepared her for this exact line of questioning.

Wembley responded, "Yet surely it wouldn't hurt to engage the criticism in the discussion of the two as elegiac lovers."

"Not at all," Tessa said, "but it's the substance of that elegiac love that's perhaps in question, and I wonder if these commentators have anything to add to its discussion."

"Even so," Wembley said, frowning.

A brief silence prevailed.

"Okay," Tessa said, as coldly as she dared. "Noted." Wembley sat back and adjusted his cap. She realized that she wasn't winning herself any points with the committee; nevertheless, it seemed that her dignity was somehow at stake. Chris, she was sure, would be writhing.

But Wembley wouldn't leave it alone. "I feel it necessary to warn you that I might not in good conscience bestow an unequivocally favorable report, taking into account a willful disregard of critical opinion, simply because it dissents from the author's own. Of course, there will be an opportunity for corrections."

"Let's change topics," said Flemish.

Strauss cut in now. "I think equally that if Professor Wembley feels able to arbitrate on what texts are being disregarded, to determine the negative space as it were, then we might ask why his own papers on the topic don't engage with, say, Plath's 'The Virgin in the Tree.'"

"Please," said Flemish. "Our purpose here is to examine the candidate. This is not a forum to promote our own biases or discuss our own work. Professor Wembley, I think you ought to consider Professor Strauss's objection in your final determination."

"But I do think the suppression of scholarly opinion is especially 'ironic' keeping in the theme of our discussion, given the project's critical interest in censorship," he said.

"As are the professor's repeated interruptions," Tessa offered.

Wembley, Flemish, and Strauss all paused and looked startled. Wembley's leer vanished. "Ms. Templeton, would you like me to wait outside while you finish?" Wembley said.

"I didn't think you'd offer," Tessa responded. Someone in the audience laughed—the administrator? She was conscious of Chris watching. She stole a glance at him. He had his cheek propped up by his hand, his elbow on an armrest.

"That's quite enough," Flemish said, cutting off Wembley, who was beginning to speak. "We'll return to our examination, on another topic."

Tessa returned her attention to her notes, aware that she had made a mistake, and yet quite happy to go at it with Wembley again if he provoked her, actually craving that he make himself a target. But Flemish commenced his own mini-lecture on the cult of Apollo as a stand-in for Augustus, Ovid's tongue-in-cheek mocking of the epic tradition and the imperial agenda overall, and commended Tessa's discussion of "terminally metamorphosed" figures in the *Metamorphoses*, Daphne being one of them. As the heat of the moment passed, Tessa became slowly aware of how stupid it was to have humiliated Wembley. Only she was capable of sabotaging a formality as straightforward as confirmation of her degree. The rest of her viva passed without incident and with only several mincing questions from Wembley; finally, Flemish concluded the proceedings.

Tessa, now worried that Wembley might withhold support or, at a minimum, require she make the emendations he asked for, could only speculate as her examiners excused themselves. Chris would have been the best person to ask how damaging she had been, and to help dissuade Wembley from holding up successful confirmation, but now Chris was following Wembley out the door.

She collected her things and made for the quad, with a feeling of total dejection, a desire to calm down, but the conviction that she was only losing more control over her temper. In considering whether to lodge a complaint she had felt so confident in the senselessness of officially censuring Chris at the risk of her own prospects, and here she was lashing out and compromising those exact prospects. She left the Westfaling quad, stepping into a thick fog on the road. Mist curdled around the mossy coping of the neighboring college. She heard someone coming quickly behind her. The person was matching steps with her now, walking silently alongside. "Well, I don't quite know what to say after that," the voice said.

"Congratulate me for shooting my foot off," she said, walking faster.

Quiet. Footsteps.

They reached the lane of trees on Parks Road, a small evergreen enduring amid the fog. "Tessa, would you please slow down?" Chris said, reaching for her arm.

"What? What do you want?" She whirled around.

Chris halted next to her; the familiar scent of his cigarettes; his hand along the lapel of his blazer; even now there was something eerily satisfying about his following her. There was indeed no one else who could mend what she'd just done. After she had presented in Edinburgh they had talked for an hour. Until last Thursday, she never would have imagined giving her viva and not debriefing with him afterward.

"You're going to have to do some damage control."

"Because of you? I'm aware."

"With Wembley," Chris said.

Tessa began to walk away again, but Chris jogged in front of her. "Will you pause for a *moment*, please."

Tessa stopped, and waited for Chris to catch his breath while he fished in his pockets for a cigarette.

"I persuaded him to only refer you to resubmission. There won't be another viva. All you have to do is emend the text."

"He's the one who wrote the dissenting review on my paper, isn't he?" Tessa said.

Chris shrugged.

"That's why you were getting so worked up about the footnote?"

Chris shrugged again. "I tried to prepare you."

"Indoctrinate."

"Tessa, darling, I admire your spirit, but please remember which side your bread is buttered on. You're biting the hand. Really chomping on it. You'll chew it off this way." He took a step closer to her. She was freezing cold, suddenly.

"I don't even know what to do," she said, honestly, now at least aware she was telling him the truth. "I don't know what to do. I cannot think of another time I've been so at a loss for words or action. I'm incredulous. To think that we had such a good—you were the one person I could depend on."

"You *can* depend on me," he said.

"It was your prerogative to write whatever type of letter you felt appropriate. And somehow you felt it appropriate to decide where I work—where I live, assuming that was your real motive. Now I'm, like, clinging to the rinds of your praise. It's humiliating. You circulated a letter that essentially calls me stupid."

"Tessa, forget about the letter. It will be so unimportant in the grander scheme of things. You'll fix your dissertation. You're going to win the OUP award, I just know it. In fact—"

"How can I possibly forget the letter? Do you not understand the gravity of what you did?"

He emitted a long sigh and put both hands on her upper arms. "Look, you're shivering." His hands were warm. "Pull yourself together."

He moved to embrace her, but she kept him at a distance with her hand.

"I don't understand," he said, suddenly growing annoyed. "I explained this to you. I thought we had moved past this. Will you stop for a moment and consider how much I've done for you?" A car passed. Tessa was surprised, even for Chris, how quickly he had switched from conciliatory to aggressive.

"I didn't realize I owe you fealty for doing your job," she said.

"Don't make the mistake of thinking you got this far on your own," he said, tossing his cigarette butt. He stamped it out, his sole making a damp sound on the wet pavement. "How am I supposed to advocate for you when you can't advocate for yourself—you're acting like a child. You look one." He flicked the black ribbon around her neck. "Look at you, dressed up for your viva. Do you really think you're impressing anyone with your repartee? The moment you said that to Wembley the man next to me laughed and said to himself, Lovely girl, complete twit."

"I'm not a twit," was all Tessa could manage. She had no better response. Words failed.

"You're doing a fairly good rendition at the moment."

Tessa's forehead grew hot and normally this meant her tongue would act on its own, but now it couldn't, or wouldn't—she knew she was cornered, and now practicality overrode her desire to lash out. She was silent, and she hated herself for it.

"What are you, buffering? Wave a hand if there's a sentient being in there. Hello?"

Tessa, silenced by rage, found herself waving a limp hand.

"Good. Did you get that out of your system? Now I need you to get yourself back on the right track. Fix your thesis. You have the conference paper next month. Present on Ovid, forget Marius. Spend the break preparing. I'll help you. Acquit yourself well, as I know you will. The OUP award is yours—it's yours to lose. Even if that doesn't happen, though I think it will, we'll spend the summer turning the dissertation into a book. But you must alter your behavior. We're going to work together. I swear it will work out. You can trust me. All right?"

Tessa nodded.

"Where are you going now?"

"I need to go home," she said at last.

"Are you sure you can be alone right now?"

She turned away from him and walked on into the fog, stupefied with anger.

"Tessa?" he called. "There are OUP drinks Wednesday." He wasn't following her. "I'll text you," he called. "I'm trying to help you!" She walked on, the humiliation blooming inside of her. The ribbon he had flicked burned around her neck; the light was declining, her steps noisy on Woodstock Road. When she looked over her shoulder, there was a youngish man, a not-Chris. She felt her eyes linger to make sure. That will have always happened, she thought. He will have always talked to you like that. And you will have always said nothing.

· · ·

A DARK MORNING—later than she usually woke, she knew immediately. Her forehead throbbed. Her hair smelled like cigarettes. She
had broken a cardinal rule and switched to whiskey at some point—
she didn't remember doing this but its taste was overpowering. She
could only remember walking into the Childe Roland in search of
total oblivion. Tessa untwisted her foot from the sheet, took her
phone, and walked, doubled over, to the bathroom. She was still
wearing her subfusc.

It was quarter to ten. One text from Claire.

> I'm sorry I didn't call you back. Very busy. I think you
> should get out of Oxford until you figure out what to
> do. Come to New Jersey. Flights are on me.

Claire. Tessa must have called her last night. She was momentarily flooded with gratitude, even though she would never be
able to admit to Claire that she needed the money upfront. Tessa's
account with Lloyds was in overdraft and her credit depleted. Hungover. Marooned. *And* insolvent. She looked at her outbound calls
and saw that she had, indeed, called Claire at 11:52 p.m., just after
dialing Ben. Fuck.

She ran a bath. The rush of water, the promise of her body being
encased in its warmth, comforted her. In the kitchen, she filled a
glass, drank it, then filled it again. The question also remained how
she would respond to the Westfaling offer of employment, which sat
accusatorily on her windowsill underneath an agate paperweight, a
gift from Chris. She went to the window and scanned it, holding the
paperweight in her right hand.

Your response is required by May first.

She had weeks to respond, but she had been informed that if she
planned on accepting the position, the administrative office would

need to begin processing her work visa as soon as possible, preferably by mid-March, which they were comfortably in, it being the
sixteenth. She would go to Westfaling and tell them she planned to
accept. What else could she do?

In the bathroom, Tessa left the ribbon and gown on the tile, the
white shirt—a brown stain on the collar, origin unknown—on a
bare towel hook, and eased herself into the hot water. She would have
killed for the refuge of Ben's presence. An escape of any sort would
be very welcome—preferably an escape from her own spinelessness
the evening before. That feeling, of being struck dumb, leached into
her and made her feel like a coward. Dangerous, these thoughts. She
allowed her mind to drift back to another, no less troubling subject.

Ben had ostensibly left because she'd not shown up to cook dinner, but of course there was more to it than that. Ben and Chris
had become strange bedfellows over the past half year as Tessa was
deciding whether to apply to teach at schools in the States, as well as
in the UK. Both of them wanted her to stay at Westfaling.

Last summer, Tessa had agreed that she would only apply
to schools in the UK. Since Gabriel was only getting worse,
Ben needed to be able to visit him, and his mother, on a regular
basis. His family was important to him—Gabriel's Parkinson's was
the reason he had moved back to Oxford in the first place. Ben
had begged her not to force him to choose between herself and his
parents. She had relented.

But finding sponsorship for a work visa in the UK was not as
straightforward as she had thought. She read on academia blogs that
it negatively affected one's chances to get a job, given the administrative hassle. Sometimes the salaries for posts weren't high enough
for the school even to legally sponsor you—the UK mandated sal-
aried minimums, and academic posts walked a fine line. Moreover,
there were more schools in the U.S., and she had done her undergrad

there. So, with fears that she would end up with nothing, she had applied to U.S. schools as well. It hadn't been easy, or cheap, but she'd done it without Ben noticing, which wasn't difficult, given he was gone, at the time, on a rare four-week dive. And she didn't feel bad about it. She wouldn't feel guilty about anything until she had to, and she wouldn't have to until she got accepted somewhere. And then she'd gotten rejected everywhere. So as far as she was concerned it was immaterial.

But last week, Tessa had come home to find Ben waiting at the dining table with a letter from UCLA in his hands. She had lunged for it, thinking it might be a letter of acceptance. This obviously wasn't the reaction he was hoping for. And seeing the text, "we regret to inform you," had left her without the mental or emotional resources to mount a defense for Ben's accusations of, basically, treachery. Betrayal. They were meant to have dinner the next day to discuss it. She had accepted the punitive responsibility for cooking, and then been goaded into an argument with Chris and lost track of time. There had just been too much *happening*. She knew she had behaved badly. But now the contours of everything had shifted. Obviously, what Chris had done altered the relativity of her bad behavior. She was the victim here, and she needed Ben.

In the living room, dressed, her ears still wet from the bath, she called him. While it rang, she could see him, settling into his bunk, a shitty spy novel folded open on the pillow, the hum of his electric toothbrush the only noise, except the HVAC and occasional shout or laughter from the mess hallway. His hair would be tousled, he'd have that tired gaze, the one that would rest on you gently until the lids closed and he fell into sleep.

"Hello," he said, even-toned.

"Ben," she said, eager to say his name.

"I suppose our rule about not phoning is null and void."

"There have been certain extenuating circumstances."

"What could those be, I wonder."

Tessa didn't want Ben to have the impression that she was calling because of Chris. "You didn't text when you got to Aberdeen."

"Did you really expect me to?"

She hadn't. She paused. "Where are you this time?"

He didn't respond immediately. Someone with a Scottish accent was shouting in the background; she'd heard about Ben's coworkers, but never met them, given how far Oxford was. "About ten hours' steam from the coast."

"What is the job?"

"Listen, Tessa, I'm knackered."

"Sorry, I just . . ."

"What?" he said.

Tessa felt something turn in the pit of her stomach. She knew she was losing him and it made it even worse, made her even worse at figuring out how to not lose him. "Have you thought about whether you're going to come home after your rotation?"

Voices picked up in the background.

"Does saying nothing mean that you haven't thought about it or you haven't decided?"

"Tessa."

"Because I thought I should tell you, I'm going to stay at Westfaling."

Ben sighed.

"And the other thing is that Chris has totally lost it."

"Tessa, please don't talk to me about Chris."

"No, it's not what you think. He's sabotaging me—"

"Tessa, stop!" he shouted, startling her. The Scottish voice in the background ceased. "I don't want to hear it," he said, more calmly now, but still heated. "I've had a long think about this," he said. "And you know how you always say how academics wind up marrying other academics because no one understands what you do, and why your field is so important to you." Tessa experienced a sinking feeling as she understood Ben had rehearsed these words, and what that rehearsal entailed. "I thought we were the exception because I loved you, nothing else mattered, and so on."

"But I love you—"

"No, no. Let me finish. Because you were right, I don't understand. I don't understand how you can care more about your field than about the people who love you."

"That's not true," Tessa protested.

"Oh? You know, it wasn't the dinner what did it for me. It wasn't the letter. But what I knew when I saw that letter from the University of *California*, was that you'd never really bothered about missing my father's funeral. You'd never really known what that did to me." He choked up, and Tessa felt her own eyes welling with tears.

She didn't know what she could have done: Stood there? Held him while he cried? "Obviously I was wrong," she said. "Obviously I was a million times wrong; if I had had any idea what it would do to you, I would never have gone." It had seemed like the right choice, to miss the funeral. Was she insane? Was she so bloodless? "I grieved, Ben, I grieved. You think I don't know what it means to lose a father? If any part of me could have been there with you, I would have."

"You know, I believed it was because of your own grief. That you going to Edinburgh was some sort of, I don't know, some sort of inability to deal with your own loss. But I was giving you too much credit. I believed that, I told myself that. I thought, Why do you always think less of her? Why do you chalk everything up to her careerism? That there's actually a person in there, not just a shell of one. But no, it's all for yourself. And that's why you went to Edinburgh."

They had had this fight before. *You told me to do whatever it takes*, she'd said. *There are limits*, he'd said. *Oh? What limits are implied in the phrase "whatever it takes"?*

"Ben, no."

"And I've also, and this is why it's my failing, really. I also saw that I was never going to be able to forgive you for that, either," he said.

"Ben—"

"Goodbye, Tessa."

. . .

TESSA'S WALK to College was charged with the weight and shock of Ben's words. She felt clammy and hot and ashamed. She was confused and uncertain about everything, unable to get her bearings. The city seemed to swerve precipitously around her. She was furious at Ben, furious, that what she had apologized for to no end, and what he had convinced her he had forgiven her for, had become his reason for letting her go.

She had cared for Gabriel—the retired carpet retailer, "a gentleman of leisure now," his humor in the face of his failing body, the way his blue eyes saw her deeply even as his teacup would make wild spirals on its journey to his lips. Family photos had lined the mantelpiece at Ben's small home in Kidlington, they were tight-knit, but Tessa had never sensed in them a need for her to play the adoring girlfriend. She'd felt strangely accepted, as if the unconditional love clearly extended to Ben also extended to her, though she'd done nothing to earn it. And that was it, perhaps, the strangeness she felt around the Duncans, that she had done nothing to merit their warmth, and so it had seemed impersonal almost, uninterested in what she did or did not achieve.

But Ben's love for her clearly *was* conditional. Ben had convinced himself she had gone to Edinburgh because of some repressed grief about her own dad, something he'd never even mentioned to her, which was apparently the thread that he had clung to since in order to believe she was a person. Not some hollow, ringing absence. *A shell of a person.* It wasn't true. Did she suffer some sort of emotional deficit? No, she had gone to Edinburgh because she was giving an important fucking paper for what was at the time her budding career. If he didn't understand that about her, that was his problem. She would not have gone, of course she would not have gone, if she had known she was going to lose him over it. But for him to come out at this hour when she genuinely needed him and lay into her for something—something for which he'd already offered forgiveness—was absolutely maddening.

What bothered her *the most*, more than him not being there, was him needing to understand her in the framework of some projection about what her dad had meant to her. About her being repressed. She could see him and his mother and aunts asking where Tessa was. She doesn't know how to deal with her *emotions*. She's not good with *loss*. No. He had been somehow *forced* to euphemize her.

The reality was that she needed him now and he was not to be made available. She proceeded to Westfaling with the slip of paper in hand, feeling like she had already forfeited every fiber of personhood, already been unraveled to a finer thread than she thought possible; what difference would it make at this point to be committed to another year of this? She wanted to stand her ground in this city, a city that over such a short period of time had begun to feel alien and threatening to her—the buses and cars drove on the wrong side of the road, the traffic signals were incoherent, everyone on Woodstock was in danger of being struck by a commuter bus, especially non-Brits, who were wired to look to their left when they crossed the street, not their right. To be a non-Brit in Oxford, you had to look both ways to feel safe, and even then, you didn't. It was overcast, of course. There was always a threat of rain, even if it wasn't raining, and a chilly breeze nipped at her face and her hands. The Westfaling belvedere peered out over the other buildings.

She had never had to justify herself here. Oxford had justified her. Chris had justified her. Here she was, now, circling back like a moth, indenturing herself and her future with a slip of paper. At the threshold to Westfaling she stopped, feeling that a run-in with Chris right then was more than she could bear, and the unreality of her situation fed on her resolve. There were so many variables that she didn't have the brainpower to evaluate, so many problems with her course of action that it was impossible to even attempt logic—the muscles of her throat constricted and she wavered against the grainy stone of Westfaling's façade. Go home, she thought. It's over. She repeated this to herself as she passed through the threshold: Go home, it's over. Give up, and go work in a fast-food restaurant.

She rounded the green toward the administrative office. Selma, the head secretary, was still working when Tessa arrived. Tessa greeted her and explained that she wasn't prepared yet to sign the official offer of acceptance to Westfaling, but she wanted to let Selma know that she would likely be accepting and the work visa would probably need to be processed.

"You certainly leave it to the last minute," Selma said.

Tessa apologized numbly.

"There will need to be some paperwork with the work visa," Selma said. "Is Leckford Road still your current address?"

"Yes," said Tessa.

"Good, we'll be sending the paperwork along then very soon."

Outside, it was drizzling. The carillon rang. Of course, the carillon rang no matter what happened. Students jumped from windows all the time and had to be wiped off the sidewalk, it didn't stop the carillon from ringing. She began her trek home back across the green, some part of her daring Chris's shadow to darken the doorstep of Staircase 7. Clouds had gathered so thickly across the sky that it was nearly dark, and just noon. In the window of Chris's office, she saw a light flicker on. Panic enveloped her. The adrenaline, of which she thought her supplies must be depleted, surged. She walked quickly away from college, taking some refuge in her knowledge of where Chris was. Inside her flat, she checked her phone and saw that Claire had texted her.

> Come to New Jersey or go to Florida until you figure this out. Funds en route.

Still numb, she opened an email notification from Lloyds bank that a £1,500 transfer was pending to her account. The email thanked her for receiving the £292.18 they were owed including overdraft fees, and she was left with £1107.82. Claire was right, she needed to get out of Oxford.

PART IV

Little false island, cut from your mothergod
to whom do you now belong, pretty one?

MARIUS,
translated by Florence Henshawe

THE ITALIAN COASTLINE ADVANCED IN MINIA-
ture under Tessa's eyes as the plane broke through a curtain of clouds and bore down on Fiumicino Airport. Tessa
had bartered with a chipper, banged preteen for the window seat,
knowing that Isola Sacra lay just south of Rome's airport, and opti-
mistic that she'd be able to glimpse it from above. She was down one
package of Cadbury Cremes for the opportunity. The last vapors of
cloud whipped past, the coast began to pixelate with boats and jet-
ties and roofs, and a slab of blue parting the mainland announced
itself as the mouth of the Tiber. There, along its north bank, was the
sliver of land known as Isola Sacra.

Tessa didn't know exactly what she had expected, but it was
less an island than a coastal appendage, separated from the mainland only by the Tiber River and a narrow canal. It looked like
it had been sliced off with a very fine knife. As they approached
still nearer, she could see nothing magnificent in its dirt patches
of fallow farmland, the weak green pastures, the smatterings of
terra-cotta roofs huddled around capillary roads, and finally, several acres of mute, glinting windshields: the Rome AirPark. Tessa
laughed morbidly to herself. Isola Sacra was now an airport parking lot. Five euros a day to park your Peugeot or your Fiat, where it
would bake under the sun or endure cold tempests off the Tyrrhe-
nian, depending on the season. She was suddenly struck by the stu-
pidity of this journey. Claire didn't know where she was. Chris had
texted her three times since she had skipped the OUP drinks. Still,
Tessa had ignored Marius for two years on account of Chris's

advice. Now she felt particularly inclined to pursue him, consequences be damned.

* * *

IN THE AIRPORT, Tessa used a *bancomat* to withdraw two hundred euros, feeling suddenly rich with Claire's infusion of cash. A
short taxi ride along the via dell' Aeroporto di Fiumicino left her
outside the *soprintendenza* lodgings, an unassuming stucco building surrounded on three sides with palm trees and on the other by
the highway. Lucrezia had texted her a code which she used at the
door and dropped her things, hoping she would have time to see the
necropolis before Lucrezia and her team returned for the day. Per
Google Maps, it was just on the other side of the highway. Upstairs,
she thought she could see it from the balcony, just next to the air
park. She repacked her bag with *I Frammenti Completi*, a folder with
her notes on Marius, including some of her own translations and
also two of Florence's, a Beinecke commentary from 1928 on minor
poets that mentioned Marius, and two peanut butter sandwiches she
had made in Oxford.

She sprinted across the highway, nearly succumbing to a speeding sedan, and hugged its nonexistent shoulder for several yards
before finding a lip of pavement that spewed onto a tree-lined dirt
track. The noise from the highway faded. A few evergreens rustled
in the breeze. After a couple of minutes, she saw a handwritten sign:
Necropoli. For a fleeting moment, her troubles seemed distant. She
let her fingers trail through a spray of oleander buds. She turned once
and saw what must be the entrance to the necropolis: the outline of a
fence, a parked white van, and, inexplicably, a navy-blue sports car,
a very expensive-looking, very sleek, Italian sports car. Two figures

stood next to it, a man and a woman, their hands intertwined. As Tessa neared, she recognized the woman as Lucrezia.

"*Tess-sa!*" Lucrezia shouted, and dropped the man's hand and ran down the dirt path to greet her. "I thought you were, like, a mirage. I'm so happy you came."

Lucrezia introduced Tessa to Alberto, who said, "Hello," but seemed to say, *Hello, I'm a fantastically handsome owner of a Maserati.* Tessa had the opportunity to stare at his jaw for a few moments while Lucrezia, who was covered in dust, embraced him, kissed him on the mouth, said *ciao* and *ti amo*, and then kissed him again, and brushed off the imprint she had left on his blazer. Why had Lucrezia never mentioned any Alberto? True, they rarely talked of their personal lives, but still. "Goodbye," he said to Tessa politely, without any real interest that she could detect, and then got into the car, which looked absurd in the idyllic landscape; the engine purred and he drove off.

"He's gone for five days," Lucrezia said. "Brussels. Business."

Tessa wondered if he kept that thing in the air park. "He seems . . ."

"I'm in love with that man. But he looks like a mannequin."

Tessa laughed.

"But you're here!" Lucrezia continued. "I'm so happy you came. I will show you the site. We have so many experts here, petrologists, numismatologists, taphonomists, osteologists, biological anthropologists, hydrologists, geologists . . . but we don't have a Latinist."

Lucrezia guided Tessa past the gate and pulled it closed behind them, its iron spike raking across the dirt. "Isola Sacra is just one part of the whole excavation, you have to understand," she began, checking her wristwatch subtly and leading Tessa down the remains of an old road, stone surfacing through malnourished grass and stray dandelions. "The old via Flavia Severiana," Lucrezia was saying, "connected the two ancient ports, Ostia and Portus." She explained how residents of both cities were buried here; it was a city of the dead in the ancient style, the living would come on holidays to drink, celebrate, remember, et cetera. Tessa caught sight of several mound-like structures picked out between the trees. Her skin prickled as they moved onward. Tombs ran along the road's course before it bent out of sight: disheveled brick buildings in various states of ruin, pockmarked, roofless, blistered.

Lucrezia explained that about a hundred tombs had been musealized after they were first excavated in the thirties, and the plan was to do the same to the various mausoleums they were working on now. Thus the necropolis reposed in near-replica of what it once had been, the huddled rinds of the tombs reinforced or the brickwork capped to prevent further decay. Even some of the epitaphs—text dedications to the dead inscribed on marble plaques—were locked into niches on the tomb façades with small metal clamps, Tessa saw as they walked. "But of course, this is not a *vacanza*," Lucrezia said. "You want to know about your Marius."

"And I'm imposing on you."

"Not at all!" Lucrezia said. "We must make time to hang out later, though, catch up."

"You can tell me about Alberto."

Lucrezia's expression broke into an uncontainable smile. It reminded Tessa of Liam with his letter from Brasenose.

"But in the meantime," said Tessa, laughing.

"In the meantime," Lucrezia echoed dreamily.

"You'd mentioned some inscriptions?"

"Yes!" Lucrezia said. "It's in the lab." She gestured for Tessa to follow her as she abandoned the track of the old road and cut through an alley between a series of tombs, walking quickly. The terrain churned with stray blocks of old masonry, but Lucrezia seemed to know each and every hazard already. "So are you working with Chris on this?" she said. "Because I think he knows my boss, Edward Trelawney."

"I'm most definitely not," Tessa said, grimacing. "Actually, if you could not mention to Edward that I'm here, if it would be all the same, I'd rather."

Lucrezia's eyes lingered on Tessa's for a moment, a glimmer of curiosity in them, and Tessa hoped she wouldn't inquire further. Lucrezia shrugged. "He won't be here until next week. It's not need-to-know." They picked their way through a copse of pine trees. "So, there is what I'm going to show you now, and there is also a verse epitaph, but I don't know if it's interesting to you."

"A verse epitaph," Tessa repeated. She was not very familiar with the genre; her favorite had always been Lord Byron's for his dog: *To mark a friend's remains these stones arise / I never knew but one—and here he lies*. "They weren't uncommon, no?"

"Not uncommon, but not normal, either. Most epitaphs only list the name and occupation of the dead, maybe the age, and some common phrases of dedication. You know, not unlike gravestones today. This one is metrical and six lines, but it's very damaged. What its literary value is, maybe you can say. But it makes no mention of Marius."

Tessa looked up and nearly tripped on a root. "Well, I don't imagine you have something that *does* mention him," she said. They were bearing down on a modern modular structure, a sort of warehouse that, when she and Lucrezia passed through its open threshold and Tessa's eyes adjusted, she understood to be the "lab." "Do you?" Tessa asked. Lucrezia smiled but didn't answer.

The interior was vast, lit with fluorescent lights that buzzed hypnotically in the rafters, a strangely sterile, industrial space outfitted with row upon row of industrial steel shelves nearly overrun with yellow trays and clear plastic bins: "They contain the fruit, so far, of the excavation, which is yet to be catalogued," Lucrezia explained. At the center were a series of worktables, some cleared, some lined with miscellaneous lab apparatus, and one occupied by a young man in a white coat and elastic gloves peering at something under a lamp. He did not look up as Lucrezia approached, speaking quietly now, "I'm so glad Westfaling paid for your flights." Tessa didn't bother correcting her. "Of course, I could have an epigrapher from the *università* come look at these, and we will, but I wanted to give *you* the opportunity if it was anything interesting. Unfortunately, I can't justify buying your ticket when Antonia Domenica would be here in a 'eartbeat with her magnifying glass."

"And her squeeze paper," the young man added ruefully, without looking up. Under the desk lamp he was teasing apart a crinkled brown roll with his gloved hand and a wooden tong.

"For publication, Antonia makes impressions of the inscriptions with squeeze paper," Lucrezia explained.

"Sometimes makes fragments of the inscriptions, too," the man added.

"About the flights, I understand," Tessa said to Lucrezia, though she felt her level of understanding would depend largely on the worthiness of whatever Lucrezia was about to present.

"Good," said Lucrezia. "Graham, this is Tessa. Tessa, Graham."

A young, angular face with the whisper of a beard met Tessa's eyes for the briefest possible instant without being rude. "Hi," he said. "Welcome."

Tessa was about to ask what he was unfurling so delicately when a line of script on the inside of the roll caught her eye. "Tell me that's not a curse tablet," she said.

Graham's face turned to Lucrezia's with a more or less shit-eating smile on it.

"It's a curse tablet," Lucrezia affirmed.

"Needs to go back in the oven," Graham said.

"Where are the ones you finished?" Lucrezia called after him as he whisked it away to a nearby table.

"Tomb one hundred fifty-five, context seven," he said. "You'll see them."

Tessa felt an insurrection of excitement as she followed Lucrezia to one of the shelves of labeled bins. She knew only vaguely about curse tablets, little petitions for revenge that ancient Romans would inscribe on sheets of lead, roll up, fix with a nail, then drop in some juncture between the living and the dead, like a grave or well, so that supernatural entities would hear the plea and visit justice on the perpetrator, blinding him, or rendering him impotent, or drowning him in a river of fire.

"They're like cannolis in situ," Lucrezia said, maneuvering a bin off the shelf. "But at forty degrees lead softens. I tell Graham he can be a pastry chef."

"Ha-ha," Graham called from across the lab.

"That we don't choose our fate, our fate chooses us."

Lucrezia set the bin on a nearby counter, while Tessa prayed to the gods both below and above that inside lay something of interest, something that would immeasurably improve her understanding of Publius Marius Scaeva, or at least place him definitively in the region. She flipped on the desk lamp while Lucrezia punched her hands into a pair of plastic gloves, then removed the lid.

One crude tablet sat faceup on the plastic sheet, scratches

of script etched along its crinkled surface, which Tessa gradually resolved into letters, some of which were missing. Its message was short. Tessa's mind filled in the missing letters.

DITE INFERI PUBLIUM MARIUM SCA   AM
DEFIGAS ET FUTU   ICEM EIUS

DITE INFERI PUBLIUM MARIUM SC[AEV]AM
DEFIGAS ET FUTU[TR]ICEM EIUS

The etching of Marius's name, inflected with an accusative ending, sent a jolt of excitement through her. For a brief moment, she lacked the resources even to process the message. "To Dis and the underworld gods," she translated softly, "may you curse Publius Marius Scaeva and his slut."

She looked up from the tablet at Lucrezia, whose face glowed next to hers under the lamp. "You read it as Scaeva?" Lucrezia said. Both their voices had quieted considerably. It seemed important to Tessa, suddenly, that Graham not hear them.

"I mean, I have to think about what else it might be," Tessa said, excitement lifting. "Scato? But Scato would inflect Scat*um* in the accusative, not *am*. Publius and Marius are clear as day, though. Look!"

"I *see*." Lucrezia laughed. "What do you make of the message?"

"Jealous wife or mistress," Tessa said, thinking out loud. "*Fututricix*, such a carnal word. Though it's added more or less as an afterthought, and she isn't named, which is interesting."

"Yes," Lucrezia agreed.

"I find it likely the author was female. It could have been a property issue; it's been opined that women were more likely to resort to magic. More likely to have to, is more like it. We didn't exactly get a fair shake in the courts."

Lucrezia listened, and Tessa wondered how much she knew; whether she remained quiet in the same way that Chris had used to, seeming to appraise her, but sometimes turning out simply to be uninformed. She knew Lucrezia, though. She would not be uninformed.

"Where did you find it?" Tessa asked.

"Tomorrow you will see. We found it in the tomb of a young woman."

*   *   *

DINNER WAS PROVIDED at the *soprintendenza* lodgings; Lucrezia supervised three of the team in a production of balsamic chicken, pasta salad, and fresh grilled vegetables, then disappeared without joining the meal. Tessa shook hands and smiled at an assortment of faces—Heloise from Vancouver, Jan and Joop from Rotterdam, others. Tessa could hardly believe what Lucrezia had shown her within one hour of her arrival, and after making polite conversation at dinner she excused herself to her room—a bare space with a bunk twin and a desk, a window through which she could hear whispers of traffic on the via dell' Aeroporto di Fiumicino, and water pipes in the walls that whooshed and churned with the echoes of laughter from the bathroom.

Yet by the time she unpacked her things and opened her laptop, the initial excitement about the curse tablet had tempered somewhat. The tablet seemed to raise more questions than it answered. She would love to place Publius Marius Scaeva unequivocally in Isola Sacra, but what of the corrupted letters in Scaeva, the missing 'aev'? Who was the *fututrix*, and who the author? Sulpicia, Marius's wife attested to in the *Suda*, seemed the most plausible candidate, though the tablet's subtext of low-rent jealousies hardly resonated with the delicate vision of domestic love that characterized the hearing poem, for example. *Intimacies / little sweet things, I would not trust to tablets.* The poems' sensibilities were generally elegant, euphemistic, caressing, not violent and profane: *I curse Marius and his slut too.* Then again, Tessa knew well the two-faced slander that intimates are capable of in the throes of anonymity, and it struck her what an interesting genre the Roman curse tablet was in its own right, in which words were meant to effect a new reality, not unlike wedding vows, or a letter of recommendation.

Speculation was idle, though, with low-hanging fruit to be picked. Did other names match their Sc am? For candidates she could consult the *Corpus Inscriptionum Latinarum*, also known as the *CIL*, a fifteen-volume compendium of all Roman inscriptions known to civilization as of 1931 (with drawings and commentary). Since the Renaissance, scholars had sketched and catalogued hundreds of thousands of these engravings found in the ruins of the former empire—from the epitaphs, plaques, and curse tablets of ordinary people to the dedicatory statues and columns of the imperial family. On her hard drive lurked a PDF of the volume of such artifacts found in the city of Rome, an immense file that featured a census-like index of all the names inscribed in its entries. She opened the file, and a full minute of scrolling ensued; the *CIL* never failed to awe with its giantism, its Byzantine beauty, its enshrinement of learning and anal-retentive excess. Finally, she reached the index, which listed numerous matches that would inflect to Sc am: Scapula, Scaenica, Scala, Scapha, and even another Scaeva. Tessa sighed.

Two knocks rapped against the door, and Lucrezia entered, still dressed in the grimy jeans and crew neck she'd worn that day, equipped with some sort of snack in her hand and a sheet of napkins.

"Comfortable?" Lucrezia asked.

"Yes, luxuriating."

"Risotto rice cake?" she offered.

Tessa took a napkin from Lucrezia and tried the cake. It was warm, crunchy, and delicious. The bed squeaked as Lucrezia sat next to her and pinched off a piece of her own, holding the rest daintily between two fingers. "Last night, Heloise tried to make risotto," she said. "I'm not saying she failed, but . . ." She paused to chew and gestured with her free hand. "Anyway, we don't throw away risotto here."

"You salvaged it?"

"Trick from my *nonna*. Good, right?"

"Amazing," Tessa said, before her next bite. "The garlic."

"Right?"

They chewed for several moments in silence.

"You told me before that Marius writes in these limping iambs," Lucrezia said.

"Yes."

"What does that mean?" she arched her back against the wall. Her eyes were bloodshot, red from dust, or fatigue, or both.

Tessa set her laptop on the nightstand and scooted against the wall herself. "Well, it means different things to different people," she said. "Really, an iamb is a downbeat followed by a beat. 'Whose woods these are I think I know' is four iambs. Whose *woods* these *are* I *think* I *know* / his house is in the village though."

"Whose *woods* these *are* I *think* I *know* / his *house* is *in* the *vill*age *though*," Lucrezia pronounced slowly.

"Right. Marius composes in iambs but blunts them at the end of each line. You can't really do it in English, but the effect is to make the line limp. A Greek poet, Hipponax, was the first to use them, and he was said to have suffered from a foot injury, a narrative I like. 'The domain of rhythm extends from the spiritual to the carnal,' a poet once said. I agree. It's *everything*, rhythm. It's the pattern of language in time. It's how any poet composes a higher reality. But Hipponax really shined writing invective poetry, really vile things like, 'What midwife wiped you up as you squirmed and mewled?' That set a precedent, so Roman poets like Catullus wrote their invective in choliambs, and so on."

Lucrezia nodded, tired, her eyes fixed on some vanishing point in the ceiling.

"Anyway, that was a long-winded way of saying that Marius shows few tonal vestiges of invective, but he nevertheless writes in that form. Thus he's a mystery or, if you think of rhythm merely as a signpost of genre, an incompetent."

"Maybe you will learn enough here to revitalize interest," Lucrezia said.

"The philandering is a great start. Way to help me rehabilitate the image."

Lucrezia laughed. "But if you link him here conclusively—"

"I know," Tessa said. "It *is* an excellent start. I'm grateful."

Lucrezia inspected the last morsel of risotto cake between her fingers. "I was thinking what other Latin names are like Scaeva," she said, before popping it into her mouth.

"Likewise," Tessa said, reaching for her laptop. "You know the *Corpus Inscriptionum Latinarum*?"

"*Certo.*"

Tessa maneuvered her computer screen to present the page of names from the volume's index. "Hm," Lucrezia said. And then, "Did you check Volume XIV?"

"Volume XIV?"

"It's the volume for Ostia specifically, as opposed to Rome." Lucrezia took possession of the laptop and began to type rapidly. Tessa hoisted herself up on the cot so she could watch. "Do you mind if I download? It's only ten gigabytes," Lucrezia said with a laugh.

Tessa didn't know of this Volume XIV, and for a moment she was filled with envy for Lucrezia's skill set. Lucrezia knew the region intimately; its material realities. Tessa knew little of material realities. She trafficked in metaphor, in obsolete rhythms.

Lucrezia opened the file and navigated to the index of names, as Tessa had done for Volume VI.

SCAPULA [4560, I A. 5309, 45]

"*Merda*," she said softly, as she scrolled through the document.
"What?" Tessa said.

Lucrezia scrolled directly to the second Scapula, number 5309, her fingers swiping the track pad. Tessa caught the name before she could put it in context.

5309 45: FISTULA, REP. DOMO SCAPULAE
P MARIUS SCAPULA

"Fuck," Lucrezia said. "I knew the name was familiar."
"*Fistula*. A water pipe, found in Scapula's house?" Tessa said.
"The Domus di Scapula is in Ostia Antica." Lucrezia groaned. "I didn't know *that* was Scapula's full Latin name."
"Publius Marius Scapula," Tessa repeated.
"He might be our philanderer."

•   •   •

ANY AMBIGUITY ABOUT the tablet's cursee was put to rest the next morning outside the tomb where it had been discovered.

"Yes, early fourth century," Graham said, brushing off a flat square brick with the back of his gloved hand. The abbreviation POST. ET. NEP. was stamped into its surface. "Postumius and Nepotianus," he said. "Consuls, AD 301."

"So the curse tablets . . ." Tessa said.

"Yes, with the brick, we can postdate them," Graham said. "Likely fourth century, but not before."

"Fuck," Tessa said under her breath. Marius's syntax and grammar were decidedly not late-empire, even if the sources had somehow mistaken his era. Publius Marius Scaeva, second century. As opposed to this Publius Marius *Scapula*, owner of a fourth century *domus* in Ostia, a not-poet and a philanderer. For a moment Tessa felt that Scapula had stolen this discovery from her, that he, an impostor, was tormenting her from the grave.

•   •   •

THE BUS HURTLED down the via dell' Aeroporto toward the south end of Isola Sacra, where the Tiber divided the island from the mainland and the ruins of Ostia. Tessa stared numbly out the plate-glass window, tracts of inscrutable farmland rushing past under darkening clouds. She had lurked extraneously around the dig site for several hours, doubt and loneliness cascading into the curse tablet fuckup, before impulsively setting off for the Domus di Scapula itself, as if intent on some retribution. She could not shake the feeling that Scapula had taken something from her—not only the curse tablet, but her tether to the ancient past, the glimmering interface between now and then that had always been made up of language, sufficient to the cause. Archaeological strata, stamped bricks, Volume XIVs—she knew nothing about these things. She was out of her depth. She was failed risotto.

An Alitalia flight attendant seemed to share Tessa's sour mood, frowning into her green ascot. The via dell' Aeroporto paralleled almost exactly the old via Flavia, and it occurred to Tessa that the employees of Rome's Leonardo da Vinci Airport commuted by virtually the same road as the workers of ancient Rome's Portus and Ostia—yet this observation felt stale, banal, mere platitude. History repeats, and so on. Frustration welled inside her. Who cared if Marius had fooled around? she thought suddenly. Now she had nothing. She was a stew of contradictory ideas and petty annoyances. It seemed an unforced error: had Lucrezia told her the tablet could be postdated from the fourth century, Tessa never would have pursued it in the first place. She lamented the fact that she could count on no one other than herself, that she was dependent on that fuckwit Eccles, *and* her friend Lucrezia, for better or for ill.

At the Ostia Antica station she stepped off the bus and was greeted by a drop of rain. She trekked past the dour turrets of a medieval castle toward the entrance to the archaeological park, its mouth disgorging damp tourists, their umbrellas blooming. Already, traces of human habitation were rising illegibly out of the ground— the moss-strewn vestiges of walls and other rubble, waving along the concourse. At the kiosk she paid her fee and obtained a map. 22. *Domus di Scapula*: about halfway into the site, southwest of the amphitheater. She made a beeline for the *domus*, past a jumble of tourists who tried gamely to ignore the drizzle. Indecipherable brick shapes loomed in the fog. Only the amphitheater was recognizable, the lip of its semicircular bowl indicating when she needed to turn.

She trudged through the fog and the armature of the old neighborhood, triangulating between the map and what she believed to be the *domus*. Roofless, it slouched before her in vague, stony outline. She entered through a gap in its desecrated wall. Overall, the house was less preserved than the others, and she could see all the way through to the portico of the once-entrance as she stepped gingerly through its scattered carcass. A half-turn staircase caught her eye; it reminded her of the half-turn stair in her childhood home in Jacksonville, but as with the Alitalia flight attendant, the likeness seemed to signify nothing. She marched through rooms and over faded mosaics, hunting a museum label, some proof of Scapula, some means to put this pointless search to an end, as rain fell cruelly into the roofless interior. Finally, on the portico, affixed to its façade, she found an ersatz stone inscription: *22. Domus di Scapula.* Okay, she thought. Here it is. Rain fell lightly but persistently, dripping into her eyes. For a minute she listened to its patter on the portico, on the *domus*'s capped walls. Of course Scapula was a dead end. Nothing had been stolen from anyone. It was her own incompetence, she knew, that assailed her. "Fuckwit," she said out loud, her breath condensing in the wet air. She left the site as directly as she had come.

•   •   •

TESSA WOKE with the team and ate shitty cornflakes alongside them, traveled to the necropolis alongside them, though she felt accused and extraneous, uncertain of her next step. At the site, they proceeded to the curse-tablet tomb, same as the day before, everyone quiet, still half asleep. Jan and Heloise unpacked their things nearby in the shadowy predawn, while Joop rattled a stray wheelbarrow over the cobbles and Graham scuffled into a pair of knee pads. Lucrezia had disappeared for the morning to attend to some bureaucratic nonsense, as she had phrased it. Tessa felt intensely alone as the sky began to fill with silver light. She noticed the tomb's epitaph enduring stolidly in the niche above its threshold. A white marble plaque. She translated:

MARCUS JULIUS CLARUS AND JULIA FABIANNA
MADE THIS FOR THEIR SWEETEST DAUGHTER
JULIA FORTUNATA, WHO LIVED FOURTEEN
YEARS, TEN MONTHS, AND ELEVEN DAYS.

"Fun fact," Graham said. "If you died young you were thought to linger around the grave site."

Tessa inhaled slowly. She was still trying to temper her annoyance with the curse-tablet situation. "The spirit, you mean? The soul?"

Graham nodded. "More likely to take the message down with you to the underworld."

Tessa wondered why he was using the second person and also if he was flirting. He seemed criminally young, twenty-three going on sixteen. Dust from yesterday still rimed his starter beard.

"Grim," Tessa said.

"Get used to it, Tessa." He chuckled. "You're in a necropolis." He stepped toward the threshold.

"Hey," Tessa said.

He turned.

"Lucrezia said something the other day about a verse epitaph. Do you know where it is?"

He nodded. "Most of its fragments are now in the lab," he said. "Tomb four hundred?" He couldn't remember the exact number. "I can't show you right now."

"You don't have to show me. Can you point me roughly in the tomb's direction?"

Sullenly literal, he shot his arm out toward the east, at a slight angle to the road, encompassing about half the site. He reminded her of one of her students, Arnold. Smart, but not that smart. Sort of clammy skin and boyish. He ducked under the threshold.

For a few moments Tessa stared up at the marble plaque, nursing her dislike of Scapula and hoping that Julia had carried out her civic duty. Jan, Joop, and Heloise moved with the soundless efficiency of dead-dawn routine, joining Graham inside with their skewers, pens, knives, aerosol containers, plastic bags. Some of the tombs had ceilings still intact; this one did not. It was average-sized, barely containing the four of them as they gathered around the lip of the sarcophagus. "Heloise, do you think you can get the *humeris* today?" Graham said—a touch of condescension in his voice—as Tessa ripped herself away, walking east, through a maze of brick and dirt that she struggled even to differentiate as tombs.

It felt odd to see history so carnally represented—words cut into stone, original bricks in their masonic patterns, the via Flavia running through everything like an artery. What she felt reading Ovid could not be approximated by bones and pumice dust. Words had always been the interface between herself and history—poetry, really, for she was not moved by the formulaic epitaphs she encountered, impersonal, sparse, legal, nearly all the same:

MARCUS PETRONIUS CRESCENS MADE THIS
FOR PETRONIA PLINIA, HIS VERY DESERVING
WIFE, FOR HIMSELF AND THEIR CHILDREN; FOR
THEIR FREEDMEN AND THEIR CHILDREN; FOR
ETC. ETC. ETC. THIS MONUMENT CANNOT BE
INHERITED ETC.

Whoever whoever whoever, etc. etc.

She searched each epitaph for signs of poetic life, the first lozenge of pink peeking over the horizon, but found little. Her mind wandered. Years ago, Tessa had needed to find a headstone for her father, and she recalled the major decision boiling down to font. She didn't remember what she had chosen. Perhaps Garamond.

After an hour or so of walking, she began to see the same names over and over again. There was Bobuensus and Bobuensus again, and good old Mercurius. It was hard to say if she'd seen the same tombs, or if everyone there had the same name, like Publius Marius Scapula and Publius Marius Scaeva. The flowers and tombs and people here seemed to be hiding their meanings from her, to be in another language, inaccessible. Birds trilled insane and meaningless warbles. Finally, she started back toward the road and the other living souls in the necropolis, seeking some sort of shelter from the fact that she suddenly did not know what she was doing there. The nape of her neck ran cold despite the sun. A few contiguous tombs reposed in her way, so she had to circle them and actually wound up even farther from the via Flavia, in a section that was still being excavated, many of the structures partly encased in earth. She heard the rhythmic pickaxe and the wheelbarrow in the distance, but couldn't see them, and she quickened her pace, intent on getting back, before she was halted by the sight of a single word, hovering in the upper right corner of a marred epitaph. *Viatori.* Traveler, wayfarer. She hovered closer to the fragment.

The marble suddenly seemed as delicate as a curtain. The millennia had been punitive. Maybe five more lines had been shredded away. She pronounced it slowly: *wehahtooree.* She stepped still closer, up on her toes so she was at eye level, her fingertips resting against

the stone jamb for balance. It could be nothing, of course. The ded-
icatee of the epitaph might be referred to as a voyager . . . whoever
whoever dedicates this to whoever the traveler.

In her mind's eye, she saw this:

$$\text{U} \; - \; | \; - \; -$$
$$\text{VI} \quad \text{AT} \quad \text{OR} \quad \text{I}$$

For if this were the verse epitaph Lucrezia had referred to, *viatori*
would end perfectly a line of limping iambs.

Tessa retreated slowly from the tomb's open mouth.

The pickaxe hammered the air into one profound echo.

●   ●   ●

THAT EVENING, Lucrezia and Tessa left for dinner at a restaurant near the Mediterranean shore, a few kilometers from their
lodgings. Lucrezia drove slowly down a narrow corridor that led
straight to the seashore, toward the sunset, past scribbles of farmland and stucco houses with terra-cotta roofs. Even though outside
was chilly and Tessa's hair slick from a shower, she rolled down the
window to smell the air, which was fragrant and crisp, laden with
fertilizer and the salt breeze. Lucrezia had been impressed that from
a single word in situ, Tessa had guessed the specific tomb where the
team had unearthed fragments of the verse epitaph. While the rest
of the team worked to disinter the remains of poor Julia Fortunata,
Tessa and Lucrezia had located the fragments in the lab store and
arranged their stone message on one of the workspaces. When Tessa
shut her eyes she saw the other three pieces of the epitaph laid out
in the lab, the in situ *viatori* hovering ghostlike where it completed
the first line.

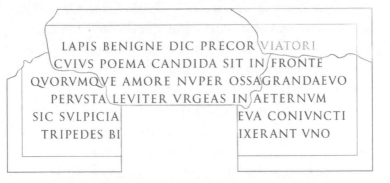

LAPIS BENIGNE DIC PRECOR VIATORI
CVIVS POEMA CANDIDA SIT IN FRONTE
QVORVMQVE AMORE NVPER OSSA GRANDAEVO
PERVSTA LEVITER VRGEAS IN AETERNVM
SIC SVLPICIA   EVA CONIVNCTI
TRIPEDES BI   IXERANT VNO

KIND STONE PRAY TELL THE TRAVELER

WHOSE POEM IT IS ON YOUR WHITE FOREHEAD

AND WHOSE BONES, SEARING, NOT LONG AGO, WITH AGED LOVE

YOU PRESS GENTLY UPON FOR ALL ETERNITY?

THUS SULPICIA   EVA, SPOUSES

THREE-FOOTED, TWO   THEY HAD LIVED IN ONE

As Lucrezia had lain out the marble pieces, she had explained that the rectangle in the lower portion had been deliberately cut away, likely to be reused in a new context—in a wall or as floor tile or as veneer. Flat marble stones were valuable in antiquity and "recycling" was very common. Tessa had translated the epitaph for Lucrezia and sketched out the meter on scratch paper, showing her where the iambs needed to be (and were), and where the caesura needed to be (and was). Finally, she had shown her the entry in the *Suda*. *Publius Marius Scaeva. A poet writing in choliambs. He married Sulpicia.* Gradually, Lucrezia had begun to share at least some of Tessa's awe and excitement that Marius and Sulpicia were, in a very reasonable realm of likelihood, buried within the tomb marked by the *viatori* fragment.

Lucrezia had then mentioned, offhand, that Ed was going to rue filing the paperwork for all this because it was so out of scope. "Ed?"

Tessa had asked. "Ed Trelawney, the one who knows Chris?" Lucrezia had responded. "My boss." This reminder had deflated Tessa with worry, and she had asked that they talk before Lucrezia tell him. Lucrezia had suggested that she and Tessa see Ostia Lido, that they go to dinner and talk there.

They were the only diners in the restaurant—it being six-thirty p.m. Tessa imagined that most places along the shore here looked exactly like this one—a jeroboam on display, a few pastel watercolors of the sea, dim lighting. Lucrezia ordered for the two of them—swordfish and mozzarella and tomato.

Tessa, slightly nervous but still alight with what she'd found just a few hours before, began right when the waiter left. "You mentioned your boss, Edward, the other day."

"You wanted me to hide you from him," Lucrezia said.

"Yes," Tessa said, then paused. "I don't know exactly how to say this."

Lucrezia reached for a bottle of olive oil. "What do you mean?"

Tessa hesitated. "Westfaling didn't pay for my flights." Lucrezia began pouring the olive oil. "Chris is actively trying to sabotage my career."

Lucrezia's eyes rose to meet Tessa's in what appeared to be disbelief. "What?" she said. Tessa watched the pool of olive oil thicken and stretch and threaten the edge of Lucrezia's plate.

Tessa pointed: "Lucrezia."

"*Cazzo*." Lucrezia tipped the bottle just in time. "I don't understand," she said. "What are you talking about?"

Tessa put her silverware down, and before she even started talking, she felt the emotion rise to her face. "In some sort of ploy to keep me at Westfaling next year, he wrote a 'recommendation' letter for me that was radioactive." Her voice trembled. "It was so ridiculous, in fact, that someone sent it to me via anonymous email, like some sort of whistleblower. It torpedoed my applications to work anywhere else."

Lucrezia's eyes widened. "But you're going to work at Westfaling next year?"

"It's the only place I have an offer."

"Oh, *porca puttana*," Lucrezia whispered. She asked the questions that Tessa had come to expect, how bad the letter was, whether she had confronted Chris, what his motive could be. "And what are you going to do now?"

"I don't know yet," Tessa said, though she felt less diminished by her uncertainty than she had even that very morning. "What I most want now is to know what the rest of the epitaph said."

"And for it to name Marius, too?" Lucrezia said. "Well, you can begin with the *CIL*—as you know, they usually draw the inscription, so you can see if there is a shape out there that fits. Look through all the Mariuses in Ostia. But you'll be hunting the needle, you know. Most likely it's lost."

"Will you give me some time to look?" Tessa said.

"You can have all the time in the world," Lucrezia said. Their waiter emerged from the kitchen bearing two sizzling plates laden with swordfish. "You will love this," she said.

Tessa had no appetite after the discovery; worry overwhelmed her, that she was missing something, or that the discovery would be taken from her like the curse tablet.

"I mean, can we wait to tell Ed?"

Lucrezia looked to the heavens, savoring her first bite. "So you no longer trust Chris?" she said.

"That's correct," Tessa said.

"And you think Edward will tell Chris if he sees it?"

"Do you?" Tessa asked.

By way of answer Lucrezia explained that Ed was held up in

Tunisia, where he was acting as advisor to a sister excavation on the ancient Roman port of Carthage. He anticipated returning to Isola Sacra on his way back to Oxford. "We could ask him not to tell Chris, or anyone, explain the situation," Lucrezia said, but she seemed unconvinced.

"And would Ed be sensitive to that?"

"He could be," Lucrezia said, breaking eye contact.

"Okay, so he wouldn't be."

"He would be sensitive to it," she said. "But he's not the kind of person to break with protocol, for something that's none of his business. We have a whole legal document, you know, a *documentazione di scavo*, and there are provisions for discoveries that are not in scope, you involve relevant experts, people who have their Ph.D.s, unfortunately, unlike you."

"So?"

"So for now I think we will have to not tell Ed." Lucrezia's eyes glittered.

"Really?" Tessa said, grateful and surprised. "I should mention that I'm giving a paper on Marius in Oxford next month."

"So we will tell him before then. Now try your swordfish."

•   •   •

SCOURING THE FIFTEEN VOLUMES of the *Corpus Inscriptionum Latinarum*, hunting its vast archive of Roman Mariuses for a marble inscription that would fit their four fragments like a jigsaw piece, Tessa was visited by an accompanying sense of geometric coldness, of dread, as if she saw in the hundreds of jagged fragments queued on her screen a reflection of a part of herself. She worked in the harsh fluorescent light of the lab, not far from Lucrezia, who had

been asked by Ed to change the color scheme of a major presentation
at the last minute. "He's, like, I don't know about this purple, maybe
more of a lavender"—mentor-mentee friction that seemed enviably
normal to Tessa, though at least Chris had never subjected her to
PowerPoint.

Tessa felt the momentum of what she'd found at Isola Sacra
gathering—even the epitaph in its current state would be enough,
in combination with the *urinatores* and the "false island" poem, to
cause a stir when she presented on Marius next month.

For Tessa had learned that Isola Sacra once constituted only a
vague stretch of the Italian mainland, bordered on two sides by the
curving mouth of the Tiber, and on a third by the Mediterranean. It
was not even an island until the emperor Claudius sliced a channel
along its northwestern plane—today's Fiumicino Canal. The metapoetic landscape of Isola Sacra would play well as explanation, more
resonant as background, she thought, than the gloss provided in the
1928 commentary by Beinecke, who believed the "false island" poem
was really addressed to a "false" or inconstant woman, and the "amputation" referred to their divorce. Florence's translation went thus:

> Little false island, cut from your mothergod
> to whom do you now belong, pretty one?
> the tiny sprout of Tiberinus or the Ocean
> God himself? You're between men. Marry.
> Rumor flies, but needs no wings to know your damage.
> What may be salvaged, salvage, and do not be afraid.
> What's left to fear from fame? News of your amputation?

Yet as Tessa scanned the digitized *CIL*, the irregular, craggy
shapes of inscriptions—none of them rectangular—she felt taunted

by Marius's puzzle, which seemed to articulate only new and ever-rippling fissures, and in whose solution Tessa sensed no promise of catharsis or wholeness. It occurred to her that each time she had arrived at breakthroughs in her career—after her father's death, during Gabriel's funeral—some terrible sacrifice had been made, and now once more she felt herself on the brink of revelation within the turbulence of upheaval and loss—of Ben, and even of Chris. It would never again be like that afternoon at her parents' house: the fuchsia flowers, the pond, the ease of unbordered pouring out of one's soul, the excitement of transformation, before transformation itself became an occasion for despair.

When Tessa could no longer deny to herself the futility of finding the missing piece in the *CIL*, and she saw that few of the more modern compendia of inscriptions had troubled with drawings, she abandoned her search. Through the lab's open warehouse door, twilight gleamed. A full day had elapsed. Lucrezia's foot kicked the leg of her stool with nervous energy. They had paused only for lunch; had otherwise been locked in their trances of monotony.

"Hey," Tessa said.

Lucrezia sighed. "He's very particular, which makes him a good archaeologist, but reassigning RGB codes in appendix figures is not how I want to live my life."

"I'm sorry," Tessa said. "That's a disaster."

"I'm full of adrenaline and also bored out of my skull," Lucrezia said.

A bird twittered somewhere up in the rafters.

"Oh, I almost forgot," Lucrezia said, rising. "Look here." She abandoned her laptop and led Tessa to the neighboring workspace, whose cluttered surface she illuminated with a click from its desk lamp.

Littered across the table were the pieces of a human skull. The spectacle of their inert shapes—the bowl of the cranium, the curve of the mandible with its inset teeth—caught Tessa off guard. They seemed oddly map-like, the way they were laid out below them, some familiar, some not. The piece that Lucrezia now indicated resembled something like a seashell, a scallop. "This is a temporal bone," she said. She lifted it with two fingers and pointed to where the bone seemed to swirl delicately around a tiny aperture, like water spinning around a drain. "This is the ear canal." Jutting into the canal's narrow tunnel was a series of bony nubs. "You see the exostoses?"

"Yes," Tessa said.

Lucrezia laid the bone back down on the table. "Maybe if you place Marius at Isola Sacra, Ed will agree that they are a skeletal marker of occupation. Not a bone anomaly from the *thermae*, the cold baths."

"Skeletal marker of occupation," Tessa repeated. "I think I have one of those in my lumbar."

Lucrezia laughed and returned to her laptop, leaving Tessa to marvel in solitude. She heard the bird twitter again up in the rafters and stared at the assortment of bones. That an occupation, or a career, could actually mark one's skeletal remains seemed disturbingly true. Disturbingly real. That it might also render one in some way senseless seemed equally true and disconcerting. A hardening could occur, an armoring, somewhere in the most delicate regions of one's being. Tessa felt a sudden assault of sadness, of regret, puncturing somewhere deep inside her. It lasted only a moment, and then passed.

· · ·

SHE AWOKE the following morning in the dark to the sound of rushing water in the pipes. She switched on the light, dressed quickly. A knock on her door, then Lucrezia's dim form slipping into the room.

"Ed will be here until tonight," she said in a hushed voice. "If you're here, I'll have to explain who you are. So maybe go enjoy yourself for the day." She shut the door behind her.

•   •   •

A SHOWER, then a taxi to the metro station and an hour ride into Rome. She could make it to the Borghese, then to the lovely restaurant in Prati she'd taken a shine to when she lived there for a month, two summers before, doing research at the Vatican Library. Identical six-story buildings gave way quickly to pine forest and farmland, then a series of commuter suburbs, small houses capped in terra-cotta. The closer her train got to Termini, though, the more agitated she became. What if Lucrezia showed Ed the fragments in the necropolis, and he told Chris?

Yet in the flurry of people outside Termini Station, she became suddenly, not carefree, but unburdened. There was nothing else she could do at the moment, and nowhere she needed to be. She idled in the flock of hurried, purposeful people, feeling pleasantly anonymous, then wandered to the concourse outside, drifting north, through Rome's casual beauty, its garrulous architecture, its undulating side streets. *Viator*, traveler, she thought, as she tacked left and right, and what did it mean that she did not know where she felt most at home? In Jacksonville, Tessa and Claire were oddball children, "fucking nerds," they'd been called, though Tessa experienced a brief spell of popularity her sophomore year when some of the less intellectual boys decided, fleetingly, that she was hot. Sometimes Tessa missed the way she'd brown while hitting tennis balls back and forth with Claire, missed the salty taste of sweat above her upper lip, the ribbon palm in front of their house, the whorls of her mother's orchids, but mostly she didn't miss Florida at all.

Tessa glimpsed the crown of a stone pine at the end of via Giacomo, evidence of the tree-lined edge of the Borghese gardens. She made the eleven a.m. entrance and was the first inside. She was immediately struck by the marble, the sheer quantity of it in the floors and the columns and the walls.

She took in the shadowy Caravaggios, his *David and Goliath*, in which he was said to have painted his own face onto Goliath's, decapitated, and his lover's onto David's. *Judith Beheading Holofernes* was there on loan, and to round up the gory medley, another *Judith Slaying Holofernes*, by Artemisia Gentileschi. In it, Judith raked a giant dagger across Holofernes's throat, while her knuckled fist drove his face into the puckered seams of his coverlet. It struck her that Judith would have gained more leverage with her fingers splayed, not knuckled, her palm against his ear, but the use of her fist made her seem repulsed, as if she did not want to so much as handle his skin, even in the act of taking his life. Or perhaps Artemisia had wanted to show Holofernes's expression, and if Judith had gotten her proper grip, her fingers would have covered his eye and cheek. Either way, it was an arresting image, with a less delicate Judith than Caravaggio's, a Judith who seemed to be going about her business, to be doing what was necessary, and what was necessary was not a delicate thing at all.

Other museumgoers moved quietly around her, so many with audio guides, the gallery resembled a silent disco. Tessa continued her wander to the third floor, and toward the Apollo and Daphne room, feeling the statue's presence before she even laid eyes on it.

They faced away from her, her first glimpse—and this was not by accident—always disorienting. She saw the backs of two figures in motion. The whorls of Apollo's garment, like a hovering mollusk, the satiny curves of an arm, a hand, a leg, a breast. The statue required one to circle it, so that its narrative unfolded in motion, suitable for Ovid's passage that, at 115 lines, had its protagonists almost entirely in movement. A frond of laurel leaves burst from Daphne's left thigh, sprigs of foliage sprayed from her hair to her outstretched hands; darting up her leg was a sheet of bark. Her mouth was agape. Then Apollo's face in eerie serenity, or ignorance, of Daphne's drama. He could see, perhaps, a crescent of her cheek, the tip of her nose, while the viewer was left to imagine what Daphne saw in this final moment, her screaming eyes pointing into the statue's negative space. Their bodies continued to twist as Tessa circled—then Apollo's toga curved around his muscled torso, billowing behind him, and then she was again behind the figures. Tessa was always in awe of how Bernini could make marble seem so light and airy, like a meringue, if he chose, or as dense and speckled as granite. She finished her first orbit, knowing she would do still more.

She had bought a version of this statue for Chris, here, two summers before. A paperweight. It probably still lay somewhere in his house, among his collection.

Love, of course, meant ironically. Love falling short.

But Ben's love had fallen short, too. What would his look like, adapted to statue form? she wondered. It wouldn't be adapted to a statue, she felt suddenly. It couldn't move stone like that.

"It's a chase scene."

Tessa turned to find the owner of this American voice, which was neither loud nor soft, but somehow pitched correctly for a museum. She took in a face, smooth skin, boyish, a few freckles that brought out the brown of his eyes, handsome.

"Hollywood spends millions on chase scenes with actual cars, to less effect than Bernini, with stone," he continued.

Tessa found herself agreeing and began to circle the statue again, more slowly. He followed her. "Art historian?" she said over her shoulder.

He bent forward, toward her. "I'm in film," he said.

She laughed at his light irony. He didn't look like an actor; his quarter-zip hung long and boxy, his expression seemed thoughtful and vaguely introspective. Screenwriter, maybe. Or set design. "Maybe you chose the wrong medium," she said, slightly provocative, continuing to circle.

"Stone can be very stubborn," he responded.

Not in the right hands, she nearly said, but she didn't. She stopped to read an inscription on the pedestal, underneath Apollo's grasping arm—two lines from the *Metamorphoses*, *in frondem crines, in ramos bracchia crescunt / pes modo tam velox pigris radicibus haeret*, into foliage her hair, into branches her arms grow, now sluggish roots cling to her swift foot.

"I didn't mean that exactly," he said, after this silence.

"What did you mean?" Tessa asked.

* * *

AN ENDLESS ARCADE of umbrella-shaped trees came silently past Tessa's reflection in the taxi window, voices jabbered on the radio in Italian, and signs reared their indecipherable messages in the plowing white beam of the headlight. She had splurged on a taxi back to Isola Sacra, and in the dark she recalled the strange day in company with this man, the statue man, Quarter-zip. They had left the gallery together, and after twenty minutes of wandering the Borghese gardens, she had made a joke about the ever-enlarging fact that they had not yet exchanged names, and they had continued to omit this basic formality through the early afternoon, relishing it, calling one another stranger playfully as they shared information—she talking on a surface level about teaching at Oxford, he admitting that his "mediocre" novel was being adapted into a movie in Rome ("Rom-com?" "Bank heist.") and he'd been invited to the set and then told summarily to fuck off when he tried to exert some creative control, of which he had none; she had lived only in Florida and Oxford, he everywhere, North Carolina, Georgia, Washington, Texas, he was a navy brat, "Worst kind of brat," "Bratwurst," "The title of your bildungsroman." They walked for hours, the sun wore gradually through the dark bruising clouds, and on their way to Prati Tessa glimpsed a navy-blue Maserati and who but Alberto stepping out of it, walking quickly onto a serpentine side street. She'd become incensed—he was supposed to be in Brussels—and Quarter-zip had gamely come with Tessa as she chased Alberto's clicking loafers to a restaurant, feeling strangely proprietary about Lucrezia's heart, wondering aloud what defense he would come up with, whether she would tell Lucrezia, how Tessa would confront him—hello from Brussels. But when they'd entered the restaurant she'd seen it was not Alberto at all, this man was older, with silver in his hair, a craggy face, meeting two adorable daughters and their grandmother for lunch, and following this, Tessa wondered aloud to Quarter-zip if she'd seen Alberto because of a latent envy of Lucrezia's relationship, a desire to see it dashed against the rocks of infidelity or mendacity, and Quarter-zip confessed to how he had discovered his girlfriend in L.A. cheating on him, how humiliating it had been, how it had led to him accepting the empty-gesture invitation to come to Rome, where he was now in limbo with a free room nevertheless at an expensive hotel near Termini. Their jaunt through Rome had gone from conspiratorial and fun to a more heavy and perhaps emotionally laden journey, and on their continued walk, Tessa found that not exchanging names had become something solemn and protective, insulating and permissive, a minor elision at first that had widened and could contain more emotionally, and into which they began to spill more personal details—childhood narratives, most embarrassing stories, where they lost their virginities. She thought of Apollo and Daphne, not of the chase, nor of Daphne's wordless scream, but of the sensuousness of their bodies folding into one another, and a subcurrent of desire lingered with her through dinner in Trastevere, where Tessa spoke about her father, his philosophical tyranny, his inability to question his own tenets, the way he'd needed the women in his life to reflect back his putative worldview. Yet here, in the pause when Quarter-zip used the bathroom and her fingers clutched a fold of table fabric, she felt a shift, the beginnings of resistance to this person, and the sensation that she had trusted too far. Afterward, when he began to direct their course back toward the expensive hotel, she didn't object, and she thought maybe she could disappear into Quarter-zip's clean sheets, buy a new pair of shoes, get a massage, get drunk on martinis. Let go. Be in the moment. For a few seconds it had seemed like maybe Marius didn't exist. She let herself slide into this possibility, its contours. They had a drink in his hotel bar, but finally it had become clear to Tessa that they had exchanged too much, that it would feel somehow wrong to exchange names, too, that what had begun as an exciting game had led them to a strange and uncomfortable loneliness, and she felt her hold on something important slipping, she was slipping away, and when he signed the bill in the bar she looked away from his signature, as if he were a stranger undressing. When she insisted she return to where she needed to go, he told her not to, asked at least for her name, for her number, to see her again in Rome. "What is this? Cinderella? Are you a pumpkin? You can't be serious. At least tell me your name."

It all felt ignominiously like her relationship with Ben, an encapsulation of its failure, her unwillingness to open up, to be seen. And yet the prospect of meeting this man again in Rome or telling him her name gave her a shiver of repulsion, even now, as the taxi pulled into the driveway of the *soprintendenza* lodgings, and Tessa exhaled a breath of relief.

In the bathroom upstairs, Tessa found Lucrezia brushing her teeth. "Fun day?" Lucrezia asked Tessa's reflection. Tessa nodded, smiling. She was glad that she had taken her advice.

* * *

TESSA WOKE the next morning to a bright backlit curtain and utter silence. In the kitchen she found Heloise making an omelet, and she explained that it was Sunday, everyone was sleeping. For a few hours, Tessa attempted work in her room as gradually the team began to stir. A day trip was being planned. A wine tasting. Graham and one of the Dutchmen were arguing Malvasias versus Trebbianos in the hallway.

"Tess-*sa*," Lucrezia called.

The invitation was extended.

"I haven't really seen Ostia yet," Tessa said.

"No?"

"Has everyone already been there?"

"Of course. But if you haven't seen it, you should. One hundred percent."

Tessa couldn't tell whether she'd heard a ripple of condescension in Lucrezia's "one hundred percent"—after all, Ostia Antica was for tourists, not archaeologists. Everything there had already been discovered. Yet practically all the inscriptions in Volume XIV had been found in Ostia, and along with Pompeii it constituted one of the few large-scale relics of a Roman city. Also, after Tessa's last trip, she felt almost as if a reconciliation were in order. On the short drive over, she regretted her decision less and less, as the group played captive audience to Graham and Joop's debates. "Is Graham even old enough to drink?" Heloise said.

They dropped her at the foot of the medieval castle, and she proceeded once again past the graffitied gateposts, on to the long concourse entrance—a blazing strip under the day's cloudless sky. Despite the warm sunny weekend, only a handful of tourists shared the pine-lined walkway, and the effect was slightly eerie. Already the city's skeleton was visible; dilapidated walls faced with flat square stones rose around her. At the ticket kiosk, a single group of thirty or so fair-haired visitors milled about, and after Tessa paid her entrance fee she glommed onto their amoeba just as it was trailing away behind a tall, middle-aged woman whose long skirt swept around her ankles. Tessa liked her look more and more— nose ring, tresses of dark hair—and the cluster of bodies soothed a mounting assault of anxiety. In the clarity of the sun, without rain or fog, the ruins took on the full proportion of a human habitation, yet hardly any tourists dotted its landscape. Drained of its viewers, the ancient city seemed to ascend a plane of reality more or less equivalent with that of the present.

The group drifted and crept forward into the site until the guide paused at two towering, disheveled stone walls on either side of the old road. "*Guten tag*," she sang in a husky, Italian-inflected German. "*Ich heisse Nadia.*" Impelled at first to bevel off and go her own way, for she barely understood German, Tessa nevertheless felt herself drawn to Nadia's incomprehensible song, to the obedient Germans like children on a field trip, to the promise of an itinerary. A commitment to stick to the group for five minutes renewed itself for another five, and then another. She understood the Latin names: for the city gate, the granaries, the shopfronts, the apartment blocks. She struggled to understand the German, of course, but it seemed many of the Germans did as well: *Wie bitte?* one would say. *Wie bitte?* and Nadia would gesticulate and try a new melody, or a new pitch. They moved in a muddle of preverbal song, and no one complained that Tessa had latched on. The group saw the baths, the amphitheater with its half-moon shape, a tiled floor strewn with mythological mosaics—Theseus, Romulus and Remus, Actaeon with his murderous dogs. It felt good to be guided, to follow blindly, and she drifted for what felt like hours, until Nadia's voice grew hoarse and the shadows slanted sideways off the ledges of ruined masonry.

Deep into the tour, what felt like miles from the entrance, Tessa caught sight of the half-turn brick staircase that had reminded her of the half-turn stairs in her home in Jacksonville. The Domus di Scapula. In its ruinous state, the stairs led only to their own landing. It was a stairway to nowhere, a feature that hadn't seemed odd or even occurred to her last time. Over the next quarter hour the group approached it obliquely as Nadia devoured in German arpeggios the objects of interest in their way. Again Tessa advanced on the *domus*, again its deteriorated walls afforded a vista all the way from one side to another, as the group thronged under the desecrated portico. "Domus di Scapula," Tessa caught, and she felt a twinge of painful recognition. "*in einundfünfzig ausgegraben*," Tessa heard—excavated in 1951—and then she lost Nadia's meaning again, her spritz-canto carrying upward into the open sky as Tessa mounted the staircase. Maybe in a year or two, she thought, the curse tablet will feature in this part of the tour. She climbed the first ten steps and made the turn up the next set, then stood on the staircase's bare shelf. *Peristyle*, she picked up. *Triclinium*, where the Scapulas would have eaten. She looked down into the *domus*; a breeze picked up and whipped her hair around her face. Publius Marius Scapula, *et fututricem eius.*

Even at home, she'd seen her father carry on with other women: a hand on the small of a back, a peculiar smile, none of which she'd comprehended at the time. They weren't discussed, the series of romantic entanglements, mostly with "subordinates"—Claire's phrase, when illumination came years later. It hadn't at first seemed odd to Tessa that her mother would take no responsibility for Dean's care, when responsibility was being allotted. Only later did she wonder, and pick apart the miserable cliché of his habits. *Nymphaeum*, she heard. *Tablinum*. For most of her adult life Tessa had resented how she was conscripted at seventeen, in a family of ostensible care providers, before she'd even realized there may exist something that would constitute her own volition. She associated the house in Jacksonville not only with the pain of Dean's death but with a previous version of herself, whose form she could barely perceive and whose remains she did not even know when she had lost. The Scapula house seemed familiar, now, with its half-turn stairs and its utter desecration, as if it were there to immortalize her own insignificant melodramas, which were irrelevant anyway in the scope of human history. And yet, though all these thoughts were familiar terrain to Tessa already, she encountered a new emotion, or at least the absence of one—for as she descended the steps back into the *domus*'s dubious enclosure, it occurred to her that where she had so often felt total aversion to the teenage girl who knew nothing through the prism of innocence, she was now visited by an inexplicable urge to retrieve her.

Several pairs of eyes had locked onto Tessa; her extended stay on the staircase had disrupted the easy rhythm of the group. She inhaled deeply and gradually reacclimated to Nadia's voice, its tarantella waltz, the wave of emotion subsiding. The group filed obediently toward the far side of the house. The echoes of *Wie bitte* had tapered off, more likely from futility than from any dawn of comprehension. Tessa caught the Latin word *spolia* and understood that many of the tiles in the floor of the atrium had been reused. Plundered, recycled, salvaged, whatever you wanted to call it. Risotto rice cakes, she thought. Tessa walked over the rectangular patterns and rhombuses of *portasanta* and *cipollino*. At the center of one of the arrangements was a rectangle of cut marble. Its outline appeared to her as if out of a dream.

MARIVSQVE SCA
CIPITES CORDE V

•   •   •

THE NEXT EVENING, Tessa sat curled on an armchair near the balcony window when she saw an email from Claire, subject matter: *??? Where are you???*

Tessa paused typing into a Word document the text of the epitaph, the sixth of Marius's extant poems, and responded only: *Italy. Claire, I found Marius's tomb.*

"Hey," a voice said behind her. Lucrezia.

Lucrezia hadn't reacted with the torrent of enthusiasm Tessa had rather uncritically anticipated when she'd shown her the picture on her phone, the record in 1951's l'Année épigraphique, the "reused" piece from Marius's epitaph, principally because Tessa had accompanied the revelation of the missing fragment with a request—admittedly phrased more as a demand at the time—that Ed be kept in the dark, just for the time being. Lucrezia hadn't been happy; Tessa's plea for discretion now turned on the fulcrum of a somewhat remarkable discovery, as it was clear to Lucrezia from the size and shape of the *domus* tablet that a mason had stripped the marble from Marius Scaeva's epitaph in Isola Sacra to be used as the centerpiece in Marius Scapula's tile arrangement, out of malice or thrift or some combination thereof. From the photo and measurements, they had been able to sketch the absent pieces alongside the ones in the lab.

```
LAPIS BENIGNE DIC PRECOR VIATORI
CVIVS POEMA CANDIDA SIT IN FRONTE
QVORVMQVE AMORE NVPER OSSA GRANDAEVO
PERVSTA LEVITER VRGEAS IN AETERNVM
SIC SVLPICIA MARIVSQVE SCAEVA CONIVNCTI
TRIPEDES BICIPITES CORDE VIXERANT VNO
```

Meanwhile, the complete epitaph raised more questions for Tessa, especially the line *Tripides bicipites corde vixerant uno*. Three-footed two-headed and one-in-heart they had lived. Was that meant to be taken literally? Was the epitaph telling her that Marius was indeed handicapped, that he, perhaps, had only one leg? Or was the meaning somehow figurative, as *one-in-heart* surely was? But could they tell if Marius had one foot when they exhumed him? Limping iambs, chosen not because of orthodoxies about meter, but as the prosody of his human form. This hypothesis had set Tessa into new mental torsions, and her mind had pivoted to the human remains themselves. Could Tessa be there when they opened the tomb? "I'm not saying hide it from Ed, I'm saying tell him later," she'd pleaded. "You know that this is the right thing to do, even if it's not the correct thing to do," she'd said. "Please, I beg you, give me the first crack at this." Ed was gone until mid-April, more than three weeks. Time had stretched out voluptuously in all directions.

Now Lucrezia was showered, in bare feet, wearing a bright yellow sweatshirt, and carrying two beers. Tessa took the beer gratefully.

Lucrezia pulled another chair from the dining table so that it faced Tessa.

"Yes?" Tessa said.

"Can I see the letter?" Lucrezia asked.

It seemed a reasonable request, but for some reason Tessa felt stung. Lucrezia wanted her to prove what she was saying was true, as if she could have concocted the whole story. Or more likely as if she simply believed Chris had recommended her appropriately, that she just wasn't a very good classicist. That she was so convinced of her abilities . . .

"Of course," Tessa said. "You want to ensure I'm not some psycho."

"Basically," Lucrezia said.

"The fucked-up thing," Tessa said, oddly relieved by Lucrezia's candor, "is that the words, like, worm their way into your head, and actually do make you question yourself." She pulled her phone out of her pocket. "I thought, Maybe I'm the crazy one. No, he admitted it to me, he even showed me the, quote, real one he wrote." Tessa unlocked her phone and searched "reconsider" and "Eccles" from the email message. She opened the email and handed Lucrezia the phone. "Do you want to strip-search me as well?" she asked.

"No, this is enough," Lucrezia said. She pressed on the screen to open the picture file. Lucrezia's eyebrows rose. "Oh my," she said. " 'I have heard that she acquitted herself well.' "

"Please," Tessa said. "I've read it."

Lucrezia waved her hand in apology. She handed Tessa her phone. "I'm sorry," she said. "I just needed to see it."

"I get it," Tessa said. Trust, but verify, Chris used to say.

"What's fucked up is that the person who wrote this offered you a job."

"That's one of the many fucked-up things about it," Tessa said.

"I'm sorry this happened to you," Lucrezia said.

•   •   •

"ALBERTO GETS THESE CYSTS just above his ass and his doctor told him having hair there makes it easier to get them. But he can't reach, of course. So I shave it for him every week."

"That's repulsive," Tessa said. They were sitting on the balcony in the dark, their feet up on the wrought-iron parapet. They had moved out into the unseasonably warm night as they drank more. Lucrezia drank straight from a bottle of red wine.

"It's intimate," Lucrezia said. "I love to do it." She took a long drag of her cigarette.

"Every week you shave your boyfriend's ass?"

"Every week."

"The most I ever did was pop a zit on his back," Tessa returned. "Never again."

"These are not like zits, though," Lucrezia said. "They're like the size of a chestnut, and totally black, and they smell like eggs. And they're painful, they're no joke. Alberto cried like a little baby when he had one."

Tessa laughed. "No, I get it."

"Do you have the same boyfriend, Ben was his name?"

"No longer." Tessa tapped the ash out on her own cigarette.

Lucrezia looked over at her with an expression that seemed to say, *Want to talk about it?*

Tessa made a walking motion with her fingers.

Lucrezia nodded and stared back into the horizon.

"He just left. It wasn't long ago," Tessa said. "Two weeks."

"Damn," Lucrezia said. She put her free hand on Tessa's wrist. "I'm sorry."

Tessa felt momentarily tempted to share how Ben had left just as she was discovering Chris's letter, and how he wasn't there for her when she needed him—she knew she could count on Lucrezia for some Ben-bashing. But she also knew it wasn't the full story, and she had prevailed on Lucrezia's sympathies enough for one day.

For a few moments they stared into the gathering darkness above the courtyard. Chatter from below melded into a low-grade buzz as it dissolved into the sky like a mist.

"Do you think Chris is in love with you?" Lucrezia asked.

"I don't know," Tessa said. "Probably. Maybe. If you can call it that."

"It sounds like passion."

"Stop."

"I know, I'm kidding. That's terrible. But Alberto is always flying to Brussels or London and I don't know what he does there, and I miss him, sometimes I wish he would kidnap me along, you know?"

Tessa found it difficult to empathize, but Lucrezia was tipsy, and it was vaguely endearing.

"And besides, he's not entirely unattractive," Lucrezia persisted. "How old is he?"

"Forty-four," Tessa said.

She nodded. "He's short, but he punches above his weight. His wife was really beautiful, no? I thought he had a *je ne sais quoi*. Sorry, I'm not being sympathetic," Lucrezia continued, "but I talked about going to Jordan for sixteen months and Alberto said, 'If that's what you want.' I became so fucking angry. If that's what I want?"

Tessa had never found Chris repulsive per se, it was the idea of doing *that*, and how low it would feel, how that would compromise her sense of achievement, everything she held dear, that made his eventual lechery so unsavory. But in her first term, had she not once worn that backless summer dress to their meeting? And had she never once looked in a mirror before she knew she was meeting him? It didn't really matter; it wasn't as though she were about to forgive him.

"So what are you going to do with Marius now?" Lucrezia asked.

"My question is, what are *you* going to do with Marius now?" Tessa countered. The alcohol had blurred her arguments, prepared earlier. But her closeness to Lucrezia now made her feel that perhaps she wouldn't need them. That perhaps Lucrezia already knew what she wanted to do, and only needed Tessa to help her do it.

"You mentioned that Marius wrote in these limping iambs, and you thought he might have a foot deformity," Lucrezia said.

"Yes, like Hipponax."

"And do you think the word *tripedes* might refer to that?"

"I think it could."

"Well, we'll know if there's any bone pathologies when we exhume him," Lucrezia said.

Tessa was quiet for a long time, listening, hoping that "we" included herself. "And will I be here when you do?"

*   *   *

re: ??? where are you???
Italy. Claire, I found Marius's tomb.

CHRIS FOUND IT decidedly amusing and bloody resourceful how Tessa had separated her wealthy sister from some of her money so she could fly to Rome. He was sure Diana would have deployed a similar sort of ruse when she was young and needed her father's money, but she had never had to as an adult, with an allowance. Tessa had called Claire—what they talked about, he did not know—and Claire had sent her a text telling her to go to their mum in Florida, or come to New Jersey, where she lived, funds en route. Very clever, Tessa. Playing a little tune on the heartstrings.

Ordinarily Tessa could have come to Chris for such a request. If she had really found Marius's tomb, a prospect Chris was still handling with some skepticism, he would have immediately found travel money for the both of them. Clearly, though, with the whole recommendation letter business, she wanted to skirt his influence. And yet he couldn't help admiring how she had skirted him so.

Chris stood and shook out his legs. He was in his mother's room at Hampshire Hospice. He had arrived perhaps forty-five minutes before, but Dorothy was still deep in a morphine nap. The wireless connection in her room was surprisingly strong.

Chris had been very good about respecting Tessa's privacy for almost a week, but she had not responded to texts or emails, and she did not answer her door, and when he had passed her flat the lights were not on, and he had grown genuinely worried. She had so few friends in Oxford that if something happened to her, god forbid, it was conceivable that several days would pass before anyone would notice. He had been genuinely shaken, and genuinely concerned for her safety as he had logged into her account and found that she was in Ostia. Ostia! He had thought it likely she had left town; he had worried that she had gone to Ben's mother's house, or flown back to the States, as her sister had requested. But no, she wasn't taking a vacation, she was following up on a lead. He loved it. What grit. What steel. She had flown there to meet Lucrezia Pagani, one of Ed Trelawney's underlings—Ed, who often complained about the bureaucracy around Ostia. The *documentazione di scavo* had taken him years to get approved.

"Connor?" his mother said.

"Yes?" said Chris. She always asked for Connor, her favorite of the hospice nurses. He placed his laptop on the small console and went to his mother's bed.

"Connor, you look like my son."

"Oh?" said Chris.

"Yes. He was always a sly little boy."

"Well, sly is a strong word, no?"

"I caught him looking through me purse once. Don't know what he thought he'd find in there. Never did tell him, just let him look. What's the harm? I thought to meself. He was a regular Jacob, that one. Would've put on a pelt to deceive his father, if he had an Esau to do it to." Or a birthright to inherit. "Shifty man. Never would've come clean unless you made him." Here she winked at Chris. She knew it was him. "Did good for himself, though. A clever one. He teaches at Oxford now."

"And this Chris fellow, do you love him?" Chris asked.

"Despite meself, I do. He's all I have left. But he's off now, in Oxford, never comes back to visit his poor dying mum."

She found it hard to move her hand with its brace still on, but she moved it on top of his.

"Chris?" his mother said. "Did you feed the kiddies?"

"Old Nutley did," Chris said.

His mother's eyes had gone gray again, and her belly was distended; a lifelong teetotaler, she was experiencing many of the symptoms of jaundice, due to the spread of the cancer. Even on holiday, Dorothy did not touch alcohol. Chris had certainly not inherited his drinking habits from his mother; and yet it was as if she were paying for them with her own flesh. Then again, he remembered the way she used to thump him with a rolling pin when he ignored his chores or talked back to her.

"Back along I'd give you a good larruping if you didn't feed the kiddies," she said, as if following the same train of thought.

Chris wondered if he could draw a straight line between his inclination toward bending the truth and his mother's willingness, when he was a child, to use force. If he didn't keep up with the endless chores in the house, Chris would lie and say he had. Chris did not know what these disciplinary sessions would look like to him today, as an adult. He did not know if she just gave him a few nips with a switch or the rolling pin to set him straight, to an adult's eye. To him as a child, she had seemed ogreish in her strength. He recalled welts along the back of his shins that bled into his socks. He didn't know if, once or twice, good old-fashioned discipline had crossed imperceptibly into the realm of something else. He would lie, lie, lie, even under the switch, sometimes until his mother's arm would fatigue. He would not be made a farm boy.

Perhaps this was why he hadn't wanted to admit to Tessa that he had written her the recommendation letter, perhaps it was why he lied about his intention when doing it, perhaps it was why he could not tell her that he was in love with her, and why he still prowled around her, lying.

"Do you think Chris is happy?" Chris asked.

"No," she said. "No, he's an island, that one."

Though Dorothy was drifting in and out, and seemed only partly lucid, she said this with more conviction. It hurt Chris—not that it had never occurred to him before, but that he was unhappy, and that he was self-centered, was difficult to hear confirmed by his mother. It made it more difficult to mount a counterargument to himself—that he had had a bad year, for instance. That his mother's terminal illness had caused some loss of control over himself, or some need for control over something, it was hard to say. He could justify some blurring of boundaries, as Tessa had alluded to the week before. But that he had always been an unhappy island, a dysthymic isle, an archipelagous malcontent, suggested that he always would be, a prospect with a definite edge to it as he held the bony fingers of his last direct relative.

"And do you think you played a role in that, Mum?" Chris asked.

Her eyes rolled backward so she looked at the ceiling. "If I did, God will judge me for it."

A non-answer. Though Chris knew he was being cruel, accusing a woman as weak as this. Yes, leave these riddles for us nonbelievers. Thank you. He sighed. The bladder bag hanging from the bedrails began to fill with dark yellow urine.

"Do you need water, Mum?"

"Yes," she said.

Chris filled a small cup from the tap. Connor had told him that eventually they would have to use a sponge to keep her lips moist and give her water, it would become so hard to swallow. He poured some water gently into her open mouth.

.   .   .

LEAVING THE HOSPICE, Chris was intercepted again by Elizabeth, the attractive young nurse-office-manager who reminded him, wrenchingly, of Tessa. Again, she wore lipstick—something Tessa rarely, if ever, did.

"Mr. Eccles," she called, when she saw him, as he passed the reception desks in the lobby.

He knew what it was about, but for a moment allowed himself to indulge the fantasy that she simply wanted to chat. He turned toward her and smiled.

"Yes?"

"Did you manage to find the advance decisions document?"

Chris's hands moved into his pockets and his right clenched around the pages, which had been folded and folded into a hard cube. He approached the reception desk, so that he would not have to shout. When he lost his temper, it was always worse if he shouted. "You do realize you're asking if I had the chance to hasten my mother's death?"

Elizabeth pursed her lips and folded one hand over another. She was standing at the desk. "So you're aware of its directions? And yet you haven't seen it?"

"Even with the antibiotics, the jaundice is still advancing," he said. "So what difference does it make?"

Elizabeth held his stare. There was nothing she could do, except incriminate him with her eyes.

"I can't bloody find it," he added.

Whip whip, smash smash.

●   ●   ●

THE DRIVE BACK to Oxford had become routine. He no longer needed to use his phone to help him navigate when he turned out of the gravel courtyard. He noticed, every time he passed, the same rupture in the verge guardrail three kilometers into the A34 heading northwest, evidence of some spectacular crash, an event his imagination returned to unwillingly. Was it a lorry that had skidded off its path in some lashing storm? Or had it involved multiple cars, one punished for another's momentary lapse in attention or judgment? He was past it in a moment, but the rails, bent and twisted as if made of taffy, lingered with him as he drove on, pondering the email Tessa had sent to her sister.

If Trelawney's excavation really had come across Marius's

remains, it could ignite some interest in his work. Marius had been deemed merely an enigma by scholarly opinion so many times over the centuries that there never seemed anything there to resurrect. He was like a black hole, an opaque entity that annihilated any illumination one attempted to cast on it, even sometimes annihilated the scholars who did—George Bale, for instance. He had only reluctantly allowed her to incorporate Marius at all into her dissertation, insofar as one fragment of a poem seemed to feature a monologue in Daphne's voice, which could be argued to be the first surviving reception of Ovid's version of the myth.

But if Marius did surface as a man of interest, Tessa would be rather well equipped to exploit it, he observed, as he accelerated around a lagging gray Peugeot. She had already written a chapter on his unusual use of choliambs. She was familiar with his manuscript tradition and all the, admittedly sparse, commentary on his work. She'd have an immediate foothold in an area that Chris himself wasn't an expert in—Silver Age poetry. His recommendation, or lack thereof, would matter less for her prospects.

And so what if he did matter less to her, from a professional standpoint? His fear of such a scenario was of course due to his knowledge that she did not in fact love him. But some of that ambivalence must be chalked up to circumstance. That she had met Ben before Chris had truly, unabashedly fallen for her. That Chris had been in a marriage, albeit an unhappy one.

Perhaps the most practical course of action was to cease his meddling and beg her forgiveness. He was already more or less certain that she would not receive another offer for employment next year. Only Case Western University had interviewed her, and they hadn't been in touch since. Granted, it sometimes occurred that an offer was made and then turned down—rarely, with tenure-track positions—which extended the cycle. And who knew how long some of those American schools took? But another academic year meant an entirely fresh start for the two of them.

Chris took his hands off the wheel and let the car float between lanes. There was hardly any traffic. The wheel's bias was ever so slightly to the right, which agreed generally with the road's curvature, and they sped along, Chris and the Fiat, the Fiat driving. As the road angled back toward center, they drifted into the right lane, and the verge lit up in the headlights, and the sleeper line pounded the wheels and rattled through the car and through Chris's body, and he wanted to wrench the wheel back toward the road—but the motorway had angled up just slightly, and the wheel turned back of its own accord. They hadn't even hit the guardrail. They were back in the lane, floating again, and Chris's hands had not left his lap.

• • •

CHRIS SIPPED from a piping-hot mug of tea at his desk at home in Jericho. He had slept surprisingly well after returning from Hampshire the night before, and after debating whether or not to call Ed Trelawney he had decided not to, for now. He would simply wait for Tessa to return to Oxford and ask her to her face. He would encourage her, now, to pursue Marius as a topic. In fact, if she was going to be doing sustained research on any Silver Age poet she would want to have Beinecke's four-volume commentary on Silver Age fragments, or at the very least Volume IV, which had, he remembered, a section devoted to Marius.

And so, after dodging Martesi's request to play tennis and responding to some other emails—sometimes he felt he neglected his own inbox in favor of Tessa's—and watering the garden, he walked through the cool late-March afternoon toward the OUP bookstore on High Street. He found the four-volume set, and paid for volume IV (£115), and then decided to stop by College, feeling good about his purchase. He would wrap it in red. Or even some other color he'd never seen before—it would be a further relinquishing of control. Perhaps she would notice. He would ask someone for help. But what was Tessa's favorite color? He was quite sure it was red.

He nodded to Max at the Porter's Lodge and nipped up to his office on Staircase 7. College was practically deserted, it being between-term. The cucumber in his fridge was rotted and there were no limes left—nothing to flavor the water with, something he liked to do. Usually Tessa would bring him limes or fresh cucumber. Was he insane? What had he done? He was going to lose her, and she was perfect. She had genuinely cared about him once, and he had sullied her reservoir of goodwill. He thought of his mother languishing, alone, in hospice, with that surrogate Connor, and for a moment he thought he would cry. Any lingering desire to call Ed Trelawney deserted him and was replaced by sadness and violent regret. Instead, he emailed Martesi back and said he would take him up on that game, in fact, and then walked despondently through a thickening crowd of tourists to the Covered Market, where he bought two cucumbers, to slice up and add, with ice, to his water.

* * *

IN THE MORNING Tessa was tasked with carrying the bag of sandwiches and chips to the van, which idled in the dark deserted street, doors ajar, while Tessa and the others slung their gear beneath its seats. They seemed to arrive with the dawn.

Tessa, Lucrezia, and Graham unpacked all kinds of equipment: a lamp, paintbrushes, plastic bottles, gloves, knee pads, hats, aerosol containers, skewers, pens, knives, clipboards, stratigraphy sheets, assorted pegs, a shovel, a pickaxe, a trowel, plastic spoons, a box cutter, a tarp, and some foam pads. Then they walked to the tomb. The dawn was rising. It was pink and ocher and Tessa could smell the ocean and the air was crisp.

Tessa knew, now, exactly where the tomb was, had oriented the whole necropolis around it, but it struck her as they approached how ordinary it was, how much it resembled those around it—all of them the size, perhaps, of a woodshed, their dark entries made by the hollow of stone. Blistered brick walls and the epitaphs, or lack thereof, on the lintels above the entrances.

It was hard to see anything inside the tomb until they set up the lamp. They plugged it into an extension cord that ran twenty meters to a generator, like some primordial serpent. Then the whole rocky interior was lit like a surgical theater. The craggy particulars of every square inch were visible, except where shadows were cast by the living. There were two arcosolia—half-moon recesses that presided above the sarcophagi. A massive slab, a single cuboid piece of limestone six feet by two-and-one-half and nearly six inches thick, covered each sarcophagus.

"Let's do the northwest today," Lucrezia said to Tessa, and Graham, who crouched in the center of the tomb, unable to stand to his full height. "We'll be able to see if it's the male or the female when we get to the skeleton."

Ten minutes later, the coroner arrived, already wearing latex gloves and carrying a clipboard, along with two men in white work pants, with heavy work gloves and boots. They were wiry and grizzled, their skin tan from outdoor work, one of them perhaps in his late forties, with gray stubble around his otherwise bald head, and another in his early thirties, round-faced, heavy.

The six of them crowded in the tomb, breathing the same dank air. Tessa stood back and watched. Lucrezia spoke to the two men in

Italian, and they dusted off their hands and approached the northwest arcosolium, where, presumably, the remains of either Publius
Marius Scaeva or Sulpicia, his wife, rested.

Lucrezia said, *Prego*, and the two workmen positioned themselves
low on either side of the lid, with Graham in the middle. In the
lamplight every mote they kicked up was visible. Graham crouched
between them and worked his fingertips under the uneven edge of
the slab. Lucrezia was talking quickly in Italian now with the workmen and translating for Graham. "You're going to pull it towards
you first. *Prego*."

"*Uno*," said one of the workmen.

"*Due*," they both said.

"*Tre*," said the three of them.

Feet scraped against gravel. Graham awkwardly tried to leverage his body, but it was clear his grip wasn't very strong. The two
workmen were able to get more lift on it—the slab made a horrible
groan as it raked several inches across the rock lip of the *cubiculum*. Feet screeched back. Tessa, Lucrezia, and the coroner retreated
as well. Tessa could make out almost nothing beyond the three
bodies and, without asking Lucrezia, she ducked into the tomb and
crouched by the other arcosolia and the lamp.

A cloud of particles teemed in the blade of light just above the sarcophagus. Graham coughed. Tessa put her hand over her mouth. A
few more words in Italian, some pointing, Lucrezia said: Again, just
pull it towards you.

"*Uno*."

"*Due*."

"*Tre!*"

Again the scraping and exhalations and feet scrabbling for traction. Tessa wondered if she would smell death, but there was no odor
except a more intense miasma of concrete and dust. There was noth-

ing young enough to be rotting in there. It smelled like they were cutting stone, which she presumed they were—abrading the jagged surfaces of huge blocks. Now she could see the lid rested about half-way on, halfway off. Graham and one of the workmen held it steady while the other talked quickly in Italian to Lucrezia who was nod-ding. Lucrezia left the threshold of the tomb and came back inside with four round pegs made of cork.

"It's too heavy, Pasquale's saying. He doesn't want to lay it on the ground," Lucrezia said to Graham and Tessa. "Help me put these out," she said to Tessa.

The coroner stepped to the edge of the tomb and looked inside while Tessa laid the pegs out in a rectangular shape, slightly smaller than the lid's. The workman, Pasquale, started to point and speak to Lucrezia again. It was very crowded inside as Tessa and Lucrezia and the coroner stood on the periphery of the chamber and the lid's des-ignated space. Tessa tried to peer over the far edge of the lid, but she still couldn't see anything in the sarcophagus. Lucrezia was nodding and she said something to the coroner who said something back, shaking his head. He pointed at his latexed hands.

"What's wrong?" Tessa said.

"Okay, can you go ask Jan or Joop to come? We need another."

Tessa looked at the space and realized they wanted another man. Tessa hesitated. "There's no way we can fit another person in here and be able to put the lid down."

The workman, the one with the gray stubble, Pasquale, looked at her. Graham reached his hand around and rubbed his lower back. The coroner's assistant coughed.

"Then you can wait outside," Lucrezia said, pushing the lamp farther up against the edge of the tomb.

"Let me do it," Tessa said.

Lucrezia looked at the lid and then back at her. The workman said something, she heard, *ragazza!* "Tessa, please, we pay these men by the hour."

Tessa realized she would want to kill herself later if she allowed herself not to be here for this moment. "If three of them can do that, then four of us can fucking well do it," she said. She saw the word "fuck" register with the two workmen. She was sweating. Grit caked her forehead. Her lips were dry, and she could taste dust on them. Lucrezia hesitated for a moment and then seemed to remember why she might want to be there for this. She said something and the workman shrugged. They started talking again in Italian.

"Okay, you're going to stand there," Lucrezia said, pointing. Tessa positioned herself up against the wall, behind the crouching Pasquale. Only three people could fit around the niche, but once they pulled the lid out, she would have to swoop in and help them hold its full weight. Tessa's knees were inches away from Pasquale's rear. His back, in the tattered shirt, was roped with muscle. "When they pull it out, you're going to pick up the other end," Lucrezia said. "Then you all place it on the pegs."

"Okay," Tessa said. She crouched down and nearly toppled onto Pasquale. She used the wall for support.

"*Uno.*"

"*Due.*"

"*Tre!*"

More scraping and scrabbling. Pasquale's back rose, she could see his neck straining in a rhombus of light. She hopped forward as they slid the lid out and she got her hands under the rough stone. The weight was otherworldly. All eight hands were plunged down for a moment before Tessa got her legs under it. She thought it was going to take her down with it. She felt her legs strain beyond their limit as she refused to let go. The slab seemed to hover and then elevate just enough for the four of them to regain their balance. "Cazzo!"

Pasquale exhaled. Graham got lower. They carried it the next six inches and lowered it onto the pegs.

Everyone stood up from their exertions. Lucrezia and the workmen were laughing and joking in Italian. Graham dusted his hands off. Tessa turned toward the sarcophagus. She had to crouch again to get a look inside, and the lip of the *cubiculum* cast a shadow over most of its contents. She peered through a haze of swirling dust and pulverized concrete, wiped her eyes and licked her lips, and looked closer. Teeth. They were still intact and connected to the mandible. And a definite eye socket, into which dirt and dust had gathered. The bones nearest her resolved themselves into an intact skull. Marius? He was surrounded by dirt, despite the stone enclosure, and much of the back of the cranium was covered.

"Bring the light over," she said, gesturing.

Shadows moved in front of her. Bodies were exiting the tomb. Tessa turned to see why no one was bringing the light over and saw the coroner still there. Pasquale and his associate had gone. Graham was gone as well. Lucrezia held a camera. "Lucrezia, can you?" It flashed, blinding her momentarily. With the lid occupying the center of the tomb, there wasn't much space for the lamp. With her free hand Lucrezia attempted to move it around the lid.

The more of them that tried to see in, the more shadows they cast.

The light moved, and suddenly the whole *cubiculum* was illuminated. The skull was canted toward the tomb's interior. The hands seemed to have been facing palms up. There was a mound of dirt where she presumed his ribs would be—but no, when she looked closer, there was what seemed to be bone protruding from the mound in several places. The pelvis was fully exposed and, it looked, partially fragmented. Two long bones extended from it, which articulated with more bones and then what Tessa presumed were the feet.

"Don't touch it until we've photographed." Lucrezia crouched next to Tessa and looked closely at the pelvis. "This is probably the male," she said.

Marius.

Tessa inched herself to the other side of the grave to look at the feet. Lucrezia's flashlight illuminated them. Light raked over the small bones, which were mostly interred in hardened clay. Lucrezia crouched next to her and for a moment she could only hear the two of them breathing, could only see the beam of light flooded with motes of dust and matter.

"Looks like a talus," Lucrezia said, pointing at one of the bones. "Metatarsals, there. The other talus."

Marius's skeleton. Lucrezia put her arm around Tessa's shoulders. "Tessa, there he is."

"I see." But Tessa didn't see. She didn't see yet. "Can you tell anything from his feet?" she asked.

Lucrezia was looking with the flashlight held up to her shoulder. "For certain, not yet. They seem to be normal. But we won't really know until we've disinterred them, cleaned them, et cetera."

Crouched in the bright light, sweat trickling down her back, Tessa did not have a single logical thought in her mind. He's dead, she thought. As if you needed to confirm that? *So then why the limping iambs?* she wanted to ask him. *Cur choliambi?* She had thought that this moment would feel a certain way, and it didn't. He seemed to her as inscrutable as always.

• • •

THAT EVENING Lucrezia and Tessa discussed logistics on the balcony again. They had spent the rest of the day beginning to disinter Marius's remains. After photographing him, they had to draw the skeleton; Graham would hold a plumb line from a measuring tape that had been laid out over the sarcophagus, from which he'd give Heloise measurements while she drew. "Twenty-one centimeters," he'd say. "Easternmost tip of the femur." Tessa would sieve the rubble. Lucrezia had been busy managing other members of the team.

Now Lucrezia appeared at Tessa's side, without saying hello, just standing at the balcony, looking out.

After a moment, Tessa said, "Can we wait on telling Edward?"

"Possibly," Lucrezia said.

"Possibly?"

Lucrezia kept her eyes on the horizon and said nothing.

"Maybe there's a way we can be reticent about a second century poet's remains being found. Maybe the narrative can remain: A new skeleton was disinterred. Of nobody of consequence. A Marius Scaeva, Roman citizen, occupation unknown. For as long as possible," Tessa said. "Honestly, I didn't realize until today the extent to which I was hoping to find something abnormal about the skeleton. Club foot, I thought, for sure, something like that."

"Well, we don't know yet," Lucrezia said. "You can't tell anything without disinterring the bones."

Tessa paused. "Well, assuming the skeleton is normal. I mean, it's still an interesting discovery in its own right. I just don't know what it tells us about Marius. I mean, the meter is still the big question mark around his work. And that hasn't been resolved."

Lucrezia nodded. "It's still significant to find his tomb."

"I know," Tessa said.

"But we will be able to disinter the feet tomorrow," Lucrezia said. "And if we don't find anything with the skeleton tomorrow, I might ask you why I should not tell my program director about the discovery."

Tessa nodded, feeling she was losing control, frustrated. But she didn't see how she could argue. She had no leverage except Lucrezia's goodwill. She would write her paper on the landscape of Isola Sacra and how it illuminated certain metaphors in Marius's extant work. The question of meter would remain unresolved.

"I get it," Tessa said. "Can we talk about it tomorrow night?"

Lucrezia gave her a look of exasperation. "No, I can't. If it's not clear to me what is to be gained by waiting any longer, then I have to tell him. Clear?"

"And if we find something that will make a difference for me?"

"Then we'll talk."

That night Tessa checked her email, but there was nothing back from Claire yet. She felt that this was a situation in which she could really use her sister's advice; at the same time, it was hard to fault Claire for growing weary of dispensing advice, given Tessa's increasingly poor track record of following it. Yet Tessa found it frustrating that she couldn't tell whether Claire was simply too busy to respond to her, or if Claire was experiencing Tessa's flight to Italy as a betrayal and a willful misuse of her funds. Obviously it *was* a willful misuse of her funds, but it was always hard to tell if Claire cared.

Tessa managed a few hours of sleep. She woke to the sound of Graham's alarm next door, her cheek at rest upon an open page of *I Frammenti Completi*, the nightstand light still aglow. She could hear a drizzle outside her window. When she saw the team in clear and blue ponchos drinking instant in the hallway it occurred to her that she had no rain gear. She wore acid-washed jeans and a crewneck sweatshirt, cotton.

"You don't have a raincoat," Lucrezia stated.

"It's fine," Tessa said. She looked out the window for confirmation, but above the clothesline, which was sheltered by an eave, ribbons of water cascaded onto the balcony.

"Graham, do you still have an extra poncho?" Lucrezia asked in a clipped voice.

"Jan is using it," he said.

Jan shrugged.

"Shit," Lucrezia said, and walked swiftly down the long, tapered hall back toward her room. It was a dark, cold morning, and Tessa felt like a fucking burden. She stood there feeling like an ass, while the rest of the team ignored her. Finally she followed Lucrezia down the hall.

Lucrezia was in her room, which was only slightly larger than Tessa's, but completely lived-in. The small twin had a duvet and a cover; there were posters on the walls; a sitting chair with garments of clothing draped over it; a closet that was crammed with apparel and into which Lucrezia had embedded herself, and from which she emerged holding something long and shiny.

"This is all I have," she said, taking it off the hanger.

It was a red lacquer raincoat.

"Bold," Tessa said. "I can't wear this on the site."

"You can, and you will," Lucrezia said, handing if off to her. Tessa looked at the label. Burberry.

Reluctantly, she took it. She was going to look absurd.

.   .   .

THE VAN CUT through the rain, which was falling in torrents, down the highway to where it could U-turn, then back toward the necropolis. There were no flashing lights of planes overhead. Tessa had seen Graham suppress a laugh when she returned to the breakfast hall wearing the coat, but now it seemed eminently sensible, under cataracts of rain. Lucrezia drove solemnly; the windshield wipers squealed, as if objecting to being overworked.

"Did you cover everything completely?" Lucrezia said to the dim silence in the back.

Graham grunted in assent.

The site was muddy and dark. Marius's tomb had been completely covered with a black tarp the day before, and in its imper-
meable darkness, it appeared even more primordial. Tessa struggled
along the stone path toward the tent that Graham and Jan and Joop
were pitching near the tomb. Under the tent, she contemplated it
at a closer view. With the tarp on, the tomb looked somehow sin-
ister. It suddenly seemed to Tessa that the tomb had manipulated
this human-made shelter for its own ends, as it had manipulated
the earth-made shelter of sand before. The tomb had its own survival instinct. It roosted there, unperturbed. You don't dig Marius;
he digs you. You don't excavate the tomb, the tomb excavates you,
she thought.

Graham and Lucrezia painstakingly chipped the dirt and debris
from around each bone: the twenty-eight phalanges, the two metatarsals, cuneiforms, naviculars, the cuboids and calcanei and two
tali, then fibulae, the tibiae, the patellae. The morning wore on,
and in the dry pauses in the storm she sieved the little mounds of
debris from inside the tomb, walking with the sieve to the edge of
the necropolis in Lucrezia's shiny red coat. Lucrezia, Graham, and
Jan were moving achingly slowly. They were all huddled unnatu-
rally over the short stone niche, like animals at a trough—Lucrezia
drew carefully on a sketch pad while Graham held a plumb line over
Marius's lower half, and Jan used a ruler to give Lucrezia measurements. Tessa was aware of the deadline Lucrezia had imposed; that if
they didn't find anything new of note, Ed would be informed they'd
found Marius's skeleton.

By afternoon, they had removed each talus and were working
around one of the tibiae. Tessa was losing hope that anything new
would surface, and was preparing for Lucrezia to tell Ed the next
day, and for word to then make it back to Chris about the discovery

quite quickly. If only the Oxford conference were sooner, or if she could buy more time; she wanted to be the one to break the discovery. When the coroner arrived again, Tessa was surprised.

"We're going to exhume the other remains," Lucrezia told her.

"But there are only a couple of hours left in the day," Tessa said.

"What do you want me to do?" Lucrezia said. "He's here, I'm not going to tell him to go. We're paying him. Do you want to help or do you want to get Jan?"

Tessa, frustrated they had to pause exhuming Marius, went to find Jan, who was huddled over an open tomb with Joop, not far away. She then walked, in the rain, down the old via Flavia and out of the necropolis, onto the path that led down from the highway. The little oleanders drooped under the onslaught of rain. Her feet squelched in the muddy track of the road. Doubt suddenly seeped into her mind. Somehow, this was going to be taken from her.

She turned back toward the necropolis, back through the fence, into the realm of the tombs. As she trekked back along the old via Flavia, doubt seeped still further. She would write a paper about the discovery of Marius's tomb. It would be a curious novelty for Latinists specializing in the Silver Age of Roman verse, and then the discovery would wither away from view, would decay, and she would be ignored again, and she would be forced to continue at Westfaling indefinitely. It felt like Chris had orchestrated her failure, putting her in red so he could watch, as a final laugh.

As the tomb came into view again, a curious stillness seemed to have taken hold. The coroner's bag still crowned the table under the tent, and everyone else's things were still there, but Tessa could see no human shapes, nor even any shadows through the entrance. The tomb was too small for that, really—were they all huddled on top of one another? Were they playing a trick on her?

She continued along the stone path. Her feet slipped on one of the stones. She, unthinkingly, quickened her pace. Something seemed out of place—like someone had been hurt. Where were they? Thunder rumbled above her, and a fresh cascade of rain began to fall. It struck her that perhaps something inside had collapsed, and the others had gone to get help? The tomb seemed to smile at her malevolently as she trotted faster. She cleared the tent and ducked under the entrance, into the musty wet smell and acrid interior, breathing hard and soaked, nearly tripping over the new slab that now carpeted the *cella*, Sulpicia's cover. Graham, Jan, Lucrezia, and the coroner were huddled around the open tomb, looking inside. Lucrezia held a light.

"What is it?" Tessa asked.

Lucrezia turned abruptly. "Look at this," she said.

Tessa stared over the four heads at Sulpicia's skeleton. Lucrezia's light directed her toward Sulpicia's lower half. Her pelvis looked normal, with two long bones extending from it, but then one of them stopped short, and while her left leg continued to the end of the grave in an articulating line of bones, her right leg did not. It was clear that in Sulpicia's grave there was only one tibia, only one talus, only one calcaneus, and one foreshortened femur. Tessa looked at Lucrezia, who was smiling in the half dark. Tessa stepped forward, dumbstruck. She crouched next to her, and for a moment she could only hear the five of them breathing, could only see the beam of light flooded with motes, and Sulpicia's femur, which was shorn off at the end. Lucrezia put her arm around Tessa's shoulders.

"Tessa, look."

"I see," she said.

"Now, that is an interesting skeleton," Lucrezia said.

"Do you think it was a birth defect," Graham asked, "or something else?"

"Look," Lucrezia said, pointing at the femur. "Are those striations?"

Tessa kept staring at it. A missing foot. Marius was the poet that they always thought might have been clubfooted, and he was buried with someone who, even worse, was missing a foot entirely. But surely this must have been Marius's real grave. "Did we mistake it?" Tessa asked. "Is this Marius's grave?"

"The sub-pubic angle is definitively female," Graham said.

"Those are definitely striations," Lucrezia said, pointing with a caliper.

"So you think it was amputated?" Graham asked.

At the word amputate Tessa's mind pivoted.

"Then the question is whether she survived it," Lucrezia said.

"But we'll be able to tell, right?" Graham asked.

"Bone would have grown over it if she survived, so yes," said Lucrezia.

Now Tessa began to shudder. It didn't compute—there must be some mistake. The historical record, but they knew that Marius was the author. It is not the evidence itself, but the peculiarity of the evidence. "Marius is Sulpicia," she said out loud.

Lucrezia was laughing, her face shining in the vivid light.

Tessa's tongue caught in her throat and she couldn't speak. A molten unease churned inside of her. Marius is *not* Marius. But how? What was done to her? Could this be? Everything fractured for a moment in the lamp's raking light. The coroner's latex hands. Jan's illuminated strands of wayward hair. Graham's ear, whose cartilage the klieg light penetrated like a screen, causing it to glow red. Lucrezia's cackling laughter, the joyous whites of her teeth. The draped rim of the raincoat, glistening in radioactive red. Amid her stupor and exhaustion Tessa felt her adrenaline surge, lending everything a harsh, striking clarity.

• • •

A WEEK PASSED. No word from Tessa. He met Martesi twice at Bury Knowle, where they would rally and play a few games. Twice he passed Tessa's flat on Leckford Road, and twice there were no lights on inside, no evidence of someone living there. Chris flipped through the Beinecke a few times and read parts of Marius, but found it opaque and uninspired. He returned to a paper he had started years before on Ovid's *Amores*, the apostrophe to Elegia, the personification of elegy herself, the one with a leg shorter than the other, to imitate the elegiac couplet. He let himself be tempted to hack Tessa again, to see where she was now. He returned to Hampshire to see his mum over the weekend. He did not drop by her house, though he told her that the garden looked marvelous. That the snowdrops had come in beautifully, that there was nary a weed.

It was the beginning of April, and in the Hampshire Hospice garden some of the regular spring flowers were blooming. Tulips and hyacinths and daffodils. He noticed that one of the staff—perhaps Connor—had clipped some early tulips and set them in a vase in Dorothy's room. She would look at them dolefully, when she could.

"And have the tulips begun to bloom?" she asked him.

"Yes," he said. "Old Nutley's having a fine time keeping the kiddies away."

"Oh, they'll eat anything. And you, Connor, tell me about your life. Do you have any romances?"

Chris had told Dorothy months ago that Diana had left him, but it was unclear where his mother's mind was at. She would call him Connor, though she seemed to know she was talking to Chris, and even when she knew she was addressing Chris, it would be hard to decipher what year she was in—it could be 1999, when he was single, or 2002, when he and Diana were married, or April 2010, the present moment. He did not know. And did it matter, really?

"Mum, I'm in love with a student of mine."

His mother smiled. "A student. Chris," she said, "you can't go round having it off with all your students." But there was mirth in her eyes. "That's lovely, dear."

Chris offered her a cup of water. She looked better today—Connor told him that they had drained bile from her midsection with a tube.

"What's her name, love?"

"Tessa," Chris said.

"Tessa."

"She's American."

"I can see it in your face. Your eyes lit up."

Chris smiled in spite of himself.

"And are you together?" his mum asked.

He sighed. "No," he said. He held her arm and looked down into the taut white sheet.

"You'll find a way," Dorothy said, and patted his hand.

Chris laughed darkly. "Mum, I've been—I found a way to read her personal correspondence. Well, her emails. I know it's wrong, but I haven't found it in me to stop."

He looked at his mum. What was he seeking? Permission? Punishment?

She nodded. She said, "When I heard you were becoming a teacher, I was in church that Sunday and the vicar was reading from the Book of James. I remember the verse he read, 'Not many of you should become teachers, because you know that we who teach shall be judged more strictly.'" She enunciated these words slowly. "I thought to meself, Chris ought to mend his ways, if he hasn't already. But then I looked around meself, and your father was dead, and you'd been made fellow and professor of this and that. Sometimes I thought, He would'nt've been happy here. And he never would've got out if he didn't have some of the old Nick in him. So's I thought, So long as he isn't hurting anyone, let him be. I thought, Chris's lies were the only path to his truth, in a way."

Chris found this speech from his mother moving. He had always resented her religion. That she was willing to relinquish some of it for him was touching, and not something he would have counted on. She would not normally divide her loyalties from God, and moreover, she was on her deathbed, approaching her Savior.

"Chris?"

"Yes, Mum?"

"I want to go home."

The door to the hospice room opened and Connor stood in the threshold. Chris barely noticed him; he was still processing his mother's words. Connor ignored Chris and put a hand on Dorothy's shoulder.

"Feeling much better today, I hear?"

She nodded.

"Yes, the bilirubin can cause discomfort and itchiness and can make you less lucid. Chris, your mother was saying that she remembered where she kept the document we asked you to fetch for her."

"The icebox," Dorothy said. "It's in the icebox."

Chris looked at Connor and held up his hands. "That's wonderful news," he said. "Never would have thought of that. Didn't even think to check it. I'll pop over there at once."

"Good," Connor said, fixing Chris with an incriminating glare. Did she call him Chris? Chris wondered.

． ． ．

CHRIS DROVE VERY FAST to his mother's house, uncertain what he would do. The knowledge that he actually had nothing to fetch and no purpose once he would arrive actually made him drive faster, hasten even more. He let the window down to a slit, so he could feel jets of warm late afternoon air as he accelerated through the narrow back roads, something to remind him that he had skin, had neurons, was an actual person, his sense of himself fragmenting as he scanned the horizon line of his own past and misdeeds. When he arrived he let himself in with the spare key and this time pocketed it, thinking that he would be returning. He felt a sudden shock of fear that Old Nutley had stopped feeding the sheep and that one of them would have wandered off or, worse, starved. He looked out onto the yard, which was flowering with everything Dorothy had planted last year. Old Nutley had been watering, but it was near-choked with weedy overgrowths; the picture he had painted for his mother was of course, a lie. He tore through the back door and through the garden to the shed, where he laid eyes on Feddy, Neddy, and Betty. Thank Christ, he thought. They looked at him curiously, hungrily. The trough was full of water.

Chris walked back into the house, which was eerily tidy, but unlived-in. Every surface had accumulated a layer of dust, though there was no clutter at all. He stood for a moment, uncertain what his next move was. The document, of course, was not in the ice-box. He turned the lights on and looked out into the garden again, then he took the pages out of his pocket and opened them: *refuse all med prolong life.*

Outside, Chris sat down against the shed in the shit-smelling dirt and straw. He took a cigarette from the front pocket of his shirt and lit it.

"*Baaa*," said Feddy.

"You think so?" Chris said.

"*Baa*," Neddy confided.

Chris had never spent very much time with the three siblings, given that they were born well after he had left the house. But he had known their mother, Jetty, so named for her jet-colored wool. She had been born just before his father's suicide, and though black sheep were traditionally considered a bad omen, Dorothy had kept her and raised her in the house. When Chris came home once a year from uni or his graduate schooling, he looked forward to seeing Jetty, who became an immense dark puff, because her wool was useless at the market, unable to be dyed. When he and Diana married, he had wanted Jetty to be the ring bearer. Diana and her parents vetoed it.

The first time he'd seen Diana she was wearing a red wool coat— an extraordinary red, a radiant carmine. It was the first meeting of the first graduate course he'd been given as a young lecturer at Cambridge with a monograph on its way to publication. The next class she'd worn a red belt, then red flats, it drove him mad, as if she knew he was attracted to her and just wanted a laugh. Soon she had asked him to look at one of her papers, which he had done enthusiastically. It was on Etruscan funereal structures. It was one of the chapters of what ultimately became her dissertation. Her prose was good but not excellent. For instance, sometimes she had difficulty with subject agreement in compound sentences, of which she had many. Chris made a note of this to her in his comments while they flirted. A month later, when he read one of her newer drafts and noticed that she continued making the same mistake here and there, he was satisfied that he was her real motive for asking for help.

Chris had not strayed once from Diana, not a single time, perhaps out of some vestigial respect for his parents' union of thirty-one years. He had strayed in spirit, though, gradually, imperceptibly, through the first two years of mentoring Tessa, and then abruptly when Tessa's scholarship launched into a new realm of excellence. He recalled the turning point—she had stalled out in her writing on Virgil, sent him nothing ahead of their meeting in his office. "I'm sorry I don't have more for you," she'd said. "More would imply you had something to begin with," he'd responded. "More of nothing is just more nothing." It was the first time he had been rough with her. In a month he had a draft of Apollo and Daphne on his desk.

Chris lit another cigarette and toiled through the garden's weedy overgrowth to the shed. All three sheep looked at him with their mothers' maudlin eyes. Diana's family had vetoed Jetty as ring bearer, which was not unreasonable for a wedding of two hundred fifty at Hedsor House plus a luxury glass marquee. Diana's father had been a bond trader before bond trading was massively lucrative, and a bond trader still when it became massively lucrative in the eighties. So, eager to forget where he'd come from, Chris had allowed himself to become a sort of plaything, a trinket whose status derived from its Oxford pedigree, and from how far he'd come from humble origins. He had been swallowed into the oblivion of her family and their money. Only loving Tessa had loosened the death grip on his childhood.

Rams were more likely to have black wool than ewes, so Jetty had been a true rarity. Jetty, Jetty, Jetty. He had loved Jetty. When she littered, they weren't surprised to see that her children were all downy, soft white. Dark wool was a recessive gene. He and his mother hadn't spoken for years when she called him to say that Jetty had died. He had helped bury Jetty, a few meters away from where he sat just now. He wished that Tessa would have had the chance to meet Jetty. He thought they would have liked each other.

Chris stubbed out his cigarette and looked down at the kiddies, uncertain what to do next.

* * *

HE BEGAN WITH the low weeds. Chickweed. Purslane. Henbit. There was a trowel in the shed but he could do these with his hands. The sun had dipped very low, but he could still see the shapes of their stalks in the gray glow of twilight. He tossed them into a wheelbarrow. He was careful not to uproot any of the flowers. The tall weeds were easier—dayflower, quickweed, pigweed. Glad he had been playing tennis, he crouched into the earth, getting covered in lignin and soil and petals and root systems. The clothes he wore were not his—his mother had kept some of his father's clothes, along with the tallow smock he used to wear, and Chris had donned a frayed pair of trousers and a shirt for the job. He would ruin the clothes, even as they smelled of the antique wooden drawers and his father's sweat, cured over decades, as they smelled of his childhood. The bulb in the garden light had blown and he couldn't find a spare, so when it became dark he taped a torch to an old hat and wore it like a miner. The taproots proved trickier; if they resisted, they could take out the entire root systems of the flowers. He had to dig around them carefully with the trowel and coax them out, convince them they would be better off elsewhere. They had to want it, the taproots. He imagined himself in a game of persuasion with them. They could reach as far as a foot into the topsoil. He whispered to each one how lovely it was aboveground, how they, too, could drink in the sun's rays when loosened from the earth's chokehold, how the leaf system had cut them, the roots, a raw deal, had systemically oppressed and submerged them over the course of their shared evolutionary pasts. He told them a weed is just a flower in the wrong place. He garnered their trust. He told them lies with his trowel, which he used gently, encouragingly, and he piled them into the wheelbarrow with their cousins, under a dark collapsing night, after he ripped them cleanly from their beds.

•   •   •

WHEN CHRIS RETURNED to the hospice early next morning, Elizabeth was again at the reception desk. After he had weeded the garden, he had dusted the house, then fallen asleep in his father's filthy clothes. He strolled into the reception area in his own trousers and blazer from the day before, produced the advanced decisions document, and asked if he could also move his mother to part-time home care. Elizabeth looked surprised, but then said they would begin the paperwork immediately. Chris asked if he could take his mother for a walk through the garden while this occurred.

After the nurse unhooked Dorothy from all her machinery, helped her into a wheelchair, and strapped the bladder bag and catheter to her thigh, Chris did take her through the garden, which featured some lovely Japanese maples. Chris signed the paperwork authorizing the hospice to transfer her from in-house to house-visit patient and he accepted liability for her health.

•   •   •

HIS PARENTS' BED looked very large with Dorothy in it. He propped her up with pillows to ease her breathing and draped her favorite Southdown wool duvet over her legs. There was so much space between her feet and the foot of the bed—he recalled watching his mum and dad sleeping there once, how little room there was for the two of them. Dorothy was taking very long, slow breaths that made him think each one was going to be her last. It had his nerves on edge.

"Mum," he'd say, just to see if she was still there.

She would nod or make a very soft noise.

Chris had no idea how much longer she had left, or if she was even aware that she was at home now. He presumed that the lack of antibiotics would hasten the rest of her journey, but he also worried about the vagaries of a dying human body, none of which he could predict. He hadn't eaten anything that day himself; he felt nauseous, and wished he could have a drink of something, but there was no liquor in the house. He wanted to call someone, but he contented himself with sitting by his mother's side on an old hand-built wooden chair and trying to remain calm while her breaths seemed to stretch out into eternity. After perhaps an hour of this, she began to moan softly, and to grimace. She became more lucid.

"Chris, Chris—it hurts."

"I know, Mum, Connor is on his way."

"Are we at home?"

"Yes."

"I thought so," she said. Her body, too weak to writhe, registered all its pain on her face, which was mottled and contorted. Chris began to worry. Some instinct told him to pull his chair closer to the bed. Her hand appeared from under the duvet and found his. For another hour they sat like that, he holding her hand, which still had a Hampshire Hospice wristband on it, she breathing and groaning. There was birdsong. Time dilated.

"Goldfinches," Dorothy managed to say, once.

Just as Chris sensed his mother might be nodding off, he heard tires outside. He opened the door and Connor walked past him with a medical kit.

Connor had a wrapped lunch from the cafeteria, one each for

Chris and Dorothy, and some more paperwork for Chris to sign. He showed Chris how to pulverize the morphine pills and mix them in with water, and gave him a handwritten schedule for her dosages. There were fiber capsules and laxatives, a bedpan, changes of linens, a handbook. Connor would make a house visit again tomorrow and stay for the afternoon while Chris returned to Oxford to collect his things.

Before it got dark, Chris found some mixed grains in a sack near the shed and fed the sheep. Their rough tongues and the smell of lanolin from their coats recalled him deeper into his childhood, submerging him, he felt—he kept finding himself short of breath—it was an experience much like drowning, he thought, recalling childhood. His mother's labored intake of oxygen wasn't helping, the rattling noise her breath made, the definite sense that her lungs were slowly taking in fluids. The sun, falling, seemed to cut against the clouds, abrading them, and there was a rawness to Chris's sense of loneliness and failure that he hadn't quite encountered before, hadn't quite reckoned with. He sat for a long time on the wooden chair, in the dark, next to Dorothy, composing a short text message to Tessa, listening to the long labored breathing of his mum, the breaths that could take thirty seconds, even a minute, each one seeming to mess with him, to say, *Will this be the last?* His face glowed in the dark room as he composed the text.

PART V

dear tessa, there are no words

TESSA HAD NOT READ ANY OF CHRIS'S TEXTS since flying to Italy, but this one raked across her screen and she couldn't avoid seeing the way it began.

dear tessa, there are no words

She didn't open it at once, but the confessional mode of its beginning made her think he had reevaluated his position. She was next to a Danish woman who was traveling to London at the invitation of her sister, who hoped to reconcile with her after years of neglect. Her sister had done well as some sort of business process consultant and moved there, and now had two kids and an equally successful husband, and had ghosted Isilde five years ago. "Your first mistake is that you're going to London," Tessa had coached her. "If she wants your forgiveness, she would have come to you." Tessa gave Isilde her number because, frankly, she seemed hopeless. Her sister was going to run roughshod all over her.

Tessa's own sister had still not responded to her, a fact that had perhaps biased her against Isilde's own laconic London sibling. Yet Tessa felt enlarged by the events of the past few weeks. As she took down her bag and deplaned along with the mostly Danish and British passengers, she allowed herself a moment of unadulterated pleasure, recalling the sleeplessness and desperation that had vaulted her to Italy, the fear and the headaches, and her fingernails bitten practically down to the cuticles.

She wasn't in the clear yet at all, not by any stretch of the imagination, which she was reminded of as she scanned the rest of the messages on her phone, one from her management company, which had not received a rent payment for April first. Today was the fifth.

After disinterring Sulpicia, Tessa had been left with the mystery of how the record in the *Suda* attested that Marius, Sulpicia's husband, was the poet responsible for all the verses concerned with amputation and written in lame iambics. It was so clear to Tessa, after establishing that Sulpicia had undergone the literal loss of a foot, a literal amputation, that she was the author. None of the amputation metaphors were metaphors. The limping iambs were the meter chosen by someone who literally walked with a limp. Tessa had flown to Copenhagen, where the foremost scholar on the *Suda*, Greta Deloitte, was a professor of classics. Tessa had canceled her rent payment on the first of the month and used her university stipend, deposited the day before, to pay for the flight. Greta had helped her track the record in the *Suda* to a lost scholia from the late antique grammarian Probus. This was exciting to Tessa: this was the same Probus whom Giorgio Valla, a Renaissance scholar, had quoted in a commentary on Juvenal. The quotation contained some of the only surviving lines of an ancient Roman female poet, also named Sulpicia.

si me cadurci restitutis fasciis
nudam Caleno concubantem proferat

if, when the mattress straps have been restored
it might reveal me lying naked with Calenus

Of course, none of Probus's original scholia still existed. All that existed were secondary quotations from it, like Valla's. Valla himself had thought the two lines he was quoting were from a Sulpicius, a man, and it wasn't until another Renaissance scholar observed that Sulpicia the poet and her husband Calenus appeared in two of Martial's epigrams that the record was corrected to show that Sulpicia, not Sulpicius, was the author of the verses. The point was that a later commentator had mistaken the gender of an author quoted in the Probus; if Valla had done it, what precluded the author of the *Suda* from doing it, too? Tessa had been surprised at how quickly she was following paths of thinking that led to a destination where Sulpicia was the true author. In previous years, at previous talks about Roman female poets, for which there was almost no surviving work, and the authorship of all of it contested, she had found herself objecting to bias on the part of her female colleagues. She had felt that they were looking for data to support their conclusions, and it had made her uncomfortable. There was so much noise, so much uncertainty—there were poetic personae, corrupted manuscripts, a complete absence of corroborating records—they were like early Spanish explorers thinking they'd landed on the shores of India. Because they were looking for India, they saw it where it wasn't. Not like Henrietta Swan Leavitt, who had simply observed her Cepheid stars closely and allowed what she saw to bring her to a conclusion—the correct one. Tessa had feared becoming someone who fit the data to the conclusion; and yet, now she worried she was doing just this.

•   •   •

IN OXFORD, Tessa was relieved to find that her key opened the door to the flat—the landlord had not changed the locks. And yet immediately upon turning on the light in the main room, she felt a pang of discomfort—the same discomfort she had experienced before leaving for Italy. There was the dark side street. The windows seemed very large. Anyone could see into the room. *there are no words.*

She pulled the curtains closed and locked her door.

What had Chris written to her? Some sort of apology?

Tessa had kept her cards somewhat close to the vest with Greta but eventually told her it was possible there had been a material discovery relating to Publius Marius Scaeva. Greta had responded point-blank that that would be very interesting indeed to numerous editors across the globe; any convergence of material culture and philology was nothing short of amazing. "God forbid we should be the people to turn classics into a collaborative field," she had said, shaking her head, "where we share our expertise between archaeology, history, philology, et cetera, to find out what happened in the eras we study." Regardless of the success of a paper on Sulpicia, though, Tessa couldn't just leave Westfaling and go live in her sister's house in New Jersey next year. Oh yes, the hottest new Latin scholar, Tessa Templeton, straight from her sister's couch in Hoboken. She could imagine the placard: *Distinguished Visiting Couchsurfer.* Tessa Templeton, on any publication, without an affiliated university next to it—people would think her some hobbyist. It would definitely damage her credibility. And adjuncting would be a major step down, assuming she could even find a position this late in the application season.

She unlocked her phone and read the message.

> dear tessa. there are no words that could make apology for what I've done, and I say this with all sincerity, I will do anything to make this right. you are a most exceptional scholar and individual, and your career will flourish with or without me, I promise you that. please agree to meet with me if you are in town. I am worried about you. yours, chris.

Tessa did not understand every word at first; just reading a message from him unsettled her in a literal sense—since she had seen the recommendation letter any word by his hand seemed to coil into malignant insincerity. It occurred to her, as she read it again, that it *had been* words that had constituted his action, his crime was constituted of words, a different text was the physical embodiment of what he had done to her—and now he was using words to attempt to persuade her, convince her what a terrible mistake she would be making not to trust him. Where did action enter into this? She felt it was right for him to suggest action as a path toward forgiveness, and to suggest an existence that didn't include him as its destination— and yet it was apparent that he could say anything. She did not even consider his morality anymore, or lack thereof. It would be like considering cancer cells immoral. They do what they do.

The way she saw it, bringing a complaint against Chris would be like undergoing chemo. Sure, it might get rid of the cancer. But it would undoubtedly poison you in the process. You have to evaluate the risk-reward. Ideally there would be a targeted surgery, some sort of precise incision, that would remove the tumor. It was part of why she had been so circumspect with telling anyone, especially in the classics community. It would be like spreading it to the lymph nodes.

I am worried about you

It reminded Tessa of Apollo in his speech to Daphne, as he chases her, how he worries that she'll scrape her legs as she runs. It's like, *Thanks, Apollo, for taking my well-being into consideration.*

A text from Lucrezia slid across her screen.

tutto bene? did you arrive ok?

Lucrezia was planning to tell Edward they'd uncovered a femur whose shaft was cut short at the distal end, with striations that resembled those of a surgeon's saw. But she would not yet mention anything about Marius and Sulpicia, at Tessa's request.

Tessa called her.

"Where are you now?" Lucrezia asked.

"Oxford."

"Did you get what you needed from Greta?" she asked.

"Yes, it was exceptional."

"So what is next?"

"A trip to the Bodleian."

Lucrezia laughed. "All the way to the Bodleian? That's too far."

"I don't know," said Tessa, smiling. "My flat has decent proximity to the M40."

"So you could maybe make that."

"The last leg, I hope," said Tessa.

"Yes! I told Ed about the femur, and he was very excited and looking forward to seeing it when he comes back to the site. I didn't tell him about the epitaph, so he doesn't know anything about Marius or Sulpicia, and as far as I'm concerned, I don't know, either. In a week or so, I'll call my old friend Tessa Templeton from Oxford and ask her to look at the fragments of a verse epitaph."

"At which point I'll inform you about Marius Scaeva and Sulpicia in the textual record."

"And I'll tell Edward that we've exhumed a poet, or poets," Lucrezia said.

This plan required Tessa to sacrifice some of the credit in the official narrative—how she had tracked the Conti testimony and *urinator* detail to Isola Sacra, and how she had picked Marius and Sulpicia's tomb out from one word of the epitaph. She was willing to sacrifice this for Lucrezia, though, who was providing cover at her own risk and giving Tessa time to assemble the necessary evidence for her thesis about authorship.

"Poet, I think," Tessa said. "I think it was Sulpicia."

"*Che grande!*" Lucrezia said.

Tessa found herself smiling; she already missed talking to Lucrezia. "And how is Alberto?"

Lucrezia laughed and said something that didn't come through. ". . . he doesn't listen. I'm, like, I have sixty-two deaf male skulls lined up in a lab. I don't need another one at home."

Tessa laughed. "That's funny. What did he say?"

Lucrezia laughed. "Ah. It doesn't translate."

There was a lull. "So, Chris just texted me," she said.

"What did he say?"

"He basically said, you know, I'm sorry. He asked to see me if I was in town. He probably has no idea where I've been. I never told him, of course. He said he's 'worried' about me, which, like, if he was worried about my well-being he wouldn't have sabotaged my fucking career."

Lucrezia laughed. "So are you going to meet him?" she asked.

"I don't know," Tessa said. "I'm maybe slightly curious about what he'd have to say. Like, what he hopes to do to ameliorate the situation. And there's this Westfaling offer letter hanging over my head. I have to respond to it eventually."

"Well, maybe you should hear him out," said Lucrezia. "It would make my life a lot easier."

"What would?"

"If you and Chris could be a team again. Then I could tell Edward. You know, I don't like sleeping around."

"Do you mean, sneaking around?"

"Ha! Yes, of course. *Sneaking* around. Sleeping around, that can be okay."

Tessa laughed. "I won't tell Alberto."

"He wouldn't hear you anyway," said Lucrezia.

"Well, if you do have to tell Edward . . ." Tessa said, "again, please let me know first."

"And likewise to me, if you have to tell Chris."

They hung up after agreeing to keep in touch and to see each other when Lucrezia was back in Oxford, or, as Lucrezia suggested, when Tessa had secured grant funding to come back to Isola Sacra. Tessa imagined Lucrezia on the balcony of the *soprintendenza*. It would be warm there now. They could sit there under the clothesline and look out at the landscape, the landmass that always felt like it would drift away with all of them on it, but which had remained, somehow, for thousands of years.

Before Tessa went to sleep, she responded to Chris's message.

3 o'clock, Nero?

*   *   *

CHRIS'S SPIRITS LIFTED when he saw the text. He pulled tufts of the kiddies' wool out of his briefs and out of his hair as he sat up on the couch. It was light out. He heard Dorothy's wet breathing in the next room. It was nearly eight a.m.

Normally, he knew, Dorothy would be up and about by six. He had put her to bed at ten, but she hadn't slept; at midnight he had needed to help her use the bathroom, and at four she had extracted him from a deep sleep with groans of pain. She had been due, at that point, for more morphine, and he had administered it generously.

Connor was to arrive at noon, which would leave Chris more than enough time to get to Oxford, pack his things, and pick up the Beinecke and wrap it before meeting with Tessa. He felt that he badly needed to see her. In the kitchen, he made breakfast for himself with some leeks from the garden and mashed fruit and oatmeal into a bowl for Dorothy, when she awoke. He made some tea and wondered whether Tessa had really found anything in Italy—and what his approach would be that afternoon. He needed to get her back on his side. There must be some indispensable service he could offer for her work on Marius. Something more than just a book.

He stepped into the next room quickly and watched his mother for a moment—she lay facing the ceiling, and her breathing was labored, but she was breathing.

As he stood over her, coaxing a last thread of leek off the rim of the bowl with his spoon, he recalled Dorothy on the floor of the barn, with straw in her hair, struggling to breathe. He had been just a child then. Perhaps he would never have even thought twice about the other beatings if it weren't for the rake incident.

Chris had scored well on his eleven-plus exam, so well that he became eligible to apply for scholarships to pay for his expenses at grammar school. She had discouraged him from applying for scholarships. He had forged her signature.

When she found his acceptance in the post, she had chased him into the yard with the rolling pin. He ran into the barn, knowing she would follow, and when he heard her steps outside the door he swung the handle of a rake across the threshold. The crack was such that he thought he had struck steel, and the vibrations ran through his entire body. Both his mother and the rake clattered to the floor. She made a noise like a dying animal, a desperate croaking, and it took him a moment to realize she was straining for air. His hands were shaking. The rolling pin lay next to her. She was staring at the barn ceiling, and he was looking at her blue eyes, dilated with fear. There was straw in her hair. Uncertain whether she was still dangerous, he kicked away the rolling pin, then knelt at her side.

The next day she told him it was a blessing he was welcome somewhere else, because he was no longer welcome there.

His mother had given up on him, or she was afraid of him, he did not know. Either way, after the rake incident, she had wanted him gone. The rake incident was embedded in their shared past. He had never told anyone about it.

      •   •   •

AT TWO KILOMETERS onto the A34, Chris readied himself for the mutilated verge railing. He guessed that there would be shredded turf from wheel treads and fragments of multiple undercarriages, bits of busted headlights, but he wasn't quite sure if he had ever seen these things. He always passed so quickly. His heartbeat quickened slightly and he could feel his foot on the pedal relax, the Fiat slow. He had become like some Pavlovian dog. He crossed into the right lane, and he saw the billboard in the distance that was near the accident, and below it—men. Men in vests, a light shade of gray to him, but he knew they were Day-Glo vests. Neon, Diana had once called them. From νέος, *neos*, new. They were reconstructing the barrier. The damaged link had been removed—he saw it on the median, laid out behind them in the sun, like a slain animal, completely ignored—and they had a new one they were going to fit in. One of the construction men looked up as Chris passed—he had slowed considerably—and Chris thought they made eye contact for a moment, though he didn't know if the man could see him, and then he whipped past and was gone.

    Well, now he would have nothing to mark the time when he drove between Hampshire and Oxford. But perhaps it was a good omen—this mending. Still, he resisted it, and felt foolishly resentful. This was what everyone did. They made it look like nothing ever happened.

Chris arrived at his house shortly after one. He packed his leather carryall—an expensive gift from Diana—with enough clothes for four days and included a sheaf of work he had been ignoring, mostly applications for graduate studies work that required his signature to secure funding. He threw in a bottle of his favorite peaty scotch. He didn't need much else, really. He had his laptop and toothbrush and chargers and phone. He would need to go to the college, though, for the Beinecke, which was fine, since the college was just next to Nero.

As Chris walked, he felt suddenly very ill at ease with how little he knew of Tessa's Marius affair. If they had found something that would merit funding, he would need to be the one to make the request—Tessa not even having her degree yet. And moreover, it would have to be done in conjunction with Ed Trelawney. It suddenly seemed to Chris that, even though he had decided to cease violating Tessa's privacy by logging in to her email, it wasn't any additional transgression if he made some inquiries to find out what exactly was going on in Italy.

He stopped in Debenhams to buy wrapping paper. There were some wonderful solid crimsons and a burgundy, shading into gray for him, as well as a kind of burnt-umber stripe print that he loved. But perhaps she wanted some other color—what was that dress she wore to the classics ball the other year? She said it was green. Perhaps it was neon.

"Can I help you find anything?" a young saleswoman asked. Her hair was very light—dyed, he thought—and her lips glossy.

"Yes, perhaps you could. I'm a bit colorblind, you see, and I'm trying to find a good, rich green."

"Well," she said, "this is a nice peppermint here, with little pink spots that make it pop." Her fingertips alighted on a gray tube with barely perceptible lighter gray spots. "And this is a solid, darker green, blue almost. I think it's technically called Nile-green." Her fingertips alighted on another gray tube.

Chris sighed. "Which do you like?" he said.

"The peppermint is lovely. It's bubbly with the spots. If it were me getting the gift, I'd like that one."

"Excellent," Chris said. "I'll take the Nile."

*   *   *

CHRIS HAD ALWAYS enjoyed wrapping gifts. He was good at guessing lengths and distances, and he felt he could guess exactly how long to cut the paper so it would wrap around the gift, exactly how much space to leave to press down the corners. He used scissors well, cut perfect, straight lines; sometimes he didn't even need to use the natural edges of a roll. Perhaps it was the generations of shepherds, of Eccleses working with their hands, shearing the Southdown ram, which was a notoriously difficult sheep to shear, since the wool grew so near to their eyes. You had to be extremely careful, and dexterous, when you sheared around their faces. Chris wrapped the Beinecke in so-called green paper, using a minimum of clear tape, at his desk at Westfaling, and when he was finished, it was quarter past two. With nothing to do now, he felt the anxiety return. He needed to collect as much information as he could. He decided to phone Ed.

He picked up on the third ring. "Chris, old boy, how are you?" Ed said, in his gravelly voice.

"I'm well, Ed. I'm not interrupting anything, am I?"

"Nothing terribly important," Edward said.

"Tremendous," Chris said, running his finger along a seam of the wrapped Beinecke. After a few more pleasantries, he said, "So. Marius."

There was a pause on the line that Chris did not know how to interpret. "Who?" Trelawney responded.

"The grave site, in Ostia," Chris said, wondering if Ed was being coy.

"Isola Sacra?" Ed said.

"Yes."

"What Marius is of interest?" Ed said.

"Publius Marius Scaeva."

Ed was quiet again. "I'm sure I don't follow."

Chris laughed, now certain that Ed was playing as if he had found nothing. "Ed, I know Silver Age is not my specialty."

"Hold on—a Silver Age poet in Isola Sacra?"

"Yes, well, his remains."

"This is news to me," Ed said.

Chris paused. He didn't think Ed was this good a liar. He seemed genuinely surprised. "So there is no Publius Marius Scaeva, husband of Sulpicia, buried in Isola Sacra?" Chris said.

"Well, Chris, I would have to look into it. I don't have the names of every specimen in three different dig sites memorized. Where are you getting your information?"

Chris considered backing off. Yet Ed might still be bluffing. "Perhaps it was bad information, but it came from one of my pupils," he said truthfully.

"Chris, I truly do not know what you're talking about. But I'll ask my site manager about it tonight."

"Will you let me know what you find?" Chris said. "It's probably nothing, some mistake."

"Well, I don't know what to think, Chris. I hope you're right, of course, but I'd bloody well hate to be the last to know."

Chris, flummoxed, immediately decided that he needed to see for himself what Tessa had been up to these past two weeks. He quickly unpacked his laptop, opened the backup software, and logged in to Tessa's account. He cursed the university wireless connection as he watched the progress bar stall and then move and then stall out again, like a horse with the yips. It was ten to when he got in. He scanned through the messages for something with Ed Trelawney, but saw nothing. There were mostly exchanges with Lucrezia Pagani, who a quick internet search revealed to be in charge of the dig site at Isola Sacra. Edward Trelawney was not on any of the lists of recipients. On the second of April, Tessa had apparently flown to Copenhagen (he could see the e-tickets), and from there sent Lucrezia a pleading email not to tell Edward yet. Okay, so Edward *was* in the dark. They referred cryptically to a "specimen," which, when Lucrezia sent Tessa a note confirming evidence of the serrated edges of a surgeon's saw, as well as amputation-related bone remodeling, Chris immediately knew belonged to Marius.

·   ·   ·

CHRIS WAS FIVE MINUTES EARLY to Café Nero, carrying the green not-green gift and wondering at how Tessa had manipulated Lucrezia into concealing information from her own supervisor. Was this a revolt against supervisors the world over? Advisees of all nations unite? He would have to say that Ed told him in order to address the issue of Marius at all, and he considered that the bluff was probably worth it. Or he could ask her where she had been and see if she told him the truth. The more important thing was reconciling with her.

He walked through the bookstore up to the café. They had met here once, when he began advising her. He remembered—they had had a table in the back room overlooking Broad Street. It wasn't too crowded, it being off-term. Trendy music played softly from a speaker. He didn't see Tessa. He ferreted out a table in the back, the same one, he was quite certain, they had once met at. He draped his coat over the chair and left his gift on the table, then went to order his double Americano and a pot of black tea with a dash of honey for Tessa. He looked at his watch. He was two minutes early. He should have had a cigarette.

It was a fascinating discovery, really. But how did she know to look in Isola Sacra? That was what mystified him. And were they really sure that this leg, this amputated femur, belonged to Marius? Celsus, the early doctor, had discussed medical amputations, how he would create a surgical flap over the amputation site, how he would pack wounds with vinegar-soaked sponges. That would be almost contemporary with Marius. But no one had really found any evidence that these amputations had succeeded. Marius would almost surely have died from such a procedure. And yet, if the limp had anything to do with his decision to write in choliambs, perhaps he *had* survived, an interesting prospect for the field of ancient medicine in its own right.

"Double Americano and pot of Earl Grey!"

Chris brought their beverages on a tray to the table. Tessa was now five minutes late. He took a long sip of his double Americano and stared at the empty teacup and wrapped gift that awaited Tessa. When he looked up again, there she was.

"So, you're going to ply me with gifts and hope that I forgive you?"

She sat down. Her face was slightly darker, tanned, and it brought out her eyes.

He chuckled, affecting nonchalance. "And tea," he said. "Don't forget the tea." He lifted the pot and offered to pour some, and she nodded, looking him for the first time in the eyes. She seemed almost afraid, he thought, as he poured; her eyes were shifty. Maybe she was simply uncomfortable with hiding information from him, like the Marius discovery. But she sat calmly, composed, in a boxy wool sweater he had never seen her wear before. It was not flattering. "You look like you've caught some sun," he said, attempting a cheerful tone.

"Is that a question or a statement?"

"Both, rather. A statement, of course. Have you been in Florida these past few weeks?"

"No," she said tersely. "And what have you been doing with yourself?"

So, she hadn't lied. But she had changed the subject to avoid further prodding. An espresso machine was sounding off, reverberating through the little side room. Chris leaned forward, resting his elbows on the table, so that Tessa could hear him better. "The usual, really. Peer reviews, finding funding, preparing lectures, shirking Library Committee responsibilities." No smile. "And I've taken my mother out of hospice and brought her home."

Tessa's expression didn't betray a reaction to this. "In Hampshire?" she asked. "You're staying with her?"

He nodded. "She's in her last days."

"I'm sorry, Chris," Tessa said coldly. But Chris felt more leverage with this truth. He wouldn't milk it—Tessa was too smart for that. "Shouldn't you be with her?" Tessa asked.

"I will be after this. I had to pick up my things this afternoon. There's a hospice nurse with her at the moment."

Tessa nodded. Tapped her finger against her teacup. He wondered what she was thinking, what was going on in that head of hers right now. Was she sympathetic? How much capacity did she even have for sympathy?

"So you're still upset with me," he ventured.

"Of course I'm still upset with you," Tessa returned. Her voice cracked just so when she said it, which Chris found strangely touching—that there was sadness there, underneath the anger. An onlooker might have believed she was upset with him because of some romantic jealousy.

"Look, I thought your dissertation needed another year, which I'm not entirely wrong on. Perhaps I was preparing you too long. But now you're ready, I can see that," Chris said.

Tessa nodded. "No, you're right. Clearly I let my ambitions get out of hand."

"Well, it's good to be ambitious," said Chris.

"No, I see your point. Because of some deep Machiavellian hunger in me, I believed that after earning my dPhil from Oxford I could begin a teaching career with my advisor's blessing."

"Right," Chris said. "I deserved that."

"I mean, tell me if I'm being 'argumentative,'" she added.

"Tessa."

"Yes?"

Chris had nothing. He wanted to tell her how he was working to get her the OUP monographs award, but he knew now that she would be better off never knowing.

"It was refreshing, in a way," she said. "Reading all the things you were really thinking about me and my work."

"But Tessa, that's not how I really feel about your work."

"Is it not?" she said. "I don't know what's true anymore. But when you live in constant fear that you're not good enough, to hear that confirmed by your mentor, it's a relief, in a way. To have some certainty."

"Oh, please," he said. "Don't play the victim."

"I'm not playing the victim. I am the fucking victim."

"You're milking it," he said. "Look, I won't make light of what I did. But look at it in context. There's nothing that I want to see more than your professional success, and haven't I acted accordingly for all the time we've known each other? I won't take credit where credit isn't due, but the guidance has been solid, no? For years I've been your biggest fan. You've taught me as much about the classics as I've taught you."

"Is this what we're really talking about, Chris? Professional appreciation?"

Chris paused, wondering genuinely at first what she was referring to. "You mean, the nature of my affections?"

"Yes," said Tessa. She was toying with a leather strap on her handbag.

Chris felt suddenly self-conscious, felt he was suddenly under her gaze. Of course she knew, had always known. But he had never thought she would confront him about it. Some part of him wanted her to know—but it would be such a poor showing to make a declaration here now. "Tessa . . ." he stalled.

She waited. He simply could not tell her this now. Not until they were on better footing. She could know, but he would not let this be where and how he told her.

"Chris—" she began impatiently.

"Tessa, it will never happen again. This year, you can send the letters yourself. I will open myself up to you. Anything you want to see, I will show you. But stay at Westfaling, work with me on Marius. It will be entirely your project—"

"Marius?" Tessa said. "Who said anything about Marius?"

It hurt Chris that she would keep this from him—and then try to bluff her way out of the knowledge. She had become so protective. "Tessa," he said. "Really?" He pushed the wrapped gift across the table.

She looked at it like it was some flattened reptile, then back at Chris, confused and alert. "Who said anything about Marius?"

Marius, he thought. Marry us. "Ed Trelawney did, the head of the excavation at Isola Sacra?"

Tessa's eyes widened and she uncrossed her legs. She would be a miserable poker player. "There's no use beating about the bush," said Chris. "That is quite a discovery. I'm so impressed by you. But you need help, Tessa. Why do this all alone? You're always so hard on yourself." He reached across the table and put his hand over hers, quieting her tapping finger. "You're the one, Tessa. You don't have to hide. You're the one who made the discovery. How can you think that you're not good enough?"

* * *

"I'M GOING TO use the bathroom," Tessa said. She stood up from the table in a daze, utterly bewildered. Ed had told Chris, which meant that Lucrezia had told Ed. Or somebody had told Ed, possibly Graham? She stalked out of the café into the adjoining Blackwell's and up the stairs to the bathrooms, pulling her phone out of her jeans pocket at the same time. She immediately dialed Lucrezia, who would probably still be on site now. Tessa looked down the stairs to see if Chris had followed her. There was only someone in a blue sweater, ascending slowly.

"Tessa?" Lucrezia said.

"Chris knows," Tessa said. "Did you tell Ed?"

Lucrezia made a sound that Tessa did not like to hear. It was a sort of scoff. Like, of course. "No, Tessa, I did not tell Ed."

"Chris just asked me about Marius and told me he had talked to Ed."

"*Dio mio*, Tessa, are you shitting me? What did he say?"

"He said, 'Ed Trelawney, the head of the excavation at Isola Sacra, told me about Marius.'"

"And you believed him?"

"Well, I sure as shit didn't tell him," said Tessa. "You didn't tell Ed?"

"No," said Lucrezia.

"And he hasn't said anything to you?"

"No," said Lucrezia. The blue sweater continued to ascend. Tessa rested against the windowsill. She heard the espresso machine in the distance down the stairs. "Fuck, you know, I was trying to help you," Lucrezia continued. " 'One more day, please, Lucrezia, one more day.' You don't consider that I was the one at risk? Not you?"

"Lucrezia, I didn't tell him, I swear to god."

"How did I let myself get talked into this?"

"Could it have been Graham?" Tessa asked. "Could someone on site have figured it out?"

"How would Graham tell Chris?"

"He would have told Edward."

"Why do you think Edward wasn't told by Chris?" Lucrezia asked.

"How would Chris have found out?" Tessa said. Lucrezia didn't answer. "Are you saying that I told Chris?" Tess asked.

"Are you saying you believe what Chris says?"

"I don't!" Tessa nearly shouted. The blue sweater was turning the corner. Tessa ignored her. "But this makes no sense. How would Chris have found out?"

"I don't know."

"And further," she said. A cold suspicion had instantly seized her. "How would Chris know that I'm involved if Ed told him, unless you were the one who told Ed?"

"Tessa, stop. I don't know if you are a liar—"

"Me, the liar? How does Chris know I was there, Lucrezia? Are you trying to take credit for this?"

"I don't know if you are a liar, Tessa, but either way, I'm finished with this. I have to decide what I'm going to say to my boss now."

"Lucrezia?"

"It doesn't matter. Just, I wish you the best, okay? Good luck to you."

Lucrezia hung up.

It must have been Graham.

It wouldn't have been difficult to put the pieces together, really. A literature scholar shows up out of thin air and then a particular tomb is excavated, out of order. He wouldn't have needed a day in the library or even a particular aptitude for deduction. The names, and an internet connection, would have sufficed. Then he tells Ed, who tells Chris.

Lucrezia's job would survive this. Tessa hoped it would survive this.

Tessa shifted her weight on the windowsill. She had been away for over five minutes. The thing about Chris, she now realized, was that it was possible she hadn't needed to hide Marius from him at all. Chris genuinely wanted her to succeed, as long as she stayed near him, or as long as there was the potential for their lives to merge. She saw this now. It was twisted, but accurate, she felt. He could make her life much easier; he had before.

Tessa descended the stairs slowly. Chris was still there—he had taken out his laptop. The ever-diligent Chris. He flipped it closed when he saw her. Shouldn't he be getting back to his mother? Perhaps his mother wasn't real. Did it matter? Tessa sat down across from him and picked up the gift, encased in crisp green paper. Perhaps it was the Beinecke, Volume IV. "You're wrapping in green now," she observed.

"It's called 'Nile,' I'm told."

"It has hints of blue."

"I wouldn't know."

Tessa opened it carefully, unfolding the tabs, removing a piece of tape, and undoing the creases. From the weight and shape she knew it to be a book, yet she felt like she was handling unexploded ordnance. But as she tore through she saw the familiarly stippled dark back of the volume. Of course it was the Beinecke. Ever the best mentor there could be. It infuriated her. It was the perfect gift.

"What do you think?" he said, smiling.

She inspected the cover and then put it down. "Is this a joke?" she said.

He looked confused. "It would be a rather expensive one."

"It's going to cost you more."

"It was a show of good faith—"

"A show of good faith would be never mentioning Marius again. You wanted me to have nothing to do with him before, and you'll have nothing to do with him now."

Chris put his hands up in mock defense.

"Do you realize how horribly insufficient this is? Did you really believe for a moment that you could pop over to OUP and—what? Make amends?" she said.

"You know when you get cross a vein bulges just under your chin," he said. "And your face gets all fiery. It's charming."

"Are you trying to provoke me?"

"You wear your anger like some svelte fabric."

Tessa arced her shoulders toward the edge of the table and began to leave her seat.

"Wait," Chris said. "I'm sorry."

"Chris, don't make the mistake of not taking me seriously."

"I realize you're upset."

"Upset doesn't begin to cover it."

"Look," he said. "I didn't think I would hand you a book and go scot-free. As I said, it's a sign of good faith. Good faith that I will be the most diligent and tenacious steward of your project you could ever hope for or imagine. Let me prove my worth to you. There are all sorts of things that need to be dealt with. Ed will have a *documentazione di scavo*, there will need to be an outside expert—difficult for you on your own, as they'll not take on someone without her dPhil. There will be costs associated—airfare, taxis. Funding will need to be secured. But with a formal relationship, it won't be an issue. Even a per diem, usually. There's a nondisclosure agreement, which will keep lips sealed about your discovery until it's time to present your findings. A per diem, Tessa. Think about it."

Tessa listened to Chris, each sentence a prying finger on her resolve. An image of her and Lucrezia on the balcony, in the summer, when it was warm. Shouts in Italian tearing through the darkness. Perhaps she'd gain leverage to prevent Ed from taking action against Lucrezia. A per diem. She could pay back Claire. Chris was scribbling out a check.

"For your travels," he said. "The grant will reimburse me." He pushed it across the table. Two thousand five hundred pounds. Tessa stared at it. A dark yearning was taking shape somewhere in her stomach.

"And in return?" she said. She didn't quite understand this new desire, which had an edge to it, a sharpness. Was it the tantalizing oblivion of giving in to Chris? Of the ease of it? Or something else?

"Be kind to me," he said. "Entertain the notion that this was one isolated mistake, and not a reflection of my character. That's all I ask."

Tessa had believed that Chris would try to make himself as useful as possible in this meeting, and he had outdone her predictions. He had made himself too useful, she believed. But she was torn. She knew she had a capacity for self-sabotage, and she wondered if she wasn't engaging in such a capacity now. She stood up from the table and began to dig in her jeans pocket for change.

"Oh, come, now," Chris said.

She dropped a two-pound coin. "For the tea," she said.

"At least take the book," Chris said, in a tone that seemed to suggest sadness.

"Why would I?" said Tessa, feeling that she was losing control of herself, that her anger would brim over and spill everywhere. "In a year it will be obsolete."

*   *   *

TESSA WAS PERSPIRING under Claire's sweater when she stepped outside, walking quickly as if she could walk away from her own words, which had come from somewhere injudicious and frighteningly bold. It made her uneasy. The sweat around her neckline cooled as she walked determinedly toward the Bodleian, without thinking about what her destination really would be, consumed with what had just transpired. Truth be told, she would have loved to take the Beinecke and add it to her library. She would have loved not to have to retrieve a tattered copy from the Bodleian or the Sackler every time she wanted to review the only decent English-language scholarship on Marius; to have her own copy would be not only convenient but sentimental. Moreover, with the upcoming paper she was going to be giving at the conference on April sixteenth, she needed ready access to all the resources she could get.

As Tessa walked, a new suspicion about Chris germinated somewhere in her mind. It wasn't quite logical, but it emerged from what she perceived as the lack of logical explanation in the situation. Yes, Lucrezia might have told Ed herself and then lied to Tessa about it, in order to take credit for the discovery. Or Graham may have told

Ed, but would Graham really be able to connect all the pieces? She
didn't think he'd even caught her last name. The only other way
Chris could have possibly known was if he was corresponding with
Claire, which was absurd. Claire was the only one Tessa had told.

But this possibility supplied the idea that Chris might know the
password to her email. She remembered the oddness of him asking
how she knew George Bale had sent her the first rec letter, how he
had borrowed her phone that morning, had seemed to know ahead
of time she'd received the anonymous email. What if she had left
her computer on that night she had passed out in his house, and he
had done something to it? Tessa had heard of software that recorded
your keystrokes. If that was the case, she could change her password. But if Chris had hacked her, she would need to know. Changing her password wouldn't tell her anything.

* * *

TESSA HUMMED as she put the finishing touches on an email to
herself. Who knew that for ten dollars you could buy a .edu email
address? They were advertised for student discounts—she pictured
her brother-in-law Stan, a reward fiend who worked in consulting,
drooling over the .EDU EMAIL page, which listed all the massive
discounts students received on Spotify, Netflix, iPhones. Guns?
Trafficked organs? A first-class citizen, the student in the twenty-first
century. .EDU EMAIL CUSTOMIZED was an extra ten dollars,
and she was happy to be upsold. It wouldn't have worked with any
.EDU email. She had written out a list of the schools she'd applied
to, just so she could visualize their names.

UCL / University of College London / UCLondon
University of California Los Angeles / UCLA / UCLosAngeles

UC Irvine
Brasenose College Oxford
Trinity College Cambridge
Wake Forest
Northwestern
Berkeley
St. Andrews
Grinnell
Bates
Stanford
Case Western Reserve University / casewestern.edu / case.edu / cwru.edu

Thank god for obscure schools in the Midwest. UCL was an obvious no—Chris knew too many people there even if she could find a permutation of their email address that was available. UC Irvine was a possibility, but then she discovered that the school actually used multiple permutations of its email address—UCI. edu, UCIrvine.edu were alternates, and besides, UCIrvine looked odd to her, suspicious, even if it was authentic. Northwestern, an obvious no. She wouldn't be able to get a "northwestern.edu" email address, or a "northwesternuniversity.edu" one. Same with Stanford, no, Bates, no. But Case Western . . . all three permutations: casewestern.edu / case.edu / cwru.edu looked equally viable to her. She wouldn't be able to pick one out of a lineup. It was also the only school that had interviewed her. Sure, she hadn't been to the campus, but if the email looked real enough—plus Chris didn't know anyone in Ohio.

Tessa was in the Westfaling College computer room. She'd left her phone and laptop in her flat and walked back to the college, where she knew she could use a public computer. Now, as she sat here, the email was going to arrive from an address that she had forged from a discount scam site. Ovid claimed to have invented the epistolary genre with his *Heroides*, in which he assumed the personae of numerous abandoned women of myth—Dido, Ariadne, Medea— and wrote letters to the unrequiting objects of their affection. She was doing Ovid one better. For wouldn't Dido, in her pain, ventriloquize a letter from Aeneas, before writing a letter to him herself, which could do nothing? Wouldn't that be a more honest reaction to her rejection? Cameron Voorhees, the man who had emailed her for her Skype interview and who had said he would be in touch, Cameron.Voorhees@case.edu officially, was sending her an offer letter for employment from Cameron.Voorhees@cwru.edu, complete with signature and official university logo at the bottom of the message.

Dear Tessa Templeton,

She wrote,

We're pleased to inform you that you've been recommended to the Department of Liberal Arts and Sciences for the position of Assistant Professor of Classics at Case Western Reserve University . . .

Tessa was halfway finished with the letter when the door clicked open and a young woman in a pilly wool cardigan entered. It was Florence. She looked at Tessa with surprise.

"Hello, Professor Templeton," she said, which struck Tessa. All her students called her Tessa. "I've never seen you in here before."

"Computer problems," Tessa said. It was never fun to have a student witness you in a compromised situation. Florence let down her bag next to one of the computer stations in Tessa's peripheral vision and began to tap at the keyboard. Tessa, genuinely worried about fucking up the slightest detail in her email, decided to finish before making any conversation, or asking Florence why she was here over break. She had doubled back to edit Voorhees's email signature so that it read cwru.edu instead of case.edu, and she had blown up the pixels and was whiting, graying, whiting, blacking with a little paint-can skeuomorph on the screen.

But the silence seemed to irk Florence, seemed to accuse her of something. Or perhaps she felt guilty, because after a few minutes she said, "Actually, I'm checking on summer law schemes and I haven't got a laptop."

Tessa looked over at her.

"I'm transferring to law," said Florence. "At the end of term."

"Oh," Tessa said. "Oh, Florence." She turned her chair fully toward her. This news landed like a blow.

"I've been catching up on coursework over the break. I'm sorry I didn't tell you."

Florence's face was pained; she was earnest and bright, and clearly she had not made the decision lightly, but it weighed hard on Tessa now.

"And don't you need a signature from your tutor for that?"

"Chris gave it to me."

Tessa threw up her hands. "*Florence*—"

"I don't have what you have," Florence insisted. "I'm not clever enough. I wouldn't make it as a classicist."

"You don't know that," Tessa said. It was strange to hear someone who genuinely believed Tessa had "made it" in classics. She didn't know quite what to say; Florence could make a valuable contribution to classical scholarship, she believed. She also believed she could become a translator. She also felt betrayed. "But there's an old adage, a good American one," Tessa finally said. " 'Whether you think you can or you can't, either way you're right.' "

Florence nodded and seemed to gulp.

Perhaps Tessa was being too rough.

"You said 'speak to me' on my translation," Florence said.

"I was just going to tell you that you're a beautiful translator," Tessa said. "I can't translate the way you can."

The *u* in the email signature still looked like an *e*. Another few minutes passed and Florence stood up to leave.

"Wait," said Tessa. Florence turned. "Did you get any acceptances?"

"There was no word," said Florence.

"You'll get something," Tessa said.

. . .

GATHERING MATERIALS for the paper presentation proved challenging without Lucrezia's help, but not impossible. Lucrezia had shared three crucial photographs with Tessa after she had left Italy: one of the epitaph with drawn missing pieces, one of Sulpicia's right femur, and one of Tessa holding the femur under the white work tent, dressed in Lucrezia's red lacquer trench. Tessa had never in her life taken pleasure in an activity involving PowerPoint, until she dropped this last photo into a slide. In it she wore an unmistakable expression of exhilaration; a few strands of wet hair clung awkwardly to her forehead; the camera hadn't been exactly upright, so she and the femur hung slightly askew; on the left, behind her, the blurred outline of someone *else's* disembodied leg, captured in motion, mid-step. So often Tessa had been presented with a photograph and her eye had fixed on herself instantly to make an assessment of how she looked. In this photo such an assessment could not be made favorably—the skin under her eyes drooped, her smile was too big for her face, her hair resembled a nest for small rodents; yet she felt a surge of recognition for the childlike excitement lighting up her features.

Tessa also felt she could look at the photograph a thousand times and see something different with each view. That she wore an expression of unadulterated joy, she could not deny. That there was something hideous and barbaric about biological anthropology, she had no doubt. She held a woman's remains, one of the last traces of her physical being, one of the few that had not been obliterated by time. Sulpicia, she thought. Please forgive me.

She would be either at the Sackler or the Bod, depending what books she needed for the day, when the doors opened. She was one of a small cadre of researchers who haunted the stacks, wearing call numbers on their wrists and thousand-mile stares. There was a quiet to the city that she let envelop her. The weather was varied, insane, frantic—pounding showers were interrupted by piercing sunlight, a dense fog would preside over the city center, oozing into the narrow, cobbled side streets, then shred and dissolve in gusts of manic wind, and for two afternoons, cloud streams gouged the sky.

At first her body had retaliated against her work ethic with drowsiness and aches, bleary eyes and headaches, and what she swore were swollen feet. Her stomach had clenched with anxiety and undigested energy drinks. She had acquired jitters and cramps and blurred vision. But after a few days, her body adapted to her new conditions. It learned not to act up. It did not meddle in her affairs. It was a vehicle to get her head to the Bodleian and back again. It was a sort of golem, a construct that was more like Claymation than biology. She believed that her neglect of it was only temporary, that she could come back whenever she wanted. She didn't eat or exercise. She lived on sugar and caffeine and then binged on chips. Empty Styrofoam containers were competing with filthy dishes for real estate. She felt like a renter rather than a body-owner. She had no long-term investment in the corporeal property. She'd mortgaged her body for her paper. She'd leased it out. It wasn't hers.

•   •   •

"TESSA'S THE NAME, right?" Max called out as she rushed through the Porter's Lodge toward her office. She needed the Baehrens, 1882. She was quite confident the volume of Baehrens was in her office.

"Right," she said.

"Your pidge needs to be cleared out."

As she trotted toward her office across the quad, she noted a single cigarette butt on the grass, within throwing range of Staircase 7.

In her office, Tessa scanned the mail quickly and opened a large envelope from the classics faculty. Her suspicions of what it contained were correct.

MINOR POETS AND PSEUDEPIGRAPHA:

NEW APPROACHES TO OLD PROBLEMS IN

NONCANONICAL TEXTS

16.IV.MMX

IOANNOU CENTER FOR CLASSICAL STUDIES,

OXFORD UNIVERSITY

She opened the pamphlet to inspect the schedule of proceedings. She was slotted for two-thirty on the sixteenth, just after a Hellenist from University of Virginia whose name she vaguely recognized, and two slots before Chris, who appeared to be rehashing a paper on the *Halieutica*, a fragment in the *Appendix Ovidiana* concerned exclusively with fishing, true author unknown. *Go Fish: Four Readings of Authorship in the* Halieutica. Her title, from when she had submitted a preliminary topic, was: *Marius and His Limping Iambs: The Mystery Endures.*

Tessa retrieved the book she needed, a volume on minor poets from the German scholar Baehrens, published in 1882, and tucked it into her bag. She locked her office door and took the stairs down as she normally would, not attempting to minimize the groans of the old staircase, which she knew Chris would be able to attribute to one of three people, her being the most likely, from within his office, if he was there. She prepared herself for a confrontation—for how she would deflect him and his attentions—if his door was open and he called out to her, as he had many times before. But once she turned the corner she saw his door was shut. She stopped, let her bag fall from her shoulder so she held its strap in her hand, considered looking under his door for the telltale band of light. No, best to get home.

She was down the steps and out the door in a moment, into the serenity of the quad. She heard a peal of disembodied laughter as she walked toward the Porter's Lodge, though there was no one else in the quad with her; it was either from an open window above, or from the neighboring quad. She was just observing how sound could make such serpentine journeys through the quads, caroming off the stone or reverberating in the arched passageways such that a conversation a hundred yards away might seem to be occurring just behind your back, when a checkered blazer she recognized emerged from the shadows of the Porter's Lodge and began to walk toward her. He must have been in there already, otherwise she would have heard the latch of the wicket door. He carried some papers, and a bulky leather carryall hung from his shoulder. He saw her, and her breath caught for a moment, and she immediately attempted to recompose herself for a conversation, as he continued determinedly around the jarring green of the lawn and then, having made the corner, toward her. She looked him in the eye and slowed her steps but was amazed to find that he simply nodded to her and continued walking. She felt a pang. She stopped and watched his journey to Staircase 7. He had nodded to her as if she were some acquaintance. As if he hardly knew her.

● ● ●

ANOTHER TRIP to Hampshire, this time with materials on Marius. The Beineke, Baehrens, and a 1940 volume entitled *I Frammenti Completi di Publius Marius Scaeva*, edited by Sergio Conti, which he had tracked down on short notice through Fredericka Sotheby-Villiers, the only classicist he knew personally who had ever published a word on Marius—they bounced on the passenger seat as he accelerated down the washboard lane to his mother's house.

Inside, he met Connor, who needed to rush off to another client, and in a moment Chris was at the foot of Dorothy's bed; Dorothy, who was asleep, whose dwindling shape he could not grow accustomed to. Outside, it rained lightly, *mizzled*, as she would say. He found his place on the sofa outside her room.

For three days Chris pored through the extant criticism on Marius, the notes Tessa had produced when she was editing Sotheby-Villiers's paper for *Hellenistic Derivatives*, and the emails between Tessa and Lucrezia Pagani in the week after the discovery. He was being good, and not logging in to read any new correspondence—in any case he doubted the hot spot from his phone would have sufficient bandwidth to run the backup software—but he could revisit the last download he had made before he had met with Tessa at Nero.

He found three photographs sent by Lucrezia Pagani to Tessa:

the epitaph, which scanned as limping iambs. Marius's femur, with Lucrezia's accompanying note about striations and amputation. And one of Tessa, in a red raincoat, holding the femur.

Chris hoped that Tessa would come to her senses and agree to work with him and Ed on the Marius discovery, but he feared she would do otherwise. It bothered him that the moment she had the smallest amount of success he was completely forgotten, and he worried that if she did not work with Ed Trelawney she would poison any possible future relationship with the excavation team. She had already circumvented Ed once; doing so again would be catastrophic. Indeed, he had received an email from Ed Trelawney, followed by several more form letters with agreements that he had signed and returned in Oxford:

> Your intelligence was accurate, I'm both disturbed and excited to say. Let's keep this portion of the story between us, shall we? I'll make calls to bring you on officially as the outside expert. There will be some boilerplate agreements that I'll get to you soon. Cheers, Ed.

He worried about what Tessa was planning for the conference as he watched Dorothy diminish before his very eyes; he could do nothing for either one of them.

•   •   •

THE MORNING OF the sixteenth, Tessa woke to gilded curtains and the wrenching fear that she had misquoted one of her sources. Gusts of wind swirled outside but her window no longer rattled in its sashes—the April warmth had returned its wood beams to their original size. The result was a room in eerie quiet and repose, a repose that she was not used to and did not trust.

The length of sun across her bedspread and the fact that she had slept past the dawn worried her; everything seemed a bad omen. In a fit of anxiety, she skipped the welcome ceremony and went to the Bodleian to run a double-check on her work. At ten, satisfied to the extent she believed possible, she doubled back to her flat to shower and put on something appropriate for her presentation. The wrought-iron gate squealed when she entered the building's forecourt and, after inputting the code to the front door and walking the half level to her floor, she was confronted by a bright orange page taped to her door.

NOTICE . . . DERELICT . . . RENT

She stopped reading immediately and went inside. She couldn't—not now. She opened the nearest drawer to the hallway in the kitchen—the cutlery drawer—jammed the missive facedown over a pair of old chopsticks, and banished it from her mind. In a moment, she was under a scalding shower, focusing on the presentation ahead. Steam rose around her. She found it hard to breathe. The nerves were kicking in. Beneath the lavender aroma of shampoo she felt the urge to vomit. Mentally she dressed herself. That satin white shell top. Her fishbone blazer. Black slacks.

•   •   •

VOICES ECHOED FROM the next room in the tinny glass atrium where Tessa registered with Liam, the conference administrator and general factotum, who was pleasantly going about handling the entirety of the conference bitch-work.

"There you are," he said, handing her the packet that would doubtless contain the presentation handouts, schedule of proceedings, and a laminated name tag. "There was a switcheroo in the spot before you, but no worries, it won't affect your timing at all."

"A switcheroo?" Tessa said.

"Chris had a conflict at four, so I gave him the spot before you."

Tessa felt her grip tighten on the coarse paper packet.

"What was the conflict, did he say?" Tessa asked.

Liam looked at her quizzically, with that amused light in his eyes. "I didn't ask," he said.

This peculiarity dialed Tessa's anxiety up further. She affected calm as she passed into the break room, a lengthy and bland interior space distinguished by two industrial-sized coffee makers and a cappuccino machine at its far end, a machine with which Tessa was intimately familiar, but which she could not now see for the sixty-odd individuals contriving conversation before her. With a glance she took in the assortment of people, saw the illustrious names from the schedule in the flesh, looking completely ordinary. Philip Barr in a navy blazer and with a swish of brown hair, talking to what looked like Fiorina Miristakos, her slight figure and rippling brown curls unmistakable, even from behind. Was that Colm Feeney stirring a lump of sugar into his thermos? Good god. He wasn't scheduled to speak, and yet he'd shown up to spectate. Tessa noted Phoebe Higgins, dressed seriously down, in a dark patterned dress over tights and gray sneakers, laughing cautiously at something a tall, brooding man was saying, her crooked teeth bared.

Lacking anyone to glom on to, Tessa darted through the crowd toward the coffee. Normally she would be on Chris's arm, cracking jokes and making small talk. She felt wayward, lost, even injured. She didn't belong now, and felt herself nursing antisocial fantasies of rendering everyone irrelevant with her brilliance. She accidentally nudged someone in billowy khakis as she passed, "I'm sorry," she said, "I'm so sorry," recognizing on his name tag the Hellenist who had been scheduled to go before her. John Fitzwilliams. He shrugged. She was over-apologizing. Flustered, Tessa continued through the crowd of faces, most of whom she recognized, none of whom she felt comfortable chatting with. She knew everyone and no one. She glimpsed Colm Feeney again and saw he was talking to none other than Chris himself, hunched over a Nero cup. They were in a serious dialogue. She had no one to attach herself to and Chris was in a serious dialogue with Colm Feeney, who stirred sugar in a thermos. Tessa bolted past the coffee machines for the backroom, under the pretense of finding more coffee.

The pantry was dark and cool. She shut the door behind her and took several long breaths, letting the darkness envelop her. The whir of the refrigerator was soothing. She groped around for the small counter and sat on it. When she had given her paper at Edinburgh, she had run through it with Chris twice beforehand. She remembered the first idea she had, what he had called the naïve reading of the Daphne and Apollo sequence. He had flayed the idea in private, down to the sinew, but had left what she considered its toughest substance. Afterward, she could not have imagined presenting her first amateurish musings without his coaching. Now she felt massively out of her depth. Why are you presenting architectural findings at a philology conference? a voice in her head said. This is inappropriate. Do you have permission from the excavation director to be doing this? the voice asked.

The door opened. Light bled into the pantry, blinding her for a moment.

"Are you all right?" Chris's voice.

"Yes, I'm fine," Tessa said instinctively. She didn't feel it. She was glad Chris was no longer talking to Colm Feeney. He wavered. "Go out or come in," she said.

He closed the door slowly, and she knew he stood just there before her, though by what sense she could not say, it was so dark. She could not smell him. She could not see him. His shape had disappeared; her eyes had not readjusted. She could not hear him breathing over the refrigerator and the bustle of voices outside, dampened by the door. He was just out of reach—she could not have touched him. Finally he spoke. "You don't seem it," he said.

"What about you, are you all right?" she asked.

"No, not at all," he said. He took a step away from the door. She thought she could see his outline leaning back against the fridge.

She waited for him to say more. Would he mention a position at Case Western Reserve University?

"You see, I have this worry you're going to make a presentation on the Isola Sacra findings."

He had not, she took small comfort to find. So perhaps he really had heard about the discovery from Ed Trelawney. It took her a moment to capture any new import in his words. "What is that supposed to mean?" she asked.

"Will you extend me one iota of trust that that would be a very stupid move?"

"I think you can understand why that might be difficult."

"Tessa, you need to wait. We both need to wait, and then the discovery can be handled properly."

"With you taking credit for it."

"With you showing respect for an ongoing research process, and not spilling the beans in dramatic fashion without even informing the director, who'll never let you on site again. And I wouldn't blame him! Please, see reason. There are protocols about how to disseminate information, which you would know if you would listen to me."

Tessa wavered. She felt totally alone. She wasn't confident that the audience would buy her argument about authorship. The link between Sulpicia's pathology and the poem seemed precarious, and she would be subjected to the probing of the audience in the Q&A—not an unsophisticated crowd. Chris could have been helpful in the analysis.

"There's still a chance for you to own this," Chris said. "Just don't talk about Isola Sacra today."

There was an acrid taste in Tessa's mouth. She hated public speaking. She hated how logical Chris sounded, the notion that he was right.

"If you assure me you won't, then I'll give my *Halieutica* talk," Chris said.

"As opposed to giving some other talk?"

"The Isola Sacra one, of course," he said.

Tessa was stunned. "*You're* going to present on Isola Sacra?"

"If you don't see reason."

"That's why you switched with the Hellenist?"

She heard his fist pound the counter. "I'm trying to help you—"

Tessa fled the pantry. Back into the break room. Everyone was thronging toward the theater on the other side of the hall. Liam was shepherding stragglers away from the pastry table. Waves of horrified anger crashed over her. He was wearing her away, working on her resolve inch by inch, he was going to get his way. And she could do nothing!

"Liam," she said. "Let me go first."

His brow furrowed. "You mean before Chris?"

Chris emerged from the pantry and walked slowly past them, toward the theater.

"Chris," Liam said. "Do you want to switch with Tessa?"

He waved Liam off and kept walking, without even looking up.

"Hmm," Liam said. "I think you have your answer."

He didn't say it maliciously; he said it kindly. Liam was so large—he stood a head taller than Tessa—he seemed like a footman before a castle. His physical presence was suddenly intimidating. Tessa proceeded toward the theater in a kind of daze. She was going to have to watch this. And then afterward, say what? *No, I was there, he wasn't?* Show them the photograph of her at the dig site? No one would care. The reveal would seem childish. Tessa walked slowly through the threshold into the auditorium, feeling as if she were attending her own funeral. The rage was gathering in the back of her throat. It was in her sinuses. She could feel her nostrils flare. She was just conscious of the restful faces pointing toward the podium as she climbed the theater steps toward an empty seat in the back, a shadowed nook from which she would bear witness to the crumbling of her dreams, and as the cherry on top, as the bonus to it all, she caught sight of Florence Henshawe's young face in the opposite corner. She had come. She was looking on, alone. Tessa sat amid the squealing of bleachers and coughing of academics. Liam took the podium to introduce Chris. Silence prevailed.

"The first presenter of our afternoon session needs no introduction, though I'm going to give him one anyway. In addition to being my dissertation supervisor, Chris is distinguished by his publication of four books, including *Subversion and Play*, which won the 2004 Demosthenes Prize, and he is the author of over fifteen articles. He is the Sterner Robinson Professor of Classics at Westfaling College, Oxford, where he is head tutor. Please welcome Christopher Eccles."

Applause. Chris rose from the second row and took the podium. She had only caught an impression of his appearance earlier—the mussed hair, the gray blazer. His button-down was gray too—it looked foolish. He probably thought it was one of his olive-toned shirts. He looked haggard. There were deep shadows under his eyes.

Yet his demeanor was light. He repositioned the microphone, which jutted out above his forehead, due to Liam's height. "Sorry," he said. "Need to adjust here from my more lofty predecessor." He flashed a smile at Liam. Disarming joke about his height. Check. "His scholarship is equally lofty, I assure you," Chris added. He found the right place for the mic. "You'll have to adjust, too, I'm afraid, for my scholarship." He smiled at the audience. A few chuckles. "Descent in quality begins now." Smiling. More chuckles.

He placed his reading glasses over his eyes and squinted at the paper in front of him, then stopped. "Oh, you'll have to forgive me. The talk I'm going to give is not on the *Halieutica* as indicated on the conference schedule. I want to talk to you today, instead, about Publius Marius Scaeva, that elusive and oft-ignored Silver Age poet, for whose work a recent discovery in our sister field of archaeology, I believe, may shed new light. I don't have a proper handout but I do have a few slides. I hope you'll forgive the change in topic."

He began: "That Marius has long been a peculiarity of known classical Latin poets is no secret in this room. Indeed, mysteries abound. The manuscript we have of his longer poem is lacunose, and much of the verse we have cryptic. At times, it is difficult to identify subject matter. The speaker of his long monologue, for example, a fleeing woman, has been connected with Daphne, fleeing Apollo. And yet in the very same poem, we have allusions to everyday Rome. The mythic and the contemporary intersect in ways that suggest the poem was perhaps once many poems, and was collated incorrectly. This is just an example, one of many that have plagued scholars over the centuries.

"But the central mystery has always been the meter. As many of you know, all extant poetry composed by Marius is in the choliambic meter, which takes its name from the Greek adjective for 'lame,' and is also known as limping verse. It was pioneered by Hipponax in the Greek and adopted by Catullus for some of his more choice invectives. It can also be found in Martial and Persius. It is much like an iambic trimeter, but with its pattern reversed in the last two feet: an iamb in the fifth foot and a spondee or trochee in the sixth. This unexpected change in the cadence results in the 'limping' effect for which it's named.

"Just as a matter of arithmetic, there are some three hundred extant lines of choliambic meter written in classical Latin, and one hundred and ten of those belong to Marius. It is striking that nearly half the quantity of verse written in this decidedly intracta-ble meter should belong to one poet, and one poet, moreover, who betrays no familiarity with the tradition of invective that had so long been the hallmark of the choliambic meter, whether to mock poetic pretensions or question one's parentage or inveigh against stubborn mistresses.

"Speculation about Marius and the rationale for his metrical choices have ranged from timid steps in a dark room to headlong postulatory sprints . . . also in a dark room. That these scholarly expeditions have met with little in the way of solid footing is not for lack of effort. One Italian commentator speculated, I do hope in jest, that Hipponax was the true author of Marius's verse, and that Mar-ius was his pseudonym for composing Latin lyrics, the gap of five centuries be damned. If so, Hipponax should be lauded for pioneer-ing time travel, in addition to the choliambic meter." Some chuckles.

"Other scholars have speculated more conservatively along these same lines: Latin poets drew from their Greek predecessors, they sometimes drew style and subject matter, and they often drew meter. I don't think anyone in this room would disagree with that. One need only allude to Horace's famous quip, 'Greece, though captured, cap-tured in turn her savage victor.' *Graecia capta ferum victorem cepit*, to put Marius into a Hellenist context. So yes, perhaps Marius was sim-ply that: a devoted Hellenist, of a peculiar sort, adopting particular Hellenist meters for his particular poetic goals, whatever those may have been. This has more or less been the extent of Marian scholarship for hundreds of years, and it's rather unsatisfying, I think you'll agree. Now allow me to change tracks for a moment. I do promise I have a destination in mind."

Chris took a sip of water and shuffled his pages around. Tessa simmered with anger and terrible, searing regret. Her mind raced for a solution, some way to wrest the situation back into her control, but Chris was taking from her the one thing she had going for her: the element of surprise. He was going to reveal the findings, and he was going to be loved for it.

"Prosody," he said. "The patterns of rhythm and sound used in poetry. To me, personally, it is most sublime when the symbolic meaning of a word or idea can be reincarnated, somehow, in the physical expression through which that idea is being conveyed. Take, for example, the inimitable Jackie Wilson in his 1967 hit 'Higher and Higher.' The height of Wilson's love is denoted by his words: *Your love, lifting me higher.*' And these words are conveyed along waves of sound whose frequencies are themselves ascending—otherwise known as a rise in pitch. Note how the lyrics culminate an octave higher between the end of the first verse and the beginning of the refrain." Chris sang, "*Your love, lifting me higher . . .*" His voice then rose an octave. "*You know your love.*"

Chris had an excellent voice, the legacy, Tessa knew, of being forced into choir at an early age. It seemed overly theatrical to Tessa but she saw where he was going with his line of thinking.

"There are many people who don't see beauty in this, I'm given to understand. Why us literary critics find it sublime when a poem or a song finds some physical expression that embodies its meaning, I do not know. Perhaps it has something to do with the age-old concept of the spirit and the body, which finds its corollary, here, in the abstract and the concrete, the ethereal meaning of a word and the thing in itself, whether that physical thing be the waves of sound, or impressions of ink on parchment, or light pixels on a screen.

"The Latin poets knew this, and perhaps Latin best exemplifies these prosodic possibilities, which abound in a language unencumbered by so many pesky articles and prepositions. Take the line from Ovid, *Metamorphoses*, describing Python after Apollo has shot him full of arrows: *innumeriis tumidum Pythona sagittis.* The lyric locates 'swollen python' within the 'countless arrows,' a representation in word order of the image we have of the snake, like a pincushion, stuck with Apollo's feathered agents of death. How would this appear in English? *Uncountable swollen python with arrows?*

"Catullus Eight is one of those other extant classical Latin poems written in limping iambs. In true Hipponax homage, it is an invective poem, invective towards both Catullus himself and Lesbia, who has rejected him. *Miser Catulle, desinas ineptire / et quod vides perisse perditum ducas.*" Chris recited the two lines again in Latin, emphasizing the length of the syllables at the end of each line, and the rhythm of the iambs that preceded them. The iambs bounced along smoothly, symmetrically. The trochee at the end of the first line, and spondee at the end of the second, fell arrhythmically, awkwardly. And yet one could see that with five, ten, twenty lines, the meter would bestow a sort of rhythm, a sort of odd, indeed limping grace. Then Chris translated the two lines, in a curt and monotoned way, to emphasize how very boring it sounded in English: "*Wretched Catullus, stop being a fool, and consider lost what you see as lost.*

"It is a wonderful poem, but does it have what we've been discussing, this instantiation in form of its meaning? No, I don't believe so. Catullus Eight is exactly what scholars have tepidly, gingerly called Marius: a Hellenist imitation. Catullus is imitating Hipponax, for Hipponax also wrote invective in limping iambs. Just as Virgil imitated Homer's dactylic hexameter, so Catullus does here. 'Greece, though captured, captured in turn her savage victor.'

"For a presentation on Marius, I have quoted remarkably few lines from his work. Hardly any of you would have thought I'd quote the lyrics of Jackie Wilson, and not the verses of the poet ostensibly under discussion; or perhaps you would, if you'd suffered through one or two of my lectures before. But in any case, we now move on."

Chris wielded a clicker from under his pages on the podium and turned toward the projector screen behind him, which presently flickered into an image of two lines of limping iambs and their translation underneath. He read, " 'But lest you be unaware of the rules of shearing off land / here you will learn how one is made two.'

"This opening to perhaps Marius's most cryptic poem—in which he describes a landmass being separated from another—is also written in limping iambs. Why? The poem has nothing to do with invective and is in fact decidedly didactic in tone. The other poems—a love poem which seems to occur in the same landscape as the didactic one, and another with perhaps a Daphne-figure fleeing Apollo, also do not fit within the category of invective, with the exception of a few lines voiced by the Daphne-figure. And so, the one place of sure footing that scholars felt they had established in the dark room of Marian scholarship, that Marius was imitating Hipponax wholesale just as Catullus did, is really not so sure at all. It is, in fact, precarious, wobbly.

"Allow me just to give some details of this archaeological discovery I alluded to at the beginning of my talk, in what I'm certain seems like eons ago." A few chuckles. The audience seemed to be hanging on his every word. The device made an audible click and the projector screen now lit up with an image of Marius and Sulpicia's epitaph, and the sketch Lucrezia and Tessa had made of the missing pieces. There was a murmuring in the audience.

LAPIS BENIGNE DIC PRECOR VIATORI
CVIVS POEMA CANDIDA SIT IN FRONTE
QVORVMQVE AMORE NVPER OSSA GRANDAEVO
PERVSTA LEVITER VRGEAS IN AETERNVM
SIC SVLPICIA MARIVSQVE SCAEVA CONIVNCTI
TRIPEDES BICIPITES CORDE VIXERANT VNO

KIND STONE I PRAY TELL THIS TRAVELER

WHOSE POEM IS ON YOUR PRETTY FOREHEAD

AND WHOSE BONES, NOT LONG AGO SCORCHED WITH LONG-LASTING LOVE

YOU PRESS GENTLY ON FOR ETERNITY?

THEY WERE SULPICIA AND MARIUS SCAEVA, HUSBAND AND WIFE

THREE-FOOTED, TWO HEADED, AND ONE IN HEART THEY [HAD] LIVED

"Let me quickly add some background. Isola Sacra, an island just outside of Rome and very near Ostia, is an active dig site. This is a photo of an epitaph recently excavated there. As you can see, it is of a Marius Scaeva. Of course, there may have been numerous P. Marius Scaevas in the Roman Empire. Publius is of course a very common 'praenomen.' Marius is a common 'nomen,' from the gens Maria. The 'cognomen' Scaeva was again common. And yet, it is the name of his wife, here, along with the meter of the poem, that conquer even the most obstinate skeptic, who would say the Marius buried therein is not the Marius who authored these poems."

Chris clicked again, and an image of Marius's entry in the *Suda* appeared on the projector.

Publius Marius Scaeva. A poet writing in choliambs. He married Sulpicia.

More murmuring in the audience. Chris smiled.

"Isola Sacra is an island artificially created by Claudius in the first century, when he dug a canal from the Tiber to the Mediterranean in order to admit larger boats to Rome's main port, known as Portus. Recall the lines from Marius's poem discussing the amputation of land, and the formation of an island, and you will begin to see some of the resonances between these once-cryptic verses and what would have been Marius's surroundings."

There was an energy in the room now; not a single gaze strayed from the podium. Listeners who had previously only affected this role were now riveted. Some scribbled furiously. Most wondered at how they could have not received word that this discovery had been made. Tessa could see George Bale tapping his fingertips rapidly against his uplifted brogue.

"Prosody," Chris said. "What does this all have to do with the limping iambs of Marius's verse? There is one additional discovery made within Marius's tomb, which I think will lay the foundation for further inquiry, but undoubtedly establishes a peculiar similarity between Marius's physical form, as it once was, and his choice of poetic meter."

Cold beads of sweat had begun to form on the back of Tessa's neck. She felt one plummet between a crease in the collar of her top and seep into the satin fabric against her back. When Chris clicked again and an image of Sulpicia's femur appeared on the screen, she felt she had been struck physically. It was on a white table, with a ruler next to it for size. "Marius's femur," Chris said, and paused. Had she heard him correctly? Had he said Marius? Chris continued talking and now had a laser pointer in hand, but Tessa's confusion roared in her mind; she could hear nothing he said. Had he said Marius's femur? She wanted to ask the woman next to her, but she did not need to, as Chris continued.

". . . no osteologist myself, it has been made known to me that Marius's femur is a very odd femur indeed. These striations you see here," he said, running the red dot along the cut marks on Sulpicia's femur, "are undeniably the serrated edges of a surgeon's saw." More murmurs in the audience. "And again, I apologize I have to be the one to demonstrate this, so nonexistent is my expertise, but the area you see here"—he denoted the femur's stump—"shows amputation-related bone remodeling." Someone gasped audibly.

Chris smiled and then wrapped up quickly, "In any case, this recent discovery encourages the view that Marius's choice of meter was somehow related to what would have been a literal limp, a literal alteration in gait that cannot be disassociated from his verse. What we have here, in other words, is in some way the prosody of his human form. Further research will be done as the excavation is finished and I'll answer any questions to the extent I can then, thank you very much for your attention and the time you've given me today. Following me will be Tessa Templeton, who was also involved in this discovery. Thank you very much, that is all."

A moment of stunned silence prevailed and then thunderous applause. Chris smiled, bowed, and took his pages with him off the podium. Sotheby-Villiers stood and shook his hand when he sat down. Colm Feeney reached out and patted him on the shoulder. He turned and accepted thanks from everyone around him.

Tessa's confusion lasted only so long. Assuming her sensory faculties had not betrayed her and Chris had just proclaimed that

Sulpicia's femur was actually Marius's, she would have the opportunity, now, on stage, to correct the record.

Liam took the podium again. "I'm certain we will be very interested to hear more from Tessa Templeton. A recipient of an O'Neill Fellowship, Tessa is a doctoral student at Westfaling College where she expects to receive her doctor of philosophy in a few short weeks. Please welcome Tessa Templeton."

Some of the energy in the room had subsided; Tessa understood this as she approached the podium, pages in hand. Nonetheless, eyes followed her expectantly. There was a tangy, acrid taste in the back of her mouth; nervousness; a dampness in the armpits of her blazer. Its tag was abrading the skin along her spine, itching her. The room was quiet.

"Well, first I'd like to thank Chris for that riveting talk," she heard herself saying. "I'm quite pleased to see him make some of the associations he has made in his paper, for reasons that will become apparent shortly. And I will no longer have to take pains to introduce these broader questions about meaning and rhythm and the word-as-object, as Chris has already done so for me."

Tessa would now have to skip over the section of her paper that revealed the Isola Sacra discovery to the audience, as well as the epitaph, and the resonances between the amputation and the verse subject matter. "As Chris noted," she said, "when we take as a premise that the author of these poems lived on or near Isola Sacra, new meanings become available. Of course, there is the 'terra amputata' poem, in which a description of the canal can double as a description of bodily amputation. Knowing what we now know about the remains discovered in the tomb, it seems impossible not to identify this once-abstruse section as a dramatization of the author's own amputation through the metapoetic landscape of Isola Sacra, as well as a highly personal account of unimaginable pain."

Tessa's voice faltered slightly. None of what she had written would have the same impact; it was just more detailed analysis of what Chris had presented. But she kept reading.

"Other new meanings are activated when considering Isola Sacra and the region around it. Indeed, there are two lines that have given scholars a particular amount of trouble since the Renaissance, and they translate as follows: *Were I deaf to you, my love, like a diver / to the bird's call.* What have others made of this simile? Most have believed it abstruse. That it is tackling a question of sound and the ability to hear is certain; but why a person who dives would have a hearing impairment is less evident. One might imagine the surface of the ocean as a membrane between the diver, who is submerged, and a bird, which is airborne, perhaps a gull. Scholars have certainly done so: in 1904, Williamson hypothesized as such to clarify why a diver would be separated from the sound of a bird's call. It's a little unsatisfying as an explanation.

"As a quick aside, to illustrate how out of favor Marius has been in this century and the last, the word used for diver is *urinator*; *urinator*, in addition to being an unfortunate homonym in English for 'one who is micturating,' refers specifically to salvage divers in ancient Rome. Salvors, you may call them. Diving weights, used by these brave amphibians, have been discovered amongst numerous shipwrecks along the Mediterranean coast. These were men tasked with retrieving goods from sunken ships around the harbors; there is epigraphical evidence for a *collegia*, or guild, for the *urinatores* in Isola Sacra, though Williamson would not have known that because the region was not excavated until the 1930s, when Mussolini's 'grandeur of Rome' propaganda machine had the paradoxically humanist result of excavating nearly all of Ostia and Isola Sacra in four short years. That no one specifically made the connection between *urinatores* and the guild at Isola Sacra since Mussolini is illustrative of how little attention has been devoted to the works in modern scholarship. But even if one had, it wouldn't have told you very much until quite recently, when the excavation"—here she added, "that Chris alluded to," and returned to her pages—"began to tabulate certain osteological abnormalities in the population of male skulls found in the necropolis in Isola Sacra."

Tessa used the clicker to navigate to the first image from her slideshow, that of the temporal bone specimen with evidence of auditory exostoses. "There are sixty-two male skulls from the necropolis that show evidence of what we now call surfer's ear, and no, I'm not going to sing lyrics from the Beach Boys to illustrate this point . . ." No laughter. She continued. "Surfer's ear is a bone protrusion in the ear canal, a bodily response to repeated exposure in cold water. Early results suggest that these bone protrusions in the skulls at Isola Sacra are skeletal markers of occupation: the *urinatores* being the excavating team's prime candidates. As you know if you've ever used earplugs in a plane, or been in a relationship with the sleep-apnea-afflicted, occluding the ear canal does make it more difficult to hear." A chuckle, but she felt that she was losing the audience.

"*Were I deaf to you . . . like the diver / to the bird's call,*" she continued, "takes on new meaning when we suppose that many of the *urinatores* could have been at least partially deaf, their hearing canals interrupted by overeager bone formation. The simile is more poignant—dare I say better—if we can take it to mean a permanent separation, actuated by biology, as opposed to a temporary separation, actuated by submersion underwater."

Tessa felt the room—it was lukewarm. Chris had covered this major theme. She would not get her point across with her written speech. She faltered and read the next sentence. "My purpose here is to establish a framework for investigating the tomb at Isola Sacra, the verses attributed to Marius, and this extraordinary opportunity we have . . ." She stopped. The room spun. George Bale's brogue drooped from his kneecap. Phoebe Higgins scrawled a note on a sheet of paper. It occurred to Tessa that she could not merely claim Sulpicia as the true owner of the femur; she sensed instinctively that she would have to do so in memorable fashion. To do so tepidly, timidly, to do so in a fashion that would spare Chris embarrassment, in a fashion becoming of a junior academic, a dissertation advisee, would enable him to recover from his error and continue smothering her role in the discovery. She would not be smothered. She needed to embarrass him. To render any association he had with Marius and Sulpicia so fraught as to require him to be amputated from them.

As the silence dragged on, three, four seconds, eyes began to look up at her. Liam's expression traversed from mild boredom to concern. A pearl of sweat clung to the small of her back. She carefully turned her pages over and placed them facedown on the podium.

"Although Chris would have you believe from his talk that he was, is, or will be involved in this discovery, that happens not to be the case at all," she said, addressing the audience now directly, without the medium of her written words. "You may ask him how he came upon it; presumably Edward Trelawney is bringing him in as an outside expert. Suffice it to say that Dr. Trelawney would not have been aware of Marius and Sulpicia had I not brought it to the attention of his site manager. I don't say this to stir up trouble; the narrative of how any of this occurred is not proper for this context and I'm content if it's lost to posterity. I do not want to fight about it here."

Tessa could feel discomfort take hold of the room immediately at her change of tone. She didn't care. She didn't look at Chris, but she imagined that his expression would betray no discomfort. Not yet.

"But what I'm not content to lose is the story of Sulpicia. And perhaps I really should have begun by correcting the record on one important fact. The femur that Chris refers to did come from the *mausoleum* that Marius was buried in, yes. But it did not come from the *sarcophagus* that Marius was buried in. There were two people buried in the mausoleum: Marius and his wife, Sulpicia. The femur, which I agree is the linchpin in this broader question of meter and the mysteries of the poetry's meter, was Sulpicia's femur, and therefore it is the prosody of Sulpicia's body, and Isola Sacra as written is a metapoetic landscape of Sulpicia's experience, not Marius's." Tessa felt her face flush; she could tell all eyes were on her now, and the only thing she could hear was the sound of her voice. The room was quiet. Phoebe had put her pencil down. Tessa's eyes locked with Florence's for a fleeting second.

"How Dr. Eccles came upon this misinformation, I do not know. You will have to ask him. However, he seems to have made the assumption that the femur from Isola Sacra belonged to Marius, purely because it came from the same dig site as Marius. I can assure you, this is not the case. Photographs, forensic drawings, and carbon sampling will eventually bear this out. I know this because I was in fact there." Tessa flipped the clicker so that the image of her in the white tent, holding the femur, appeared on the screen. "This was taken less than a month ago. You'll have to forgive my choice of parka for the day." Someone laughed nervously.

"I don't know how the transmittal of data to Dr. Eccles occurred, but it seems that in trying to scoop the discovery Dr. Eccles mishandled some key details." Some chuckles, but mostly stunned silence. Tessa chanced a glimpse at Chris, and noticed that his face had whitened considerably.

"Does this mean that Sulpicia was the true author of the poems we have associated with Marius? I believe so. It would seem that

Chris Eccles believes so, even if he would try to convince you otherwise, so strong is his conviction of the link between our limping
poet and their limping iambs. But who was Sulpicia? What can
we know about her? We know that women composers of memoir
and poetry existed in ancient Rome; we know Agrippina's memoirs
existed, as well as literati sufficient to provoke Juvenal's misogy-
nistic anger at them. And yet why is it that we have only six short
poems by a Roman woman, and a few fragments and spurious
letters? Why does the writing of almost no pre-Christian Roman
woman survive? Do mice and mold and fire and flood simply prefer to consume women's writing? Are they the ones with taste?" A
volley of laughter.

"I only want to bring your attention once more to Chris's mistake, because it serves as a moment in which we can see, in almost
real time, a sort of common error that repeats over and over again in
history, and which I think offers a potential avenue for understanding why we do not have more of these works.

"Let me draw a parallel, if I may. Indeed, there is yet another
poet named Sulpicia in the written record, who may in fact be our
Isola Sacra Sulpicia: we know of her through two epigrams of Martial (she was a contemporary), and a healthy tradition of reception
in late antiquity. She is apostrophized with the likes of Catullus and
Sappho in a poem by Sidonius Apollinaris in the fifth century, and
around the same time an anonymous author assumed her identity to
write sixty hexameters, titled *The Complaint of Sulpicia*, widely available in your copy of Baehrens, Volume IV, published 1882.

"Do not be impressed that I have this Sulpicia's entire extant
oeuvre memorized. It grieves me to say that it consists only of two
lines of iambic trimeter quoted in the scholia of Juvenal by the
Renaissance scholar Giorgio Valla, to provide commentary on an
unusual word: *cadurci*.

si me cadurci restitutis fasciis
nudam Caleno concubantem proferat

If, when the mattress straps have been restored
it might reveal me lying naked with Calenus.

"May we just pause to note the reappropriation of lust, which generally functioned as a male prerogative, as well as of the male gaze, in this fragment. Sulpicia is offering us an image of herself in the nude, in a subjunctive clause wishing that the bedding be repaired so that she and Calenus may resume their copulation. Posthaste.

"It is no wonder that this Sulpicia did not make it through the monasteries; can you imagine devoting valuable copying time to a woman writing verse of this nature? The transmission of literature from roll to codex was laborious and operated under a selection process that's more familiar to us than that of mold and mice and fire and flood—a human one, with human biases. When I say it is miraculous that we have even these two lines of Sulpicia, I do mean, specifically, that it is a miracle that Giorgio Valla took Sulpicia to be a man—his commentary attributes these lines to one Sulpicius, and it was another century before Pierre Pithou matched the lines with the poet Sulpicia, alluded to in Martial's epigrams, married to Calenus. So we must be thankful for Valla's ignorance, which preserved so unwittingly these two precious trimeters.

"Indeed, we find ourselves in a paradox in which ancient Roman women's work that survived only survived because it has been mistaken for a man's. In this context, we must be thankful that Sulpicia, the wife of Marius, has been taken for Marius since at least the *Suda*, until the present day, even. God forbid she be identified as the true author of these verses; we wouldn't have them today. And we should thank Chris now, for illustrating this so vividly." She chanced another glimpse at him; he was shaking his head, as if in shame of her. On her behalf. Well, the crowd would judge.

"I'll end my remarks here. Thank you," she said.

Tepid applause from most, resounding palm slaps from Phoebe and George Bale and a couple others she didn't recognize. Tessa collected her pages and walked as fast as she could back to her seat, feeling suddenly exposed and uncomfortable, the unimaginable words she'd just uttered following her like an aroma. Chris had his head resting against his fingertips, shaking it. His eyes were closed.

Liam's voice from the podium microphone followed her as she found her seat: "Well, we have much to digest, but one more speaker before dinner. Please welcome John Fitzwilliams . . ."

Applause. The Hellenist whom Chris had switched with took the podium.

"You really went after him," the woman next to Tessa whispered.

"I had nothing to lose," Tessa said.

"Well, good for you, dear," she said.

Tessa hoped the audience had taken her point about Chris's mistake. She hoped they would recognize that Chris had baldly stated that a body part belonged to someone it didn't; that they would not be able to forget what he had done. She glanced at the back of his head several times in the front, a few rows ahead. Before Fitzwilliams started speaking, Chris got up from his seat and promptly left the room. Tessa felt shame, fear, and triumphant rage as she sat through the presentation, glad that Chris was gone, but wanting to escape the crowd as soon as she could.

After the presentation, amid the applause, Tessa darted out of her seat and crossed the proscenium into the hall. She was nearly to the exit when she heard footsteps behind her and then a voice.

"Tessa, won't you come to dinner?"

She turned and saw Phoebe Higgins following her.

"Of course I'd love to, but . . ." Tessa looked desperately through the plexiglass into the porter's office, seeking some excuse.

"If you won't come to dinner, at least walk with me for a moment."

Tessa didn't feel she could disagree with this. Phoebe took her arm and led her to the glass door and outside onto St. Giles'. They walked for a few moments, the sun casting long shadows to their side, the road relatively quiet, an occasional bus. Phoebe fumbled under a nest of scarves in her bag for something.

"That was quite a presentation," Phoebe said.

"Thank you?"

"I felt I knew more about what was happening behind the scenes than most may have," Phoebe added. Amid the scarves she produced a package of cigarettes and offered one to Tessa, who accepted it. They halted on the pavement while Phoebe lit them. The first classicists were emerging from the Ioannou Centre behind them, off to dinner. Tessa took a drag and they kept walking toward Broad Street.

"Come to UCLA," Phoebe said, without preamble. "Harris Withers is retiring, so an assistant professorship will be opening."

"You're kidding," Tessa said, inspecting Phoebe's face for humor. "I don't understand, you need to source a position for the fall?"

"The following fall," Phoebe said. "But you could adjunct next year, then I can push for you as an internal hire." Phoebe took a long drag as they walked; Tessa wondered if she could take this as an endorsement of her presentation. Her nerves were still kicked into high gear.

"Well, I'm grateful for your interest," Tessa said, wanting to make Phoebe understand her gratitude.

"Don't be. You deserve it."

"I take it seriously."

"Good."

"Can I think about it?" Tessa asked.

"No," said Phoebe. "Of course you may."

Phoebe took another long pull; streaks of smoke billowed out of her mouth in the wind. Tessa wondered how much of a hardship the last three cigarette-less hours had been for her. Chris couldn't even sit through a long movie without a cigarette.

They were approaching Cornmarket and Broad; Tessa led the way along Broad Street to avoid the crowd on Cornmarket. Boxed flowers, hanging from a streetlamp, were blooming. Tessa proceeded cautiously. "Obviously, if I took an adjunct position and then wasn't hired by you, I'd be worse off, career-wise," she said.

"I know," Phoebe said. "It's a slight risk. But the best I can do."

They reached Turl Street and turned right.

"How do you think the crowd took my presentation?" Tessa asked.

"Chris will be embarrassed. Overall, we were spellbound. Of course, one keeps hoping to find more female authorship from the period. I assume you were correct about Sulpicia, in which case, the presentation will be very memorable indeed."

Tessa nodded and was very pleased to hear this confirmation.

"But I worry that Chris will become a gatekeeper to the excavation, whether you like it or not," Phoebe said. "Inevitably, you have to decide what matters to you. Is it Marius and Sulpicia? Is it Chris? Is it a tenured professorship?"

"How would Chris matter to me?"

"Well, sometimes one desires retribution more than what is good for one. And sometimes anger, even justified, is a mask for something else."

Tessa snorted. "That's not what's at issue."

"Okay," Phoebe said. She took another drag. Had she said it slyly?

"Believe me."

They walked in silence for a few moments, and at the end of Turl Street, Phoebe began to turn left toward the Old Bank.

"I'm going the other way," Tessa said. They actually had gone the complete opposite direction from where she lived.

"You're sure you wouldn't like to come to dinner?" Phoebe asked. "I'm sure you'll be asked after."

"I need to decompress," Tessa said. She didn't want the pageantry of a dinner right then.

"That's fair," Phoebe said, stubbing out her cigarette. "Well, the show continues in the morning. I'll see you tomorrow." She smiled; Phoebe didn't smile very often, and it seemed like a wince, but Tessa appreciated it. Tessa waved, Phoebe walked off toward the Old Bank with Magdalen Tower in the distance, and Tessa took Queen Street the opposite way. Not wanting to run into all the conference-goers, she began to twist through the backstreets toward Jericho.

She felt harried and tired and annoyed and elated. Bold and intimidated, confused and clairvoyant. She had struck a blow against Chris, a legitimate blow. When it surfaced that the femur belonged to Sulpicia, her presentation, however dramatic, would be remembered favorably. When the world came to understand Sulpicia as the author, she would be remembered as the one who had made this observation; no one else.

And yet, it saddened her, all the words she had not been able to read. She produced the folded pages from her blazer pocket; they were heavily creased now.

Yes, she had sacrificed any entertaining of the notion that Marius had written the poems.

It is tempting to view the metrical choices as the stylistic innovations of a devoted husband, giving verbal expression to his wife's pain

Nor any of her more thorough arguments for Sulpicia-as-author

The feminine surda, the domestic imagery

She had never gotten to her read on the hearing poem.

Appropriate word choices for a poem about the sensory experi-
ence of hearing, whose rhetorical objective is to dissolve the bar-
rier between lover and beloved

"Deaf to you," meaning unable to read your world into mine

They are two, but one

Soon she was on Gloucester Street, behind the White Rabbit; she walked around the Ioannou Centre and then back onto Woodstock Road, toward her flat. By the time she opened the wrought-iron gate and punched in the code at the entrance door, she was exhausted. She would lie down. She would sleep. She clambered up the staircase to the second-floor landing and, ignoring another red sign on her door, keys dangling from her hand, attempted the lock. The key jammed. The lock looked oh-so-slightly different. There was sawdust on the floor. She tried it again. Jam. She read the notice.

•   •   •

TESSA THRUST the small iron gate open and strode out onto the pavement, the gate clanging loudly behind her against the brick retaining wall, shattering the quiet peace of the side street. She was on her mobile, yelling something. Chris couldn't make it out. She'd startled him. He had thought she was in for good. He was idling at the opposite end of her street in the Fiat. She wavered for a moment in front of her gate, listening to whoever she was speaking to, then set out slowly toward Woodstock Road, away from him. He shifted into first gear.

He had seen her crossing Walton Street as he had been heading south, toward Hampshire. He'd doubled back and followed her with no real intention in mind, simply lost in thought and emotion, grateful that she'd skipped the dinner—the idea of her assaulting him with their colleagues over Pinot Grigio and roast duck was almost too much to bear.

The Fiat teetered forward just as Tessa turned the corner onto Woodstock. He accelerated to the end of the street and then slowed; at the corner he peered down Woodstock Road. She had hung up. She tarried near a bench in the sun, then sat on the coping of a wall next to a shrub. She still wore her blazer and slacks from the presentation and had her shoulder bag. Her hair glinted in the light. She stood up and tried a new number on her mobile, crossed the street, and walked toward the Old Parsonage. A car blew its horn behind Chris. He turned the corner and brought the Fiat to a stop in the bicycle lane on Woodstock. Tessa was just ahead of him, standing. He rolled down his window and started clapping. She turned.

"The last thing I need," she said.

"Joking. Tessa, come, now."

She put her mobile away and took a step toward the car.

"You skewered me good and proper," he said.

"It was merited."

She was leaning down, her arms wrapped around her stomach, clutching her blazer around herself.

"You didn't go to the dinner," he said.

"I cannot believe you tried to take credit for that," Tessa said. "That was a new low for you." She looked down into the window.

"If you had been the one who broke it, Trelawney would never have let you near the site again. But I broke it, so he'll have to take it up with me."

"Sure," said Tessa.

"I'm trying to save you from yourself," Chris said.

Someone slammed the roof of his car—a biker. "Arsehole!" Chris heard as the biker zoomed past.

"I'm rather in the way here," Chris said.

"Where are you going, anyway?"

"Hampshire," he said.

"Of course," said Tessa, lifting her hand to her forehead. "I forgot."

Chris shrugged. "Can I help you get somewhere?"

"Not unless you have a crowbar and a screwdriver." She rested her hand on the roof of the Fiat.

"You lost your key?" Chris asked.

"It's a little more complicated than that," she said.

Tessa explained that she had spent her rent money on a flight to Copenhagen to meet with Greta Deloitte about the *Suda*. Chris nodded, recalling the Danish Air ticket in her inbox, and was incensed when she explained that her lessor had changed the locks.

"But that's absurd," Chris said. "How could things have got that tight with you? I could have lent you money."

"We haven't exactly been on the best of terms, Chris," she said.

"But to be thrown out on the pavement like some tramp." He was overcome with a strange emotion, an indignation, even, and a searing sadness that Tessa would not turn to him in a time of need. "But Tessa, please, you know what I'm going to suggest."

"ARSEHOLE!"

"I'm not staying at your house, Chris."

"Tessa, I won't even be there. No one is using it. You must. You can't afford a hotel, clearly."

She wavered.

"Get in, please, for the love of god," he insisted.

"I just insulted you in front of everyone in the community," said Tessa.

Chris shrugged. "I don't care."

"And you just attempted to derail me again by taking credit for a discovery that I made."

A young girl, probably a sixth former, rang her bell at them loudly as she approached from behind, slowly, in the bike lane: *cling cling cling cling cling*. Her eyes bored into Chris's in the rearview mirror. He sighed. Tessa gave the girl the finger and the girl scoffed, horrified, and pedaled around them.

"Thank you," Chris said.

To Chris's eternal happiness, Tessa went around the front of the Fiat and opened the passenger-side door. He pulled out into the car lane and made a quick right back toward Jericho.

"Didn't find another unwilling recipient of the Beinecke?" Tessa said.

It was on the backseat.

"You're the only unwilling recipient I want," Chris said.

He slowed at a speed bump, then accelerated to the intersection of Walton.

"You know I'm sparing you a lot of choice words because you're on your way to your mother's," Tessa said. "And I understand the situation is serious."

"I appreciate your restraint," he said, smiling. "I can see how difficult it is for you."

"Can you take anything seriously?"

He didn't feel the need to respond to this. Yes. No.

Chris double-parked in front of the house and reached back for the Beinecke as Tessa got out of the Fiat. Then he thought twice and left it there. He followed her to the door and let her in, rushing ahead to make the house look like less of a terror before she saw it.

"I would offer you one of Diana's jumpers but I'm afraid there are none left," he said, rushing up the stairs. "You're welcome to use anything of mine upstairs," he shouted behind him. In the bedroom, he snagged jumpers and trousers and books off the floor, dumping them into the mostly empty top drawer of the dresser. He hastily made the bed and then realized she may want her own sheets; he yanked those out of the linen closet in the hallway along with a towel. There were no extra toothbrushes—tragic that Diana had taken all of hers with her. Soap, shampoo, there were extras— but the idea of Tessa in his shower nearly felled him with emotion. It was something about the ordinary, domestic image. He leaned against the hallway wall for support. Back in the bedroom, he thought he could smell something off but wasn't sure—he tied off the hamper and left it. He really did need to be going to Hampshire.

"Sadly there aren't any extra toothbrushes," he called on his way downstairs, his hand gliding along the balustrade. At the base of the staircase, he saw her in the kitchen, facing away, toward the French windows, a glass of water in hand. She had shrugged off her blazer. The top she wore was sleeveless, white, soft-looking. The sight of her bare arms filled him with desire; she was so achingly beautiful.

"Well," he said, his throat dry, approaching. "You know where everything is, mostly. Text me if you can't find anything."

She turned and leaned against the kitchen island, one hand on her opposite forearm, the glass of water in her other hand. "I guess I have to thank you," she said. "Obviously I will be out of here tomorrow."

"Please take as long as you need," he said. He stepped into the kitchen. Tessa stood there, the sun streaking in from the garden, a silhouette. In her work clothes, like Diana would have been after a presentation, an image he'd seen thousands of times, locked in by habit, as if in amber. A strange wave of emotions threatened to overtake him.

"Are you okay?" Tessa said. "Are you crying?" She didn't step nearer to him, as Diana might have.

"No, god, no," he said. He took off his glasses and rubbed his eyes.

"I'm not going to hug you," Tessa said, still not moving. The bottom of the glass clinked on the counter as she set it down. "I *am* sorry about your mother."

"Of course," Chris said. "Spare key is in that drawer just behind you." He gave her one last look. "If you get around to it, the flowers in the garden could, you know . . ."

"I will," Tessa said.

．　　．　　．

IN HAMPSHIRE, Connor was naturally unamused that Chris turned up two hours past when he was due, but Chris had prepared for this with a £200 cash tip. Diana had left nearly £68,000 in their joint checking account—chump change to her—and Chris was intent on spending as much as humanly possible before it occurred to her to do anything about it. Connor was due back in two days, on Sunday, so Chris would be with Dorothy for the next two nights, if she made it that far.

"She's meant to get her antibiotics at four, but I left it for you," he said, patting Chris on the shoulder.

If possible, the pallor in his mother's face had increased. Her lips were very cracked, and on the nightstand was a sponge in water that Connor had been using to hydrate her.

"Chris, I want to take a walk in the garden," she said. Chris was touched that she had called him by his name.

"Tomorrow, Mum," he said.

It was dark by this time, and Chris hoped the garden would look spectacular the next day. He poured himself a full glass of Laphroaig and sipped it as he did his chores. He fed Neddy, Betty, and Feddy, and put a pillow next to his mother's bed, where he sat on the floor and checked his email on a hot spot from his phone— of course his mother didn't have internet. He imagined his coevals in this situation—George Bale, for instance, who had been raised on a country estate in Northamptonshire, no doubt kitted out with wireless internet by now and servants to change his mother's sodden linens when she would pass her last days.

Chris could not help feeling massively proud of Tessa, and that pride was tinged with the poignancy of the moment. His mother's wet breathing. The warm peaty scotch. The bed that he used to burrow into for warmth, between his mum and his dad. It had seemed large as a park. He imagined Tessa as a child, a bright bundle of joy, a bobbing blond head on a sun-dappled beach in Florida, a tropical climate, a beach that undulated gently into the waves, not like the coasts here, the sheer chalk cliffs, the headlands whose drop would leave you long enough to see your life flash once, twice, maybe three times before you shattered the water's surface—at that speed, a surface like tempered glass. Freezing water whose churn would feel like thousands of knives. Florida. From Latin *floridus*. Florid, flowery. He wondered what flowers she had had in her garden as a child, and what it would have been like to see their colors.

Dorothy slept till nine again. Chris had administered the same dose of morphine early in the morning. She didn't want to eat anything—she only took some water, and it was clearly difficult to swallow. She was barely producing waste, and this worried Chris, though Connor had warned him it might happen. Occasionally she winced with pain, and she insisted on holding Chris's hand, but when he prepared to give her the next dose of morphine at ten, she told him no.

"Please, Mum," Chris said. "Let me give it to you."

She pressed his palm lightly with her fingers. "No," she said. "Wait. Take me to the garden."

Chris looked at the wheelchair, which Dorothy had barely been able to hold herself up in before. "Mum, I don't think you'll be able—"

"Chris," she said. "Take me to the garden."

The wheelchair seemed to swallow her, she had shrunk so much. She breathed slowly, so slowly. He placed her feet on the stand so that they wouldn't drag, and slowly he began to push her through her house, into the kitchen, and to the back door. Sunlight cut through the open window, motes of dust and tangled threads and dead cells teemed in its shafts. When he opened the door, bird-song, and the garden's fragrance. Dorothy was smiling through her pain. He doubled back to the bedroom for a blanket—it was a slightly chilly April day—then he wheeled her the rest of the way into the garden.

The daffodils had wilted, and he knew he would need to clear them away. But the primroses had bloomed, and the tulips, and without the weeds clogging the garden their lovely shapes popped. Dorothy had been at work before she fell ill. He wheeled her farther into the soil, and she ran her finger along the felt-like whorl of a ranunculus. He admired the red azalea, whose color was impossible for him to miss. Dorothy smiled.

"You did well, Mum," he said, kneeling next to her.

She sat like that for a while, feeling the flower. Then he heard what sounded like a sob. He saw wetness in her eyes, which startled him—she had such little hydration left.

"Mum, what's wrong?" he said.

"I shouldn't of sent you away," she said.

Chris's heart churned. He recalled the dormitories, how they turned the heat off between terms.

"You was just a little boy," she said.

He felt his grip on her hand and the wheelchair back tighten. Her hand was so delicate, not like the burnished metal spindle supporting her. Yet she was in so much pain already, his grip didn't seem to frighten her. God, this was the path he had taken to the barn, that morning, when he struck her with the rake. His grip tightened. She was so young then, so large. She looked younger now, suddenly, like a young woman. He breathed, a long deep breath.

He said, "Do you remember when I used to ask you the colors of the flowers, because I couldn't see them?"

Dorothy began to say something. Chris leaned nearer to hear. "Sometimes," she said, "I told you they was different colors. From what they were."

Now Chris was there again, holding his mother's hand. He laughed. "What's that one?" He pointed at a magnolia. "A nice pink?"

"Yes, a blushing pink," she said, smiling.

"And this one?" He pointed at a primrose.

"Lavender," she said.

He laughed. He could not detect the truth. "I used to think I could smell their colors," he said. He put his nose up against the petals of a tulip. Its smell was perfect. He was taking in its essence. The cell structures that made it reflect light the way it did—they affected its fragrance. It was something he could pick up on. It made mutinous loops in his sinuses. It conjured every good thing that existed. "Is it yellow?" he said.

Dorothy nodded. He still could not tell if she was indulging him.

"Will you let out the kiddies?" she said.

Chris did so and brought his mother some feed for them. He left her alone with them in the garden, the three of them nuzzling her and licking her hand, so that they could say their goodbyes. Chris returned after a few minutes, and Dorothy made him promise to take care of them. He did.

"And the goldfinches, Chris. You always need to plant the thistle. They eat the seeds. And they use it to build their nests."

"I'll remember, Mum," he said.

Chris could see that his mother was exhausted, having spent an hour in the garden. She began to wince more and more. She was shutting down. She moaned softly. Neddy chewed on some of the wilted winter jasmine. Feddy had wandered off somewhere. Betty was back in the shack. Chris wheeled his mother to her bed and gave her the next shot of morphine. Exhausted himself, and hungover from the scotch he'd drunk the night before, he poured himself another few fingers, and eventually fell asleep, too.

• • •

THE FUNERAL WAS on a Tuesday. There were few mourners at the cemetery. A handful in black huddled around the coffin and the ditch; the hearse had been needed elsewhere and quickly drove off as soon as it had left its freight. A light drizzle pattered down. The vicar finished his final prayer and Tessa watched the few clods of dirt land on the surface of the coffin with a meek thud. They were using a shovel to toss the soil, and Chris bent into his work, sinking the shovel's face into the mound—dutifully left by the backhoe, which had borne the brunt of the labor just hours before—and tossed earth with impassive diligence into the hole. After a minute Chris handed the shovel to a fragile-looking old man in a deerstalker cap and severe black suit, who seemed barely able to manage the implement, whether due to age or grief, Tessa could not tell. Gradually the shovel traversed the small ring of mourners. Diana was not even among them.

Tessa had spent the past three days living in Chris's house and attending the rest of the conference. Her public scuffle with Chris had generated more than just a gossipy dinner at the Old Bank: before dinner George Bale had called Edward Trelawney about the discovery, and gotten a busy signal because Fiorina Miristakos was already on the line with him. Philip Barr had heard that a specimen, believed to be evidence of the first medically successful amputation in the ancient world, was arriving at the Royal Laboratory in London in two days. Edward Trelawney confirmed it belonged to one Sulpicia, wife of Marius, and by the time Tessa arrived at the Ioannou Centre in the morning for pastries the only acceptable topic of conversation was the Isola Sacra discovery. Tessa became the most sought-after person in the building. Meanwhile, she discovered later, Phoebe Higgins was expertly letting others know she had inside information that supported the theory that Chris had had little to nothing to do with the discovery, and had made a hasty presentation in an attempt to strong-arm Tessa out of the publication process. Phoebe even thought it possible Ed could be convinced to relieve Chris of his duties from the excavation.

On the surface, the conference had proceeded as normal, with each paper occurring in its accorded time slot and with interested and pointed questions from the audience about the topic. But in the seams, during the coffee breaks and the meals and at the water closet, the attendees talked mainly about the discovery and how it had occurred. Apparently Ed had not known for weeks that he had excavated a renowned poet—Marius was renowned now. Arguments were made about whether to call it Marius or Sulpicia's work. Rumors spread about where Chris had gone—that he was hiding out on his father-in-law's yacht in Corfu. Tessa navigated this landscape smoothly, understanding quickly that she *had* achieved what she had hoped with her speech, that once the room had verified how wrong Chris was, it turned on him, and without him there to defend himself, she was able to indict him as much or little as she liked.

In short, Tessa had spent two days methodically dismantling Chris's reputation, even going so far as to say, when others asked where he was, that she did not know, perhaps it had been embarrassment that had caused him to leave the conference—for could she herself really believe that his mother was sick? There had been no corroboration from any other source besides Chris that she was, and Tessa had decided to make it protocol to believe nothing from his lips unless it could be independently verified. When she received a text that Dorothy was dead and that Chris did not know how he could cope if Tessa wasn't at the funeral, at Hampshire Church on Tuesday the twentieth, she was in Chris's study, trying to word an email to Ed to petition him to terminate Chris as outside expert to the excavation. She had felt a stab of guilt.

Tessa considered all of these things as the shovel made its way to her. It had struck her as sad how few mourners there were when she first arrived at the church. She had not comprehended how desolate Chris's life was—had become. His wife was gone. He seemed to have no real friends. His origins were humble. The notion that he was on a yacht now seemed cruelly unfair—she believed it was George Bale who had said it, jokingly. George Bale, aka Lord Bale. Moreover, he had said nothing about the Case Western offer: not at the conference, not at his house afterward, and not in their brief conversations since. Her worst suspicions about him were unfounded. The guilt she now felt about Chris metastasized and seemed poised to overtake every recent decision she'd made in her life, things she had felt indignantly righteous in.

She'd been convinced she was right about Ben, since Ben was the one who had left her. Yet she'd barely thought of him since he'd left. He had never mattered to her, it seemed now. She'd been convinced that Claire was abusing her with her silence. But Tessa had extorted her sympathies for hard cash. She'd been convinced Chris had everything coming to him even though he was maybe in love with her, albeit pathologically. Tessa had even cast doubt on the existence of Chris's sick mother, whose body she was now helping to bury, whose body she was now literally covering with clods of damp, gravelly dirt, as the shovel had been passed to her, the last in the ring, its slightly wet handle and iron sheathing warm from the meager series of hands that had gripped it as it made its journey through those who had known Dorothy Eccles and had loved her. Tessa scrabbled for control over the wet rung. She thought of Sulpicia and how she herself had fastened upon her bones in elation, the way she had transacted on Sulpicia's body to achieve higher renown in a self-absorbed community of self-anointed keepers of culture, and she felt a wave of self-loathing so pulverizing she felt she might disintegrate and be swept away if a slight breeze picked up.

She had been bent to a dry and self-interested purpose. She felt wretched, and it showed on her expression, she knew, because when she looked up at Chris he was watching her with what seemed like pity and immense gratitude.

•   •   •

TESSA HAD BORROWED Liam's car to get there, a finicky black Honda whose interior smelled of old sports equipment. She followed the small motorcade to Dorothy's house, led by Chris in his red car. They all drove slowly; it rained; Tessa had never seen the downs before, and so she tried to take in the swaths of rolling land around her, tried to meditate on their beauty. She felt raw, unhappy, and desolate. She had believed she would discharge this last favor to Chris coldly and impersonally; it would be the last thing she did for him before severing him entirely. She had not anticipated her own vulnerability.

The motorcade occupied a stretch of two-lane road that became a narrow one-lane paved road. An empty cattle pen, abandoned, collected rust on the shoulder.

Chris's need for her had impressed itself upon her from the first text:

> If it's rather too much I understand. I'm not quite sure
> how to communicate to you how much it would mean
> for you to help me through this.

Tessa had been struck that he had used the word "much" twice in two sequential sentences. He would never do something like this ordinarily; he was too vain about his prose style. He was unpolished, he was raw.

Chris's car slowed in front of a gnarled elm tree where the narrow road branched; to the left was an unpaved lane with two bands of gravel and a streak of unkempt grass. The gravel ground audibly under Chris's wheels and they proceeded under leafy boughs amid the drizzle, which was forming muddy runnels along the road. After a few short minutes, she saw a building flicker behind some branches. It was small—a dark stone thing, brick and what looked like granite, and though it had a small gable, it resembled a block, enduring amid a small clearing, a wooden shed recognizable behind it. For a moment she could not help but associate it with the tomb. She idled on the gravel path and shuddered. They thronged nearer to it.

Tessa could foresee the fresh mud on the heels of her black sling-backs, so she parked as close as she could to the front door. The other mourners left their cars and headed inside. Chris stood beside his, seemingly unaware of the rain, drops collecting on the inside of his eyeglasses. Tessa rolled down the window. "Sandwiches and tea inside," he said to a thin, severe-looking elderly man as he hobbled inside. "Sandwiches and tea inside," Chris said to two elderly women. He was saying it like a prayer. They shook his hand and one hugged him. They stood in mud. Tessa listened to the rhythmic swish of the windshield wipers in her front seat, watched the fog for a moment, which wreathed the edge of the woods at the margin of the clearing. "Sandwiches and tea inside," Chris said to a heavyset young man with a goatee. Tessa rolled up her window and stepped out.

Given that Tessa had had no access to her flat, she wore exactly the same outfit to the funeral that she had worn to the presentation days before: gray slacks, white shell top, the fishbone blazer, and a pair of black slingbacks. She wore a parka on top, a transparent thing she'd found in Chris's closet, probably Chris's. She felt odd approaching Chris in this same outfit; looking back on the presentation, she felt like his executioner. Now she wore protective plastic, as if to repel the blood splatter. She squelched through the mud toward him, wondering if he would give her the same mechanical refrain. There was some regret for not at least offering him the comfort of a hug in his kitchen. She felt she owed him one now.

The plastic crinkled between them. A weird prophylactic that, for Chris's grief, was not an effective barrier. His desolation sank into her. "I'm so, so sorry," she said, and she meant it. She drank in the tangle of his emotions. The fibers of his blazer were soaked under her hands, but his back was warm.

"I thought I would be fine, but I'm not fine," he said

matter-of-factly. He lit a cigarette and offered one to Tessa. She wanted to go inside and be dry—her feet were already wet through her shoes. But she accepted it.

She wondered now if his grief was real. She felt it, as if it were hers. But did *he* feel it? Maybe he felt nothing. Maybe he was trying to draw her in. This proposition fascinated her; what did he feel, was he feeling? He sniffed loudly. It was hard to distinguish between tears and rain.

"You will be okay," she said. "Time heals," she lied. They stood smoking for a few moments. She felt they couldn't be farther from Oxford.

"Do you want to meet the sheep?" Chris said.

Tessa thought he was referring caustically to the people inside. "I guess it's about time," she said.

Instead of going inside, though, he began to walk around the edge of the house.

"Where are you going?" she asked.

He turned. "To meet the sheep."

Oh, literal sheep, she thought. Fuck it. She committed fully to the mud and skirted the house behind him. "Are you trying to avoid your guests?" she asked.

"These are the true intimates of my late mother," he said, a billow of smoke whipping over his shoulder. "But yes, I consider avoiding them a bonus." He unlatched a gate and shepherded her into the backyard. The shed loomed over it, a dark shadowed interior, in which she could hear scuffling, and from which she could smell animal and dung. This aroma mingled strangely with a powerful floral effusion. Whites, yellows, fuchsia, carnelian. Flowers, lots of flowers, none of which she had been able to see from the front of the house. A few bags of fertilizer and feed sat under a small tarp. A rake leaned against the shed wall.

"They don't eat the flowers?" she said.

"Not if my mother tells them not to," Chris said, reaching under the tarp and digging his hand into one of the opened bags. "Palms?" he asked.

Tessa held her hands out and he filled them with grain. They both stepped to the shed. The patter of rain on its roof was pleasing. One of the sheep approached from within the shed's gloom. She heard the rustle of straw.

"Tessa, meet Neddy. Neddy, Tessa."

A *baaaa* emitted from the puff of white hair.

"Reach your hand in," Chris said, "like this."

The tongue was surprisingly rough and abrasive, almost like sandpaper, but it was diligent and probing and strong.

"Neddy is not the brightest one. More of an Epimetheus. But he's upbeat, a good chap, a good lad. Betty and Feddy are more lucid creatures, and as you can see, they're grieving."

Chris tossed some feed in, and they heard a chapfallen *ba* from inside.

"Did you know that when sheep go to butcher they cut out their tongues?"

This was very Chris. To get a rise out of her. But he seemed to be also trying to get a rise out of himself. He lit a new cigarette. She was still working on hers. You're a weird, violent little man, she thought, for a moment. "It's called offal, Chris," she said.

"Yes, I suppose they're just meat at that point anyway. Perhaps we should have called one of them Philomela." He sighed. "I'm sorry for being morose."

"You have every right to be."

"It means so much to me that you're here. I can't even say." Now he sobbed, once. The sound struck her. "It means so much to me, that you can *comprehend* a fucking reference to Philomela. Even if it's sordid." He issued one more sob. Tessa felt herself move closer to him. Her hand reached around his shoulder. A gaping discomfort widened inside of her; but it felt good to be of some use. His grief was real. His grief was bizarre.

"Fucking Neddy and Feddy. Fucking sheep." He sobbed again, and then laughed sadly. "What's going to happen to them?" he said. A few tears flowed down his cheeks.

"They'll be okay," Tessa said instinctively. "You can have someone feed them."

"Fucking sheep. Fucking mutton. They're not going to live without her."

"You don't have to send them to the butcher, Chris," she said. Christ, she wanted him to stop crying. *Stop crying*, she wanted to say. She had forgotten how much she hated being in proximity to grief, being imposed on by the grief of others. Perhaps she had doubted the reality of his grief because she was resisting its imposition. She was entangled now in its web. His tears looked hot; the mist from the damp earth seemed to be rising from some liquid sadness.

"Generations and generations of shepherds. And this is all that's left?"

.   .   .

TESSA AND CHRIS came in through the back door, Tessa first, which led into the kitchen. Inside, Chris's guests were gathered around a coffee table in the front room. She heard soft chatter and the clink of teacups on saucers. They had found their own way to the sandwiches, too, it seemed, not that Chris appeared worried about a dereliction of hosting duty. The tall, wispy-looking man seemed to have picked up the slack, and he offered to take Tessa's parka when she came in, carrying her flats, which she set at the front door, where there was a mat.

"Nutley," he said, shaking her hand. "Alistair Nutley."

She gave him her name and her parka, then poured herself some tea in the kitchen.

In the front room, Tessa met Sophie and Lyra, who were both old friends and church members with Dorothy, and she heard how many of their friends had passed recently. She met Connor, the hospice nurse, who said that Dorothy had been like a mother to him, that she had helped restore his faith in God.

Chris sat on the swaybacked couch between Tessa and the long, reedy Alistair, whose thin, gnarled fingers curled paternally around Chris's shoulder. Her relationship to Chris went undiscussed, though she was told how good it was of her to be there. Chris talked about how this was the couch he had slept on for the past couple of weeks, how he could hear Dorothy from there when she needed something—he alternated between calling her Mum and Dorothy. As he talked Tessa felt their knees touch and he seemed to stutter when this happened, as if the touch had electrocuted him, and it occurred to Tessa that she hadn't been touched in weeks. There had been Isilde's forearm on the plane, and Greta had patted her on the shoulder in Copenhagen, but aside from that, nothing she could recall. She felt like one of those collector's dolls you leave in the packaging because someday they'll be worth something. When her knee touched Chris's she noticed that he seemed to draw strength from it, to talk more quickly and with more animation, and to slide nearer to her. No, she thought, no. But her power, which seemed to bestow life on him, was now intoxicating, and when she was asked how she knew Chris, she said he was her mentor. She told them that she studied classics, and Chris said that she had already eclipsed him, that he was constantly in awe of her abilities, and that she was going to take his job from him. He said it only half in jest, she thought, and suddenly everyone else in the room seemed to know that there was something between them. And it was odd because Tessa knew there was something between them, too, but she didn't know what anymore, exactly. She only knew that she still planned to send a poisonous email about him to Ed later on, and that she could somehow feel close to him in the meantime, could at least temporarily separate the person who harmed her from the person she'd known and cared about for years. His face looked sallow and haggard, his hair was still wet, and his white button-down was damp along the front where his blazer hadn't covered him from the rain; it clung to his skin. His appearance seemed to authenticate his need.

But he still talked with charm and added in small jokes that kept Lyra and Sophie smiling. He maintained his slick surface, which Tessa knew required energy, but she saw now that he derived the energy from her, that he was performing for her, most of all. After an hour, she knew she had put in her time and it would not be untoward for her to leave, but she remained, and had more tea, and even a sip of Chris's scotch after he and Alistair poured some, which warmed and fortified her.

Finally, toward the late afternoon, Sophie and Lyra agreed that what Dorothy would have wanted, were she there, would be to hear a song. Sophie, Lyra, and Nutley stood and debated which song, until Lyra insisted that Dorothy's favorite was one called "Shepherd of the Downs."

Connor insisted that he knew that one and he joined them standing. Sophie then asked Chris, "Won't you join us?" And Lyra insisted. "You had such a beautiful voice as a little one." It was not possible to tell from Chris's expression whether he welcomed their invitations—Tessa watched him closely. Finally Nutley coaxed him off the sofa and the five of them began to sing, right there, in the little front room, while Tessa listened. In the first refrain, Tessa began to feel chills along her arms. She thought that she could see saucers rattling on the coffee table from Nutley's baritone, and Lyra and Sophie's sopranos seemed to be bursting at the low ceiling, pressing for the open skies. Connor had sung the first line of the refrain, and the second had been sung as an ensemble—she had not seen them even coordinate this. Chris sang in a calm tenor.

> He drank of the cold brook he ate of the tree
> Himself he did enjoy from all sorrow was free
> he valued no girl be she ever so fair
> no pride or ambition he valued no care
> no pride or ambition he valued no care

Everyone took a breath and began again on the next verse. Nutley sang the first refrain this time, his neck wattling with emotion. Everyone's eyes were angled toward different corners of the room; they were communing in the sound. Tessa was able to gaze at them unchecked. She was no longer there.

. . .

CHRIS HAD TOLD HER that he would see her in a few days—he was staying in Hampshire to tie up loose ends with the estate—and the skies were clear by the time Tessa left the house. She was treated to a memorable sunset on her drive back to Oxford. The fog had lifted, the sun was falling—but it seemed not to fall entirely for a very long time, to be transfixed on the brink of the horizon, to be waiting for her to return safely back to Oxford before it let the night begin. Above her hung a few lazy clouds whose undersides shifted from orange, to pink, to blood-red, to an almost bluish color. She hit the outskirts of Oxford and drove up through Cowley, where Liam lived, to drop off his car. She found herself craving company; she didn't want to be alone. Was that a strange reaction to a funeral for someone she didn't know? She wasn't sure.

She idled for a moment outside Liam's flat, where she texted him to let him know she'd arrived. A pink curtain in a dormer window puffed outward on the second floor. It seemed remarkably peaceful. He emerged from the front door with his wife, Lara, in a breezy white dress and gold bangles.

Now, as Tessa put the keys into one of Liam's large hands, Lara said with worried eyes, "How is he?"

"You know, his mother died, so."

"Yeah," said Liam.

"He'll be all right," Tessa said.

"Liam told me about the conference," Lara said, and then added dryly, "We thought you two were getting a divorce."

Tessa noticed Liam cut Lara a look. "Slender, marmoreal thing," Chris had once described her. "She runs a food blog. Describes sourdough starters as 'life-affirming.'" What previously had been total apathy toward Lara curdled to dislike. Lacking an appropriate response, Tessa merely turned to Liam and thanked him again for letting her use his car. He wore a white button-down tucked into dark jeans, belt buckle gleaming in the streetlight.

"We could drive you back to your flat if you'd like?" he said.

Tess instinctively reacted against this—either him understanding that she was staying at Chris's place, or having to go through the charade of pretending to enter her own place. "I'm okay," she said.

"Really, it's no bother," Lara said.

It wasn't too difficult for Tessa to dissuade them, and after another thank-you they left for their dinner, or whatever social event awaited. Tessa walked in the direction of Magdalen Bridge, annoyed at Lara's remark. Of course she was aware of how they'd always appeared, she and Chris; that their absorption with one another had seemed like romance masquerading as intellectual chemistry. But she had taken some intensely private satisfaction in knowing that there was nothing going on, that Chris had found her purely by way of a paper she had written, that his marriage had been intact, that public perception is vulgar.

Yet what had happened at the funeral, exactly? Now she felt momentarily more at peace. The emotion seemed odd and she assumed transient, given she had no place of her own to live until May first, when her next stipend would clear, and that her prospects next year remained uncertain. But she felt that her preoccupation with her own prospects had altered. Perhaps it was death's ability to trivialize concerns that once seemed monumental. Maybe. But whatever validation she had been seeking, now that it was within reach, seemed far less desirable than it had just weeks before. And Chris, though a scoundrel, seemed to covet his position less than she did. This posture seemed more authentic, and perhaps worthy of emulating. She carried this strangeness with her all the way to Jericho, up St. Clement's and through the roundabout, over the bridge and along High Street, up Walton and to Chris's home.

Inside, she flicked on the lights and found her laptop on the kitchen island next to the Apollo and Daphne paperweight that Chris did, indeed, still have; it was the only one left in the house, in fact. It held down a stash of papers—Library Committee documents, she believed. It was a replica of the Bernini sculpture, in real marble. She picked it up off the counter and ran her hands along the smooth figures—Daphne groping for escape, Apollo clutching her, her body transforming already into the laurel tree she would become. It had cost her over fifty euros, and she recalled the way its

pedestal had jutted under her shoulder blades, stuffed into her knap-
sack, on the jetway back into Heathrow.

The quiet in the kitchen was tranquil but poignantly lonely, and,
standing there, Tessa felt an urge to compose a letter to Claire, an
apology letter, and to that end, the French window that opened onto
the garden caught her attention. She would write it in the fresh,
warm air. She returned Daphne and Apollo to their nest of library
committee papers and poured herself a glass of chilled white wine
from the refrigerator and stepped outside. The garden was fragrant
with flowers and damp soil.

She recalled the first time, three summers ago, that she had been
in the garden. It was June, maybe, and Diana and Chris were both
working at the round glass-pane table, on which had sat an assortment
of paperweights—granite and celadon, marble and limestone—they
were mostly sculptures of moments in classical mythology. Pali-
nurus falling backward off Aeneas's ship, Priam holding Hector's
corpse, in the manner of a pietà. Papers had been strewn all over the
table, for they were both reading funding applications, and Chris
was also marking several dissertation chapters, and it was breezy, she
recalled the sound of the patio umbrella billowing—one corner of it
was loose and it flapped around in the wind—but not a single page
was lost or disrupted in the twenty minutes Tessa stayed and chatted over tea. Tessa recalled a tangle of emotions—she wanted this
in her future, she was covetous of Diana's existence, but not of her
husband, no. It was something in how the paperweights had clearly
been collected over years, from all over; that these two people had
evolved into this space doing classics was something she loved.

She set her glass of wine down on the glass table. It was wet. The
umbrella was folded.

Inside, Tessa had trouble finding a towel. There were certain basic things that were missing in Chris's house, things that presumably had belonged to Diana. She took a few sheets of paper towel and came back to the table and dried it off.

When Tessa did finally open her email, she saw her unfinished letter to Edward Trelawney.

Dr. Trelawney,

Some of my colleagues mentioned they would reach out to you regarding whether it is appropriate for Dr. Eccles to serve as outside expert to the Isola Sacra excavation for guidance relating to the work of Publius Marius Scaeva. I'm reaching out to you directly to underscore my own qualifications to do so, following the formality of the confirmation of my dPhil in May. The importance of . . .

She thought of Dorothy, for a moment, watching her undermine her son. She closed the email with a small spasm of discomfort, as if banishing a bad spirit. She took a long gulp of the white wine, which was pungent and strengthening, craning her neck back slightly, seeing the vines climb the trellis up the brick wall, the second-story window, the shadows of the soffits in the night, and when she finished she set the glass down, and in front of her, in the lightly billowing curtain behind the French windows, stood a figure.

"You left me there," a familiar voice said quietly. It was Chris.

"I thought you were staying for a few days," Tessa said into the darkness, which seemed impenetrable. She had thought, for the briefest second, that he was Dorothy's ghost. She closed the laptop and extinguished its white light. He stepped through the threshold into the garden and wavered against a rack of gardening tools. Her eyes began to adjust. He held a bottle and a glass.

"I'm sure you're aware of why I came back," he said.

There was something accusatory in Chris's manner that made her both afraid and emboldened. "I can't say that I am," she said. "I'm quite sure you said you needed to stay in Hampshire. Did I mishear you?"

"Please don't mess me about," he said. The bottle clinked on the glass counterpane as he set it down. Her eyes were adjusting. "Sitting there with you today, you must have known. And you left me."

Chris's need paralyzed her momentarily. Because she did know, had known. "Chris, do you think I'm the best person to be with you right now?"

"How could you ask that?"

"Surely it must have occurred to you to be with family."

"What family?" he said. "You're the thread by which I'm hanging."

"Chris," she said.

"No, I have to tell you." The pitch of his voice rose. "Because today I was thinking about the soul and whether or not I believed in it."

"The soul?"

"My mum was devout. All her life. I wasn't. A friend of my mum's used to say, you may as well believe in God, because what do you have to lose? If you believe, and He's real, you'll go to heaven. If you don't, and He's real, no heaven. You lose nothing by believing, so why wouldn't a logical person do so? I thought he was very clever, and for a while I told my mum I believed in God and such was my reasoning, which of course infuriated her. 'There's no love in your heart, if those are your reasons,' she said." He took a drink from his glass. "If I have a soul, though," he continued, "I know, if I do have one, it exists for you. I—whatever I am—will simply cease to exist, if I lose you. I might still have legs and arms, and a tongue and face, but I would be a shell—a nothing. Which is how I know that

I'm not just a body, I'm not just matter. That's how I know, how I believe. It's more than just me."

She didn't move for a moment, didn't let her body betray that she had understood or even heard him. "I don't know why you're saying this to me," she said.

After a silence he said, "Because I'm in love with you."

Tessa was aware initially of a coiling in refusal and annoyance, which tempered to gratification, which traveled back to annoyance and skepticism. She could feel heat moving to her face. "I know that you think you are," she said at last. She could barely make him out. They were two voices.

"*Think* I am? I *love* you, Tessa."

"You're not in love with me," she said.

"You consider it an infatuation? An infatuation of three years?"

"You don't need to define it as something else to know it's not love."

"You're idealistic."

"You sabotaged my career and lied to my face about it."

"To be nearer to you—"

Again, Tessa's color rose in annoyance. "That's why you wrote the letter," she said.

"Yes."

"Thank you for admitting that. Although it's a little late. I guess that shouldn't be a surprise to me."

"I lost my sense of boundaries."

"You did indeed."

"I'm in love with you."

"Whatever sensation you think you're experiencing, Chris, it's not love. God help the person you're in love with."

"Tessa, you understand nothing."

"Please don't argue this with me, Chris. You don't want me to be angry with you right now."

"You'll not persuade me that I don't feel what I feel. And what's more, you've known it." Chris's figure moved through the shadows toward the table. "You use my feelings for your own ends when it suits you, and as soon as it doesn't, you act surprised, you pretend to be naïve, as if you never encouraged anything. I don't say that to excuse what I did, it doesn't, I say it because it's the truth." The garden chair opposite Tessa creaked as he sat down, and the bottle clinked against the table. "You knew all along how I felt about you."

No, Tessa thought. She would not concede this, even if she knew it was true. She would concede nothing to him. Her anger rose, and for a moment she was blind to the fact that he was mourning. "In fact, Chris, you're the last person I know who I could ever believe to have loved me. Any stranger on the street has had a more positive effect on my well-being than you have. Forget the pragmatic consequences your letter had on my future, a betrayal that I perhaps could eventually find it in myself to forgive you for; the words themselves have been scarred into my consciousness. *You're a joke,* that letter says. *You've spent the best years of your life on a joke, that would be funny if it wasn't so sad."* She took a breath. "And when I first read them, part of me thought this couldn't be real, but part of me also knew that it was, not because of the Garamond or the signature, but because I knew it represented your true opinion about me. It was the most authentic thing I've ever seen or heard you express, because you thought I'd never see it!" She breathed again, becoming aware of fresh waves of anger toward Chris, becoming aware of new feelings toward him, or at least the proper way of articulating them. He sat in dark silence. "That rec letter is the closest thing to a love letter you'll ever be capable of—full of enmity, spite, supercilious, demeaning dejection of someone else's value with an underlying purpose of pinning them even more certainly in your control. That's love to you. That's the most real thing I've ever seen you do, Chris. That's your truth. And the fact that you're able to disguise it as love to yourself is maybe what's most appalling." Tessa stopped now because she could no longer ignore the bitterness that emanated from his dark silence. "And it's too bad, it's unfortunate, because you had meant something to be me before, Chris. Don't you understand that?"

She was breathing hard and her face was hot—red, she was sure. She had sat up in her chair and was preparing for what he'd say next, so she could rebut it. She wished Dorothy had not just died, for she resented any strictures of decency on her temper. She was in the midst of a sumptuously hot flash of anger. The bottle of whiskey made three glugs into his glass, and its edges gleamed momentarily in the moonlight. He would say something like, *I'm elated finally to know your true opinion, now that you have little to gain from me professionally.*

"And who do you love?" he asked.

They were not the words she had expected, and they struck her with a peculiar force, engrossed as she had been that day with how few people she had in her life, with how few people loved her—or, if she was truly honest with herself, whom she herself loved. No one, she thought. She said nothing. Her reflections went undisturbed for several moments, and then for several minutes. Finally she heard the bench scrape against the garden tile as he stood up, and without a word he went back inside.

This is who we are, he'd said to her in Edinburgh, and in some ways he was right. It was appalling that he thought he loved her, and yet it wasn't at all. She hardly had a firmer grasp on the vagaries of interpersonal romance. Each time she'd felt herself on the brink of another person, she'd turned away. The love that she idealized, by which the borders of one's person dissolved and integrated with some other essence, had only ever been approached through the vehicle of poetry. She thought of the ride to Edinburgh in Chris's Fiat, the damage it had inflicted on Ben, and the scythe-like potency that overcame her onstage as she heard her own voice, commanding, over the nervous pound of her heart. For a moment in time, she had been perfect. She would always have chosen to go, and perhaps her ideas of love merely exceeded the enclosures of reality and the flaws of individual people, including but not limited to herself. It seemed certain, though, that some threads of her entanglement with Chris had been real, some moments shared beyond the confines of that reality.

She had called it a love letter as an insult, but it struck her now how primal the rec letter had been, in addition to insidious, and the idea of the letter *as* love letter was so academically interesting that she felt herself momentarily transfixed by the concept. Still, Chris doomed her to arrive at new revelations in his presence. To some degree, it was exhilarating, the lengths he'd go. What her own desires consisted of, she could hardly say; was it not a type of love, that he would risk his own position, in addition to compromising hers, to have her near him? Would she not be utterly repulsed right now, if she felt nothing for him in return?

Inside, Chris was making up a bed on the couch that occupied the middle of the living room—between the kitchen and the garden doors—the couch she had slept on weeks before. He did it wearily, hunched over the cushions, tucking the sheet under them, but slowly, without any force, as if the cushions might overpower him.

"You don't have to do that," she said.

"It's for me."

"Oh," she said. He managed to work the sheet around the corner of the cushion and glanced at her as he patted it down.

"Chris, I'm sorry. I shouldn't have lost my temper." She took a step closer to him, and stood with her head slightly down, staring intently at the gnarl in one of the wood floorboards.

He tucked the last corner of the sheet around the couch cushion and turned to face her.

"I've lost a wife. Maybe a job," he rasped. "And now my mother has died, who I can't so much as mourn because you're still the only thing that matters to me. Can't you see that?"

She nodded and took a step toward him, but stopped.

"And yet, I love you. I love you even when I'm the one you trample upon, and it's not because I'm a masochist, Tessa. I'm just in love with you."

Tessa continued nearer to him as he spoke. They were close enough to touch now, but not touching.

"And it's very you to seek to undermine the emotion I'm trying to express, rather than simply tell me you don't feel the same way. I thought I might make my declaration and find out how you feel, but instead I'm met with skepticism and disbelief. An interrogation. The epistemology of love. You don't need to take such pains to reject me. Tessa, just shoot me down. I know you have it in you."

She closed the remaining space between them and took his head between her hands, pulling his face into hers. She found his lips and, after pressing his forehead hard to hers, she kissed him deeply, forcefully. He tasted of tobacco and scotch. She wrapped her arms around his neck and rubbed her temple against his, pulling herself in closer.

"You know I can never do what you tell me to," she said.

He gave her short kisses on her mouth and inhaled deeply between each one, as if she had literally deprived him of breath, and they took small steps together just to balance. She could not recall, since junior high, ever kissing someone her own height, and she wondered that this novelty hadn't occurred to her before she had initiated the kiss. He continued to breathe deeply, now through his nose, an audible huffing, though he moved her gently, as if a great effort were being expended to hold himself in check. And as he lay her down on the couch, his arm on the small of her back, it was thrilling how far he'd go for the possibility of a moment like this. *Rocky beginning. Witnessed an improvement in her work ethic. Culminating . . .* the thought of the letter as love letter was so perverse that it actually heightened her pleasure as she wrapped her legs around his torso and pulled herself against him. She began to unbutton his shirt—the same white shirt he'd had on at the funeral—and his expression now was similar to the one he'd worn as she'd shoveled, though more agonized by lines in his brow and a shaking in his jaw. As she ran her hands through the wiry tangle of hair on his chest she realized that she really would be capable of working herself into a state of arousal. Her last words to him had opened a lane of opportunity to say, *Don't remove my trousers*, or *Don't remove your slacks*, as a rhetorical command to do just those things— but Chris was beyond words. The sheet was already loose off the cushion, its elastic band cinching up in her hair, and the extemporaneous nature of what they were doing furthered her desire. She began to peel off her own slacks and Chris immediately did the same to himself, his belt buckle clinking on a floorboard. He removed his briefs also, hastily, one of his dark-haired legs flexing for balance as he pulled them off his other foot, and he bounced around the room for a moment and produced a condom, then climbed back on top of her and they were in the moment once more. She was again surprised at how good it felt when they actually commenced, soon she was panting along with Chris, and for a short time she forgot herself completely. When Chris began to slow, she pushed against his shoulders to suggest a turn and they did so, she got on top, and she watched him—the lights were all still on, his eyes closed, his face in a paroxysm of something— pleasure, pain. What did he think was happening?

"Do you love me?" she asked.

"Yes," he panted.

Tessa found herself stopping. Was this cruel? "Wrong answer," she said. His eyes opened, questioning. She disentangled herself from him and stood. "I'm going to get myself another glass of wine," she said, "and you can think about whether you want to give me a different response." She sensed his disbelief and the tendril of need pursuing her as she walked to the kitchen, retrieved a glass from the cabinet, and filled its bowl with the cold sauvignon blanc.

"Tessa, please don't play games with me right now," he called.

She pinched the stem between her fingers and returned to the couch where he lay.

"This isn't a game at all. I'm entirely serious." She watched his face. He was a wreck. He was weak.

"Tessa, you don't understand, I need you."

"I do. I understand, Chris. I understand perfectly. You can have me. But let's be clear about our terminology here."

He grabbed her arm and the wine sloshed in her other hand.

"Do you love me?" she said.

"Yes!"

She struggled against him, wine spraying over their skin as the glass dropped to the carpet; she pushed his neck as hard as she could, slapped his face. He shouted in pain.

"Do you love me?" she said.

"Yes, I love you, I love you."

She tore her nails down his back.

"Tessa, please. Please." He struggled for her again, and as his hands fumbled around her hips she found his ear with her teeth and bit the cartilage hard, grinding her teeth into it, so that he yelped again and she tasted his blood.

"Stop lying!" she shouted into his bleeding ear.

"Okay. I don't love you."

They paused. She searched his eyes. His hands slackened from around her wrists.

"Do you love me?" she said.

"No," he said. "No, no," almost whispering, like a mantra as they began again. Pleasure radiated through her body. She buried her face in his neck, his grainy cheek against hers. She continued faster, kneading into him, the spark of arousal still very much alive, the shadowy texture of her own desire beginning to coalesce. They lifted as they pulled into one another, the glow of pleasure enlarging even as it fell inward, enveloping her, locking her in its dizzying ether. She felt her hair being gathered into his right hand and his mouth murmur into her ear, "I love you," and then abruptly she was yanked backward by her roots so that she saw the ceiling and its bright recessed bulb. His left hip crested hers and he was on top, his hand pressed against her face. In an instant her mind shifted, a vast distance opening between them while he drove against her. She struggled to coax herself back, but could think only of the sting along her scalp, her surprise, and the ease with which he'd once wounded her, because "love." She groped for some new signal of this love's power but found merely the weight of Chris's form, the heaving breath from his lungs. She pulled away and looked for his expression, but he was a blur, a silhouette in the ceiling's light, a corona of mussed hair.

"Chris."

She pushed against his shoulder and he paused. "Yes?" she heard. Space and time were returning rapidly.

"This has to stop," she said.

She began to disentangle herself from underneath him. For several ominous seconds he did not move or speak. Then he said, "The marriage is over."

This comment confused her for a moment—so distant had

Diana seemed, having failed to show for the funeral. "I hadn't questioned that," she said, maneuvering out from under him, which he
neither helped nor impeded. Tessa regained her feet and stepped
away, brushing back her hair, trying to gather her thoughts. Everything seemed to have lagged behind the accelerating moment, and
now the scene hung in an unnatural stillness. He held his pose while
she retrieved her slacks and dressed quickly; he was nearly prostrate,
statuary. She suddenly wanted to leave, though of course she had
nowhere to go.

"Unless you tell me not to I'm going to sleep upstairs," she said,
struggling to regain control. "I'm sorry," she said, and then added, "I
thought you were going to be gone." None of these phrases seemed
equal to the rush of her beating heart, and he continued to stare into
some vanishing point in the torsion of white sheets. "I'll find another
place tomorrow."

Chris raised his head so he could see in front of him but did not
turn his gaze toward Tessa's. For a second she questioned herself;
why she had stopped it. "Well, good night, then," Tessa said when he
didn't respond. She fetched her laptop from the garden outside and
walked soundlessly past him and up the stairs.

In the bathroom, she washed her hands and inspected herself in
the mirror. She looked thin and pallid, but her face was red, and her
hair raised. She brushed it down with her hand. Who are you? she
thought. Her stomach lurched with confusion and violence. What
he felt was not love, it was something else. Something she did not
know, did not know what it was. Get a grip, she thought.

•   •   •

TESSA WOKE EARLY the next morning, showered, and slipped
out the front door before Chris could rise. She hustled through the

subdued Jericho side streets in a sort of fugue. The sun feathered painfully against her eyes. In the Porter's Lodge at Westfaling, she inquired in a low voice with Max whether any student rooms were open at the moment, in the off-term. He squinted at her for several seconds and then said, also in a low voice, that a fresher had been sent down just before Easter. He produced a key attached to a labeled fob. "Till Saturday."

In her office, Tessa sent an email to her management company requesting access to her flat and assuring them that her rent was forthcoming. She checked her inbox—she had not dispatched the email to Trelawney she'd been drafting when Chris arrived, and its image sent her into a mental spiral that she could only arrest by banishing it to her drafts folder. This left space for her to observe that she had one hundred and eight unread emails. She felt capable only of dealing with simple requests. A new student had asked for the suggested reading list for his Trinity term Latin paper, a simple matter of attaching a file from her hard drive to the reply email—and Tessa was momentarily grateful for a task she felt up to completing. Several more small undertakings were discharged. She went down Staircase 7 and made coffee. She attacked the stack of unread emails again. There was one from the *Classical Journal of America*, which had never received her edits on the article that had been accepted for publication. The question of the footnote was still outstanding.

Dear Ms. Templeton,

Though we have been looking forward to publishing your work in our fall issue, we are nearing the point where we need to make final decisions. Please let us know how you would like to respond to the edits that were suggested for publication. In particular, the issue of how to footnote your discussion of Apollo on page four.

When Tessa reread the relevant section in the pdf that was attached, it suddenly did not seem so important to her. If others had believed that Ovid referred to Apollo's love for Daphne without any sense of irony, that was their prerogative. She was willing to make this concession. Yes, she had read Yelland. They would not be able to shout that she had never consulted Yelland. She was ready to move on. She was ready to move on to Isola Sacra. She responded with a short email, saying that she accepted all edits (the rest were cosmetic), and that she very much hoped she had not exceeded their time frame.

There was, of course, the additional question of her offer to work at Westfaling next year, and the lack of any other enticing opportunities. A decision about Westfaling had to be made by May first, a mere ten days off. Phoebe's offer to adjunct at UCLA would be a step down, at least for a year, and was in no way a guarantee she would get the tenure-track position opening the year after. But Tessa felt that it was more than just pure pragmatism that made her want to remain at Oxford. UCLA would make it difficult to have any continuing association with Isola Sacra. Staying at Westfaling would be tricky, but would enable her to access the excavation again. That's where she wanted to be, she realized. Oxford and Isola Sacra. She could untangle how she felt about Chris somehow; she felt that she could keep him under control, especially as he had less and less power over her future. His recommendation letter, after the Sulpicia discovery became formalized and circulated, would not be required. It would not matter. It would merely exist, as a token of his true opinion, his innermost burning. And what had happened last night, exactly? The encounter seemed blurry, indistinct. Some impression of pleasure lingered, despite what he'd done with her hair, which had occurred so abruptly as to resist interpretation, and whose roughness in retrospect it was difficult to gauge. Her eyes alighted on the meat tenderizer key chain, the gift from Ben in the mug on her desk, attended by a distant sadness for things past. Nonthreatening, even amusing, but only because he never handled her without tenderness, as though she were fragile, some delicate glassware he might break.

Several hours later, Tessa crossed front quad toward an early dinner in Hall, her slingbacks clapping the pavement under a warm April sky. A voice called behind her, "Tessa," before she'd reached the shadow of the archway, and she turned to find Selma, the office administrator. Selma jogged to catch up, her stockinged thighs straining against a black pencil skirt. "Sorry to bother," Selma said, short on breath. "But I haven't got your work visa sorted. One of the forms needs a signature from Chris."

"Okay," Tessa said, waiting for more.

"He's not responded to me in weeks—I thought you might send him word?"

Tessa took in Selma's harried expression and felt a pang of responsibility. "His mother just died," she found herself saying, feeling almost protective, the insulation between life's menial tasks and his bereavement.

"Oh, poor thing," Selma said, her eyebrows contorting in concern. Tessa knew this fact would now spread through Westfaling almost instantaneously.

"He's around, though," Tessa said. Some of her things were still, in fact, in his house. "Do you have the form?" she asked. "I can probably take care of it."

"At my desk," Selma said, relief washing over her face. She beckoned for Tessa to follow her. "The Home Office keeps a strict deadline. I'd hate for your future to be dashed 'cause of a bit of paperwork."

· · ·

AFTER A QUICK MEAL Tessa walked back to Jericho with Selma's pages in her bag—an application for her certificate of sponsorship, on Oxford letterhead, lacking only Chris's signature. She wondered how Chris was holding up. He needed space to mourn, perhaps. It wasn't unlikely that he would return to Hampshire for a period. The last rays of sun were trickling over the horizon when she arrived at his door, produced the spare key, and went inside.

Light leaked down the staircase into the dark vestibule; she made her way into the kitchen—the trash was gone, and the floor had been mopped. A breeze ruffled the pages under the Apollo and Daphne paperweight on the kitchen island. The mop was out, leaning against the dishwasher, which was running, and it smelled of cleaning solution, and the floor was spotless. There was even a box of latex gloves next to the sink. The French windows were half open at the opposite end of the living room. "Chris?" she called. The curtain billowed. She walked past the couch, which was still unmade, though the rest of the room had been cleared and aired. There was Chris at the round table outside, typing away on his laptop, his face bathed in digital blue light, a mug steaming next to him. He wore a clean white undershirt, and his hair looked just slightly damp from a shower. He looked good, refreshed, revived, a sight that encouraged Tessa's belief that he was reacclimating. She felt her shoulders relax. She hadn't realized, even, that she had been tense.

"There you are," she said, as she pushed open the door.

"Ah, and there *you* are. How is Westfaling? Is it still there?" he said cheerfully.

She smiled. "Still there, amazingly. You look . . ." she searched for a word.

He raised his head.

"Clean," she said.

"You're unerring in your observation," he responded.

She took one of the wrought-iron chairs across from him and put down her bag. She wasn't sure that she wanted to tell him, now, that she was going to accept the Westfaling position. It would be difficult to ask for his signature without doing so, however. "And back to your diligent self," she added.

"I'm always diligent," he said, and took a long sip from his mug. He put it down and stared at her.

"What?" she said, reaching into her bag for the paperwork.

"You never told me about the job," he said. His tone was less jocular, but still somewhat playful. Tessa's eyebrows rose. So, Phoebe had mentioned the UCLA position to someone at the conference, who had probably sent him an email about it just now. Could it have been Liam? Chris probably wouldn't think that she would take an adjunct position over a lectureship at Westfaling. She let go of the pages.

"How did you find out?" she asked.

"I have my ways."

She shook her head and laughed lightly.

"I'm still head of classics at Westfaling College, you know. Despite your best efforts."

"And despite yours," she replied.

He chuckled. "Well, of course you're not going to take it?"

"Well, why wouldn't I?" She expected him to say that it would be bad for her career, which was how he would normally couch his arguments. But he seemed more open, more vulnerable to her now.

"After what's just happened with us?"

"What's just happened with us?"

"I'm in love with you, Tessa."

"I'm sure you mean that in an ironic sense."

A bird sang in one of the treetops. Some of the early foliage rustled lightly in the breeze.

"You know there's a deadline for accepting Westfaling's offer," he said, with a bit of annoyance in his tone now.

"I do know," she said.

"You can't string us along forever," he added.

"No, just until the deadline."

He stood up from the table, his chair raking the garden tile.

"So you haven't forgiven me."

Tessa laughed. "I don't even know how to begin to answer that."

He gave her a look of growing frustration and shook his head. "You're babbling nonsense."

Tessa sighed. She saw that she would need to have a longer conversation with him before he signed the papers; that boundaries would need to be reestablished. "Do you mind if I make some tea?" Tessa said, standing up.

Chris followed her inside. "Will you please decline them tonight so I can have some peace of mind?"

She went to the kitchen sink and filled the kettle. She nodded at him to see if he wanted any and he shook his head.

He lingered around the kitchen island for a moment, then said, "I've just heard we have a fresher coming next year, who's from Florida, like you, studying classics. Tell me that's not marvelous?"

"That's marvelous," Tessa admitted.

"Tessa, there are things at Westfaling that other places don't have," he said.

"I'm only too aware of that, Chris," she said.

He ran his hand along the hem of his T-shirt. "I found a thousand more quid for you next year. From the vice chancellor's fund. You won't have any trouble with a visa, it's going to put you over the minimum qualifying level. I know it's not tenure-track, but come on, have you ever been to Ohio, you'd hate it."

You mean California? Tessa thought. The words were on the end of her tongue, when she remembered the Case Western email. She took a step back. All at once the horror and certainty descended upon her. He was on the other side of the kitchen island. Papers, paperweight, et cetera between them.

"Tessa?" Chris said, coming around to her. He offered a hand. She swiped it away. "Are you all right?"

She gathered herself. The kettle began to bubble. Her hairs stood on end. "How did you hear?"

"Come, now, Tessa. You know how small this world is."

"What are you talking about?" she said, advancing on him now. "How did you hear it, Chris?"

He placed his hands in his pockets. He said very clearly, "Fredericka told me. Sotheby-Villiers. She's friendly with their chair. She wanted me to extend her congratulations, actually."

Tessa looked closely at his face. She couldn't detect a single abnormality; it was so difficult to tell when he was lying. She wanted to memorize the tics he made when he said this, for when he might lie in the future, but she couldn't for the life of her find one. He took his glasses off and rubbed them with the inside of his T-shirt. He put them back on and looked her straight in the eye.

"What?" he said.

"I'm going to give you the opportunity to change your story."

Chris scowled. "How do you mean?"

"That's impossible Fredericka told you that."

"Why do you say that?"

"You're lying to my face."

"Tessa, stop. You're making a fool of yourself."

"If I were you, I'd be very careful about the way you speak to me," Tessa said. He took a step back. He looked affronted. "It's impossible someone told you I was accepted at Case Western, because the only piece of information that's ever said that came to my account from a fake address that I created."

Something in his face did alter now; he flinched.

"I'm going to give you ten seconds to admit what you did or I swear to God, Chris, I will prosecute you. Ten," she said. "Nine. Eight. Seven." The kettle began to shriek. "Six. Chris! I will take you to court."

"Okay," he said. "Okay, I did it."

"You're going to fucking jail!" she shouted.

"No, Tessa, wait," he said.

Tessa's skin crawled. She had to leave. She stalked past him toward the door, but then recalled her bag, with her laptop, in the garden.

"Tessa, please," he said, following her. "Let me explain."

"Get away from me," she said. She marched through the living room to the garden, her world spinning. She clenched the handles of her bag and took it inside through the French windows.

"Tessa, please."

Chris was imploring her to give him an opportunity to explain. He took her arm and she whipped it away. She got to the kitchen and he ran in front of her, closing off her path.

His face was altered yet again. Now heaving with emotion. He seemed on the verge of tears.

"Let me through," she said.

He took a step closer and made to wrap his arms around her, but she held her hand up between them.

"Tessa, come back to me," he said.

"Chris," she said. She was unable to process it yet. She put her hand on his forearm—he clung to her. She dropped her bag. "Chris," she said again, trying to push his forearms off.

He resisted. "Come back to me," he said. He moved his head off her shoulder and she saw his face up close, just in front of hers, and the agonized lines in his forehead were back, his expression, unseeing, possessed, the whiskers, the red blotch on his nose, the individual strands of his eyebrows, and in an instant his lips were on hers, his tongue burrowing into her mouth—she dropped her bag and pushed his head away with her hand instinctively, but his grasp around her tightened in response and she felt his forehead boring into hers, wedging her further into his arms. She writhed and pushed harder, and when she felt him overpowering her she became sensible only of panic. Their foreheads connected as he pushed her against the kitchen island, stunning her. Her body went slack. He lifted her onto the counter, scattering papers around them, and her hip knocked something heavy across the granite surface. She winced as his hands marched up her thighs. Somehow, the faucet had been turned on. She heard running water. Her forearm, splayed out, encountered the heavy and irregular object that she had displaced from on top of the papers. Her fingers wrapped around it. It was smooth and solid in her grip, and as Chris raised his head from her stomach gliding upward toward her face she swung it down with all plausible force so that the edge of its pedestal connected with his head. Chris's eyes swam. He attempted to steady himself with his hand, but the joint at his elbow folded and he disappeared behind the edge of the counter, followed immediately by the crack of the kitchen tile against his skull.

Tessa slid off the counter. "Chris?" she shouted at him. She prodded his crumpled leg with her foot. He was out cold. Her heart pounded in her ears. She crouched next to his face and turned it toward her, but his eyes were closed. What did you do? she thought, the referent of you unclear. It occurred to her to check his pulse, but she didn't know how, not at that moment. She put her finger, which had gone cold, to his neck, but she could only observe that he was breathing. She stood up and ran to the phone—she needed to call A&E. Did she need to call A&E? There was a landline in the vestibule and she took the phone off the hook and dialed 999. It rang. She looked back into the kitchen, where she could see his feet behind the kitchen island. "What emergency service do you"—a foot kicked, and then turned on its toe. Was he standing up? Tessa slammed the phone down and ran back into the kitchen. Chris was pushing himself up.

"Chris," she said.

He looked at her. His eyes were still glassy. She stood a few steps back. "You hit me," he slurred. Blood trickled down his forehead and matted in the thicket of his eyebrow.

She held out her hand. "Chris, you should sit down."

He touched his finger to his face and stumbled toward the vestibule, Tessa stepping out of his way. Was he coming for her? But no, he tottered past and toward the bathroom, holding his hand to his eye.

"Chris," she said again.

He opened the medicine cabinet and hovered for a moment, seemed to lose his footing, and then collapsed in a heap between the door and the lip of the bathtub.

"CHRIS!" she shouted. He didn't move. She had no doubt, now, that he needed an emergency room. Please be okay, she found herself saying as 999 rang again. She looked at her other hand, and saw to her surprise that she was still gripping the paperweight. She crouched down to put it on the floor. She had to consciously command each finger to release it. A sob threatened to overtake her.

"What emergency service do you require?"

"I need an ambulance as fast as possible," she managed. "My supervisor hit his head." She gave Chris's address. "He's unconscious."

"Just wait," the dispatcher said. "Don't move him."

Tessa hung up the phone. The water still ran in the kitchen. Chris didn't move or make a sound. She darted over to him and crouched at his side. He had fallen, crumpled, really, and she saw now that his hair was slick with blood. "Chris, wake up," she pleaded. There was a gash along his scalp. "Chris, no no no no. Wake up."

A minute passed. Tessa felt helpless. She was afraid *for* and *of* him, and it felt absurd to just sit there and do nothing. It occurred to her that Claire would know what to do. Claire was a doctor. She dashed over to her bag and yanked her phone out as she jogged back to the vestibule. She dialed Claire, praying she'd pick up, listening to each ring.

"Long time," Claire answered. The sound of her voice brought some sense back to Tessa.

"Chris is out cold, Claire."

"What?"

It only took a moment for Claire to register the urgency in Tessa's voice.

"He came at me and I hit him on the head with a paperweight," Tessa continued, "and he's out cold in his flat and I'm here and the ambulance is coming now."

"How long has he been out?" Claire asked.

"I don't know, three minutes. He got up and walked and then collapsed."

"He's breathing?"

Tessa crouched next to Chris again and put her hand under his nose. "Yes. What can I do? I'm just standing here." Her voice cracked.

Claire paused. The water ran. Tessa was about to speak again when Claire said, "Okay, don't move him."

"I know."

"How hard did you hit him?"

"I don't know," Tessa sobbed. "Hard. His arm, like, fucking gave out under him. His head hit the tile."

"Okay, okay," Claire said. "Is he bleeding?"

"Yes, there's a gash on his head."

"Okay," Claire said.

"What do I do?" Tessa said.

"Okay," Claire said. "Can you see any clear liquid coming out of his nose or ears?"

Tessa took a moment to process this. His ear facing the ceiling looked dry, albeit lightly chewed from the night before. "I—I don't know."

"Look."

"I can see one ear and it looks dry."

"Check his nose and other ear."

"I don't want to turn his head."

"You have to look without turning him."

Tessa got down on her hands and knees and looked—there was nothing under his nose. She got to his other side and ran her fingers under his ear, the one just off the tile. It was slick with something. She looked at her fingers—it was a clear liquid.

"His ear, his right ear," she said, picking up the phone, her voice mounting in panic. "What does that mean?"

"Okay, listen to me. How long ago did you call the ambulance?"

"I just called."

"Where is he?"

"What do you mean?"

"Describe his surroundings."

"He's—in the entry bathroom, it happened in the kitchen and then he stood up and wobbled and tried to get a Band-Aid or something and collapsed. He's on the floor, the door is right there—"

"Okay, stop—stop—could he have hit his head on the bathroom tile?"

"No, he fell when I hit him."

"Tessa, listen to me. Is it possible that that's how he hurt himself?"

"Claire," Tessa said. "Claire, no."

"Tessa," Claire said, in her most exacting, determined tone. "You have five minutes to decide if you're going to let this man ruin your life or not."

"No, Claire."

"In fact, you have less than five minutes because you need to be sure there's no blood in the kitchen."

"No," Tessa said.

"Tessa, please," Claire said.

Tessa felt her legs buckle. A horrible torpor was claiming her limbs. She heard herself begin to cry.

"Get a fucking grip Tessa!" Claire shouted.

Tessa turned back into the kitchen—the tile was spotless. Papers were strewn on the floor. Tessa hung up the phone.

She turned off the faucet and collected the library correspondence, which had been scuffled all over the kitchen floor and island, then left the bottle of white wine in the place of the paperweight so the papers wouldn't fly away in the breeze. The French windows would have to remain open. Back in the vestibule, she inspected the paperweight for any damage but it was pristine; having no idea what to do with it, she placed it in her bag. She heard sirens. What happened? she thought. I don't know. She opened the front door and heard the sirens blare louder. I don't know what happened.

A white and neon Oxfordshire ambulance came to a halt on the street, a woman and a man, paramedics in matching neon, came out of the back, moving quickly but not quickly enough, and Tessa wanted to shout, *Why are you walking?* Tears of fear and worry saturated her eyes. They both walked briskly toward the open door and Tessa stepped back into the vestibule with them.

The woman crouched by Chris to check his vitals and the man said, "What happened?"

"I don't know," Tessa said. "I just came back in and he was like this."

"Bring the gurney," his partner shouted.

In only a few moments, they had Chris strapped to a stretcher. His eyes were not open. "We can take you in the ambulance," the man told her. She went to retrieve her bag from the vestibule. "What happened?" the woman asked, as she packed up her own bag.

"I don't know," Tessa repeated, noticing the visible bump in her bag's canvas from the paperweight. She shouldered the bag such that the protrusion was hidden, the lump knocking against her with each step, jutting up against her shoulder blades.

PART VI

A shadow, that's it, a hand on my
upper arm, a voice, and a breath
on the nape of my neck. Shocked,
I ran, and heard this voice, behind me.
"Stop," it called, as I ran.
"You know not who you flee.
I know all things, I'm the son
of this and that. To me all things belong.
I invented healing and
all creatures gather to hear my song.
I'm not a shepherd or a mountain dweller
I don't watch cattle or stand in a field.
Love is the cause of my pursuit.
Slow down, how it would pain me
if you fell or your lovely legs
were marked by the bramble bush."
Legs, I do miss them, and all the rest

arms and feet and hands, the arm
you took and shook—my hair
once collected in that headband.
Now, if you shook me, leaves would fall.
I don't have to wait for Time to wrinkle
my skin. I'm clad in bark, the better to
grip me by, the better for making
tar. Did you foresee, to whom all things
are known, that my hip, once dear to me
would be felled and fashioned
into the bowel of a ship? Or that every
time a war was won, my hair would be cut
my laurel wreath worn by a general or
an athlete whose forehead smells with sweat
and blood, that I would be shucked
until I grew again? Shucked and plucked
plucked and shucked, that's what my future
holds in store. My body and hair and
belly and hand, is this what you deem them for?
Did you think about your approach
about where you might plant
that first kiss? Did you think you'd
pluck me from that forest path
and shower me in bliss?
Sometimes when a wind whistles
through my leaves I recall the steamy
gust of your breath you breathless
on my toes. You feared my legs would be
marked by the bramble bush? Marked
indeed, now I *am* the bramble bush.

It is a love indeed if to have me
you account it cheap to have me treed.

SULPICIA?
translated by Florence Henshawe

A S DR. TESSA TEMPLETON SHUFFLED TOGETHER the pages of an essay by one of her favorite young students, a red maple leaf blew off the roof of Westfaling College Hall and drifted down to rest on the quadrangle before her. First leaf of fall? she wondered, looking up from the paper, which was engaging nicely with Beinecke's analysis of the poem cycle once attributed to Marius, and which included Florence's full translation of the poems. The leaf, a veined, pronged thing, lifted off again in a light breeze and continued its journey along the quiet green grass. Tessa returned to the pages, which were making excellent use of the criticism, showing where Beinecke was still relevant, and where he would need to be updated. Florence, she thought, with pride, you have come back to classics with a vengeance.

It was now early October, first week, and she was taking advantage of the lovely weather to read outside in the cloisters while she waited for Lucrezia to show for their meeting. As interim head of classics at Westfaling, Tessa had so far been able to devote considerable time to her students. Since term started, she had managed to elude committee work, a Senior Common Room feud over who owed who cake, expense form duties, invitations to drink claret with two old dons, and sundry other attempted leechings on her time and attention. She had spent the summer in Italy on a high-profile excavation effort, which seemed to have bestowed her with enough significance that, when she did not reply to emails or invitations in her pidge, neither another email, nor an escalation to her temporary supervisor, Edmond Martesi, followed. She had not won the OUP monographs award, to her very transient disappointment, but she was rumored to have confirmed, through a preponderance of archaeological, osteological, and philological evidence, the true identity of the author of the corpus of verse once attributed to Marius, as his wife Sulpicia. It was even possible, it was rumored, that she would soon be able to show that Sulpicia Marii was the same Sulpicia mentioned in two of Martial's epigrams, a woman who, after suffering from osteomyelitis and receiving a medical amputation, had been cast out of wealthy urban Roman society and divorced by husband Calenus, leading her eventually to Isola Sacra, where she had composed poetry under her new husband's name.

Tessa hoped that the telltale click of the wicket door and then footsteps from the Porter's Lodge presaged Lucrezia's arrival—it was five after eleven, after all. *Welcome to Italy*, she would say, and indeed, Lucrezia emerged into the blaring sunlight and began to walk around the edge of the quadrangle toward Staircase 7, which, presumably, Max had pointed her toward. Her wedges clapped loudly on the stone walkway and Tessa was surprised to see her in a demure black dress, not the colorful pastels Tessa had known her to wear. She watched her from the shadow of the cloister, uncertain whether Lucrezia had noticed her yet.

Tessa had been attempting to reach and to apologize to Lucrezia for months, to no avail. Ed Trelawney had agreed to hire her back to the Isola Sacra excavation, but Lucrezia had ignored him as well. In September, Tessa had googled her to see if she had been attached to a different excavation, but found only a nuptial announcement in an Italian tabloid between her and one Alberto Giardello. Tessa slipped Florence's pages into her bag and crept out of the cloister to greet her.

"Lucrezia," Tessa called. Lucrezia stopped and noticed her, pushed her sunglasses onto the top of her head, and strode right toward her. She gave Tessa kisses on her cheeks and then they hugged.

"*Dio mio*," she said. "You look so beautiful. You are so tan!"

Tessa smiled. She did not want to go into where she had acquired the tan; she did not know if Lucrezia had guessed, or if it would be a sore subject.

"Come," Tessa said. "Let's go inside. Thank you so much for meeting me."

"Well, I was in Oxford," Lucrezia said, following her to Staircase 7. "How could I decline? I needed to see you here, you've had a promotion, no?"

"Of sorts," Tessa said, leading the way up to Chris's old office. She hadn't *wanted* to take it, but at the same time, the postdoc whom Tessa had shared her office with needed more space. "It's provisional, there's a search committee for a new head of classics, which I'm on, incidentally." She was also the top candidate, which she didn't mention. She pushed the door open—light cut through the casement windows, which were open. The musty aroma of the leather chesterfield coupled with a fresh breeze, which mussed the edges of more student pages, weighted down by a smooth marble paperweight.

"Ah," Lucrezia said, standing at the threshold. "It's perfect. It's just right for you."

Tessa sat on the top of the wood pedestal desk, where the pages were, facing the room, while Lucrezia moved inside, still observing. "It makes me feel decades older," Tessa admitted.

"Decades wiser," Lucrezia responded, her wedges clomping on the floorboards. She peered out the windows into the fellows garden, then circled to the desk and Tessa and the figurine on it. "Bernini, nice," she said, running her hand along it. "I saw your Daphne paper in *Classical Journal of America*."

"And I saw the announcement in *Il Giorno*. Congratulations."

"Thank you," Lucrezia said, and her face flushed with what seemed to Tessa like happiness. For a moment, this upset Tessa. That

she seemed so unambiguously pleased, so ordinarily pleased. Lucrezia circled to the bookshelves, which Tessa had not yet entirely filled,
and then took a seat on the chesterfield and folded her hands over
her lap. The time for pleasantries had ended.

"I owe you an apology," Tessa said, from her perch on the desk.

Lucrezia nodded in agreement.

"So I will just say, I am so, so sorry for how I treated you, not just
for blaming you when Chris found out, but even initially for asking
you to hide our doings from Edward. I acted terribly. I'm so sorry."

Lucrezia looked away for a long time, and Tessa waited, the
gravity of the moment increasing, the regret and shame she had
experienced over this in the past few months seeming to flood the
room. Finally Lucrezia said, "It's okay."

"Can you forgive me?" Tessa said.

"Of course I can," Lucrezia responded.

"I am very glad to hear that," Tessa said, and pushed off the desk,
feeling for a moment a wonderful lightness and relief. Lucrezia gave
her a pained smile and stood from the couch. They embraced. Tessa
was filled with a sense of well-being. She leaned back against the
desk and thought for a few moments, wondering if she could share
any more about what had occurred with Chris. "I figured out how
Chris learned about the discovery—" she began.

But Lucrezia waved her off. "It doesn't matter," she said.

"I can tell you—"

"No, please. I don't want to know," she said more firmly.

Tessa sighed. "Okay," she said. "The only other thing I wanted to
ask you is, won't you please come back to Isola Sacra?"

Lucrezia turned away and moved toward the window and the
light arcing through it. Laughter seeped in from the fellows garden
outside. Lucrezia's hair was pulled back into a chignon; she shook

her head. "It's too late," she said, still looking outside. "I am planning a wedding," and now she gesticulated like her old self. "You'd be surprised how busy I am, I don't have time for, you know, the dead. They can be very demanding." She turned back into the room and smiled.

"But just a wedding? What about after the wedding?" Her replacement, one Mattia Castellini, was fine, but Tessa wanted Lucrezia back.

Lucrezia sighed. "After the wedding, hopefully, there will be kids."

"I'm sure we can figure out a way to accommodate—"

Lucrezia shook her head. "Tessa, I'm happy. Really. I'll come back when I want to."

"Well, when you want to, the offer is on the table," Tessa said. She worried that Lucrezia was being vindictive, and she held out hope that she would come to her senses, once she became bored with her domestic existence.

Lucrezia crossed the room again. "I missed these old Oxford floors," she said, bouncing a bit in her shoes. "Creak creak. How is Chris? I guess no longer head of classics at Westfaling?"

"Nope," Tessa said. "He's not well. He suffered a traumatic brain injury in the spring."

Lucrezia's head turned just slightly. Genuine worry creased her face. She stood close to Tessa. "I hadn't heard," she said.

"Yes," Tessa said, looking Lucrezia in the eye. "He hasn't fully recovered consciousness. Some horrible domestic accident."

Lucrezia's eyes widened even more with this sensational news. "My God, I can't believe what I'm hearing. What is the prognosis?"

"Well, it's an injury to the brain stem. He's in what the doctors call a minimally conscious state. They hope he will recover in some ways, but it seems unlikely he will recover the use of language."

"But that is truly, truly tragic," Lucrezia said. "Even if he was not great to you, I know that must be difficult for you. You were so close, at one point."

For a short moment, terror gripped Tessa's limbs and she felt her breath go short. The room swerved and she tried not to hyperventilate as Lucrezia's attention turned back to the marble paperweight. Pass, pass, it will pass, Tessa knew, and it did.

"Are you okay?" Lucrezia said.

"Hm, yes," Tessa managed. She recalled the polite officer who'd asked her questions in the hospital hallway, while Chris underwent an emergency craniotomy. They'd talked to the administration at Westfaling, even Selma, who confirmed that she had asked Tessa for help with reaching Chris. His chart had shown elevated blood alcohol content, and the contusion along his temple was consistent with the blunt force of a bathtub rim, his gash with the edge of his medicine cabinet. The officer had asked about some bruising to the patient's ear, but without a request from next of kin for an investigation, or an autopsy initiated due to death, this peculiarity had been forgotten.

Lucrezia looked at Tessa for a moment, and then picked up the paperweight.

"I always loved the Apollo and Daphne sculpture. It's a beautiful story."

"It is told beautifully."

"And he just loved her so much. That passion always spoke to me."

"Well, I don't know if you remember how it ends."

"Of course I do," she said, running her fingers along the textured sheath of bark on Daphne's bare thigh.

"I used to think it was beautiful," Tessa conceded. "But if you read it, you know, it's attempted rape. Obviously, he was the one who should have been terminally metamorphosed, if there was any justice in the world."

"That's a big if," Lucrezia said, putting it back down. She smiled. "I have to go. I'm meeting Alberto in London."

Tessa walked her back to the Porter's Lodge, saying how happy she was to see her, and that she would take solace in their meeting being half successful, and reiterating that Lucrezia should call her if she changed her mind, but Lucrezia left with an air that made Tessa think she had been wrong, that Lucrezia would not be calling. Tessa lingered outside the Westfaling gate and watched her recede down the arcade of yellow-brown plane trees; a tourist peeled some bark off the nearest one; a leaf or two fell; Lucrezia didn't look back. Tessa returned through the wicket door, and remembered suddenly that she needed to buy a cucumber to bring to Chris when she visited him; that would be a good thing to do, for he had always liked the way they flavored his water.

ACKNOWLEDGMENTS

MY GRATITUDE TO the Iowa Writers' Workshop, the Truman Capote Literary Trust, and the Sun Valley Writers' Conference for supporting me and the novel as I wrote it, and especially to Connie Brothers, Jan Zenisek, and Deb West at Iowa for making everything happen. In Iowa City, I'm also grateful to Gabe Bodzin, who's heard more about this book than any living soul should have to endure. Thank you to Henry Dunow, my agent, for loving the manuscript at first sight and promoting it tirelessly through thick and thin. Thank you to Helen Thomaides for giving the book a home at Norton, for her sharp editorial instincts, for letting drafts wander, and for always guiding them back. I'm grateful to Ethan Canin, Sam Chang, Charlie D'Ambrosio, and Paul Harding, who gave essential direction and encouragement during the manuscript's earliest stages. Frankie Thomas, Allie Dokus, Eric Wohlstadter, Keenan Walsh, Sophie Klimt, Molly Dektar, Nina Cochran, Miriam Ritchie, and Alex Black—and, crucially, Emma Kurz—all took time to give intelligent feedback when they didn't have to (and sometimes when they did). I'm eternally grateful to the brilliant Margot Livesey, this book's first guiding light and *sine qua non*, for her otherworldly generosity, her dedication to Chris and Tessa, and for navigating me through the tricky waters of a first novel.

Before I wrote fiction, I was blessed to have learned Latin from

Donald Connor, and literature from Tom Sullivan, John Limon, Stephen Fix, Karen Swann, and Jeri Johnson. Strauss Zelnick helped me see that I needed to start writing every day. Ted Thompson taught the first fiction class I took (and second, third, fourth, fifth?). Andrea Barrett and Chris Castellani provided early encouragement at Bread Loaf and vital support over the years.

I turned to many gracious experts for questions about Isola Sacra, material culture, and verse composition. Thank you to Leah Agne for general research help over the years, and to Laura Moser for crucial feedback on my "translations." Fernando Contreras at the Sanisera Archaeology Institute let me tag along for field school. Stefania Gialdroni and Paola Salvatori left no stone unturned in their tours of the Isola Sacra necropolis and the ruins at Ostia Antica and generously answered my emails in years following. Credit to Ray Van Dam for any successes in this novel's rendering of epigraphy and to Max Hardy for the Latin epitaph. I am grateful for their patient coaching. All errors and implausibilities are entirely my own.

Thank you to Muhcheese for the love and support, the medical insights, and endless sanity checks (sometimes nightly).

Thank you to my parents for their patience and encouragement, their eternal open-mindedness, and the great lengths they forced my imagination to go for all instances of questionable parenting in this novel.

Thank you finally to R.D.B.H., the Countess, and all the denizens of Selfdom, without whom this novel would not exist. Keep bashing.

A NOTE ON SOURCES

IN WRITING THIS NOVEL I drew from a variety of written sources, the most crucial of which follow below.

I came to Isola Sacra by way of an article in the *Lancet* titled "A Surgical Amputation in 2nd Century Rome" by D. S. Weaver et al. (August 19, 2000) detailing the "only unequivocal available case in classical Rome paleopathological samples . . . of the practice of, and survival after, surgical amputation"—an adult left femur found in an ossuary collection at Isola Sacra.

While the Sulpicia to whom Tessa alludes at the close of her presentation in Part V is a historical figure, the story line of Marius and Sulpicia's burial at Isola Sacra is entirely fictional, as is all poetry attributed to them (excepting the two lines quoted by Tessa at the conference). For the historical Sulpicia mentioned in Tessa's presentation, and Giorgio Valla's misattribution of her two trimeters to one "Sulpicius," I relied on Amy Richlin's "Sulpicia the Satirist," and Holt Parker's "Other Remarks on the Other Sulpicia," both in *The Classical World*, vol. 86, no. 2 (November–December, 1992).

Marius and Sulpicia's epitaph owes a debt to Helvia Prima, whose funereal inscription from Benevento can be found online or in the *Corpus Inscriptionum Latinarum* I² 1732. David Califf's *A Guide to Latin Meter and Verse Composition* helped me begin to write limping iambs in Latin, and Persius's *Prologue* and Catullus 8 and 31 made for essential blueprints. Thomas Carper and Derek Attridge's *Meter and Meaning: An Introduction to Rhythm in Poetry* was especially useful as I composed the poetry in translation, during which Peter Green's *The Poems of Catullus* and the Loeb texts of Ovid's *Metamorphoses* I.452–552 and Tibullus 3.8–18 were always near at hand. For those interested in the poetry of the *one* ancient Roman woman whose work survived antiquity in non-fragmentary form—yet another, different, Sulpicia—see especially Tibullus 3.8–18. Adrienne Ho's translations of 3.13–18 in *91st Meridian* (Winter 2006) made for further inspiration.

Note that while the *Suda* is a real tenth century encyclopedia drawing from many *scholia* like Probus's that have since been lost, the entry in the novel for Marius and his wife Sulpicia is fictional. Likewise, though the *Corpus Inscriptionum Latinarum* is very much real, the entry in Part IV is not. The Marius scholars Sergio Conti, Beinecke, and Williamson are works of the imagination, as are the Ovid scholars Yelland, Chambers, and Hoy.

For the *urinatores* and their ear ailment I was inspired by "Water-Related Occupations and Diet in Two Roman Coastal Communities (Italy, First to Third Century AD): Correlation Between Stable Carbon and Nitrogen Isotope Values and Auricular Exostosis Prevalence" by F Crowe et al. in *The American Journal of Physical Anthropology*. For evidence of the *urinatores* at Portus and Ostia see *Corpus Inscriptionum Latinarum* XIV 303 and *Supplementum Ostiense* I 4620. The connection between external auditory exostoses and the *urinatores* is, to my knowledge, fictional and my own.

For the Domus di Scapula, I depended on the Domus del Protiro at Ostia Antica and information from www.ostia-antica.org. The reuse of a portion of Marius and Sulpicia's epitaph is modeled on a similar instance of reuse at the Domus del Protiro (see *Scavi di Ostia* IV, vol. 211, no. 402 and *L'Année épigraphique* 2005, no. 306). I am indebted to Daniela Urbanová's "Between Syntax and Magic" in *Lemmata Linguistica Latina,* vol. II, and in particular to tablet 8 therein (p. 161), for Scapula's curse tablet.

As far as I know, the phrase "terminal metamorphosis" was coined by Katherine De Boer Simons in her 2016 dissertation *Death and the Female Body in Homer, Virgil, and Ovid.* Charles Martindale's *Redeeming the Text: Latin Poetry and the Hermeneutics of Reception* became important reading in later drafts of the novel. *Texts and Transmission: A Survey of the Latin Classics* edited by L. D. Reynolds, *Scribes and Scholars: A Guide to the Transmission of Greek and Latin Literature* by L. D. Reynolds and N. G. Wilson, *The Oxford Handbook of Roman Epigraphy* edited by C. Bruun and J. Edmondson, and *Ovid's Metamorphoses: Books 1–5* by W. S. Anderson were likewise essential.